TOTEMS

OF

SEPTEMBER

ROBIN LADUE & MARY KAY VOSS

BOOK PUBLISHERS NETWORK

Book Publishers Network
P.O. Box 2256
Bothell • WA • 98041
PH • 425-483-3040
www.bookpublishersnetwork.com

10 9 8 7 6 5 4 3 2 1

Printed in the United States of America

LCCN   2013948145
ISBN   978-1-940598-00-0

Editor: Barbara Kindness
Cover design: Laura Zugzda
Interior design: Stephanie Martindale
Illustrations: Rhys Haug
Title page Illustration: Donald Voss

Totems of September is a work of fiction. All names, characters, and incidents are the product of the authors' imagination or are used fictitiously. Any resemblance to actual persons, living or dead, is purely coincidental.

This book is dedicated with loving appreciation to Helen Lucile LaDue. Her grace and spirit have rarely been seen in this World. I owe her everything.

AND

Roy Frank LaDue

Wesley Charles LaDue and Dove Louis LaDue

Who Survived the Boarding School Holocaust

AND

To Charles Vernon LaDue

Who did not....

Contents

Acknowledgements

Robin would like to acknowledge:

There are many people who have been a part of creating this book. It is not possible to thank them all but we would be greatly remiss to not acknowledge all of their contributions. To the special people in my life with whom we have been blessed, we owe you a debt that can never be repaid. So, a special thanks to Dave and Debi Plekan and to Bailey the Wonder Horse, my own red pony. A heartfelt thanks to Gary and Carolyn Luther of the Diamond L Guest Ranch who passed my red ponies, Bailey and Bo, through their loving hands to mine. I am so grateful to you for them and my yearly sanctuary at the Diamond L Ranch.

Thank you to our readers who gave graciously and endlessly of their time in editing and discussing the characters in this book as if they were old friends: Deborah Romaszka., Sheila Koenig, and Ken Foster. Thank you to Janelle Ostlund, my "executive editing consultant," who spent countless hours at Anini Beach, Kauai, listening to the stories and watching the waves of the Pacific roll in.

A very loving thank you to Juanita LaHurreau, my Potawatami friend, who has gone to Merritt with me, laughed with me, and consumed endless pounds of salmon with me. Who would have imagined a bus trip through Rome would have brought us this far?

A special thank you to Bruce, who gave of his time to help while we wrote and rewrote. Finally, a thank you to the Old Men, who quietly came to tell the stories and to share the gentleness of their lives.

Mary Kay would like to acknowledge:

Thank you, Robin, for including me in this very special journey. It has been an eye-opening experience to learn more of our country's history from an entirely new perspective and a privilege to share these beautiful stories.

To my husband, Didrik, who is my wind; always there to support my various endeavors with love, time and wisdom.

Thanks to my high school English teachers at St. Agnes Academy, in Houston, Texas. Sr. Mary Hugh, O.P. and Sr. Bernadine, O.P. were two very talented women who shared their love of the written word and proper grammar, and encouraged my writing. No, I did not become a teacher in the traditional sense, but definitely in many other ways.

We could not have gotten this to press without Sheryn Hara of Book Publishers Network who saw the value in these stories and moved us through this publishing process with loving prodding and lots of professionalism and talent. Thanks to our editor, Barbara Kindness, for her wisdom and input; to Rhys Haug for his amazing pen and ink drawings that captured the essence of every one of the chapters; and to Donald Voss for his beautiful drawing of the falcon.

Also, thanks to my friends and family who supported my endeavors and work. I hope you all are inspired by the sagas of these families.

⇥ 1 ⇤

Devils Tower

Devils Tower, Wyoming   **September 10, 2001**

Arrows of sunlight reflected off the helmets of climbers as they maneu-vered through the crevices and chimneys of the indifferent monolith. Sun-scattered dust and the aroma of pine mentally transported Lola's thoughts back to adolescent nights spent under summer stars. She turned away from the Tower, back towards the parking lot, where Auntie Louella dozed in the rental car. Her foot lolled out the car's half-open door resting on the pavement, head back against the seat. If Lola guessed right, there would be a tiny string of drool connecting Auntie's lip and outthrust chin.

Years before, she had first gasped in awe at its power. Devils Tower stood as a magic marker of time and space in Lola's mind. They had made this trip, a journey of two generations, as part of a bargain. Auntie had turned ninety the previous Spring. She had, in her inimitable manner, requested that Lola take her on her final life trip to the Black Hills of South Dakota, to see Crazy Horse on the mountain. Auntie had been in the process of dying for nearly thirty years and Lola had no doubt she would see another thirty before leaving this world. Lola's price for making the trip east from the Pacific Ocean to the Black Hills had been that they come to Devils Tower. Auntie Louella had grumbled about the long drive and her old bones, but east they came with this detour to Devils Tower.

Lola's reward for the long journey had been seeing joyful tears running down the creases of Auntie's beautiful face as she stared into the eternal gaze of Crazy Horse on his pony. The shared heritage of Auntie's Cowlitz blood and that of the Sioux chief mingled in the sun that late summer day. The light reflected equally from the white stone and Auntie's tears. In that instant, Lola understood that Auntie had told the truth—this was to be her final journey.

Lola and Auntie Louella drove through the plains and woods of South Dakota to the red rocks of Wyoming. The warm September air brought the sweet smell of cut barley mixed with the pungent aroma of the last survivors of Sitting Bull's buffalo herds. They enjoyed those many miles sharing companionship, bottled water, and bags of chips and beef jerky. Every piece of gossip, snarky LeFleur family history, and bad joke had been discussed and re-dissected. Every night in the sacred sweat lodge was reviewed by the time Lola drove up the ridge outside of Hulett, Wyoming. Then, Devils Tower came into view.

The silent Tower rose majestically from the surrounding hills, reigning over the landscape for hundreds of miles. Thousands of birds made their homes in the gray, green and brown vertical columns. They darted from the hidden cracks and ledges, circling and wheeling, calling across the woods and rocks of the monument. A jumble of boulders lay scattered at the base of the Tower, dropped by the unmindful hand of the Creator. It was apparent the woods around Devils Tower had burned in the recent past. The pine trees' skeletons lent a haunting eeriness to the place long held sacred by the Native people of the land.

As Lola approached the base of the Tower, she tilted her head back, searching the blue canopy of the sky above. A Red-tailed Hawk screamed as it rode the air currents that lifted it up, up, up, past the climbers to where Lola could see the faces of the sisters as they hid from their brother, the bear. Lola guided the car into a parking spot, making sure Auntie was out of the sun. She turned towards Auntie with a questioning look.

"Go, girl," Auntie Louella chuckled. "Go, go! Give my blessing bundles to the altar. Go, child, let an old woman sleep in peace."

Lola laughed. "I won't be long, Auntie. Be good while I am gone and leave the old men alone."

Lola climbed out of the car and, drawn by the power of the Tower, began her walk up the path. A short way up, she came to the altar with the prayer ties and offerings left by the Native people who came to honor the Creator and the Old Ones. She fingered the small figurine of a black owl hanging around her neck. Its smoothness comforted her as she knelt in the pine needles mixed with the red dirt of Wyoming.

"Give me grace, Creator. Give me the heart to go on in this world. Give me the clarity of the sight of the owl. Creator, if you are there, please, bless this world and especially Auntie. *AHO!*"

Lola placed her red cloth-wrapped scented and sacred offerings of sage and tobacco at the base of the altar. From her pocket, she pulled several animals carved from a variety of stone. They included a wolf, snake, horse, elk, crow, falcon and wolverine. Each of them was festooned with a feather and tiny stones and hung from simple black strings tied with a double knot.

She whispered a quick prayer to the Creator, stood and walked on. She listened to the stories of the chickadees, jays, and crows, singing in the trees. Her thoughts were slow and languid, bits of voices, bits of song. Time seemed suspended and the only movement was that of a small brown rabbit sniffing at her dusty sneakers.

Lola began walking closer to the Tower, off the path and into the brush, finally stopping to press her body against the embracing heat of the stone. Above her head, she heard the clink of metal clasps and the voices of the climbers calling to one another. She tilted her head as far back as she could, trying to catch a glimpse of them on the monolith, but saw, instead, startling white clouds racing over the top of the Tower..

Suddenly, she felt a sense of vertigo and of time slipping away. As she lay across the heated rock, the Red-tailed Hawk cried again, its call chased by the sounds of tumbling rocks, cries and screams.

A small rock fell from the top of the monolith, gathering speed as it rolled towards the ground below. Other small rocks joined it and soon a torrent of dust, stones, boulders and trees began to fall towards Lola. She covered her head in terror, looking for a place to escape the onslaught. Glancing up in horror, she saw bodies dropping out of the sky, landing at her feet with the sound of a muffled thud. Ash and dust from the crumbling Tower swept over Lola as it rolled across the landscape, down the valley to where the river ran cold and blue. Screams of panic and the smell of death surrounded her. The sky turned black as crow's wings as the Tower disintegrated.

⇥ ⇤

Through the dust a beautiful woman emerged. She was dressed all in white and was smiling. Her black hair swirled in the wind currents of the circling storm. Two young men, identical in feature and dressed in military uniforms, came forward, each holding the young woman's hands. As the three figures disappeared back into the swirling, murky dust, a small, black-haired child in a yellow shirt appeared and ran after them.

⇥ ⇤

Grey and black debris reached the river where a man sat on the bank, holding a revolver in his clenched hand. A petite black-haired woman stood behind him, her tiny hands caressing his neck. Two older men stood on a huge boulder that had fallen from the Tower, their gray braids blowing around them in the howling storm. A bloodied white bird flew by and called to the white raven perched on a tree at the edge of the debris. Down through the valley and into the distance the dust spread, the blackening sky foretelling the end of the world.

⇥ ⇤

Lola jerked awake. She felt the rough surface of the stone against her cheek. The pleasant aroma of warmed ancient dust had been replaced with the smell of ashes, fear and death. She could hear faint cries of pain and anguish. She shook her head, clearing her mind. Slowly, she realized the sounds were actually the calls of the descending climbers congratulating each other on their success and bravery in mastering the Tower. Looking around, she saw the black asphalt of the path encircling the base of the Tower, its macadam softened by the heat. The voices of walkers coming around the bend grew louder, returning her abruptly to reality.

"Well," Lola mumbled quietly, "that was odd. I must have fallen asleep. I better see to Auntie. She will be fussing and fuming, convinced I've deserted her in her hour of need."

Lola glanced about her one more time. Pieces of casual conversation drifted back to her as the other hikers strode past. Despite their presence, she felt anxious and unsettled. Much of the heat and joy of the day had vanished. There was a heavy feeling deep in her heart and soul as she walked the path back to the car. She felt as if she were both deaf and blind. There was a chill in the air and the birds were strangely quiet. She hurried her steps, suddenly convinced that something terrible had happened to Auntie. As she reached the far side of the Tower, she could hear deep, anguished sobs coming from the woods. Lola began to sweat and broke into a run towards the car. Her breath was ragged, panic rising in her chest as she finally stumbled to the car where Auntie sat motionless.

"Auntie, Auntie!!" Lola cried. "Oh, God, Auntie!" She could see Auntie's head against the seat. No movement came from the tiny body.

"What, girl? What's chasing you?" Auntie jumped as she was startled awake "What is the problem? Damn it, child! I was dreaming of birds and rivers. You ruined my dream!"

Lola sagged against the side of the hot car, her legs buckling with relief. Auntie struggled to sit upright as Lola slumped to the ground, shielding her eyes against the setting sun.

"Auntie Louella, I was so scared. I heard voices and screams. There were tears and fear. Auntie, there was death." Lola's voice faded as she realized Auntie was fine and back to her usual grumpy self.

Lola remained nervous and worried as she slowly walked around the car, opened the door on the driver's side, and took one long, last look at the Tower. Sliding behind the steering wheel, she prepared herself for the upcoming drive to the north. Once again, she could see the colors of the tree leaves, blue sky and clouds. Slowly, Lola reached across Auntie's lap and pulled her door shut. Auntie sat back in her seat as Lola closed her own door and started the engine. She turned to look at her aunt, who was sitting quietly and casually looking out her side window.

Finally, Auntie spoke, her voice low and somber. "Lola, the things you heard, were they in the past or the future?"

"The future," Lola replied softly.

"Yes, girl," Auntie said, "I believe you. I know the truth of what you heard."

Lola turned to stare at her aunt's profile, confused at Auntie's calm, serene voice. Louella looked away from Lola, peering out the window as the car moved down the hill and past the erect prairie dogs, always the silent sentinels. A Red-tailed Hawk soared overhead. Turning her head forward, Lola gently braked at the stop sign. Without saying another word, she entered the highway and as she accelerated to the north, the Tower disappeared behind them, along with the cries of fear and the smell of ash.

⇥ 2 ⇤

The Towers

Minot, North Dakota   **September 11, 2001**

They had driven through the afternoon and late into the night to reach the motel in Minot, a dour northern plains military town. After eating her order-in cheese pizza, Auntie demanded Lola turn out the light and let an old lady sleep. She never had trouble dropping into slumber, flat on her back, arms at her side and her chin dropped to her chest. Snores rumbled up from Auntie's throat, exploding as each hit the air. They had settled in for a well-earned rest, but all night long Lola had tossed and turned in her narrow bed. The thin pillow and scratchy sheets only increased her irritation. She could not escape the sounds and smells of her time at Devils Tower. Itchy and unsettled, she counted the minutes of the too-short night, listening to the rain splash in the dust and the trash blow around the corners of the gray, washed cinder block building.

Her thoughts wandered over the past four days since she and Auntie set off on their pilgrimage. The train ride from Seattle to Minot had started off calmly enough. Auntie Louella and Lola settled their bags into the luxury sleeping car Auntie had demanded. They made their way down the aisle to the viewing car, Auntie clutching Lola's arm to keep her balance against the train's rocking motion. They took seats across the aisle from a slender blonde woman who was dressed in a pinstriped blue suit, fluffy white blouse, Hermes scarf, and prim matching pumps. Auntie settled back into her seat with a sigh and instantly relaxed. She peered out the window intending to absorb every detail of the passing scenery.

Barely an hour into the trip, the train lurched and screeched to a stop after hitting a red car that had been abandoned on the track. The passengers grumbled to each other about the cause of the accident and what it would mean for the timing of the rest of their journey. Auntie cackled her elderly laugh as an hour later the train slowly lumbered back into motion. As Auntie and Lola passed the crumpled car, now lying at the side of the track, Auntie pointed at it, her bony finger trembling.

"Lola," Auntie said, "your grandmother and I used to take the train to Portland. We saw lots of cows and pigs lying on the tracks. I used to wonder about the sights we saw, but girl, I never once saw a car on the tracks. Glad to see that there is still something new in this world."

"Auntie, what if there had been someone in that car?" Lola had a tendency to always imagine the worst. She could easily hear the screams and feel the panic of the people in the car as the train raced down upon them. She imagined their hands pressed to the windows, eyes bulging in fear, disbelief clouding reason from their mind. A cold sweat broke out on her forehead as she leaned her face against the cool glass of the window.

"Lola, girl, for goodness sake! I saw the old drunk driving that car get out and lean against that shack well before we were near. Wish I had the courage to do something like that!" Auntie smiled her impish grin.

The small blonde woman with the elegant hairdo peered over her tortoise-shell glasses in clear disdain of Auntie and Lola. She returned her gaze to the thick stack of papers cradled in her lap. Auntie, never one to be deterred, nudged the woman's slacks-clad leg with her clunky shoes.

"What are you reading there, girl?"

Clearly annoyed, the woman turned away from Auntie who, taking no notice of this message of disengagement, nudged her again.

"Where are you going, girl?"

"I am going to the Pentagon for a meeting. I'm a civilian contractor with the Navy. Not that it is YOUR business, but I don't like flying. Planes fall out of the sky and I have no intention of falling with them." The woman turned away, dismissing Lola and Auntie.

A loud gust of wind brought Lola's mind back to the small motel
room in Minot. She twisted once more on her narrow bed and finally
waded into sleep, the blonde woman's face and patrician voice fading
into the gray of a disturbed slumber.

A bare four hours later, at 7:30, the grey morning dawned unpleas-
antly damp, smelling like the old, wet woolen coat Auntie wore around
her thin shoulders. Lola pulled the rental car to a stop in front of the
tiny Hertz office . She grabbed Auntie's newly purchased white oak
walking stick and impatiently sighed as Auntie fussed at the buttons on
her coat. Auntie responded by grumbling and moaning about arthritic
joints and the lack of understanding inherent in Lola and the entire
younger generation.

⇥ ⇤

"Auntie, stop sniping at me! I will let you out. Give me a minute." Lola's
voice was as acrid as the rancid morning air.

Finally, the awaited transportation to the train station arrived in
the form of a red and gray taxi. A ruddy-faced, boozy-smelling man
emerged from the driver's side.

"Going east or west today?" he asked, his breath sending a flood
of tobacco flakes over the waiting women. He grabbed their bags and
threw them with a thud into the trunk as Lola helped Auntie climb in.
The oak walking stick hit Lola across the knees as Auntie settled herself. Lola cursed from the sting of the stick, and then climbed into the
other side. Her mood was as dark and ugly as the rank, closed sky, and
it worsened considerably as they reached the small, shabby building
that housed the train station.

"That'll be fifteen dollars!" the driver demanded, holding out his thick
but surprisingly soft hand. "Add a five-dollar tip and we'll call it a day."

Ignoring the request for the tip, Lola handed the driver a five and a
ten and then pulled the bags from the trunk herself.

"Auntie, come on! Let's go. Come on." Lola's voice was harsh and
ugly. Her mood had become even more glum with each passing second.
"Come on."

She pulled at her aunt's wet sleeve. Inside the station, a television mounted high in the corner showed male and female anchors on CNN. Lola glanced at the television briefly, noting a plume of smoke sailing across an impossibly blue sky. She shifted her attention back to her aunt who was looking around the room, seeking to identify the most appropriate of the passengers with whom she could converse on the long ride back to the west coast.

"Auntie," Lola scolded. "Auntie, pay attention! Stay here and keep your purse under your arm. Don't wander off. I mean it! Stay put. I am going to get our tickets and will be back in five minutes. Stay put!"

She left her aunt in front of the mounted television and walked towards the ticket window. After a brief exchange, she had the tickets in hand. As she turned back, she was confronted by a look on her aunt's face she'd never seen before, a look of horror and disbelief. Fearing Louella was ill, Lola moved quickly to her side. Auntie grabbed Lola's hand.

"Oh, good Creator!" Auntie moaned. "Oh Lola, my God, look at the television. Oh, my God, Lola."

Startled, Lola looked up at the TV and watched in silent horror as a screaming plane plunged into the blue and silver tower, shattering glass, the day, and the world in a moment's time. The room spun and tilted off its axis. Auntie clung to Lola's hand as a low moan escaped from her lips. No one in the station seemed to see the terror unfolding. As a tall man in a Yellowstone sweatshirt brushed past Auntie, she grabbed him with her free hand.

"Stop, you fool. Look! We are under attack. Call the stationmaster. Someone, we are under attack. Look, you fools, look!"

The man began to pull away from Auntie's grasp when his eyes moved to the television screen. Auntie's words rippled through the room. In slow motion, fellow-travelers turned to face the screen where huge black billows of smoke were filling the blue sky as flames licked up the side of the two silver towers. A profound hush fell upon the room. No one moved. No one breathed. No one spoke. The world had come to an end.

The local police and a small contingent of National Guard soldiers had magically appeared at the doors of the station. No one was allowed in or out. Lines formed in front of the two pay phones, people standing in near-silence, their voices low and trembling as they sought news about the safety of loved ones.

At long last the stationmaster called the train ready to board, but few passengers in the station could voluntarily pull themselves away from the mesmerizing images flickering relentlessly across the TV screen. Slowly, a few passengers left the confines of the terminal, pausing at the door to look back over their shoulders, shaking their heads, expressing emotion beyond disbelief. Gradually, the station emptied as the train welcomed the passengers. Solemnly, Auntie and Lola took their places in the sleeping car, stopping each porter to inquire about more news.

There had been so many rumors, and both confirmed and unconfirmed reports of other acts of terror. Only because they had seen so much horror with their own eyes could they even begin to accept the reality of the morning.

It was finally announced that this train, with all its passengers, would be held on the siding in front of the station until they could be assured there were no explosives on the tracks between Minot and Seattle.

"How in the hell will they know that?" Auntie shook her head. "The damn government never gets anything right. What are they gonna do? Crawl every inch of track?" She fumed and fussed, trying to get comfortable on the couch that at night folded into a double bed.

"Damn it, Lola!" Auntie thumped her walking stick on the floor, "Go see what's happening, girl."

Still reeling from the shock of watching the day's carnage, Lola replayed the scenes relentlessly over and over in her mind. She turned away from her aunt as her eyes welled with tears, feeling the horror of those on the planes as they careened into solid steel and breaking glass. She could feel the anguish and hear the screams of terror as the planes hit their targets. Her breath caught as she felt a pressure in her chest crushing her ribs and strangling her spirit.

"Auntie," Lola replied wearily, "no one knows anything else. There is no one to ask. There is nothing anyone can tell us. The attendant will be here soon. You can ask her but, you must understand, no one knows anything more than what we have witnessed. Auntie, this is what I heard yesterday, the screams, the fear, and the ashes. My God, Auntie, it's war. Oh, my God!"

Auntie sat upright, her tiny body shaking with indignation. "Lola, you don't really think that fool in the White House would take us to war? We don't even know who did this. I have seen enough war in my life. Lola, please, go find out what happened."

More to escape from her aunt than anything else, Lola made her way to the back of the train. The porter ignored her. After Lola tapped her on the shoulder for the third time, the attendant turned towards her.

"Don't ask me, I don't know. I just don't know anything new. Go back to your seat. I can't tell you anything. Just go." The woman's voice quivered as she turned away. Lola started to make her way back to the sleeping car where Auntie waited. She passed a line of people, squeezing their way down to the attendant, whose tears made her cheeks flush even more.

At two o'clock in the afternoon, five hours late, the train slowly pulled out of the station. As the train began to move, Auntie started thumping her stick on the ground again. "Five hours we've been here. Are we going home? What is going on? Lola, go ask again. We haven't seen the attendant for hours. Check your cell phone. Call the damn newspaper, someone must know something!"

"Auntie, I don't mean to be rude but I am out of patience here. I've talked to everyone on this train. No one can use their cell phone. We can't get reception. Don't you think I would if I could? No one can use a radio. No one has a newspaper. We will just have to wait; I can't change those facts. I don't know what to tell you."

"Don't get sassy with me. Crisis or no crisis, show me the respect I deserve!" Auntie snapped.

"Auntie, enough! Just wait until the next stop. There is nothing I or anyone else can do!"

Lola recalled the blonde woman on the trip out from Seattle, the one who insisted planes fell out of the sky. "She was right." Lola murmured, wondering where the woman was now and what she was thinking of the morning's events.

Three hours into their journey, a faint voice came over the intercom. "The President has addressed the nation. It is confirmed that four planes were used as 'missiles' against the United States. Two were hijacked and flown into the World Trade Center, and one into the Pentagon, and a fourth crashed in Pennsylvania. The President has declared that the United States will hunt down the cowards responsible for this attack on innocent people and our country.

"As of now, all commercial and private planes have been grounded. Passengers on this train will be allowed to disembark but no one will be allowed to get on the train. There will be a change of crew at the next stop, and hopefully, there will be more information at that time. Those holding five o'clock reservations for dinner are asked to come to the dining car. For those passengers who are so inclined, please pray."

Lola shook her head as she listened to the disembodied voice over the loudspeaker. She wrapped her hands around her shoulders, hugging herself as she thought of the small blonde woman who might have been at the Pentagon that morning. She could see her face and hear her refined voice: "Planes fall out of the sky." She pulled Louella to her feet. "Auntie, that's our call. Come on, I'll help you down the aisle."

The clicking of the rails sounded loud as bullets to Lola as the two women made their way to the dining car. She had a sense of falling as the train swayed around a corner. Stepping between cars, Lola got a glimpse of the tracks below. The stones in the rail bed glowed white in the late afternoon light. Auntie pushed open the door to the dining room ahead of Lola and turned to tug on her arm

"Come on, girl! I'm hungry. Let's find our table." They stopped at the second table on the right side of the car. Outside, the recently harvested plains flashed by. The only measurement of the train's speed was the blinking of the telephone poles. Off to the north, purple-colored clouds bunched up against the horizon. The flatness of the land was interrupted by stacks of abandoned cars and an occasional silo.

Sliding into the bench seat next to Auntie, Lola continued to stare out the window. She could see the plane crashing into the blue towers billowing smoke and fire, over and over again. She could hear the screams of the people and, as she squeezed her eyes shut to close out the horrifying images, she saw the tiny figure of a woman falling upside down across the face of the tower, primly holding her skirt to her legs in a final gesture of modesty, floating forever into the air…

Lost in another world, Lola shook her head as the porter, menus tucked under her arm, escorted an elderly couple to their table. Auntie, ever inquisitive, tapped her stick on the floor and nudged Lola into alertness.

"Girl, where are your manners? Say 'hello' to these nice folks. In spite of today, the world has not ended. Where are you, girl?"

Lola looked across the red table with its containers of salt, pepper, jam, sugar and ketchup in a silver holder. Both of their new tablemates were trim and attractive, with only the silver of their hair and the lines in their faces giving a hint to their advancing years. The woman wore a neon -striped blue and pink blouse with matching blue slacks, and a pink scarf tied around her neck. Her husband, dressed in matching slacks and shirt, took off his glasses and wiped his face with his scratchy white napkin.

In the woman's blue eyes, Lola could see smoke billowing into the air, blowing in a straight line across the sky. She could see the people in the building leaning out the windows, begging for help. She could not hear the words of her aunt or the replies of the elderly couple. Lola shook her head and tried to will away the anxiety that pounded through her heart and limbs.

She looked around the dining car where the other tables, filled with evening diners, seemed to be in suspended animation. She could no longer hear the clicking of the rails, feel the sway of the train, or see the darkening blue sky out the train window. She turned back to look at the older woman sitting across from her. She peered, once again, into the woman's eyes and, once more, saw the tiny figure of the woman falling towards the earth, her brown hair streaming out behind her.

Suddenly, Lola became aware of what the three other people around the table were discussing.

"We were there in August, you know, for our daughter's wedding," the man was saying. "Annie works in the south tower. We've tried for hours to reach her but all of the lines were busy. We can't find her husband either."

Lola stiffened, horror filling her body. Outside, purple clouds in the distance flickered with lightning and a wind sprinted across the prairie, brushing the tips of the stubble left in the fields. A Red-winged Blackbird flew alongside the train for a moment, and then swerved off to a distant bony tree.

As Lola's focus slowly returned to the table, Auntie leaned forward. "Whatcha talking about? You mean your child was in that tower? Lordy, have you told the train authorities? Have you asked them to let you off the train? Where is the rest of your family? Lola, get someone over here to help these folks!"

The woman across the table started to tear up. "We've tried. I told you that." She wiped her eyes in a manner identical to that of her husband. "We can't find out anything. We have to wait until we get off the train in Spokane."

Lola listened with a growing sense of anguish and fear, unable to speak. She felt a despair so strong she had to lean against the window to support herself, the sounds of Auntie questioning the couple dulled by her own panic.

"Annie and her husband were married a month ago. Our daughter was so proud of her job in New York. We went to the top of the tower and looked out across the world. Who could have done this terrible thing? Why?" She started shaking, biting her lip to hold back the tears and to maintain her composure.

"Mother," her husband murmured. "Annie is fine. We will be in Spokane soon and when we call, I am sure we will find her at home, safe and sound with her husband and the cat. Trust me. God would not take our only child from us. You know that."

The porter returned to take their orders but Lola could no longer sit at the table. She pushed past Auntie, ignoring her startled protests and the questioning gaze of Annie's parents. She staggered down the aisle of the train, the wind whistling in her ears. The thunder from the purple clouds came closer, booming in time to the pounding of her heart. As she finally reached their sleeping car, a crashing roar engulfed the train

as the lurking storm burst. Lola fell into the seat. She could physically feel her belief in the goodness of mankind fleeing her heart and soul. She pressed her face against the rough wall of the sleeping car, praying for the day to be a nightmare and for the waning sun to break through the heavy storm clouds. She could see the faces of the woman and man sitting across from Auntie. She could see the smoothness of Auntie's mottled hands and the gleam of the salt and pepper shakers reflected in the red surface of the table. Most of all, she could see the tiny figure of a floating woman, floating forever in front of a silver and blue building, tumbling downward with her skirt pressed against her legs.

Lola had no idea how long she sat scrunched into a ball in the corner of the small couch of the sleeping car. The dark of the storm gave way to the dark of night and as the skies cleared, the stars beamed, one by one. Some time earlier, Auntie had returned to the car and pulled out the top bunk, awkwardly climbing into it with much creaking and complaining. She fell asleep, tiny snores barely audible against the constant rumble of the train. Several times during the night, the train stopped but no word of the outside world infiltrated the sealed atmosphere of the train. Recalling the blonde woman on the outbound trip, Lola continued to sit hunched against the window. Off in the night, she could see the skeletons of cars, lights glowing in houses, and the occasional shadowy figure of an owl skimming the earth.

At one point, the red-haired porter stopped by the door of the car and offered to make up the bed. Without looking around, Lola waved her away, uttering a sharp "No." She could hear the low murmurings of the other passengers as they made their way down the aisle and, one by one, the lights extinguished as her fellow-travelers traded the fear of the day for restless sleep.

Odd thoughts flickered through Lola's mind. She recalled the words of the song:

"..Nighttime in the City of New Orleans, changing cars in Memphis, Tennessee. Halfway home, we'll be there by morning, cross the Mississippi River, rolling down to the sea..."

"Dear Creator," Lola whispered, clutching the small owl fetish that hung around her neck, "what will tomorrow bring?"

⇥ ⇤

The next morning, after a subdued breakfast, the train finally pulled into Spokane. Lola gathered up Auntie and all of her belongings, her gray wool coat and walking stick. She helped Auntie down the stairs to the platform. As she stepped out, she noticed that the couple they had sat with at dinner the night before was just ahead of them. They were dressed in matching tans and were huddled in front of a newspaper stand. As if a slow motion camera was watching the scene from all angles, Lola stared, transfixed as the man pointed to the enormous picture on the front page. There, in excruciating detail, was a picture of a tiny feminine figure, floating head down towards the earth, her hands vainly holding her skirt to her legs, smoke billowing from the enormous silver and blue building behind her.

Auntie was busy fussing, caught in the crowd that ebbed and flowed around them. Suddenly the passengers parted as if Auntie had waved her hand. The steel of the station seemed to vibrate from the hustle of the burgeoning noise of the crowd and the quivering of waiting trains.

"Lola, get me a paper!" Auntie demanded. "Where's the damn train to Seattle? Lola, come on, get me a paper. I want to read it on our ride home. Lola, wake up, girl. What's wrong with you? You've been acting like a ghost since we left Minot. Come on, girl. Pay attention. Get this old lady a paper and get us on the next train."

Shaking her head, Lola looked up at the monitor which was being constantly updated with new schedules. She turned to Auntie and said, "Stay put, don't go wandering or, I swear Old Woman, I will leave you here. I am going to go get us a paper. But if you move, I swear, I will leave you right here with all these people. Stay put and I'll be right back."

"Lola, girl! You ever speak like that to me again; I'll turn you over my knee!" She frowned in disapproval at Lola's words.

Ignoring Auntie's comments, Lola made her way to the front of the newspaper racks, pushing several people out of her way. She deposited the appropriate coins and reached into the rack, pulling out two copies o Spokane's *Statesman Review*. Tucking them under her arm, she turned back to where she had left Auntie. She tugged on her arm and, taking a deep breath, steered her to their waiting train. The conductor helped Auntie up the steps as Lola followed behind.

Inside the train the scene was bizarre, something out of a silent movie. People's mouths moved but no sound was heard. The doors of the train slid shut against the noise of the station. As Louella and Lola walked down the aisle to their seats, they passed rows of passengers, each with a newspaper in front of their face. The occasional sob or gasp escaping from behind the shake and rattle of the paper were the only audible sounds on the slowly departing train.

When Lola finally got Auntie situated and the luggage stowed in place, she sat down on the seat across from her. She reached forward and took Auntie's walking stick from her. Auntie's feet were flat on the floor as she sat strangely quiet. Lola pulled the newspapers she had purchased out from under her arm and, without a word, handed one to Auntie. She looked out the window as the train gradually picked up speed. Placing her own feet flat on the floor, she put her knees on either side of Auntie's. Clenching and unclenching her hands, she rubbed her eyes with her knuckles and, taking a deep breath to steady herself, opened the paper.

There it was, her nightmarish vision filling the entire front page: smoke billowing about in an impossibly blue sky above a crumbling blue and silver building. In front of the building, a tiny figure drifted down, floating into all eternity.

The train accelerated around a bend as Spokane faded off into the afternoon of the early September day. Suddenly sensing Auntie's stillness, Lola looked up. She watched in silence as a tear rolled down Auntie's nose. The single tear seemed to hang suspended and then dropped onto the paper; landing on the tiny figure of the woman floating in the air. The newspaper fluttered slightly and, with a tiny sigh, barely audible to Lola's ears, Auntie fulfilled her statement of two days earlier. Auntie Louella completed her last trip, her hands fell into her lap, and her head drifted downward, resting upon her chest, the remnants of her final tear glistening on her finely wrinkled cheek

⪻ 3 ⪼

The South Tower

Manhattan, New York   **September 11, 2001**

The day dawned cool with a cerulean blue sky. The early sun rays gleamed through the greenhouse window illuminating the dust motes floating in the kitchen air.. An old steel faucet slowly dripped into the sink, each drip making a soft *plunk* sound. A calico cat lay on the braided rug in the center of the room, contentedly grooming herself and purring loudly.

A slender man stood at the sink, twisting his still-new wedding band. He was dressed in a charcoal pinstripe suit, his shirt a cool shade of lavender complemented by a simple grey tie. The man smiled absently as he watched the morning traffic on Riverside Drive, right outside the window of their ground-floor apartment. As he stood there gazing, a small brown-haired woman clad in a short-sleeved white shirt and gathered blue cotton skirt crossed in front of the window and blew him a kiss. He waved his hand in reply and then lifted his coffee cup to his lips.

The woman pulled her purse strap up on her shoulder and hurried to the corner. She turned back to wave one more time and then disappeared from the man's view. She stepped into the street and flagged an approaching cab. She opened the door and slid inside, giving the cabbie her office address. Once settled, she smiled, remembering the night before, lying next to the handsome man, her husband of just one month. Her arm had draped across his shoulder as she gazed into his sky-blue eyes. The cab turned another corner and began its journey to Lower Manhattan.

Back at the apartment, the young man finished his coffee and rinsed his cup. He pulled back his coat sleeve to look at the slender, exquisite, silver watch, a wedding gift from his father-in-law. He shook his head realizing it was getting late and muttered about deadlines and boring meetings. Moving towards the door, he leaned down to pet the cat. A glimpse of brown leather lying on the kitchen table caught his eye just as he opened the door. Pausing, he reached for the address book his wife had left behind.

"She'll need this today. If I hurry, I can get this to her and still make my first meeting," he said into the empty room as the cat looked up at her owner. He tucked the address book into his briefcase and closed the door behind him. Just as his wife had done a few minutes earlier, he hailed a cab.

The city seemed especially lovely that day. Late-blooming flowers punctuated the steps of the brownstones and hung from the lamp posts. Tourists, including middle-aged women in shorts, filled the neighborhood, strolling along the sunny sidewalks, a camera hanging around the neck of each husband. From the window of the cab, the young man gazed up at the sky, his mind flashing back to the blue of her skirt and how it swung as she hurried away from him along Riverside Drive.

Arriving at her destination, the woman got out of the cab and paused on the sidewalk, rummaging through her purse for the brown wallet that matched the address book now inside her husband's briefcase. Hundreds of people streamed past, their shadows mingling and separating. She found her wallet, pulled out a twenty-dollar bill and thrust it into the driver's hand. The bill paid the fare as well as a generous tip, reflecting her good mood. She skipped up the building's stairs and paused at the kiosk located to the side of the entrance of the regal blue and silver tower.

"Good morning, Angus! Look at that sun! It's way too nice to work today," she greeted the mustached man standing behind the counter. He was short and plump with twinkling eyes and the kindness of an elderly grandfather. He had owned the newsstand for twenty years and knew most of the hundreds of the building's employees by name. The woman laid her wallet on the counter of the kiosk after removing a five-dollar bill.

"I'll take just a bottle of orange juice and the new *People* magazine. I have a meeting with my area manager in twenty-five minutes. I'm up for promotion and I don't want to be late. And, Angus, congratulate me! I've been married one month today! This is my lucky day."

"Well, good luck with the meeting, Ms. Annie. You look beautiful today. Marriage certainly agrees with you! Have a great day and I will see you tomorrow. I'm closing early, in about an hour. My grandson's coming to visit and we're going up to Lake Placid for the rest of the week. It's a long drive but I'm looking forward to some time in the country. Last weekend was too busy for me to even consider trying to hit the highway. I'll see you next Monday, and you'll be a manager by then!"

Annie laughed and picked up the paper sack containing the magazine and orange juice and stood at the bottom steps of the building. She paused for a glance high above her where the bright light of the September sun reflected back in prisms off the windows of the immense mirrored buildings. The sight never failed to make her catch her breath in awe.

She remembered well the first time she saw the New York World Trade Center's towers. She was eight years old and her family was living in Easton, Maryland. Annie was the only child of an accountant and a cardiac care nurse. Her parents adored her. She had arrived late in their lives after years of the heartache of infertility and multiple miscarriages. Annie's mother was a practical woman who encouraged her daughter in all of her endeavors and delighted in her intelligence and drive. Her parents had done everything they could to protect their child from the hurts of the world, so as Annie entered adulthood, it was clear she had no fears and possessed a confidence well beyond her years.

One July, as a birthday present, her dad had driven her north along the crowded highways through Philadelphia and Fort Lee, arriving in Manhattan in early evening. They had cruised past Madison Square Garden and down Broadway. Annie was thrilled at the elegance and energy of the great city. She begged her father to drive past the Empire

State Building and then up to the Guggenheim Museum, which she had read about.

After wandering through the streets of the teeming bustling city, they finally arrived at the Hilton Hotel on the Avenue of the Americas. Annie's father checked them into the classy hotel while Annie marveled at the high ceilings and marble floor of the lobby. She could barely contain her excitement as her father escorted her through the lobby and up the elevator to their fourteenth floor suite.

"Get dressed for dinner, Annie. I'm taking you to the best Italian restaurant in the city. We'll go sightseeing tomorrow after my meeting. Come on, now, get a move-on."

Annie's father was a trim man of fifty. During the week, he dressed immaculately in a coat and slacks, crisp white shirts and a variety of striped ties. On the weekends, however, Annie's father and mother dressed alike in a never-ending parade of matching polyester slacks and shirts. This habit embarrassed Annie as a teenager but as she grew older, it became one of the most endearing memories of her childhood.

As promised, the next afternoon when his meeting ended, Annie and her father took the subway to the stop under the enormous silver and blue buildings. Annie shielded her eyes against the summer sun as she strained to view the top of the buildings that towered more than one thousand feet in the air. She dashed to the elevator, demanding her father to hurry up. They rode up to the restaurant perched at the top of the north tower. They were eye level with bits of clouds floating past the windows while they ate a late lunch.

Two women and a little girl sat at an adjacent table. The youngster had huge chocolate-colored eyes and long legs, and tightly clutched a green blanket in her tiny hands. She sat on the lap of the beautiful older woman. The third member of the party was a younger woman with green eyes and high cheekbones. The three were obviously enjoying themselves and the location. The child had an odd name, as Annie recalled, something like a flower. She smiled at the little girl and offered her the pink rose from the tulip-shaped vase on the matching pink tablecloth. The child climbed off the lap of the older woman and shyly took the proffered rose, then turned back and buried her face in the lap of the older woman, clutching the green blanket close to her face.

Annie had smiled and returned to face her father. Their meal of salad and grilled steaks arrived. Delightful aromas filled the air as Annie sniffed hungrily. She grinned at the little girl and then turned back to her father.

"Dad, they look so happy together, just like our family. Aren't we lucky we are here? Can we go to the observation deck on top of the south tower when we're done with lunch?"

"Of course, Annie, this is your day," her father replied.

When they finished their meal, they rode the elevator down to ground level, crossed to the elevators of the south tower, and ascended back into the sky. Exiting onto the observation deck, Annie held her arms outstretched as the wind caught her ecstatic laughter and blew it back into her face. Annie felt that she could fly that day, swooping down and around the face of the silver and blue buildings and then back up to the heavens. Her father watched his daughter quietly enjoying her happiness and praying for a lifetime of more joyful moments.

"Annie," he said to her then, "you are the child of my heart and my soul. Whatever did I do to deserve you?"

The memories of that long ago day floated through Annie's soul as she paused on the steps of the building she had fallen in love with on that July day. Remembering that day and the image of the towers had been her guiding light during her high school and college years. Choosing accounting as her profession as her father before her, she researched the accounting firms that were housed in the towers, and pursued her dream to one day have a corner office as high as possible there. She became a Certified Public Accountant in late 1993 and, at the age of twenty-two, became the youngest accountant at the firm of Bergstrom and Hapner.

Each day—whether rainy, sunny, snowy, or even on hot, humid, summer days—Annie stood at the entrance of the building and gazed in wonder at the towers that held more workers and generated a greater economy than many cities or even some countries throughout the world.

She loved the firm where she worked. It was a relatively small company of four hundred people spread through eight offices across the northeast. Annie had met her husband at the café on the 107th floor of the north tower, seventeen floors above her corner office in the south tower. She noticed the slender man with the amazing blue eyes as he entered the café carrying a bulging briefcase. As he passed her table, one of the handles on the briefcase gave way, dumping a stack of papers on top of Annie's black pumps. She and the man simultaneously bent down to retrieve the papers and bumped heads. They both apologized and then bent forward again, once more hitting each other's head.

"Well, since we're so close, how about if I introduce myself and pick up my mess?" He smiled and held out his hand. "I'm Terry Jones and I am pleased to meet you."

Annie had laughed and shook the offered hand. "I'm Annie Smith and I am equally pleased to meet you. Imagine! Smith and Jones. Who would believe this? Please let me help you with this stuff before I have to go back to work."

Terry smiled back and reached into his pocket. He pulled out a business card and handed it to her. "Call me, please. I would love to treat you to dinner."

Thus began their romance. Terry was an art director at Minos and Associates, an advertising firm best known for its innovative ads for one of the largest coffee companies in the country. At twenty-eight, he was two years younger than Annie, and often teased her by telling her she had robbed the cradle. They married on August 11, 2001 in Central Park, with a hundred and fifty guests. The admiring crowd, at the request of the bride and groom, stood shoeless in the grass. The day was perfect—the trees rustled, children laughed, and the sky overhead bore an impeccable and impossible glow.

Annie wore her mother's wedding dress made of French satin with tiny buttons on the sleeves and down the back. She carried a bouquet of delicate pink roses with matching tiny pink buds in her hair. In their unique tradition, her father and mother wore matching black tuxedos and brilliant white shirts. Tears unabashedly slid down her father's weathered cheeks as he walked her down the grassy aisle. Thousands of memories of the small child who climbed onto his lap every night when he returned home from work were whirling through his consciousness.

He lovingly placed Annie's delicate hand in Terry's large one, kissed them both, and hugged Annie so tightly that it took her breath away. Finally, with a gentle kiss on her forehead, he gave them both a loving smile as he stepped back to his wife's side.

Terry's parents were both deceased but Annie's mother and father embraced him as their own son. Their love and approval grew even more when they saw the look of total devotion on his face as he slid the simple gold ring onto Annie's finger. Terry kissed Annie and they triumphantly turned to face the cheering crowd. As Annie held her bridal bouquet aloft, she heard the high, piercing cry of two peregrine falcons that sped across the sky towards the sun.

"Look, Terry," Annie whispered. "They have come to give their blessing."

Annie shook her head and giggled at herself for blushing when she thought about the wedding night a month ago. She stepped forward into the lobby, missing Angus' call as he waved to her, holding her brown wallet in his hand. As more people stepped up to the counter, Angus slipped the wallet below the shelf for safekeeping.

Annie entered an elevator and caught a glimpse of herself in the metal door as the box made its climb up the tower. The people in the elevator with Annie were a mix of colors and costumes, one of the aspects of working in the tower that Annie loved. The elevator finally stopped at the 90th floor and Annie pressed her way into the hallway. Two doors away was the entrance of Bergstrom and Hapner. Annie pushed through the door, calling a happy "Hello" to her coworkers as she made her way to her office. She placed the paper bag on the table, pulled out her chair, and sat down at her desk. As she settled in, she switched on her computer, noted the time of eight forty-five, and punched in the access code to her voice mail.

"You have one message," recited the mechanical voice.

"Annie, guess who? I love you!"

Annie hit the "save" button. She looked around her office in satisfaction. She loved the space the firm occupied. The offices were richly decorated and furnished in stylish oak and beige leather. She had been given carte blanche to decorate her office when she was hired. She chose a soft gray for the walls to match the thick carpet. Jiang paintings of storks and women hung on the walls and tall bookcases with etched glass doors stood in stately fashion against the far wall.

Annie's desk was simple: dark oak with a matching file cabinet. On the right was her wedding picture. She touched it gently, reminded of how blessed she was. In her mind's eye, she could again see the peregrines racing towards her, flying low over the heads of the wedding guests, and then back into the August sky.

In front of the desk was a large window that allowed Annie a breathtaking view of the north tower and the river beyond. On occasion, giggling in secret glee, she would roll her office chair to the window and hold her arms out wide. She imagined people in the other tower at their desks shaking their heads at the silly woman across the plaza. She could hear Carly Simon's voice singing, "Let the river run..."

On that sunny September day, a low hum of activity surrounded Annie as she readied herself for the upcoming meeting. She sang as she stared out her window, basking in the warmth of the brilliant light coming through the clear glass pane. The song was from an old movie, one that, to Annie, epitomized the glory of New York City.

> "Silver cities rise,
> The morning lights,
> The streets that meet them,
> And sirens call them on with a song"

Meanwhile, on the street below, Terry's cab pulled up in front of the north tower.

"How much?" he asked the driver.

"Ten dollars, sir, and you have a great day." the cabbie replied.

"Oh, I will," Terry said to himself. He leaned into the taxi to pull out his new briefcase and straightened up, stepping back onto the sidewalk. "It's almost time for her meeting. I better get going."

The sky was growing bluer by the minute. Terry could feel his spirit rise at the thought of surprising Annie. He had taken only one step towards the tower when a huge shadow passed overhead and an explosion rocked the air. Terry's head jerked up along with those of

thousands of fellow-New Yorkers. He was confused as he saw fireballs blooming out of the north tower high above the earth. Thick black smoke began to billow in the morning air and, as Terry stood in shock, debris began to fall to the ground. Broken glass fell around the crowds on the street, people panicking and screaming with the realization of what had just happened.

"What was that?" Terry yelled to a woman who had been walking by him on the sun-soaked sidewalk.

"It was a plane. How awful. It must be some type of accident. My God, look at that. The building is on fire. Good lord, what's going on?" the woman screamed at the surrounding crowd.

The busy streets came to a halt, cars pulled to the side and people stared up at the blue and silver building now wrapped in ribbons of smoke. A collective silence rolled over the tourists and native New Yorkers, businessmen and housewives. Looks of fear passed from person to person and then, as if one, people began to run down Greenwich and up Barclay Avenue.

Terry took a deep breath in an effort to calm himself as he reached into the breast pocket of his jacket. Suddenly, the air was cold and more debris began to rain down around him. He pulled out his cell phone and ran towards the overhang that covered the entrance of the south tower. The crowds on the sidewalk seemed to move in slow motion away from him as the wail of sirens filled the air. Police began to run past him towards the entrance of the north tower. Terry stood rooted in shock. He could hear the squawk of the radios, the calm voices of the dispatchers relating horrific events. Fire trucks screeched to a halt in front of him and firefighters sprinted into the stricken building. Swallowing his panic but with his hands still shaking, Terry punched in the numbers to Annie's cell phone, misdialing three times before hearing her voice on the other end.

"Terry, oh Terry! I just saw the most horrid thing. There was a huge explosion in the north tower. I can see the flames. They are telling us a plane crashed into it. We have to evacuate. No one seems to know what's going on. Terry, I am so scared."

"Annie, don't worry. Your building looks fine. I'm down here on the street and I am coming to get you."

"Terry, they won't let you up. Security is telling us to go to the elevators and leave. I will be down to where you are in a few minutes. Can you see what is happening? All we can see up here is smoke and things falling to the ground." Annie's voice rose in pitch and she seemed on the edge of hysteria.

"Honey, calm down. Stay put. I'm coming up. Stay on the phone." Terry attempted to push through the front door but a security guard blocked his way.

"I am sorry, sir," the guard said. "My orders are to not let anyone in. You'll have to go back outside." His radio crackled and the guard held it to his ear. He nodded in response to a terse dispatcher.

"Sir, we are evacuating the building. You'll have to go."

"My wife is in there! I need to get to her!" Terry was frantic as he tried to move around the guard. A policewoman stepped in front of Terry and firmly pushed him back outside.

"I'm sorry, sir. Everyone has to leave. You have to vacate these premises."

The falling debris hit the sidewalk in crashing waves around the entry to the north tower. People scrambled from the disintegrating building, shielding themselves against the pieces of metal and shattered glass dropping all around them. The flames high up on the side of the structure were building in intensity and Terry could see people coming out of the doors of the south tower.

"Annie, Annie, where are you?" Terry cried into his phone. "I can't get in the building. Come down NOW! You have to get out of there!"

"Terry, I am fine. I'll be down in a few minutes. I'll meet you at the front door." Annie hung up her cell phone and turned off the computer. Her manager stood at her door, motioning her to his side.

"Annie, you have to leave. They are saying it was a jet that hit the building. Come on. Everyone else is ready to leave. Stay close to the rest of us and we will all go down together." Annie's manager, a small, kind, middle-aged man, moved to the next office, repeating his message to the other employees in the firm. Annie turned for a moment to look at the north tower, wondering how the firefighters could possibly reach the floor the fire was on and what had happened to the people in the path of the plane. She glanced at the clock as she moved towards the door. 9:02, two minutes past the start of the planned meeting.

Annie reached into her purse to put her cell phone into the inside pocket. As she started to close her purse, she noticed her wallet was nowhere to be seen. She rummaged through her purse and then placed it on the desk. Kneeling down, she looked under her chair and around the desk. Suddenly, a horrific shock wave shook the building. The lights flickered as the building began to sway.

Annie was knocked off her knees prone to the ground. Her mind raced as explosions rocked the building. The lights flickered one more time and then went out completely, the light from the outside the only illumination. She could hear her cell phone ring. She groped for her purse but it was nowhere to be found. Outside her office, Annie could hear people screaming and calling to each other. She heard her manager's voice ordering people to "calm down" and to gather in the office's lobby area. Annie's cell phone continued to ring and, by tracking its sound, she finally found her purse. She was trembling as she flipped open the phone and pushed the Talk button.

"Annie, Annie!" Terry was screaming into the phone. "Annie, Annie. Oh, Jesus, Annie. We're under attack. A plane just hit your building. You have to get out, Annie, Annie. Get out NOW!"

"Terry, we are all coming down together. The lights are out and I am not sure if the elevators are working. Don't worry. I'm coming down. I'll call you back in a minute. I have to make sure everyone is safe."

Annie dropped the phone back into her purse and then pulled the strap over her shoulder. She felt her way through the door of her office and along the walls to the lobby. In the dimming light, she could see a group of twenty or more people huddled together in the lobby of the Bergstrom and Hapner offices. She saw her manager counting people and asking everyone to please listen.

"We're close to the stairwell," he spoke in a quiet but firm voice. "All of you—stay calm. We need to make sure everyone is out of the back offices. We need to make sure everyone is safe. Who isn't here? As soon as everyone is accounted for, we'll all go to the elevators together." His tone belied the fear and ugly awareness that was creeping through his mind.

Annie stood next to Ginger, the office assistant, a tall young woman with flaming red hair, green eyes and freckles. Annie watched as more of her coworkers appeared in the lobby. The manager returned with the last group and looked around. His kind face was creased with worry but he maintained a soothing voice as he addressed his employees.

"Okay, everyone is here. Let's all stick together and get to the elevators."

The floor beneath Annie's feet began to shake and quiver as if it was made of sand. She grabbed Ginger to steady herself and then reached for the back of a chair. In the gloom, she could make out the shapes of people filling the halls, some running to the elevators, others walking quickly with cell phones pressed to their ears.

"Don't bother with the elevators. They're not working," a voice from the hallway called. "We're all going to have to take the stairs."

A sense of panic permeated the lobby. It was as palpable as the chair beneath her hand. Annie broke out in a cold sweat on her back and under her arms. With trembling hands, she pulled her cell phone out of her purse and dialed Terry's number.

"Annie, where are you?" Terry pleaded hysterically. "Please, come on down to me. It looks like the sky is falling. Annie, what are you doing?"

"The elevators aren't working. We are going to have to take the stairs. We are all leaving now. I have to go. It is so smoky I can't breathe. . It's so dark we can't see anything and everyone is scared. Ginger and I are the last ones in the office now. Everyone is waiting for us at the stairwell. I have to go."

"Annie, Annie!" Terry screamed into the phone. "Don't hang up. Annie!"

Terry heard the terrifying sounds of trembling glass as the sky began to darken around him. People pushed through the main lobby doors, many of them holding their hands over their bloodied faces, clutching the arms of those around them. A cadre of police stood in the entrance and, as Terry watched, dozens more firefighters, carrying hoses and clothed in heavy boots and coats darted into the building.

Terry moved from beneath the overhang of the building and, through the blowing smoke and falling debris, strained to see the window that marked Annie's office. Around him, frantic people ran down the streets away from the wounded towers. In sharp contrast to the panic, fire trucks and police cars squealed to a stop, some up on the sidewalk while others parked three deep on the streets. One of the police officers pulled Terry by the arm.

"It isn't safe here, sir. You must leave the area."

"I can't leave! My wife is in there. She hasn't come out!"

Terry pulled away from the officer and backed up farther toward the building to see if he could by some miracle find his beloved wife. The east corner of the tower continued to burn. Windows, shattered from the heat, plummeted to the earth below. Terry watched as a large piece of flaming metal fell to the street only a few feet from where he stood.

A thousand feet above him, Annie tried pushing her way into the hallway. She held Ginger's hand as tightly as she could but they were separated in the crush. She could no longer see anyone she recognized and, frightened, she pulled back into the lobby.

I'll wait a few minutes, she told herself, making her way back to her office. She could see the light coming in through the window and reflecting off the glass fronts of the bookcases lining the wall of her office. She could make out the picture of her and Terry from the wedding and grabbed it to her chest. She placed it back on the desk and slowly walked to the window and looked down.

"I know you're down there, Terry. Where are you? Wave and I will see you." She dialed Terry's cell phone and, breathing a sigh of relief, heard his voice.

"Terry, I have to wait. There are too many people trying to get down the stairs now. I can't find anyone from the firm. I'm going to wait just a few minutes."

"Annie, the building is falling apart. You have to leave NOW! They are making all of us leave the area. Annie, I love you. You have to come now. Annie, I love you. Annie, Annie, Annie!" Terry began to scream as the phone went dead. He dialed her number over and over but to no avail. As he watched, the south tower appeared to sink and tilt. He stared in horror as bodies fell from the windows of the north tower. More people scrambled out of the doors of both buildings as more rescuers rushed in. The day that had started so gloriously had turned into a hellish scene of bloodied people, cascading papers, and asphyxiating dust.

Annie continued to stand at the window, the dead cell phone held limply in her hand, then falling useless to the ground. She dropped her purse from her shoulder and heard it hit the carpet. In the hallway, outside the main doors of the Bergstrom and Hapner offices, she heard the sounds of running feet and crying voices. She pressed her face against the glass of her office window, the smoothness of the surface solid against the grit-laden air. Off in the distance, she could see a last glimpse of the river. She could see the crippled north tower and remembered the day she and her father had that late lunch of salad and steak. She recalled the face of the little girl with the chocolate-brown eyes as she handed her the pink rose and, in the darkness of the room, she remembered the little girl's name: "Wisteria," Annie murmured into the empty room. "I remember now. She had just learned to say it. That's what the women were laughing at, Wisteria."

Annie began to cry, silent sobs shaking her body. She made her way back to the door and down the hallway to the lobby of the suite of offices. She called out Ginger's name and then for anyone who might hear her. She groped her way outside the main doors and slipped in among the people making their way to the stairs. A man ahead of her fell and was pulled back to his feet by other's hands. Annie caught a glimpse of the stairwell's steel door only a few feet ahead of her. She began to push her way towards the door and safety when the building began to shake again.

Frightened, Annie turned back from the crowded corridor once more. She slid along the walls to the safety of the Bergstrom and Hapner lobby. The smoke was getting denser now and the building shook again. She no longer knew whether to stay or to attempt the endless journey back to the stairs. The crowds seemed less than before but Annie was terrified of being caught in the stairwell with fire possibly above and below her. A filtered light illuminated a path guiding her back to the security of her office. As before, she inched across the floor to the now-beckoning window.

The building seemed to buckle and heave, a dying animal groaning in the throes of death. Around Annie, the air grew heavier with smoke but she could feel no heat. She saw the light of the small pewter clock on the desk. It was a battery-powered alarm clock in the shape of a sitting cat, with the clock in the belly of the cat. Her father had given her the clock on that long-ago day she'd first come to the towers.

It had been nearly an hour since the plane hit the building. She could no longer hear any voices in the hall and she resolved to make the long trek to safety down the stairs. Once more, Annie faced the door of her office. Tiny speckles of moisture marked her face. The darkness of the building seemed even more menacing as a stronger smell of smoke reached Annie's nostrils and the building continued to creak and groan.

"Oh, Terry, are you waiting for me? Are you gone? Mom and Dad, are you thinking of me? Do you know I love you all?" Annie spoke into the silence of the suite of offices. The shapes of her desk and chairs no longer seemed familiar to her, instead becoming part of the menace that Annie could feel all around her. Suddenly, she realized she was no longer alone. Hearing Ginger whisper her name, she turned towards the voice and saw a tall shadow in the doorway to her office.

"Annie, the stairs are blocked. We can't get down. I don't know where anyone is. We can't get out. Some of the people went to the roof but the doors are locked there, too. Annie, what are we going to do?"

Ginger collapsed to the floor, her hands pressed to the sides of her head.

"My son is alone in the apartment. He was sick and stayed home from school. Who is going to care for him? Annie, no one is left here with us. I don't know where they are. I'll never see my baby again."

"Ginger, come stand by the window with me. Look, you can see all the fire trucks and the police. They're coming to get us. Come and look. I won't leave you alone."

Annie turned from the window and reached out for Ginger. As she did, another large shock wave traveled through the building. The breaking window's shattered glass fell into the room, spraying both Annie and Ginger. Annie stumbled to the floor. After what seemed like an eternity, she crawled to Ginger who sat dazed and expressionless. Annie wrapped her arms around Ginger and pressed her face against her shoulder.

"Ginger, your son will be fine. We will find a way to get out. We just have to sit here for a few minutes and then go to the stairway."

"I was out there in that stairway. There are no lights. You can't see your hand in front of your face. People were panicking and leaving the stairwell to get out on lower floors. I came back because there was no place to go. Annie, what are we going to do? Tell me, please!"

Annie took her arms from around Ginger and leaned back against the bookcase. She could see a plume of black smoke streaming in front of the north tower. She shook her head at the sight and felt her heart begin to race.

"I hope Terry went home, Ginger. He was down at the entrance, waiting for me. I don't know why he came. We were talking on my cell phone and then the line went dead."

Annie twisted her hands in the fabric of her blue cotton skirt.

"Ginger, did you know today is my one month wedding anniversary? Terry and I got married in Central Park. My dad was so happy, he cried more than my mom. Terry has the bluest eyes; that's what I fell in love with. He is so kind. His parents died only six months apart. He said his dad died of a broken heart after his mom went. He always told me that he wanted to have that kind of marriage. I hope he knows how much I love him."

Ginger reached over and took Annie's hand. The women sat quietly, both of them thinking of their loved ones below. Ginger broke the silence, staring at the luminous hands of her watch.

"Annie, it's 9:50; almost ten o'clock. It's been almost an hour and no one has come. What are we going to do?"

"Ginger, do you have your cell phone? We can call for help. My phone is dead. Terry is down there on the street. He'll tell them we're here. We'll get out."

"Annie, I'm scared! Please, don't leave me alone. I'm so scared. I don't want to die. Let's go to the window. I want to see the sky. I hate the dark."

Annie pulled herself up and then reached for Ginger. Grasping each other, the two women slowly edged across the room to stand by the glassless window. The wind blew in through the gaping space. With it came smoke and debris. Annie put her hands on either side of the frame and leaned out into the endless space between the two towers. Another spasm shook the building. Annie leaned farther out the window and tried to pick out Terry from the people now fleeing from the disaster. From a height of nearly a thousand feet, the scene looked chaotic. Annie could hear the noise of the sirens and watched as dozens of emergency vehicles jammed the streets. Tiny pieces of metal and glass, paper and dust floated through the air. Down, down, down Annie looked and then she saw him. His eyes were blue and his hand was raised, calling his love to her.

"Ginger," Annie said in a voice that seemed from a distance, "did I tell you Terry and I have been married a month? He gave me this skirt."

Ginger looked up in fright as Annie spoke.

"Annie, what are you doing? You just told me that. Annie! Annie! What are you doing?"

Annie continued to speak as if she had not heard Ginger. "I really love him. Do you remember the words of that song; the one from the movie where the woman sat in the window of the building?"

Annie began to sing and, as she did, Ginger backed away from the open window.

"Listen, Ginger…
Come run with me now
The sky is the color of blue
You've never even seen
In the eyes of your lover.

"My lover has the bluest eyes, Ginger. They matched the sky this morning. I blew him a kiss as I left. My cat was lying on the rug in the dining room and Terry was drinking coffee. I never even drank my orange juice or read my *People* magazine. I never had time."

Annie smiled as she leaned into the wind blowing through the room and ruffling her hair. She stared out into the sky and then began to speak:

"I have to go, Ginger. I don't want to stay anymore. I'm sorry but I have to go. I can't stay. He's waiting for me down there. He's waving to me. I have to go."

Annie looked up into the last of the blue autumn sky. Above her, silent as the mist that came off the river on winter days, she could see two birds flying through the dust and smoke. The peregrines pointed their wings to the sky and, as Annie watched, they dove towards her. She stepped onto the edge of the window and, as Ginger screamed her name, Annie fell into space, her brown hair streaming into the wind, her hands holding her skirt to her legs.

On each side of her, a falcon sailed towards the earth. The blue and silver of the beautiful tower slid past her eyes and she thought of the man who waited below. She closed her eyes and took a deep breath. She reached out for the wings of the falcons and, as the ground came up to meet her, she opened her eyes and saw his loving face. In her final second, Annie smiled and whispered, "I love you, Terry."

◄4►

The Peregrine Falcons

Manhattan, New York   J a n u a r y   1 1 .   2 0 0 2

Falling snowflakes mixed with the dust and smoke that continued floating across the Manhattan sky four months after the morning the world ended. High up on the fourteenth floor of the 55 Water Street building, two peregrine falcons peered down at the street. Pigeon feathers littered the bottom of their nest, tiny stray pinfeathers grabbed by the wind and blown into the air. A short distance away, the remnants of the towers stood in silence, now a grave to more than three thousand voices silenced in a matter of moments. Lola stood with her niece at Ground Zero, their heads bowed both in grief and against the cold of the wind as it blew up from the river. They had come east, a journey of two generations. Lola's only requirement of the trip was a visit to Ground Zero to pay homage to those whose lives were stolen on that infamous September day.

Lola's niece, Wisteria, had flown from Los Angeles to meet her aunt four days earlier. She was a tall young woman with deep, dark brown eyes. She was twenty-seven years old and went by the unusual nickname of Istie. This nickname was bestowed on her by her Auntie Louella when she was two years old as it became clear that Wisteria could not pronounce her own name. It was a personal family amusement that

Wisteria's mother, Lila LeFleur, Lola's only sibling, named her daughter after a climbing plant. Wisteria's mother was prone to other absurdities. The final one was an overdose of Seconal, alcohol and pretzels. She was found on her bed, dressed in a yellowed wedding gown, her right arm extended over her eyes and her left hand clutching a bottle of Moët & Chandon champagne.

So, at the age of one, Istie had permanently moved in with Lola and her great-aunt, Louella. She arrived with only a suitcase of clothes and a ragged green blanket. Wanting comfort, Istie dragged that little blanket everywhere she went. Within a few days, she and Auntie had formed an unholy alliance. Lola became the bottom point on the pyramid, surpassed only by the myriad of cats that came in and out of the lives of the three generations of LeFleur women.

Lola's sister claimed Istie's father was her mysterious never-seen-or-heard-from husband. Lola had her doubts since that phantom was supposed to have had brilliant blue eyes like Istie's mother. Lola doubted that the Mendelian law could account for Istie's dark eyes. Rather, Lola suspected that Lila had been out on one of her escapades and, in reality, had no idea who fathered this lovely child.

These bizarre thoughts rambled through Lola's head as she peered through the fence to where the trucks and tractors continued their grisly work of clearing away the remnants of the once-graceful and stunning buildings. She imagined bones and pieces of clothing being scooped up by the recovery workers, never to be identified or seen again. She imagined people waiting in their homes for word of the missing; waiting for any tiny speck of hope.

Standing side by side, the two women were clearly related, but the only visible sign of their shared heritage were the high cheekbones and identical grins and grimaces. Istie was wrapped in a gray woolen coat, pulled tight around her slender body. Dampened from the cold and spitting rain, the coat evoked the sheep smell and dust reminiscent of that day in Minot when the world ended. Papers, bits of plastic and tiny pebbles blew around their feet as Lola stood mesmerized by the towers' remnants.

"I don't understand, Auntie," Istie shook her head. "Why was it so important for you to come here? Wasn't it enough watching that horror play over and over on TV? Was it really necessary to see this in person? Honestly, you are such a morbid person. How long do we have to stay?"

"Istie," Lola replied, "I had to come. I could feel the pull of those lost souls. So many of them are restless, searching for peace. They just want to go home. Can't you feel them?"

Istie shivered, shaking her head. "I swear, old woman, you just freak me out. Come on. I thought we were going to see Lady Liberty and go back to the hotel. This is not my idea of a good time. All I want is a scrumptious dinner and some time to pack. I hate your morbidity. You seem to be enjoying your misery, but I'm hungry. I want dinner!"

Lola had promised her niece a trip to South Africa to see the animals and the cosmopolitan center of Cape Town. The trip was a reward for graduating from college, but the night before, over a pasta dinner, Istie admitted she was still one credit short. She insisted it was a clerical mistake on the part of the university but Lola, knowing Istie's tendency toward both drama and laziness, had her doubts.

The two women spent their time in Manhattan exploring museums, the tall skyscrapers, Central Park, and the thousands of kiosks lining the frigid streets. At night, Lola watched as Istie sat spellbound through *The Lion King* and *Phantom of the Opera*. She envied Istie's ability to immerse herself in a world of fantasy, oblivious to the realities of life—obviously inherited from her mother. That same trait had ultimately led to Lila's death when, at the age of twenty-nine, the reality of a one-year-old daughter and no man on the horizon collided with her fantasy of the white picket fence and never having to work.

Throughout the days that Lola and Istie spent in Manhattan, the towers were never far from Lola's mind. She counted down the minutes to the time she and Istie were to leave for South Africa from JFK airport. She waited until the last day of their time in Manhattan before gently demanding that they head to the lower end of the island.

"Istie, I told you before we came, I had to see the towers. The souls are waiting for us. I don't want to talk about it anymore. I am asking for one hour out of four days. Stop whining!" Lola's voice rose in irritation as the two women stood by the chain link fence that closed them off from the haunting remains of the north and south towers. "Just give me five more minutes. I swear, you are as big a nag as your dear departed great-aunt!"

Just as Lola's words were spoken, she heard the sound of fluttering wings overhead. Lola and Istie instinctively ducked as two peregrines dove into the depths of the crater. As the falcons raced towards the earth, Lola saw the figure of a woman floating from the sky, her hands outstretched as if to touch the wings of the birds. Turning, the birds raced skyward, circling overhead and then flying off into the snowy, dirty Manhattan air. Lola trembled inside her coat and layers of sweaters as she watched the pair of raptors disappear into the distance.

"Okay, Istie. Let's go catch the boat. Don't forget the shopping bags."

The two women turned to walk down the street to hail a taxi. They had gone only a few steps when Lola noticed something wedged under a section of the cyclone fence.

"Istie, wait, let me see what this is. Wait just a minute."

It was a brown wallet, cold and wet, and empty save for a fading photograph of a young couple. Once again, Lola saw a familiar young woman , the same woman Lola believed had flown with the peregrines that fateful day. Her heart started to stutter and then began to race. She began to feel the same slippage of time, fear and horror that she had experienced that day at Devils Tower. She saw the plane speeding across the sky and plunging into the silver and blue building. The building burst into flames and smoke filled the air. Lola smelled the smoke and felt the ash on her skin. She choked on the thick smoke and swirling debris. She looked skyward and saw a small figure floating down towards the earth, growing larger with each second. As the figure fell, Lola saw the young woman, her brown hair streaming and skirt held primly to her sides. As the falling woman neared the ground, she spread her arms out as if to embrace her fate.

Lola heard the screams from the people trapped in the building and those running in staggering fear down below in the streets, far away from the crumbling monoliths. In the moments before the young woman struck the earth, the two peregrine falcons appeared in a free fall, accompanying her to the earth. In the breath before she ended her plunge, her hands were grabbed by the birds. As they soared upward, they held her hands in their talons. She rose to the heavens with the peregrines, disappearing into the endless blue sky, above the plumes of smoke and the two flaming towers.

As the vision continued, Lola clutched the open wallet in one hand and reached out to the chain link fence with the other. Sinking to her knees, she felt only darkness descending over her, surrounded by the heavy New York air. As if from a great distance, Lola could hear sobs and her niece calling her name. Slowly, Lola began to regain consciousness. She felt Istie's hand plucking at the sleeve of her coat and gently rubbing her face. Lola looked down into the bowels of the earth that were once where the silver and blue buildings stood and then raised her tear-fogged eyes to Istie's face.

"Istie, oh Istie…" Trembling, Lola turned and grasped her niece by one arm, while shaking the wallet at her.. "Oh, Istie. My God, it was her. She is the one. This was her picture. She was the one that fell. Oh, Istie, it was her parents on the train; the ones Auntie Louella and I met coming home from Minot. I know it's her.. . I keep seeing her… It *has to* be her!"

"Auntie, what are you talking about? You aren't making any sense. Auntie, CALM DOWN! You are raving like a lunatic. There isn't anyone here but you and me. Look, there is no one here. Come on! You're acting crazy and you're scaring me. I knew it was a mistake to come here. Damn you and your doomed sense of the world. Come on!"

Istie's voice rose in shrillness, sounding exactly like the cries of the peregrine falcons. Lola placed one hand on her knee and pulled herself up. She wiped her eyes and nose on her coat and, holding the wallet in one hand, leaned her back against the cold links and pulled her hat down over her eyes.

"Istie," Lola whispered, "come and look. I know it's her."

"Auntie Lola, have you lost your mind? Please, come on…this place is giving me the creeps."

Lola shook her head at Istie. This same picture kept appearing before her. She now knew that she had been with the girl's parents. She tucked

the wallet into her purse. Pulling her coat tightly around her body, she reached out to Istie and took her hand.

"Okay, my darling. Let's go down to the river and catch our boat to Lady Liberty."

As the two women hurried down the nearly empty sidewalks, Istie held out a gloved thumb. "I am catching a cab. This cold is making my teeth hurt."

Istie stepped into the road and, within seconds, a bright yellow cab pulled to the curb. Istie pulled open the door and turned to Lola: "Come on, old lady, get your bony butt into this cab. Hey, driver, down to the place where we catch the Liberty Island boat. You know, Battery Park."

"Istie! Show some respect!" Lola chided.

Istie was often demanding and abrupt, two characteristics inherited from the LeFleur side of her ancestry, traits that all LeFleur women shared but loathed to admit. The driver muttered something in Greek or Russian, the only understandable comment being "crazy woman!"

"I am not," Istie responded indignantly. "Just take us to Battery Park."

Before getting underway, the cabbie reached for his cell phone. He chatted for a few seconds and then pulled away from the curb, racing down the street. The rocking of the cab seemed oddly soothing to Lola. She sighed and leaned back against the seat, ignoring the rips in the fabric where the white stuffing came through. Istie lay down across the tattered seat, putting her head in Lola's lap, much as she had when she was a small child and had first come to live in the old house on the hill above the lake.

Istie hummed "Circle of Life" from *The Lion King* and pulled her fuzzy green gloves off her hands. She had purchased them the first day she and Lola were in Manhattan. She had forgotten the great temperature difference between Southern California and the freezing streets of New York City. She handed the gloves to Lola and began to pick at the black fingernail polish she was sporting this week. Lola took Istie's hand and turned it over. On the inside of her left wrist was a tattoo of a tiny black cat holding the stem of an even tinier white daisy in its mouth. Under the tattoo in delicate and elegant script were the words "*Le Petite Chat Noir.*"

Auntie Louella had called Istie her "little black cat," a name that enchanted Istie, who in turn insisted every cat she brought home had to be tiny and black. When Istie turned eighteen, she informed Lola of her decision to get a tattoo. Lola groaned and protested at such a permanent choice but was soundly overruled by Auntie Louella's encouragement. Two weeks after Istie's eighteenth birthday, Lola came home to an empty house and a note from Istie asking her to meet her and Auntie Louella at the Starbucks at the end of the block.

Lola knew that something had gone on that she would disapprove of and that waiting on the table at the café would be a hot mint tea and a scone. She grimaced as she read the note, while the latest in a long line of tiny black cats rubbed against her leg.

Lola made her way through the crowded coffee bar towards the table where Auntie and Istie sat. She could see their heads together, laughing and toasting one another with a clink of their coffee cups. Lola pulled out the empty third chair and put her purse on the table. As she had expected, a cup of hot mint tea was already waiting for her.

"Okay, you two. What's the deal this time?" Lola sipped her tea and waited for Auntie's reply

In unison, Auntie and Istie pulled up their sweater sleeves, showing identical tattoos of little black cats. Lola shook her head and said nothing, but silently cursed their foolishness as she stared at their newly acquired artwork.

Lola smiled at the memory and stroked Istie's hair as they drove through the streets of New York City. Outside the snow began falling again, reducing visibility. She thought of the blue sky from that September morning and again saw the streaming brown hair of the woman as she fell to earth. After a very short ride, they arrived at Battery Park. Virtually no one was in the park at the edge of the water. Off in the distance, Ms. Liberty's majestic silhouette was barely visible through the dust and the snow. She beckoned to Lola and Istie, her eternally calm gaze searching into the distance.

"Oh, Istie," Lola whispered. "Isn't she wonderful? Do you remember when we came here with Auntie? You were so little. You climbed into the crown, refusing to leave until we carried you down. Do you remember eating lunch in the north tower of the World Trade Center? A little girl gave you a pink rose. You were dragging your green blanket around. So many memories here, Istie. So many losses but maybe there is also some hope left here."

The bare trees of January rattled their bony branches as Lola and Istie sat on an empty bench, waiting for their boat. Hip to hip, leg to leg, the two women sat, entwined in the history of their blood and the sadness of a winter's day in New York City.

⋙ ⋘

The next morning, Lola awoke at seven. She glanced over at the bed across the room where Istie lay buried in the pillows and covers, one foot sticking out from beneath the blanket. Lola groaned and swung her feet over the side of the bed. She stood up and looked around the darkened room. Istie's clothes and towels were flung far and wide around the small space.

"Some things never change," Lola muttered and bent down to pick up her purse from the floor. As she did so, its contents fell to the ground, rolling among Istie's possessions. She reached under the bed and felt around. Her fingers closed on the wallet and she pulled it towards her, opening it once more. She sat back on the floor and stared.

"Why do you continue to haunt me? I wonder who you are. What do I do with you?" Lola asked the woman in the picture. "Who are you? Why do I keep seeing you? Who *are* you?"

"Istie, Istie!" Lola stood and nudged her niece's foot . "Istie, get up. We have to pack. I'm taking a shower and I need you up and packed by the time I get out. Istie, wake up."

Istie mumbled and pulled the covers further over her head. Lola sighed in resignation and stepped to the window, opening the blackout curtain to the pale winter light. She made her way over the discarded clothing Istie had thrown on the floor the previous night and finally stumbled into the bathroom. Turning on the overhead light, she winced at the brightness against the bathroom's pink tile. The countertop was cracked and the mirror had clearly seen better days. The walls of the room were covered with black and gold flocked wallpaper, a radiator chugged underneath the window that overlooked the noisy streets, its crowds, and the insanity of Broadway.

Istie had fallen in love with the hotel but Lola shook her head in disappointment over the poor quality of accommodation that three hundred dollars a night bought in this city. The only redeeming factor was the black marbled lobby that stretched nearly a block and a Starbucks on either side of the doors leading out to the busy streets. Each morning Lola and Istie had been in New York, Lola made the trek downstairs to purchase a *vente* hot chocolate and newspaper for herself and a caramel macchiato for her niece.

Lola squinted at herself in the mirror and then reached into the shower to turn on the water. Pipes creaked and moaned and finally, with much effort, the water began to flow. She continued her critical self-examination, pinching where her flesh had once been tight and shaking her head at the breasts that now pointed to the floor.

"How did I get so old? Day by day." Lola sighed at her own question, and use of the phrase she had heard Auntie Louella say at each birthday.

She stepped into the tub and pulled at the pink flamingo shower curtain. It was a poor imitation of art deco but was in keeping with the tenor of the rest of the room. She scrubbed her legs and wondered, for the thousandth time, where her knees and the firmness of her thighs had gone. Lola stood beneath the spraying water and again allowed her thoughts to drift to the young woman in the photograph, and her visions of her at Ground Zero.

"Who are you? Are you the one I think you are? Was it your parents on the train that day? Did you fall or did you jump? Who were you thinking of? Your husband, your children, your mother and father? Did you think about your death or did you think about your life? Who are you? I need to know."

A sudden thump against the door startled Lola and she realized she was still holding the soap in her hand, her fingers wrinkled from the long soaking under the shower. Another thump sounded at the door as Lola heard the faint sound of the television. She could hear Istie singing in the bedroom, her voice high-pitched and warbling.

"Auntie, I'm up!" Istie sang the words and a third thump hit the door.

Lola turned off the water, grabbed a towel and muttered expletives as she opened the door; the steam billowed into the bedroom, fogging up the window twenty-two floors above the street. As she stalked into the bedroom, she stubbed her toe on Istie's oversized green duffel bag. Contrary to Lola's hope of a clean room and a packed bag, Istie was sitting on her bed, her hair in braids, and the remote lying by her legs atop the blanket.

"What the hell are you doing out here" Lola asked. "What were you doing to make so much noise?"

Istie continued to stare at the television, ignoring Lola's question. She pointed to Lola's bed where Annie Jones's wallet lay. She then pointed to the window.

"Are you getting up? What are you pointing at?"

Lola could feel her irritation growing. She surveyed the clutter in the room with dismay and turned to go back inside the pink bathroom when Istie began to hum again and jabbed her finger at the window. Clutching the towel to her chest, Lola turned back to look out the window. Perched on the ledge outside the dirty glass were two peregrine falcons. Tear-dropped faces gazed at Lola and Istie. At the feet of the larger female bird was a white pigeon, the smaller male holding the pigeon tightly in its talons. The pigeon's head lay at an odd angle but there was no blood on its pristine white feathers.

Istie took the remote and turned off the television, patting the space on the bed beside her. Lola, gazing in awe at the falcons, slowly sat down. Istie leaned forward and wrapped her arms around Lola's neck. She nuzzled her face up against Lola's and, for a moment, their cheeks touched in a loving caress.

"They took her spirit to heaven, Auntie Lola. We saw them yesterday at Ground Zero. Stop worrying. She's fine. But Auntie, look, aren't they beautiful. You can stop worrying now. She's at peace."

Lola wiped her eyes on the rough towel and hugged her niece close to her chest.

"I love you, Istie."

On the ledge, as the cold winter sun shed its light on the side of the grime-streaked building, the female peregrine lifted off into the sky, her wings flapping and then outstretched as she soared over the wounded city. She called loudly and persistently to her mate to join her in glorious flight. Lola and Istie watched in silence, two generations connected forever by love and blood. The male finally took to the sky in response to the female's call, the white pigeon held tightly in his grasp. As the birds flew away, Lola's gazed dropped to the wallet once again. She stared at the picture but this time thought she saw an angelic smile on the woman's face.

⇥ 5 ⇤

The Flying Salmon

The three women had traveled south Wednesday afternoon. Freeway traffic had crept along the clogged arteries that ran through the heart of the cities lining the banks of Puget Sound. It was noon when they had climbed into Lola's Tahoe. The back of the vehicle was crammed with all the essentials for the evening's sweat lodge: plastic boxes, camp chairs, and cans of smudge. The warm dark womb where the Creator's spirit lived stood peacefully in the cool woods, longing for heated rocks, river water, and sage that would offer healing to the humans who sought to share in its serenity. The moon had passed into fullness at 10:55 in the morning, and the night promised to be warm and sultry—perfect for an evening around the fire and the snug heat of the lodge.

Lola's two female companions for the evening were thirty-five years apart in age but identical in loveliness of heart, mind and soul. The younger woman had been christened Alexandra but was known to all as Rona Nui, The Woman in the Moon. Rona was in her late twenties, of average height and build with skin that was always described as porcelain. Her hair and eyes were the color of fine Belgian dark chocolate. She wore a Maori quarter moon-shaped greenstone around her neck. She was engaged to a musician who made his living writing jingles for television commercials but whose true love was writing cowboy operas. Rona was a master chef with culinary talents rivaling any seen on the food channels.

Kristin, the older of the two women, was shorter with fine blonde hair shading to gray. She was the mother of two sons, born ten months apart. Both were now thirty-six years old. The eldest, River, was in the Army and stationed at Fort Campbell, Kentucky. The younger son, Chazz, was very young when he enlisted during the first Gulf War and, after a fourth positing in the desert, decided it was time to return to the green of the Northwest. Since his discharge in early summer of 2001, he and his wife had lived with Kristin in a small house overlooking Puget Sound. That is, until Chazz's most recent sexual conquest had caused him to leave Kristen's home and her daughter-in-law moved home to her own parents.

Kristin's ex-husband was a vice-president at a local software corporation. Their marriage had ended when she found him in a highly compromising position with his nineteen-year-old intern in the back of his Mercedes in the nearby Safeway parking lot. The divorce settlement allowed her to pursue her passion for art classes and three-martini dinners at the Four Seasons Hotel on a weekly basis. She never referred to her former husband by name, preferring "cold bastard" on the frequent occasions she discussed his indiscretion.

The women had spent many nights in the lodge along the Cowlitz River. This time, Kristin requested the lodge's use for an evening of healing and prayer. She brought along gifts of sage, tobacco and sweet grass to use during the ceremony. Kristin needed the healing rituals to cleanse the stress and strain caused by daily life and the impending divorce of her youngest son. She'd always referred to herself as an "energy magnet," absorbing the aches and pains, feelings and thoughts of those around her. This was particularly true of her kinship with these two women. She leaned over the back of the front passenger seat, speaking in a low voice to Rona about the poor choices of a wayward son and the approaching end of the long life of a beloved grandmother.

"My son left his wife, you know," Kristin said, as if this was new news. "He told me he could not deal with the stupidity of her family any longer. Bombastic, that's what he called his father-in-law. He just can't seem to settle down. He said it's been that way for the past year, ever since he got back from Saudi Arabia this last time. He gets so angry. He is always chasing a new skirt. Now, he's gone off to parts unknown with his latest. He calls me every morning at seven, while I'm having breakfast, just to tell me he is still alive."

Oldies songs spilled out from the car radio, one after another. Lola particularly enjoyed the beautiful notes of the instrumental portion of "Layla," the lovely words of "While my guitar gently weeps;" and the incomparable vocals of the Righteous Brothers crooning "Unchained Melody." Memories of the past fifty years meandered through her mind; visions of herself as a young girl with long curly hair and green eyes walking home from school.

Shaking her head, Lola refocused on the long lines of cars crowding the freeway all around them. She was filled with a bittersweet mix of anticipation and irritation. The prospect of the lodge with her two friends beckoned as a welcome respite from her daily grind, but the drive to the ancient land of the Cowlitz became more troublesome with every trip. Over the years, as they made the journey, they realized that there were fewer trees, more strip malls and cheaply built houses along the route. Although some saw this as progress, to Lola it always reminded her of the old song of little houses made of ticky-tacky.

"Going, going, gone!" Lola muttered to herself, glaring darkly at the intrusion of humans into the last remnants of the old forests. She sighed at the sight of the Red-tailed Hawks now regally perched on the large green signs hanging over the freeway. Wistfully, she thought of the giant ancient cedar trees that once stood where billboards now marred the scenery.

Kristin and Rona listened to Lola's gripes and complaints every time they made this same trip to the thirteen acres of land on the Cowlitz River. It was the last of the 1.6 million acres the Cowlitz tribe once claimed as traditional lands. The two women rolled their eyes at Lola and, in unison, chanted, "Where are the animals going to live, and the little birds, and the frogs?" Lola laughed and made a rude gesture to her traveling companions. Their cajoling helped her relax and enjoy the comfortable companionship.

The women arrived at the tribal property early in the afternoon. The grassy fields had recently been mowed and the trees were already beginning to turn red, gold, and bronze. A tiny mouse scurried across the dirt road in front of the Tahoe's tires, its furry body barely visible against the dusty lane. Lola pulled the car to a stop in front of the copse of trees that ran the length of the property adjacent to the river's bank. The women located the narrow trail overgrown with blackberry vines snaking across the path, reaching to snag any daring intruders.

The lodge sat to the west of a small clearing. Next to that was a picnic table and benches under a shelter guarded by two totem poles, depicting the story of the Cowlitz people. Between the table and the lodge was a fire pit, filled with the ashes of a previous lodge and a lone gray stone. Behind the fire pit was a stone altar holding rocks, crystals, feathers, and figurines of owls, wolves, cats and bears. In the comfortable silence that comes only when people have spent countless hours together, the women carried the boxes and blankets from the car to the front of the lodge.

"I think Dale and Gracie are still around," Kristin remarked, referring to an elderly couple with whom the women had shared many a sweat. Dale died in the fall of 1999 and Gracie joined him three months later. Dale had held the role of fire tender. His bear tattoos had gleamed with sweat in the light of the flames as he turned the logs and rocks that he then carted into the lodge on the end of a pitchfork. Gracie was a tiny woman crippled with arthritis but with the smile of an angel. She was always carried into the lodge in the loving arms of her husband. She sat to the north of the lodge as befit an elder with great wisdom. Their deaths were deeply mourned and their spirits of gentle guidance still lingered in the quiet sheltered space around the lodge.

"Listen," Rona said, "the jays are calling. We must have a visitor coming. I love this place. I think that when I die, I want my ashes scattered into the fire and river." The women stopped to listen to the jays scream and then smiled as squirrels answered back. Sure enough, within minutes the women did have a visitor. A fat raccoon with a huge tail strolled down the path from the field and approached the women. He waddled around the side of the fire pit completely ignoring the human intruders. After carefully checking out the rocks in the fire pit, the inside of the lodge, and the stack of wood Rona had chopped, he disappeared into the bushes at the back of the lodge. They watched as his ringed tail vanished into the darkness. They broke into laughter until they were reduced to hiccups and squatting to holding their aching sides.

Kristin knelt on the ground, her face averted from the other women as she worked to clean the floor of the lodge, pulling fern fronds and stones from the inside of the small structure.

"I think we should have forty-one stones tonight, big grandfathers and grandmothers. I need to pray for the soul of my son and those lost in the last horrid war. I should also pray for the soul of my bastard ex-husband. The only good things he gave me were my sons. That man still puts his cold arms around my heart and freezes my soul. Never once did he call his own son, Chazz, after he came home from the war, not once. He never once, not once, not one time, called to ask how he was. I don't think Chazz has forgiven his dad. He won't talk to me about it but I know he still hurts over it.

"My poor boy, he watches CNN morning, noon and night and makes daily trips to the VA but those bastards never do a thing for him. Rona, don't ever get married. Look at Lola and me. We're two aging women, ruled by our hearts. Look how we both ended up, aging and single! Stick with cats!"

Rona turned from her task of chopping wood and splitting kindling to smile at Kristin.

"Krissie!" You don't mean that! You act like some bitter old woman but I know better. I drove by your house last Saturday night and that cold bastard's truck was parked in your driveway. He can't be *that* icy. Besides, you know I am going to marry Xavier. You told me you would make my dress. I know you worry about Chazz but the only reason he left your home was to move in with his latest girlfriend. You gripe about your men but, Lady, you better think about praying for your own soul."

Rona threw a stack of kindling over to where Lola was kneeling, cleaning out the ashes from the fire pit. Then she turned her attention to stacking the rocks and wood for the fire.

"Lola, come on! Get into the conversation. You haven't said a word for the past two hours. Come on! You never say a word when we start talking about men. You aren't some virgin."

Lola wiped her hands on her jeans and reached behind her to grab another rock. She placed it in the fire pit propping kindling around it.

"You and Krissie battle it out. My luck with men isn't worth mentioning, particularly around this fire and at this place. Besides, between you two and the jays, there is no place for me to get into this conversation.

"You know, sometimes when I am here, listening to the river and the birds, I wish Istie and Auntie were with us. When I die, there will only be Istie left to come here. Our family will be as extinct as Dodo birds, Tasmanian tigers, and honesty in government."

Rona threw another stack of kindling towards Lola and picked up her ax. Her brown hair framed the side of her face, a fine sheen of perspiration glistened on her tightly muscled arms.

"Oh," Lola sighed. "If I were only young again."

"You'd do the same things all over again," Kristin smirked. "Every time we end lodge, you give thanks for your husbands, so don't give me that crap!"

"Krissie, take Rona and go get some ferns. I spend enough time with people in my head. Go away!" Lola pulled the Tahoe keys from her back pocket and tossed them across the clearing towards Rona. "I need to be alone for a while!"

Kristin and Rona turned to stare at Lola, the shadows of the leaves rippling across their faces. Silence hung thick in the air. Only the low murmuring of the river and the distant sound of the traffic on the nearby freeway permeated the denseness of the air.

"Come on, Baby in the Moon," Kristin said to Rona, "let's go. She'll feel better when she has this place set up for tonight." The two women reached for each other's hands and disappeared up the path.

Lola continued to prepare the stack of stones and wood for the fire. She could smell the sweetness of the earth as the breeze off the river swept over her. She stood and reached for a bottle of water. Resting for a moment, she sat on one of the metal chairs perched next to the picnic table. She sighed and pulled her blue denim shirt out of her pants and wiped her forehead with its tail.

"Well, Lola, that was well done," she muttered to herself. "Piss off your best friends right before a lodge. You're as bad as Auntie, bitching and griping about everything. What a nag you've turned into. Every time someone mentions those husbands of yours you get petulant."

Lola mused over Rona's accusation. It was true she never spoke of her husbands. Both had been dead for years. She focused on the fire pit and listened to the soft rippling of the river. The jays scolded again as a tiny brown mouse ran across the dirt in front of her.

"Hey, little one, didn't I see you earlier on the road?"

Lola held the bottle of water in her hands, absently turning it around and around. She thought about the history of the LeFleur women, five generations refusing to change their surname at marriage and all widowed by the age of fifty. Lola found it ironic that she was sitting in this place of water and fire. One of her husbands had drowned and the other had died in a fire. It was an odd juxtaposition that linked her deceased husbands.

Lola's first husband, James Sun Crow, was a slender, handsome man. He was an Osage Indian twelve years her senior, with a propensity for drinking matched only by his aversion to work. Lola met him when she was eighteen and instantly fell madly in love. They were married shortly thereafter and were happily married throughout college and graduate school. He disappeared the night Lola received her masters degree . The last sighting of him was at a bar in Pioneer Square where he spent the evening in a drunken stupor before climbing into his truck.

After seven years of waiting, wondering, and celibacy, Lola finally had him declared dead. Six months later, when the floating bridge across Lake Washington east of the city was demolished and the pieces pulled from the cold water, the mystery of James's disappearance was solved. His truck was pulled from the lake at Mile 3 of the Interstate, the only clue to his identity. The police came to Lola's office bearing his water-soaked and nearly disintegrated wallet asking her to come to the morgue to claim his bones. For years, Lola had visions of sparkling salmon swimming between the ribs of her drunken husband, his long black hair floating in the currents, his finely shaped lips burping into the murky water of the lake.

Lola paused in her thoughts and looked around. The sun had traveled farther to the west and the shadows now slanted across the blanket-covered shell of the lodge. The stones on the altar reflected beams of light onto the canopy of leaves. Lola moved back down by the fire pit and added more rocks to the pile. Forty-one rocks. The pile was complete. Then as she added more wood to the stack, her thoughts drifted to her second deceased husband.

Lola married Andrew Smith when she was thirty. He was a short, stocky but attractive Vietnam veteran who had been shot in the war. She knew he was a good man and overlooked his nightmares and temper, believing in his innate kindness. She had consciously chosen Andrew; his WASPishness an antidote to James, the stereotypical drunken Indian. What she overlooked were Andrew's similarities to his predecessor: their twelve-year age difference, a propensity for smoking marijuana, and a loathing to bringing home a paycheck.

Andrew died three years into their marriage, just five miles from the same place James had drowned. His pickup truck, a forty-fifth birth-day present from Lola, rammed into a bridge abutment when Andrew apparently burned himself lighting a bowlful of marijuana. The lighter caused a fire as Andrew sat unconscious, strapped in the driver's seat. The truck burst into flames. This time, when the police came to Lola's office with the identifying wallet, it was singed.

Lola shook her head in sympathy for Kristin, knowing the internal war Chazz faced was never-ending and ever-consuming. She patted the last stone, reached for smudge from the nearby can, and sprinkled sage, tobacco and sweet grass over the stack of rocks. As she added the last piece of wood, she heard the sound of the Tahoe's engine and then the banging of the car doors. Kristin and Rona came into the clearing; wet fern fronds piled high in their arms.

"Oh, God," Rona giggled. "Lola's been thinking. Well, at least the fire is ready to go. Give me the rest of those ferns, Kristin, and hand me the blankets. I'll finish getting the lodge ready. Don't go down to the river until I'm done."

Lola scowled at Rona as the young woman crawled into the lodge. She turned toward Kristin, her expression softening "You know, Kristin, Chazz will come home. Just let him know you love him and, for God's sake, get rid of that cold bastard ex-husband. The sex can't be that good. You two have been divorced for years!"

"Lola," Kristin responded, "not everyone wants to be a perennial virgin. I swear, what *is* it with you LeFleur women?!

"And in terms of Chazz, Lola, you were married to a combat veteran. Show some compassion. You, of all people, should know what he faces." Kristin's voice was soft and her face kindly. "Come on, Rona; get your butt out here. Let's go talk to the river."

A narrow path led from the clearing to the river's edge. Rona held the can of smudge in her hands and led the way, Lola followed and Kristin fell in behind. The women had traversed the tree-canopied path hundreds of times over the years and their feet well knew the way. They were hushed, enjoying the screeching of the jays and crows cackling overhead. The day was slipping into night and the frogs began their song. Peace filled Lola's heart and, for a few moments, the constant anxiety and grief that lived at the edge of her mind evaporated.

The three women stood at the edge of the water. A huge cedar log lay across the bank slopping down into the river, its surface worn smooth by years of water rushing over it during the December floods and the high waters of Spring. The women stood to the side of the log and pressed their bellies against the smoothness of the cedar log. The river ran dark and green, the swirl of the currents pulsing down toward the ocean. Rona opened the can of smudge and dipped her hand into it to pull out the mixture. She passed the can to Kristin who took a handful and then handed it to Lola.

"Say the prayers, Rona." Lola said as she held her hands high up over her head, offering them to a God she had ceased to believe in years before. She could feel the softness of the sand along the bank of the river shifting under her feet. The breeze off the river stirred again and from the woods near the lodge came the hoot of an owl. A robin chirped and then quieted again. In that quiet peace, Rona's voice was heard, its tones as perfect as those of the Righteous Brothers that had sung to them on the trip down from Seattle.

"Grandfather, our Creator, we offer these gifts back to you and thank you for the blessing of this day and of our lives. We thank you for the breath in our bodies and we pray for peace in this World. *Sagahalee Tyee*, we thank you for the river and the sky. We thank you for the hope of tomorrow. We ask your blessings on our lodge and ask that we speak our words to you in a good way. Grandfather, we ask that Kristin and her son have healing and that he comes home safely. Grandfather, we thank you for this day. *Mahsie. Mahsie.*"

The words floated out over the water as the three friends opened their hands and allowed the wind to carry their offerings aloft. At that moment, a pair of ospreys flew into view from the north. Clutched in their four talons was the wiggling body of a large salmon, its scales gleaming like crystals in the light. As the birds soared past the women, they released the salmon. It fell with a splash into the river right at their feet and then swam away. One of the pair of masked birds flew to the east, over the lodge, and the other flew to the west across the river.

In stunned quietude, the three women stood staring at the gift they had been given in response to their prayers. No one dared say a word as they turned as one and made their way back down the darkening trail to the lodge. The smell of smoke was clearly noticeable and, when the women reached the clearing, small flames and tendrils of gray smoke were rising from the stones, the fire lit by unseen hands and the rocks already warmed.

That night in the lodge was the hottest Lola could recall. The prayers offered to the Creator seemed more powerful than ever before. As the third round commenced, Lola thought back over the year since the fall of the Towers. She thought of those souls who died that day and of all those who had died since. She thought of Chazz and the struggles she knew were ahead for him. She thought of Auntie Louella and Istie and the journeys they had made.

The steam escaped from the heated rocks. She saw the shape of the twin Towers rising to the sky. She saw the souls in the Towers crying out as the buildings collapsed. As she sat in the dark of the lodge that night with two of the few people left in the world that she could truly say she loved, she saw the figure of a woman falling to the earth, accompanied by two beautiful falcons, wings outspread, matching the two ospreys they had just seen over the river in the falling light of dusk.

As the mist in the lodge cleared, thousands of tiny green, blue and turquoise lights shone through the fern fronds covering the lodge floor. Kristin sat at the west side of the lodge—the hottest spot and the place of healing—and began singing the words of a medicine song. .She was joined in harmony by Rona and then by Lola. Lola poured more water onto the heated rocks and placed more prayer ties onto grandfathers and grandmothers. The vision of the Towers gave way to the image of Devils Tower. Its striated sides stretched high into the deep indigo sky, clouds blowing overhead lit by the full moon, the bear climbing up to where his sisters huddled, riding the Tower into the sky where the stars shone brightly.

Lola opened the door to the lodge at the end of the round and looked outside. She saw the salmon swimming through the branches of the overhanging tree where dozens of babies sat, all boys, all races and colors. The babies smiled and waved as the salmon swam among them. The ospreys flew high in the night sky, their bright eyes shining through their black masks, their striped wings sleek in the air.

Rona crawled out the lodge door to stand by the fire pit where the embers glowed. The logs over the remaining stones popped and groaned. She stood for a moment, silhouetted in the light of the fire, her young, beautiful face resembling a Madonna. Kristin and Lola, two aging friends, comfortable in their skins and friendship, sat in an easy silence waiting for Rona to hand in the hot stones.

Lola sat up straight, lengthening her spine, and rubbed her hands on her muddy thighs. Softly her voice traveled across the cooling air of the lodge.

"You know, Kristin, the lodge tonight wasn't just for your healing. It was for all those lost souls and for Chazz. He will be fine, he has you. Bring him down here. Sit him in the lodge. There is a seat for him in this place of peace. I love you, Kristin, and I love Rona. She has all the

potential I have lost over the years. I feel so alone with Istie in California and Auntie Louella gone. I see you two together and I want to believe in God. I hope I am wrong about God not existing because I need him now more than any time in my life. "

Rona, listening outside the lodge, picked up two of the glowing grandfathers with the ancient and bent pitchfork and shook off their hot embers. She smiled at Lola's words and sang out, "Grandfathers coming in." She looked up at the full moon and then all around her. The lights that now lit the inside of the lodge had spread across the clearing and were marching up the narrow path to the field. Swirling down the path to meet the lights was a fine mist, a mist so soft it felt like the caress of a baby's breath. In the mist were the ancient ones, the ones that had come before. They held out their hands toward Rona. In their hands were the souls lost at the Towers. As she stood in awed disbelief, the lights and souls merged into one and soared into the black sky, disappearing among the stars.

Back at home later that night; Lola lay on the couch in the TV room downstairs. A "Law and Order" rerun flickered across the screen. Its sound was barely audible among the creaks and sighs of the old house. Lola's old lady cat lay asleep on the bed upstairs, one of Lola's nightshirts wrapped around her small, frail body. Lola's middle cat snoozed in the rocker in the corner of the living room. Curled up behind Lola's legs was the tiny black cat, her baby, and feeling its purr, she began to drift off to sleep. Caught in that sliver of time, between the light of consciousness and the dark of slumber, Lola faced the demons of midnight. Lulled by the tick of the clock, she again watched the ospreys flying toward her, the salmon clutched in their talons, its scales glittering in the sun. A brief spasm shook her back into alertness, and then she was gone, the eyes of the osprey following her into sleep.

⇥ 6 ⇤

The Wolverines of Tarrington

Cook Lake, Wyoming   **September 22, 1999**

Fall had just arrived, the nights and evenings cooler and the sunrise a little bit later each day. A windstorm had swept the valley and hills the previous day bringing rain, lightning and the odd smell of ozone. The rusty trap had lain on the forest floor for nearly a hundred years when fur trappers had decimated the populations of beaver, fox, lynx and wolverine.

The trap was spread wide, two fierce sets of teeth poised to ensnare and maim anything caught between them. The trap had somehow been avoided by generations of the remaining fur-bearing animals living in the woods. The storm the previous day had scattered leaves and brush across the trap, hiding its menacing ferocity from the eyes of two wolverines. They were slowly making their way back to their den hidden in the rocks at the base of a cliff. Inside the den were two small bundles of thick black and silver fur. The wolverine cubs were nearing their final days in the den. They were still learning to hunt and read the signals on the air and ground of the primal forest of the Black Hills.

The wolverines were a mated pair; together long after breeding season had ended. Theirs was an unusual bond, a closeness born out of the loneliness of only a few of one's kind being left alive. The male passed the trap, narrowly missing its claws and vicious bite. The beautiful female was not so fortunate.

She put her weight on the rusty spring mechanism and, in a split second, the teeth of the instrument of capture and excruciating pain had closed on her right front paw. An unearthly cry from the female brought the male to a stop. He ran to her side, trying to discern the source of her pain and inability to move. He sniffed at the rusty metal and then licked his mate, trying to soothe her pain.

The female wolverine writhed in the merciless grip, panting and crying as her blood poured from the jagged wound torn into her coat, muscles and bones. She felt her life pouring from her and, after a long struggle, stopped pulling on her paw. The male lay down next to his mate, grooming her and trying to comfort her.

The day drew to a close with the female waiting for death. Her mate, anxious and whimpering, finally left to hunt. He caught the scent of a vole and scrambled to catch the small brown rodent. Carrying it in his powerful jaws, he dropped the morsel of food near his mate's mouth. He nudged her with his nose, rubbing his muzzle across hers. She opened her eyes and took a small bite. The nourishment brought her back to a level of consciousness, but also horrid pain. Blood spatters covered the leaves and the disarrayed ground was testimony to the weakening struggles of the female.

The male wolverine rubbed against her again then left, searching for food for the vulnerable cubs hidden in the den. He hunted for much of the night, bringing mice and, finally, a rabbit to his babies and mate. Night gave way to day and still the female wolverine clung to the precious thread that was her life. The rising sun warmed her cooling body. Her mate stood watch over her as the sun rose to its zenith and then passed into late afternoon.

Tarrington, Oklahoma   **September 19, 1999**

The 1976 step-side Chevy Cheyenne pickup truck had seen better days. It had a nonexistent paint job, its color deteriorated to primer black. The bed of the truck was wood, handmade by the old man now sitting

in the cabin, hands tightly gripping the rubber-covered steering wheel. On the South Dakota license plate were the words "LIL CHY."

The driver was a stooped man in his nineties. He peered out the window of the battered truck, his mottled hands holding the wheel precisely at the 10-2 position. He wore a gray tee shirt with the picture of four Apache chiefs on it. The slogan on the shirt said "Founding Fathers." Over the tee shirt, he wore a leather vest, three of the four buttons open, the one on the bottom closed over his small paunch. Gray braids, their ends wrapped in bright red cloth, hung over his chest.

Billy Hawk was born in 1907 in Parmalee, South Dakota, an enrolled member of the Rose Bud Sioux tribe. His extended family held title to 3,780 acres of prairie, salvaged from the ravages of the 1887 Dawes Allotment Act. He was a highly traditional man, believing in the spirit of the land, the glory of nature, and the precious gift of family. He was the youngest of six children born to Boren Hawk and Shelda Wilson. Shelda was originally from the Pine Ridge reservation but had moved to Parmalee when she met Boren at a pow wow on the Northern Cheyenne reservation at Lame Deer, Montana.

Boren was nineteen and Shelda only fifteen when they met and soon after married. The wedding took place in a grange hall decorated with flyers announcing grange meetings, the price of corn, and politicians from Rapid City. An old, faded Wanted poster of Butch Cassidy dangled by one corner from the wall nearest the kitchen door.

Their first child, a son named Marcus, arrived a year later. Shelda, her tiny body strained by pregnancy, delivered a child every year until Boren died of a heart attack at the age of twenty-six when Billy was only a year old.

Shelda was a determined woman whose view of the world was one of grim reality and utter faith in the goodness of the Creator. She held this faith despite the horrors of Wounded Knee and the tragedy of Chief Joseph and the Nez Perce. Boren had been a distant relative of Crow Dog and stressed to his children the honor of a promise through his stories of the Sioux medicine man. Although Boren died when his children were quite young, the image of Crow Dog was forever etched into their brains, the only lasting memory any of his children had of their dead father.

The Hawk family lived off the land; the children learned to hunt as soon as they could walk. The winters were bitter cold and the four-room cabin offered little shelter from the frigid air that caught the breath and froze little fingers. Shelda often thought of returning to Pine Ridge but the sight of Boren's headstone standing dark against the wind and rain kept her from leaving Parmalee. Shelda drew strength on the icy winter nights from the sounds of her children's snores and murmurings as they dreamed of purple clouds and running deer.

Shelda's world came to an end when, in 1913, her six children, ages six through thirteen, were taken from her and placed at the US Industrial School in Genoa, Nebraska. Billy had stood in the doorway behind his mother when the agent came with the letter ordering the Hawk children to be delivered to Genoa. His mother sobbed as the agent read the letter and told her he would be back in four days to take the children to Nebraska. True to his words, exactly four days later, the wagon rolled away from the small wooden house. Shelda ran after it, holding her skirt in her hand and begging the driver to turn around and bring her children back home.

Billy sat next to his two sisters, Hallie and Darrilynn, in the back of the wagon. He squinted through the dust at his mother as the wagon rolled slowly down the dirt road pulled by two large golden Belgian draft horses. The horses seemed magical to Billy. Their tails docked and manes were combed and braided. He marveled at the skilled hands of the driver, guiding the mammoth steeds through the heat of August.

Darrilynn pointed to Shelda, telling her brother to remember what their mother looked like, telling him they would not see her again for a long time. Billy leaned into Darrilynn's side, his dark brown eyes taking in the dusty landscape, the small ranch house, the split rail fences, the Angus cows, and the running woman who had been his universe. He rubbed the rough wood of the wagon bed with one hand and waved good-bye to his mother with the other.

Billy spent the next twelve years at the school in Genoa. His hair was cut short, his language forbidden, his Creator mocked, and the memories of his mother and the ranch at Parmalee faded from his maturing mind. At the school, Billy lived in a dorm with dozens of other boys, their beds lined up row after row, their possessions in small trunks at the end of each bed. The matrons and masters in the school believed in the Christian adage of "spare the rod and spoil the child," not hesitating to beat those children whom they believed still adhered to pagan ways and heathen beliefs.

The brutal loneliness of the school led to suicides of many of the children, a fact disguised by the headmaster and ignored by the United States government. The lost children were declared dead of natural causes. Their parents were informed of their deaths long after the children had been buried on a cold and windy knoll at the far edges of the school property. Abuse, fear and pain were a daily part of the life faced by all of the children at the school. Many of them were Pawnee; the same people who had originally lived on the land but were banished by the advance of the settlers and the unrelenting pursuit of the US Calvary.

The school was typical of government buildings of the time—squat, utilitarian, sterile and ugly. The children, so far away from the love of their families, were forbidden to have any personal possessions. The only clothing they were allowed was provided by the school. Black wool uniforms, flaps on the shoulders buttoned with buffalo head nickels, were worn no matter the weather or temperature. During the warmer months, the children would sweat, the wool would scratch and the smell of wet sheep would permeate the room. The freedom of cotton shirts and pants was gone along with the glory of regalia, medicine bags, and buffalo skin robes.

Billy's salvation from a total surrender to despair was his older siblings and a young boy he met his second day at the school. The boy's name was Geronimo Barse and he had lived with his grandparents on a ten thousand-acre ranch outside of Tarrington, Oklahoma. Geronimo was Kiowa, as he explained to Billy, and had been named for Saint Geronimo, not the beloved Apache chief. He was named by his mother who had abandoned him to his father when he was only an hour old.

The two boys, when out of sight and hearing of the matrons and masters, taught each other their languages. They spoke of the ceremonies of their people. Billy told of the time his father dragged ten buffalo heads at the Sun Dance and his mother made flesh offerings. Geronimo listened in awe and then told Billy stories of wild ponies, eagles, wolves, and the majestic buffalo that had roamed the prairies. Geronimo recounted the tales his grandparents had passed down of millions of bison pushing across the land; the dust cloud that followed them visible for miles. He told, then, of the thousands of carcasses his grandfather had seen strewn in decaying stacks across the disappearing prairies. Billy, listening from the bunk above Geronimo, felt his heart would break and his soul would die.

The boys compared notes about their ranches and the Indian ponies that galloped across the land. They told each other of their dreams and of their sadness of being torn from their families. Geronimo, unlike Billy, had no siblings. His father, Delsey Barse, and his mother, Amanda Sharpe, a petite blonde debutante from Newport, Rhode Island, had never married. Geronimo was conceived in a barn stall, a hundred feet from the railroad tracks and the stockyards in Kansas City. His parents had just met in the lounge of the Paris Hotel where Amanda was staying with her industrialist father and socialite mother. Delsey worked as a stable hand in the barn of the glamorous hotel that catered to the very rich and the cream of white society.

Amanda's parents, appalled at the idea of a half-breed grandchild, had demanded she place the baby for adoption. She sent notice to Delsey through the bellman that this was her intent. Within an hour of Geronimo's birth, Delsey took his son in his arms and left the hotel. Amanda was sobbing with grief; her parents visibly relieved that there would be no brown child to explain to their wealthy friends upon their return to their mansion by the sea. Delsey, his infant son wrapped in furs, left Kansas City and began the journey back to the ranch at Tarrington. On a cold March day, with the wind whipping small tornadoes of dust around his legs, he gave up his son to his own father and mother. He kissed Geronimo on the cheek, hugged his parents, and left for Kansas City. There, he evaporated into the bars and back streets of the growing town, forever searching for the blue eyes of Amanda in the bars near the railroads.

Yi Pay and Emily mourned the loss of their son but were blessed by a grandson who gave them a reason to continue in the world. As he grew, it was clear he had the gentleness of his mother's heart and the independent spirit of his father. Yi Pay and Emily taught Geronimo the ways of the land and the traditions that had allowed them to survive the hard life on the prairies of Oklahoma. Despite many hardships, the small family thrived and, for six years, it seemed nothing ugly or cruel could touch their lives.

Then, suddenly, the illusion of paradise was shattered and their hearts were broken a second time. The letter from the local Indian agency arrived. It ordered their grandson to the confines of the Genoa Industrial School in Genoa, Nebraska. Emily dressed six-year-old Geronimo in black short pants, white shirt, black coat, and a black string tie looped around his neck. Yi Pay held his tears until the wagon, identical to the one carrying Billy Hawk from the north, vanished into the wavering light of the late Oklahoma summer. Emily held her head aloft. She vowed that she would see her grandson back on the land that was his birthright, a home wreathed in Kiowa traditions and enveloped in the beautiful sounds of the birds and animals of the prairie.

Day by day and year by year, time passed in the grim buildings of the school directly north of the Tarrington ten thousand-acre ranch. The birth languages and images held in the souls of the children were harder to recall, the faces of the loved ones at home now faded as old photographs. Geronimo and Billy grew into manhood in the confines of the school property. The anger of the schoolmasters grew more brutal with each passing year, beating down the souls and bodies of the imprisoned innocents. The halls seemed to ring with the pain of both past and current inhabitants.

Billy and Geronimo, forever changed, left the boarding school in 1925 and each returned to their respective homes. Billy's mother, Shelda, had remained in the house outside of Parmalee but her children had vanished into Kansas City, Minneapolis, Rapid City, and Sioux Falls. Billy, never losing his love of the land, returned to live with his mother. Occasionally, a postcard or a visitor would bring word of her other five children and then, as the years passed, grandchildren. Billy built a sweat lodge behind the four-room cabin. Every night without fail, he would seek out the heat and peace of the lodge, praying for his lost family members and for the soul of his long-dead father.

Geronimo's return to Tarrington echoed that of his Sioux friend on the ranch in Parmalee. After his twelve years at Genoa, the Kiowa language no longer came easily to his lips. His grandmother cried in her room the day her beloved grandson came home, the scars of the years of beatings visible on Geronimo's long legs. He refused to talk of his years at Genoa; instead he spent his time relearning his native language and participating in the nightly sweats he helped his grandparents prepare.

Relaxing into the heated womb of the lodge, Geronimo lay on the ground, his lodge blanket spread out underneath him wet from his sweat, tears, and the steam off the rocks. He crossed his legs at the ankles and folded his hands over his chest. He stared up at the ceiling of the lodge, unseen in the blackness that surrounded the old people and their beloved grandson. His grandfather poured more water onto the heated rocks, prayers of gratitude taking on a shape and strength of honest emotion.

One night in lodge, Geronimo sat on the moist earth between his elderly grandparents. His grandfather sang an eagle song and waved his eagle tail fan, calling in the guardians and thanking them for allowing them to live to see their grandson delivered back to their home. As the song swirled around the lodge, Geronimo felt the soft hand of his grandmother on his face, smoothing the years of separation away. In the warmth and darkness of the sacred place, he could see Billy Hawk's face and hear his voice. He felt the scars of the beatings on his skin disappear and the pain in his heart eased a little as the steam filled his lungs. A sense of hope for the future returned. And so in the north, in Parmalee and in the south, in Tarrington, the young men, survivors of the boarding school, began their lives.

Billy and Geronimo never lost contact. They married within weeks of each other. Both men had one child each. Billy's wife, Opal, bore him a daughter; while Geronimo's wife, Agatha, graced him with a son, Jerome. Each year, the men brought their wives and children to the ceremonies held away from the prying and condemning eyes of the encroaching world. The wild wind blowing across the prairies, and the dancers in their beautiful costumes provided a soothing connection back to their parents and the time before the boarding school. At the Autumnal equinox, Billy would make the day-long trip from Parmalee to Tarrington. After dinner, they would sit around the wood stove in the living room and tell stories to each other, much as they had done so long ago in the barracks of the school at Genoa.

Yi Pay and Emily died within days of each other in 1930, the where-abouts of Delsey a mystery to the end. Shelda had died of a broken heart the year after Billy returned to the cabin at Parmalee. The news of her other children's alcoholism and their lives on the streets completed the slow death of her soul, begun that horrible day back in 1913 when the wagon pulled by the golden horses had disappeared down the dusty road.

Geronimo had vowed he would never leave the ranch at Tarrington again without Billy Hawk by his side. It was only through Agatha's persuasion and Billy's insistence that Geronimo would climb into whatever battered pickup truck Billy happened to be driving on that particular trip, to head back to the Black Hills of South Dakota. Geronimo's soul always found peace and spiritual calmness when they traveled to Cook Lake, just miles from Devils Tower. The ceremonies shared by the two men strengthened the bond that had been forged in the hell of Genoa, a bond that would be broken only by the death of one of them.

In 1943, they had joined the Army and were assigned to the 15th Field Artillery Battalion, ironically named the Indianheads. The Battalion patch was of an Indian chief in headdress on a silver star resting on a black shield. The men, both thirty-six years old, with wives and children, were the only two Native men in the unit. On more than one occasion, their fellow-comrades remarked that they should be in the 442nd Regiment, mistaking Billy and Geronimo for Japanese.

After explaining their Kiowa and Sioux roots for the tenth time, the two friends began to ignore the comments of the other men in the battalion. As they had thirty years before, they wrapped themselves in mutual love and admiration, forged in the need for emotional and spiritual survival

Once again, the two friends lived in barracks, surrounded by men, lying in bunk beds, their possessions in footlockers at the foot of the bed. Leaning down one night over the edge of his bed, Billy spoke in the limited Kiowa he had learned from Geronimo during their time at Genoa:

"Nothing much has changed, has it, my old friend? Here we are, once more. Guests of the United States government, still being yelled and cussed at every day." He chuckled and slid his left leg out from under the blanket, letting it hang over the side, a gesture as familiar to Geronimo as his own, bringing back memories of the sterile halls of the boarding school.

"Well, at least this time it was our choice. Strange, isn't it? We fight for the very flag and people who so despise us. Well, we've survived four hundred and fifty years even if there aren't so many of us left," Geronimo responded in Sioux.

"I'm going to sleep. I miss my wife and son and can hear them calling for me to come home. I feel closer to them in my dreams. Good night, Billy Hawk."

⊰ ⊱

The two friends survived the assault on Omaha Beach on D-Day +1, June 7, 1944. The dead washed up on the beach in the bloody waves. Seagulls rode the red waters, their gray and white feathers stained crimson, their shrill caws echoing the cries of dying and wounded men. That first night, after grueling hours of fighting, Billy and Geronimo sat crossed-legged on a dune, looking out over the ocean. Their faces were lined and stained with the horror of thousands of deaths. The stench of battle still hung in the air and an atmosphere of somber victory colored the moods of the two men.

A patrol of ten soldiers rolled past in a canvas-covered truck, the bodies of the dead laid side-by-side, hands crossed over their chests. The soldier sitting in the passenger side of the cab leaned out the window, saluting the two friends as the truck rattled its way down the dirt road. All around them, the beach was littered with destroyed amphibious craft and rifles.

"Billy," Geronimo mused, "look out there. One more battle and more dead Indians. Huh, old news, my friend. Do you think it will ever end?

Here we are in France, and instead of enjoying the wine, we get a seaside view of chaos. Looks like we'll be moving on up the road tomorrow. All of this war makes Fort Sam Houston look inviting. Sure want to go home. I miss my family. Billy, we must have been crazy enlisting in this madness. What do we owe these people?"

Billy tapped his stained fingers against his chin, his boot-clad feet resting on a piece of driftwood. A plover ran across the beach below the men, poking its long beak into the blowing sand. The clouds to the west were dark gray with the occasional wisp of a white mare's tail sailing overhead. The remnants of beach grass, the little that still waved after the intense and unremitting battles, reminded Billy of the prairie grass on the plains. He sighed and placed his palms over his eyes, shutting out the light and the worn face of his nearly lifelong comrade.

"Geronimo, did we have a choice? Which was worse? Being hated in our own land or maybe earning some respect by our actions? But you are right. It is strange. We came to fight against a man who has committed genocide against his own people and the rest of the world and we barely survived that back home. It does no good to think about it. How can you make sense of it?

"Geronimo, when Shelda died that year after I came home from Genoa, I danced for her and an eagle flew overhead. I buried her next to my father. She and I buried my brothers Marcus and Hansen. I don't know where Howard or Darrilynn or Hallie are. Shelda told them to leave when they brought their alcohol to the house. She died lonely, without my father and full of grief over my brothers and sisters. It seems that the only thing I understand is death. And here we are again. We will go home or we won't. I can't make sense of this any more than I could make sense of any other part of my life."

"Remember what we used to hear, remember Billy? The only good Indian is a dead Indian? Well, there are an awful lot of dead Indians on this beach. So does that make us the bad guys? I'm too tired to sleep. I am an old man now, an old man.

"My friend, we became old the day they took us to the school in Genoa. Look at the gulls. They don't care. We bomb and shoot each other to pieces and they don't care. We humans, as Yi Pay said, are crazy, every one of us."

Geronimo placed his hand on Billy's shoulder and gently shook it. "Billy, remember when we used to tell each other stories at the school? You saved me then and you saved me today. We'll dance Sun Dance in Montana soon. You can come to the ranch and pick me up in whatever rattle-trap truck you happen to be driving. I tell you, Billy Hawk, if we make it home, I'm growing my hair long and I'll braid it. No one is ever going to force me to cut my hair or sleep in a bunk bed in a barracks again." Geronimo's mouth twisted in anger but then smoothed into a smile.

"Look, you young old man!" Geronimo smiled. "The sun is shining over there. It's the Creator showing us the way home."

A beam of God's Light poured down between the dark towers of clouds. The sea sparkled pink and gold under the shining sun for a brief second before closing back into the darkness and dusk of the June night.

The fighting went on for three hundred and thirty-six days; the Army pressed through France and Belgium and into the heart of Germany. The end of the war became clear and, despite the fatigue of a march of more then seven hundred miles into treacherous territory, a sense of hope grew day by day. The end of the war brought millions of heroes, men and women, home to their families. For many, the wounds did not show beyond the hearing loss from tons of artillery and endless rifle reports and the silence that grew from simply having no more words left to say.

After their discharges, the two friends returned to their wives and tried to forget the horrors of D-Day + 1 and the terror that followed. The nightmares of the abuse experienced in the boarding school merged with those from the days in combat, both men waking in cold sweats more often than not. They understood the price of battle and each, in his own way, sought to protect his family from the demons of Genoa and Omaha Beach that roamed the midnight hours. Neither man spoke of their experiences unless it was with each other on their yearly trips to the hills around Cook Lake. Then it was only in the heat of the sweat lodge where the spirits could carry them to where Grandfather waited to receive them.

Geronimo's only child, a son named Jerome, married Gloria Augustino when he was only eighteen years old. Gloria, six years Jerome's senior, was a solidly built young woman with deep blue eyes and light brown hair. She had a wicked sense of humor and an unabashed adoration of her husband. The couple lived in the small ranch house with Geronimo and Agatha, the home overflowing with love, laughter and joy.

Frank was born four months after the couple married. Geronimo adored the boy and from the first moment of Frank's life, he was the sun around which Geronimo's life revolved. Frank had the best of all worlds. His parents delighted in his every move. His dark eyes crinkled at the corners, an uncanny reflection of Geronimo's visage. Geronimo carried his grandson in a sling on his chest when Frank was tiny and on his back as he grew. He promised the black-haired child that no harm would ever come to him and that he would grow into a fearless Kiowa brave. They rode the fences around the enormous ranch together. Frank would perch on the saddle in front of his grandfather on their favorite horse, the Appaloosa gelding.

Geronimo sang Kiowa songs and told Kiowa legends to the tiny child, describing the Indian ponies running at lightning speed across the plains, thunder crashing around them.

By the time Frank was a sturdy three-year-old, he knew how to clean a sweat lodge, pile the lodge stones, and pour the water. He knew every inch of the ranch and the ever-changing variety of clouds, rain, snow and sun that flowed over the endless sea of grain, corn, and tall grass. The cries of the hawks and eagles were as familiar to him as the sight of smiling green and yellow garter snakes slithering through the waving stalks.

The paradise that was the ranch, his parents and grandfather lasted until Frank was four years old and his mother became pregnant again. Gloria was nauseous and ill for much of the time she was pregnant, delivering only four hours into a painful labor when she was seven months along. Jerome was by her bed while Geronimo and Frank sat on hard wooden chairs in the harsh glare of the fluorescent lights of the hospital's ugly green waiting room. Frank lay his head on Geronimo's lap, idly sucking his thumb and tapping his grandfather's knee.

The gowned doctor came to stand in front of Frank and Geronimo. His mask was hanging from his left hand, his right hand rubbing his whiskered chin, and his eyes tired and troubled. His words were devastating. Gloria died giving birth to her triplets, Ruby, Margaret and Belinda.

Gloria was only twenty-eight years old and had been the reason for Jerome's life. He had watched helplessly as she gave birth to his daughters and then bled out on the bed. The doctor pulled the last baby from her body as he screamed for the nurses to call another surgeon and to take the babies away. Gloria had held her hand out to Jerome, gave him a smile, and whispered the names of the three girls as her body went into a spasm and then stilled.

Jerome buried his wife in the cemetery in Tarrington next to Yi Pay and Emily and the simple stone that marked an empty grave, held in infinity for the missing Delsey. Silent in his pain, Jerome gave the care of his four children over to Geronimo and Agatha. He crawled into a bottle, pulled the cork in after himself, and died of cirrhosis of the liver only nine months after Gloria had passed.

There were more deaths over the years, each man consoling the other as caskets were laid in the ground. Geronimo's wife, Agatha, died of polio in 1952. Billy stood next to his lifelong friend, his hand reaching down to squeeze Geronimo's as the last piece of earth covered Agatha's coffin. The sky that sad day was an iron gray, clouds pressing upon the group of people that had dwindled in number over the years. Geronimo's five-year-old grandson, Frank, nestled against his grandfather's legs, his eyes wide and dry as his grandmother disappeared from his sight. Geronimo and Frank's black-wrapped braids blew in the wind that cold day, their hands chapped and cracked from the dry air of an Oklahoma winter.

Frank, Geronimo and the preacher, a short man with the pallor of a consumptive and dyed crow black hair, were identically dressed in black wool pants and coats, black cowboy boots, white shirts, and black string ties. The preacher pulled a bright yellow hanky from his coat pocket and, turning his head, coughed delicately into the cloth. The hanky provided the only speck of color to the sepia landscape.

The preacher held a seemingly enormous Bible, bound in gold with pages edged in crimson. He opened it to a page marked with a black satin ribbon. He cleared his throat, shook his body all over like a horse, sighed deeply, and read the comforting words of the 23rd Psalm:

> *The Lord is my shepherd; I shall not want; He maketh me to lie down in green pastures: he leadeth me beside the still waters. He restoreth my soul: he leadeth me in the paths of righteousness for his name's sake. Yea, though I walk through the valley of the shadow of death, I will fear no evil: for thou art with me; thy rod and thy staff they comfort me. Thou preparest a table before me in the presence of mine enemies: thou anointest my head with oil; my cup runneth over. Surely goodness and mercy shall follow me all the days of my life: and I will dwell in the house of the Lord forever."*

Frank lifted his eyes from the blowing brown dirt of the Oklahoma prairie to the sparkling blue eyes of the preacher. He felt a stirring in his soul and a wild hope filling his heart. He could see a wreath of thorns around the preacher's head and a gold tinged glow suffused the cemetery. The words of the preacher died away into the wind and the drabness of the landscape returned. Geronimo placed his hands on Frank's shoulders and squeezed them. He reached out to shake the preacher's hand and slipped a ten-dollar bill into the dry palm of the man of God.

Another generation of grandparents raising grandchildren, Geronimo mused, bathing the three little girls one night when they were two years old. They were lined up in a row in the tub, blonde hair wet and tiny pink knees poking through the suds. He could hear Frank singing to the hound dog that lay on the braided rug in front of the wood stove. Ruby, the most playful of the triplets, reached up to pull on her grandfather's braid, drawing his attention to the soap suds she had draped around her neck. "Jerome and Gloria, wherever you are, know I love your children. I miss you and Agatha but I thank you for the gifts of my grandchildren," Geronimo whispered into the air as he marveled at the innocence contained in the tiny bodies of his granddaughters.

Geronimo lifted the tiny girls out of the tub, dried them, and dressed them in identical pink long johns. He combed their fine blonde hair and helped them brush their teeth. They were so beautiful and pure,

Geronimo thought, miniature angels plucked from Heaven and given into his care.

As Yi Pay and Emily had done before, Geronimo taught his grand-children the healing powers of the sweat lodge and the glory of the bygone days of the Kiowa people. He refused to be bitter. He poured his love and hope into the four precious children he now had in his care. He bought horses for them and taught them to sing Kiowa songs to the herd every night as the big animals trotted into the barn.

He was a frugal man, wise with his money but generous with his love. His material wealth came from the graciousness of the land, a fact Geronimo could never forget. He raised corn, wheat and barley on a portion of the ranch and ran cattle on another parcel. Remembering the gifts of the Creator, he allowed two-thirds of the ranch to remain as nature had intended it:: hawks hunting for mice, rabbits and snakes hiding in the tall grasses that survived the plows and the ever-increasing encroachment of houses and shopping malls.

Over the course of the years, countless offers to buy the property came from industrialists and developers but to no avail. Geronimo, his four dark-eyed grandchildren behind him, would stare as the white men in black business suits would go over the pages of their proposals. He would never invite the businessmen into the small white house, a breach of etiquette unheard of in the Barse household. If the business-men wished to discuss their endless propositions, they had to stand in the driveway of the ranch, rain or shine, snow or heat.

Geronimo would listen in polite silence, nodding his head and shoving his scarred hands into the pockets of his overalls. Frank and the triplets would giggle, standing behind their grandfather as the businessmen became more and more frustrated, exasperated by the effort of conducting business in the presence of four snickering chil-dren. Eventually, Geronimo would utter a simple "No." Then, shooing the children ahead of him, he would saunter up the steps and into the white house, close the door, effectively and definitively dismissing yet one more unwanted stranger from the ranch.

At the age of sixteen, Frank began to attend the Pentecostal Church in Tarrington. He would dress in black wool pants and coat, black cowboy boots, a white shirt and a black string tie, the same choice of clothes he had worn at Agatha's funeral. He caught a ride into town twice a week with the neighbor closest to the ranch, a talkative widow in her seventies. Once at the church, Frank would find himself speaking in tongues and would raise his hands in exaltation of the Lord. As he became more entrenched in his new-found religion, he exhorted his grandfather to do the same. He shunned Geronimo's beliefs and their gentleness, as heresy..

Frank began to challenge Geronimo about his decision not to sell the land. He wanted to move to Tulsa, to enjoy the city life. He despised the hard work of the farm. He mocked his grandfather for his braids and refused to participate in the sweat lodge. He stopped speaking the Kiowa language, answering his grandfather only in English. He preached to his grandfather and sisters over the dinner table every night. He lectured Geronimo on the risk he faced if he did not convert to the path of Jesus.

Ruby, Margaret and Belinda would stare at their brother and grandfather. Geronimo would methodically chew his food and smile at his grandson. The girls preferred the gentleness of the Creator of the Earth and Sky versus the fire and brimstone, fear and guilt Frank thundered into the dining room every night. Geronimo would give Frank his time and space and, as he had done with the endless parade of developers, say a simple "No." He would not give up his beliefs and values, he would not go to the Christian church in Tarrington, and he would not baptize the girls. Their souls were fine, thank you. He would calmly respond to Frank and if it ever appeared they were in danger, he would let Frank know.

Still, at night, in the bed once shared by Yi Pay and Emily and once touched with the plump and much-loved body of Agatha, Geronimo would cry. He felt the same loss of soul and hope that he had in Genoa, a loss of spirit and a pain of the heart. One night, after Frank had let loose a particularly vitriolic rant against Geronimo and his Creator and all he held dear, Geronimo sat down at the kitchen table. He held a pen and a pad of paper in his hands, the only weapons he had against the rage of his grandson

September 11, 1963

Dear Billy Hawk,

Hello, my old friend. I sure like that Appaloosa gelding you sold to me at such an outrageous price. Lucky we had space for him in the barn. Saw a big badger this afternoon, looked like he was in a hurry but he would not tell me where he was going. I have been busy and the girls are getting so big. Don't know what to do with girls, Old Man. Boys are what I know. Well, I thought so, anyway. I don't know what to do with Frank. He is the angriest boy I have ever seen. Cries at night for his mother and never mentions a word about his father.

Billy Hawk, I love my grandchildren. I am fifty-six now and so are you. I want some peace, Billy Hawk. I can't fight anymore. The girls are scared of losing their brother and I am afraid of losing him and them, too.

Billy Hawk, what should I do? Tonight, Ruby, Margaret and Belinda and I did a sweat lodge. Their hair is so blonde and thick. Don't know where it comes from. Sure wasn't from me or Agatha. She was a good soul, Billy Hawk, even if she was a Sioux like you.

Billy Hawk, I cannot make sense of what to do with Frank. I love him but I don't like him much these days. I know what it is like to lose my family. You and I, we know what it is to lose the ones we love. I can't help him, Billy Hawk. So, Old Man, this is me asking for help. Billy Hawk, tell me what to do. The girls and I will be coming for Sun Dance next summer if you will come down and pick us up so, hopefully, we will see you in June if not before. I want to get three quarter horses for the girls next summer and one of your big Appaloosas for me.

Good night, Billy Hawk. You've been listening to me for fifty years. Maybe Creator will give us fifty more. Good night, Billy Hawk.

Geronimo Barse

Just a few weeks later, again at dinner, Frank began his nightly rant against his grandfather's traditions as heathen, pagan, and, finally—in the most painful stab of all—as the ignorant beliefs of a reservation Indian.

It was the last comment Geronimo ever took in silence. He pulled Frank by his arms from his chair and firmly force-marched him into his bedroom. He pushed Frank onto the bed and then began pulling open the drawers to the dresser Emily had purchased in Tulsa seventy years before.

"I love you, Frank," Geronimo spoke in Kiowa. "I have made excuses for you because you lost your mother and father. You disrespect and mock me and you condemn my Creator. You eat my food and drink my milk and take my money for your clothes. You shame your family and embarrass your sisters."

Frank's jaw dropped and he began to sputter.

"Close your mouth, boy." Geronimo continued. His voice was steady and calm despite the grief-filled rage he felt. He opened the closet and pulled out a battered forest green suitcase. He tossed it onto the bed next to Frank and released the locks, lifting the lid to reveal the stained silk lining.

"You know nothing of the world, boy. You know nothing of your blood or of the history of the Kiowa people. I fought for my life, boy, and for yours, too. Now you want me to sell my life and this land for toys and worthless junk. This ranch, boy, this land, this is of the Kiowa people and the Kiowa don't sell their land.

"Here is all you're getting from me, boy. The widow lady down the road is taking you in. You turn eighteen in two years and then you get your share of the ranch money, the share your father would have had. I'll pay the widow lady your board until you're eighteen and then you're on your own. Don't come back, Frank, until you can show me the respect I am owed."

Frank sat in stunned silence, his fists clenched in his lap. He had never heard his aging grandfather say a harsh word to anyone, never heard him raise his voice, and never heard him speak in anger. The house was quiet in the aftermath of the only confrontation Geronimo would ever have with a member of his family. The clink of silverware drifted to the ears of grandfather and grandson as Geronimo completed packing the green suitcase. He pushed the bulging lid down, snapped the locks, and stood the suitcase on the floor.

"Good-bye, Frank. It's time for you to go. Say good-bye to your sisters. I'll drive you down the road. You hate my ways, Frank. You don't have to live with them for one more second. I don't want you back on the ranch, Frank. You shame your family."

Frank stared at his grandfather in fury and started to speak, his face contorted with shock and disbelief.

"I'm not leaving." Frank began to speak in English but Geronimo had already turned to leave the room, the suitcase screeching in protest as it was dragged across the wooden floors and tossed off the front porch.

"Ruby, Margaret, Belinda, get your coats and get in the car, babies. Frank is going to his new home. Come on, baby girls. You can finish your supper later."

A few long-awaited tears made their way slowly down Geronimo's face as the triplets, now twelve and as much alike as possible, quietly got up from their chairs and hurried out to get in the '57 Chevy, all of them too afraid to say a word. The tension between their brother and grandfather had been a burden and horror. The girls all feared the loss of the only remaining members of their family.

As a light mist rose from the fields bisected by the dirt road, the eyes of a coyote reflected off the headlights, a barn owl flew level with the car and then swerved away into the night. A meteor blazed across the sky, gone in the blink of an eye, gone as rapidly as Frank was once Geronimo arrived at the widow's home. Geronimo hefted the green suitcase out of the trunk and left it standing in the dirt of the driveway. He and the girls drove off into the black night. Frank stood in the glow of the porch light, his arms hanging limply at his sides, his mouth agape at the shock of what his grandfather had just done.

⫷ ⫸

When he turned eighteen, Frank took the check that his grandfather had written. It was enough money for college, living expenses, and a ten percent tithe to the University. A thin film of wetness covered his eyes as he deposited the check. The memory of riding on the front of Geronimo's roping saddle, tumbleweed startling the horse as they rode the fence in silence, was as clear as yesterday. He had refused to contact Geronimo again, but sent long letters to his sisters, never admitting he was wrong.

Four grueling years later, Frank graduated from Oral Roberts University. He now had a degree in business and a plane ticket to New York. He took a job as an analyst for Goldman, Sachs, and within five years he reached the astronomical income of one million dollars a year.

In 1969, Frank married a young socialite named Andie Goode. He was soon the father of three young sons, Gerald, Gary, and Jerome. He moved the family into an enormous brownstone sheltered by oaks and decorated with flowers in the Spring and sparkling lights at Christmas. The brownstone had a breathtaking view of the city. The twin towers of the New York Trade Center were framed in all of the front windows.

The towers had been completed in 1970 and 1971. They were the silver and blue giants that dwarfed all other New York City buildings. Frank's youngest son, Jerome, gazed at the buildings for hours at a time. He believed that God lived at the top of one of the towers and made the wind and clouds. It was a child's belief but one he held as tightly as his father held onto his enormous gold Bible at Sunday services.

Frank loved entertaining his wife's family and, on rare occasions, his younger sisters. He flew them to the vibrant city, reveling in their awestruck expressions and laughs of joy. The four siblings, along with Frank's wife, Andie, and their three young sons, visited the Statue of Liberty, the Empire State Building, Rockefeller Center, the World Trade Center, and the Museum of Modern Art. Andie took care of the girls since Frank worked until nearly seven every evening., When the girls were in town over a weekend, however, that time belonged solely to the family and was jealously guarded from any intrusion.

Although the triplets loved all the shopping and the glamour of Broadway, they were always eager to return to the quiet life of Tarrington. The sanctuary of the ranch, the bellowing of the cattle, and the call of the hawk soothed their souls in ways that the millions of lights of the great City never could.

On one special trip for their fortieth birthdays in 1991, as the still-unmarried triplets sat in the harsh light of the waiting area of JFK airport counting down the precious minutes until boarding time, Belinda asked an obvious question:

"Frank, if you hate Grandpa so much, why did you name one of your sons after him? Why don't you call him and apologize? He loves you and misses you. If you would just say you were sorry, it would all be fine. Doesn't the Bible tell you to honor your parents? Grandpa's heart broke the night he took you up the road. He's so proud of you and misses you so much. It's been nearly thirty years. What would it hurt, Frank, for you to show some forgiveness?"

Frank stared open-mouthed at his three sisters. "Do you all feel this way? Are you all against me? Don't you remember what he said? It wasn't my choice to leave. I don't know why he couldn't join the twentieth century. Ruby, Margaret, do you think I was wrong?"

Ruby, the oldest of the triplets and the one least likely to speak her mind, reached out to touch the rich wool fabric of her brother's jacket.

"Frank, we are all proud of you but it was your fault Grandpa made you leave. You think your God is the only one but Grandpa is a good man and his Creator is no less real than your God. All of us girls go home to Tarrington and sweat with Grandpa. We go to the Sun Dance with him and Billy and we aren't evil. Frank, do you think Jesus would turn his back on a good man?"

Frank felt his heart constrict the way it had that last night in the old ranch house. He could see the three blonde heads bowed toward their plates and hear the clink of the flatware. He could smell the stew and cornbread Geronimo had cooked for them on the wood stove and hear the thump of the dog's tail on the worn wooden boards of the floor. He smoothed the creases of his dark gray slacks, and then leaned forward, with his elbows on his knees.

"Girls, I cannot have this conversation. Geronimo was wrong in turning me out. In terms of Jerome, Andie named him after our father; it had nothing to do with Grandpa. Don't think I don't worry about his and your souls, too. The old ways are long dead and they serve no purpose. My God has blessed me with wealth, a good woman, and three fine sons. What did Geronimo's Creator ever do for any of you?"

Belinda reached behind Ruby's shoulder and rubbed her brother's back. "Frank, where do you think the money came from to pay for your time at Oral Roberts University? Do you really think it came from our father? It came from Grandpa's savings. He sold cows, grain and corn every year and put the money aside for you. You owe him everything. Just call him, Frank. He's getting old. He's almost eighty. Come home, just once, Frank. What would it hurt?"

The crackling sound of the announcer's voice came over the loud-speaker, calling the triplets to board. Frank, refusing to meet Ruby's eyes, shook out his trousers and pulled himself to his feet.

"New York City is my home. If Geronimo wants to come and visit, he is welcome provided he cuts his braids and keeps his mouth shut about the old ways and the glory of the Kiowa people. I don't want to hear it anymore."

Margaret turned in shock and gaped at her brother. "I can't believe you said that. Are you that insensitive and cruel? How dare you? Go read your history, Frank. What do you think they did to Grandpa when he was forced into that horrible boarding school and then he and Billy joined the Army? I never wanted to say this to you, Frank, but you're an asshole. How could you say these things? He took care of us all those years. He gave us everything. Do you think you can just keep hurting him?

"Ruby, Belinda, I'm getting on the plane. I can't stand the sight of your face, Frank. He loved us and raised us and he was right. You are ungrateful and disrespectful. I'm leaving and going back to Tarrington. I won't be back anytime soon. Tell Andie and the boys I love them but don't call me; I'll call you"

Ruby and Belinda stood quietly to the side as Margaret pushed past and showed her boarding pass to the flight attendant. She pulled her travel bag behind her, refusing to look back at her brother. Her last vision of him was burned into her brain; a handsome man with black hair, eyes wide in disbelief, his hands hanging in defeat at his sides.

The triplets returned to their apartment in Tarrington. The weekly rites of visiting the ranch and the less-frequent trips to the Sun Dance with Billy were welcome interruptions to the rut of work. This had always been a reassuring routine. The peace of his time with the triplets was all Geronimo wanted from life and he prayed it would never end. But, as he later told Billy Hawk, some things aren't made to last.

⇐ ⇒

The trouble between the girls had started after that ill-fated trip to New York City. The scene in the airport had totally devastated all three sisters. They were unable to resolve their feelings and only knew one way to dull the pain.

The night had been cool, an early portent of autumn coming to Oklahoma, courtesy of a blustery wind from the Northwest. They had supper with Geronimo and then took an after-dinner ride around the ranch. The family stopped to watch the sun set as a prairie chicken strutted across the path, squawking a warning at the four horses. The big animals shifted their weight from hoof to hoof and shook their heads.

Margaret tucked the bottle of gin into her saddlebag, hiding it from Geronimo as he swung his aging bones onto yet one more Appaloosa gelding. She knew well the story of her great-grandfather disappearing into the bars of Kansas City and the abandonment of Geronimo's mother. She was well-versed in the dangers of alcohol and the continuing genocide it wreaked on Native people. Still, the grief in her heart from the rift in her family was more than she could bear. She reached down into the leather bag and drew the pint bottle up to her lips, then took a long gulp.

Warmth and relief flooded through her stomach and spread to her limbs. Enjoying the feel of tension loosening and flowing from her, she failed to notice Geronimo's stunned eyes staring at her. His lined and weary face was clothed in indescribable pain, the words *One more loss, one more loss…* running through his disbelieving mind.

The gin bottle was surreptitiously passed from sister to sister, the level of gin decreasing while Geronimo's heart shattered into a million pieces. In the cool of the approaching night, Ruby's horse stomped his feet, shaking a biting fly from his hock. Her arms were crossed over the saddle horn, the reins held loosely in her hands. She took a sip and then stopped. Her spine stiffened in horror as the smell of the gin reached her nostrils and she clearly saw her grandfather's heart break again. Next to her, Belinda sat on a dainty gray Arab mare. Her breath stopped as she waited for Geronimo's reaction.

Geronimo stared straight ahead. The sky faded to pink as a lifetime of memories flooded over him. He remembered standing at the graves of Yi Pay and Emily, of Agatha and hundreds of comrades buried at Normandy. The faces of lonely children and cruel teachers were still vivid in his memory. Frank's teary and anguished face came into focus, as did the bottle of gin resting on Margaret's thigh.

Geronimo ran his hands down his gray-haired braids, tying and untying the red cloth on the ends. He could feel a line of heat running down his face and a tiny spot of water dripped onto the ribbon shirt he wore underneath a leather vest. He inhaled deeply, pulled a rein to the side of his horse's neck and urged the gelding into a trot. The women he had loved and raised were left behind in the growing dusk.

The lights of the ranch house blinked a welcome to Geronimo as he rode the gelding into the paddock by the barn. He could hear the hooves of the three other horses coming up behind him and heard the voices of his three granddaughters calling to him. He slowly unsaddled the patient horse and dropped the saddle onto the floor of the barn. He rubbed the rump of the gelding as it trotted into its stall and thrust its head into the red grain holder hanging from the corner of the wooden enclosure.

"Billy Hawk," Geronimo whispered, "come and get me. I have lost everything. Come and get me. I can't go on."

Geronimo's steps were slow and burdened by the years of aloneness and the weight of loss. He took a deep, shuddering breath and lifted one foot at a time as he made his painful way into the living room of the white ranch house. A sharp pain struck him in the chest and he sank into the green recliner that squatted on the wooden floor across from the black pot-bellied stove. The bloodhound, gray on the muzzle and arthritic in the joints, stretched, sighed, and sank back onto the floor. Geronimo reached behind his head and pulled a black plaid blanket over his aching ribs and throbbing heart. The steps of Ruby, Belinda and Margaret echoed on the wooden porch and then the screen door slammed shut. The girls stood silhouetted in the light from the hallway, their faces in shadow, expressions unseen. The beat of Geronimo's heart stuttered and he listened in horror at the words that came from his lips:

"Go back to Tarrington, you three, or go to New York to be with your brother. I can't watch any more of my family die. It is a pain I cannot endure. Margaret, go home with your sisters. You are all on your own with jobs and an education. I have nothing more to offer, nothing but my ways and love. Go on, girls. Leave an old man to his thoughts."

As their father and grandfather before them, Margaret, Ruby, and Belinda gradually disappeared into the bars of Tarrington and then Tulsa and Oklahoma City. An occasional word of the girls' whereabouts floated back along the moccasin grapevine to the ranch outside the small town. Every night, Geronimo would sit in the recliner, the last smells of dinner and a full belly lulling him into sleep. He hoped, one day, that his grandchildren would remember the sanctuary of the ranch and make their way home. Night after night, season after season, Geronimo and the old bloodhound sat in the small white ranch house waiting for the phone to ring.

One winter night, two years after he had asked the girls to leave, Geronimo lounged in the recliner, the plaid blanket around his shoulders, the pot-bellied stove sending wave after wave of shimmering heat into the room. The phone rang, the loud trill giving Geronimo a start and causing the old dog to moan and roll. Hopeful, as he was every night, that the call might be from Frank or the girls, he lifted the receiver. The voice on the end of the line was as familiar to him as was his own. It was the pastor calling with the horrific news that Ruby, Margaret and Belinda had been found dead in a rundown apartment in Tulsa. The triplets had been on a binge, and died of carbon monoxide poisoning. They were trying to keep warm during a frigid night in the town on the prairie. A propane space heater blew heated and poisoned air into the girls' apartment. A neighbor went to check on them when she realized she did not hear the usual night noises from next door

Geronimo buried his granddaughters in the small cemetery in Tarrington, with only Billy Hawk standing by his side once again in the icy cold of winter. Frank refused to come home. He blamed his grandfather for his sisters' deaths, and encouraged the bitterness he felt to twine its ugly tendrils around his angry heart. Snow fell at the ranch in Tarrington and on New York City as Frank stared out the window of the brownstone.

Before him were the enormous towers of the World Trade Center. The heavy gray clouds shifted to black as they swirled around the top of the silver and blue monoliths. The image of a small boy leaning against a tall set of legs clothed in black wool floated in front of his staring eyes. A casket lay in the Oklahoma dirt waiting for the covering of earth that would seal it into eternity. He could visualize three identical coffins resting on the same earth, two old men holding each other's hands as the preacher intoned the words of the 23rd Psalm. Frank placed his palms flat on the window and pressed his forehead against the cold glass.

"I'm sorry, girls. I should have come to be with you. I'm so sorry, Ruby, Margaret, Belinda. How could I desert all of you?"

A hand tugged at Frank's sleeve. Wide, unblinking black eyes peered intently into Frank's as his son touched his hand. "Dad," Frank's youngest son, eighteen-year-old Jerome, asked, "Why don't you cry? It's okay. I'm sad, too. Dad, I want to go to Oklahoma and meet Geronimo. Mom says you named me after him. I want to go."

Frank shook his head, his eyes moist as he turned his head to stare out the window into the snowflakes fluttering to the ground. "Go talk to your mother, Jerome. If she agrees, you can go. I won't stop you. Go on, Jerome. I'll be in later. Go on."

Jerome turned to leave the room and, as he did, his father reached out to take his hand. Jerome looked into his father's face, puzzled by the emotion he had rarely seen displayed.

"Look out there, Jerome. See those buildings? Look closely and you can see the reflections of the clouds. Go find your mother. She can give you Geronimo's address. Go on, son. Leave me alone for a few minutes."

Just as Frank had imagined, three long days later, far away to the west, in the small cemetery at Tarrington,, three plain black caskets perched on the edge of three waiting graves. Two old friends held each other's hands, fingers laced in love. The prairie wind moaned as the caskets of Ruby, Margaret and Belinda dropped into the frozen Oklahoma ground.

The elderly pastor conducting the services was dressed in a black coat and pants with a white shirt and a black string tie. The Bible in his hands was bound in gold and the pages were edged in red.

A beam of God's Light, identical to that one so many years ago in France, shone for a moment on the graves as well as on the weathered visages of the old men before vanishing behind the angry black clouds of the winter day.

Just like at Genoa, Billy Hawk thought as tiny pieces of ice fell on the heads of the mourners. "More babies dead, and fewer left to sing the songs. Geronimo Barse, I am so sorry. So odd, alive and breathing and hopeful one second, and then gone. So strange."

The services completed, the pastor stepped forward. His hand slipped a letter into Geronimo's hand as the old man pressed a twenty-dollar bill into his.

"Open it at home, Geronimo. I am so sorry for your loss. I remember when we buried Agatha. Here we are again, all these years later. Too many times, huh, Geronimo? Well, time to go back to the church. Good day to you, Billy. Good day, Geronimo. Let me know if I can help. Good to see you, Billy Hawk. I'll say good-bye and God bless."

Billy took the cream-colored envelope from Geronimo's hand. The paper was heavy and thick in texture. The postmark was New York City, the return address that of the brownstone on the lower west side, a place Geronimo had never seen. The address was to: Geronimo Barse, c/o Pastor Huston Brown, Tarrington, Oklahoma. Billy tucked the envelope into the inside pocket of his plaid Filson jacket. The snowflakes began accumulating on the battered cowboy hat perched on his gray head. The two old men climbed into Billy's battered Cheyenne pickup and drove the short distance back to the ranch. The heater hummed as the friends sat in silent sorrow, the windshield wipers barely holding their own against the increasing snow.

"Read it to me, Billy. There isn't much more the World can do to me. Might as well have the rest of the pain tonight. Billy, I'm alone now, alone that is but for you. Billy, they were only forty-two, no children, no peace. Where did I go wrong, Billy? How come Creator lets me live? I should have done it differently, Billy, I should have let them all stay here on the ranch with me. Read me the letter, my friend."

Billy turned off the engine and pulled out the envelope. He slit the top with a long thumbnail. Inside lay a single sheet of monogrammed stationery, the handwriting on it stilted and prep school-perfect:

December 29, 1993

Dear Geronimo,

I got your address from the desk in Dad's office. I am sorry I am not there with you. I am coming to visit you soon. Mom is buying me a plane ticket. I want to see the ranch. Aunt Ruby said it was a magical place. I will be arriving in Tulsa on the fifth of January. Can you come and get me? Dad is very sad. I think he misses you but he is still angry. My aunties said you were a good man. Geronimo, I want to come and meet you. I am sorry I am not there with you now. Let me know, please, if I can come.

Your great-grandson,

Jerome

Geronimo sat on the cracked front bench of the ancient truck. He took the letter and envelope from Billy's hand, tenderly placed the letter back into the envelope, and smiled out the windshield.

"Billy, do you remember when we left Genoa? Remember how glad we were to leave? Do you think this boy will come to the ranch? I hope so. I have never seen Frank's children. I wonder why my other two great-grandsons, Gary and Gerald, aren't coming. I've never seen any of the boys or met Frank's wife. Can you imagine that? Let's go inside, Old Man. I've got some venison stew and my world-famous cornbread. Billy Hawk, I'm tired. Summer is a long time away. Where did our families go, Billy Hawk? Where are our wives and children? Let's go eat, Billy Hawk. Maybe Agatha and Opal can hear our words. I hope so, Billy Hawk, I hope so..."

⇥ ⇤

Tarrington, Oklahoma   **September 21, 1999**

In the past, the journey from Parmalee had taken a mere twelve hours. But, as Billy reached his eighties and then his nineties, he found himself too tired to make the drive straight through. His only concession to his aging bones was to spend the night in the ramshackle hotels that marked the exits off the concrete and asphalt roads that connected the ranches to the north and south.

Billy, alone on the long drive, would allow himself the luxury of memories. In his mind, he composed letters to his lost family members, telling Shelda of Opal's death by pneumonia and of his daughter Kathryn's death to breast cancer, just a decade after being one of the first women to receive her medical degree in the State of South Dakota. He sang lodge songs and told stories to the spirits that rode in the passenger's seat, their presence as real as the hound dogs in their crates tied in the back of the pickup.

He remembered the little girl, Janice Leary, his grand-niece who had been given into his care after her mother, Madison, and grandmother, Billy's sister Hallie, died in a fire started by an angry and intoxicated boyfriend. The shy child was now a slender and strong woman in her late forties, a stalwart friend who now cared for Billy as he had once cared for her.

Billy chuckled as he thought of the cocky young bronco rider who shared the dinner table with Janice and him. Jake, his great-grandson, had become a part of the household in 1981 when a tragic car accident took the lives of Billy's granddaughter, Joanne, and her husband, Sydney George. Jake was eighteen years old and possessed an ego and a sense of confidence that often outstripped his skills as a cowboy. His sunny and carefree disposition allowed him the freedom of expression denied to Billy in his youth at the boarding school at Genoa.

Janice and Jake had waved "good-bye" to Billy as they did every late September, wishing him well as he started the drive to Tarrington and then back to the Black Hills. Billy's indulgence of Geronimo never ceased to amuse them. They did truly understand the bond the old men shared and that time was slipping by and it would not be long before one of the lifelong friends would leave the earth. On the afternoon of his second day on the road, Billy parked the step-side pickup truck in the dusty drive in front of the white ranch house at Tarrington. He blew the horn as long and loudly as he could, calling Geronimo to the screen door and then out onto the porch.

"Come on, you old man." Billy yelled. "Get your dog and let's go."

"Is that you again?" Geronimo replied as he made his slow way down the front stairs, waving his gnarled hand in greeting. "Don't get out, Billy. I know how hard it is on your bones. Let me get my stuff and leave a note for Jerome."

"Come on, dog," Geronimo whistled for the aging hound dog, then lifted him up onto the back of the truck and into the empty crate that Billy had brought along. The cats, hearing the truck pull up and Geronimo's step on the boards above them, came running from under the porch. They meowed loudly as Geronimo loaded the hound onto the truck and wound their way around his legs.

"Okay, pussycats! Let's go inside where it's safe. Poppa's going on a road trip!"

Geronimo reached down to pet the cats and then turned back to go inside the house. He pulled out a black duffel bag, a matching bedroll, a battered Coleman cooler, and then grabbed a well-worn black cowboy hat and black leather jacket off a hook.

"Billy, my great-grandson, Jerome is coming tonight to take care of the ranch. His dad gripes about it but Jerome loves the ranch. He's driving down tonight from Norman. He's going to college up there. He's been a part-time student forever. Wants to be a journalist, he says. Expose the lies of corporate America, he says. I say he'll get a Pulitzer Prize but his dad says he will be a two-bit hack. I think Frank is afraid Jerome will write an exposé on him! Sure wish I could meet my other two great-grandsons but they never ask to come here and they're pretty much grown and out on their own.

"You know, Billy Hawk, Jerome also trained to be an EMT and that's how he pays his bills. My grandson won't give him a cent; says Jerome abandoned his family when he moved out here to Oklahoma. I swear, Billy, I never met a man more angry and bitter than my grandson Frank.

Don't know how his wife stands it. Of course, I never met her either but the girls used to tell me how nice she was to them on their visits to New York City.

"I can understand why my grandson was upset but it's been fifty years since his parents died. He is still angry over his sisters' death. All of them have been gone for years. He blames me for their alcoholism and for not selling the ranch to give him an easier life. I tried to tell him that people make their own choices but he just can't stop being angry. He forgets that it was my son, my daughter-in-law, and grandchildren that died, too. He just can't see anything beyond himself and his anger."

Billy nodded his head in agreement. It was odd, he thought, how each of them had had so many deaths in their lives yet here they were, well into their nineties and still alive. The world made no sense. But it was good of the Creator to allow them such long lives, although at times his creaky joints thought otherwise. The camaraderie, comfort and care that the old men provided each other survived no matter what went on in the world. Billy turned to the man sitting in the passenger's seat, looking at the profile of his faithful friend.

"Geronimo, we're ninety-two now. We have to let the dead lie in peace and let the young live their lives. It would certainly be a long story, Old Man, if someone was to tell it."

Geronimo sighed and rubbed his hand on the cracked vinyl of the seat. He could hear the dogs moving behind him in the wooden bed of the truck, shifting in their kennels and scratching their bellies.

"Billy, do you ever wake up at night and hear Opal and Kathryn calling you? I hear Jerome and Gloria and Agatha and the girls whispering to me. Billy, so many of us are gone. Soon, I'll be dead and that preacher man will most likely say the 23rd Psalm over me. He'll probably be wearing the same black coat and pants and same white shirt as when we buried Agatha. I think our stories would be short, Billy Hawk. *They lived, they died.* Never mind, Billy, I'm rambling like an old man! Pull over; give me a turn at the wheel!"

Billy shook his head and pulled onto a wide spot along the side of the road. They were nearing the turnoff to the forest road that would take them deeper into the mountains. The sun was rising higher in the sky, a smell reminiscent of hyacinth floated into the cab of the trunk. The old men opened their respective doors and climbed down, walking in front of the old truck, pushing each other on the shoulder as they passed.

Geronimo ground the gears as he started the drive down the dirt road that stretched for miles. Evergreen trees, their bark cracked and leaking sap, loomed above them, permitting only small glimpses of the sun and sky. Five miles and thirty minutes later, Geronimo rolled the truck to a stop in front of an enormous ponderosa pine, one of the last of the giants in the ever-shrinking forest. The dogs in the back of the truck began to bark and howl, a raucous and disturbing sound in the quiet forest.

"I'll let them out, Geronimo." Billy said. "You go take a pee against that tree over there. I know how small your kidneys are, to say nothing of the rest of your equipment!"

"You been peeking, Billy? Okay, let them out and I'll start making camp."

Billy opened the three kennels and the dogs sprang forward, howling and barking as they dashed into the woods. Their barking increased in volume, coming from a point south of where the men stood. They turned to look at each other and began to run as well and as fast as they could, to the spot where they thought the dogs had treed some pathetic animal.

The two men came to an abrupt halt, staring at an unimaginable scene ahead of them. A large wolverine stood over the unmoving figure of a smaller black and silver wolverine, baring his teeth and charging the dogs. Billy whistled for the dogs as Geronimo squatted, trying to get a closer look at the female wolverine.

"Billy, her front leg is caught in a trap. Damn these things. I thought they were outlawed in this part of the park. Damn. I think she's dead. I never thought I'd see this kind of thing again, Billy. Look at all the blood. Damn. Let's get those dogs out of here and see what we can do. Damn, Billy. I hate this shit. Damn it all. Come on, dogs, get away from there. Billy, look, she's moving, she's still alive. Come on, dogs, move! Get away from there."

Billy grabbed the collars of the dogs and tied them to a tree with his belt and the plaid suspenders he wore under his vest. He turned back to where Geronimo was still squatting and trying to fathom a way to rescue the female wolverine without losing a hand.

"Billy, I know what we can do. Let's get those dog kennels. I've got bones in the cooler for the dogs. We can open the door to the kennels and put some food inside. Once we get the male into one, we can throw a blanket over the female, wrap her up and put her in another kennel. Maybe we can save her. Billy, did you ever see a pair of wolverines together outside of breeding season? Maybe Creator sent us to this spot to save these poor animals."

"There must be small ones around, Geronimo. Let's move these dogs out of here and see what we can do."

The sun shone through the tress, illuminating the blood spatters spread over the small glade where the wounded wolverine lay. The male stood guard over her, hissing and growling as Billy and Geronimo backed away towards the parked truck. He rubbed the face of the female, looking for all the world as if he was weeping over his dying mate.

Billy untied the dogs and pulled them away from the clearing and back to the truck. He cursed the trappers as he pulled ropes out of the back of the Chevy and anchored the panting hounds to the tailgate. He climbed up into the back and tossed the kennels down one at a time. Geronimo lifted out a stack of heavy blankets from under the tarp.

The smell of the wolverine's blood tainted the summer air, gagging the old men as it brought back the terrible memories of the battles at Normandy. Both men fought down a sense of panic as they gathered the first aid kit, the kennels, and the bones from the cooler. They worked as one, their only focus saving the female wolverine.

In the glade, the hungry and exhausted male wolverine lay down by his mate. While he had fed his kits and the female through the night, he had eaten little. He lay on top of his mate, growling with the little energy he had left as the two friends came back with what they hoped would save the beautiful animal panting on the ground.

"Put the bones in that first kennel, Geronimo, and I'll get behind him with the blanket. I'll see if I can move him away from her and into the kennel. Geronimo, look at her paw. It's almost torn off. Goddamn those trappers. Do they think Creator's creatures feel no pain? I swear, Geronimo, I've lived too long. I'm sick of cruelty and blood."

Billy started to cry as he watched Geronimo prepare the kennel. He thought of all the dead soldiers on the beach, the dead children at the boarding school, and the dead buffalo piled high on the prairies. He began to talk to the wolverines in a soothing voice, asking Creator for help.

"Hey, small ones, listen to me. My old friend and I are here to help. Listen, little ones. Creator, make them hear my voice. Make them know I am here to help. Shush, little ones, listen to my voice."

Geronimo moved around to the front of the female wolverine, his ear tuned to the soothing sound of Billy's voice. The male wolverine stopped his growling and looked up into Billy's eyes. The female closed her eyes and lay still. Geronimo set the kennel down with the door open and a meaty bone at the back.

The male wolverine licked his mate one last time and, tentatively sniffing at the kennel, stepped inside. Geronimo gently closed the door of the kennel and moved it away from the hurt female. He reached behind him and pulled a second kennel forward. He could hear the dogs shuffling around the tailgate of the truck. A woodpecker knocked against a tree over the heads of the men. A chickadee perched on a branch, peering down at the strange scene below. A hundred yards away, unnoticed by the men, a white raven watched the scene from the top of a ragged snag.

Billy waved Geronimo forward with the plastic carrier. Geronimo began to sing the Kiowa song he sang to the horses every night. The air was still, nothing moved except Geronimo as he placed the kennel in front of the panting female. Billy crooned to the wolverine as he slowly slipped the blanket over her. He stared into her pain-filled eyes, willing her to hold still as he pulled the blanket higher. He studied the cruel trap that held the wolverine in its hideous grip. He spied the release mechanism, well within the biting range of the wolverine. Geronimo continued to sing as Billy placed his foot on the spring and released the wolverine's mangled paw. The female, exhausted from her long struggle, closed her eyes and allowed Billy to wrap her tightly in the blanket. In violation of her every instinct, she snuggled into his arms and sighed, choosing to trust the old man who held her.

Billy placed the trembling wolverine in the second kennel. She lay there in pain, halfway in the carrier, her face and paw resting on Billy's knee. He sat down in the grass of the glade, gently placed the cage with the female wolverine inside next to him, and dropped his head into his hands. For the first time in their eighty-six years together, Geronimo saw his friend weep openly. Barely able to gasp out the words, Billy called for Geronimo to bring the first-aid kit.

Geronimo slipped away, returning a minute later with the black case. Without a word, he pulled out a syringe of tetanus vaccine and one of antibiotics. He passed them to Billy who carefully injected the female wolverine. He pulled out a roll of gauze and tenderly wrapped her paw. The wolverine did not move, did not growl, and did not bite. Billy began to weep again, his tears falling into the thick coat of the trusting animal.

Billy carefully moved the female to the back of the second kennel. He stroked the thick black and silver fur, the luxurious feel of the wolverine's ruff soft beneath his hands. The small animal, usually so aggressive and fearless, panted, moaned and then relaxed under Billy's hand. She blinked her eyes and lay still in the plastic kennel. Billy closed the steel mesh of the gate and lifted the kennel into the air, the heft of the wolverine's weight and that of the cage causing him to strain as he slid the kennel onto the wooden bed of the truck.

Geronimo stood back from his beloved friend, a strange pain pushing against the back of his ribs. His breath felt labored and the fingers of his left arm tingled. A small cough escaped his suddenly parched lips. He cleared his throat and coughed again.

"Billy, let's go home. We can take them with us to Tarrington. No one needs to know, Billy. Creator sent us to this place today. I'm going to look for the little ones. There must be some around. Ah, Billy, don't cry anymore."

Geronimo patted Billy's shoulder. He untied the dogs again and opened the door of the truck, telling the dogs to get up and into the cab. He closed the windows leaving an inch of open space to allow fresh cool mountain air into the cab. Billy and Geronimo, hand in hand, hurried back into the glade where the male wolverine crouched in fear against the back of the kennel. In unison, the old friends lifted the cage off the ground and carried it back to the truck, placing it carefully so that the male and female could see each other and touch each other's nose.

Billy climbed up and sat on the open tailgate. A browning leaf drifted down, landing on the heated metal beside his jean-clad leg. Behind him the wolverines growled softly to each other, small noises of pain escaping the female. Billy lifted his head, squinting against the early afternoon sun. The dogs pressed their faces to the glass, their hot breath steaming the windows. With the slow movements of his advanced age, Billy Hawk scratched his forehead and the side his nose. He turned slightly to his left, his hand on the side of the truck. He shifted his weight from side to side and rubbed the back of his neck. His soul recoiled from the horror of the trap, the memory of the beatings at Genoa, and the screams of the wounded and dying at Normandy Beach. He hung his head and began sobbing again, the sound echoing through the trees to Geronimo. He felt tears coming from his own heart as he heard his friend weep.

Geronimo picked up the third kennel and headed into the woods looking for the wolverine's den. He found a pile of scat a half mile into the woods and there it was, a small opening at the foot of a cliff, hidden among the boulders and brush that littered the forest.

Two small black faces, streaked with silver, stared up at him. Geronimo placed two bones inside the kennel and placed the opening of the kennel next to the door of the den. He sat down cross-legged on the ground and waited for the kits to enter. Within a few minutes, the babies climbed into the carrier, enticed by the smell of the bones. Geronimo closed the door and took a deep sigh. He pulled himself up with the aid of a nearby tree and picked up the cage, two small black bodies squirming as he carried the kennel to the black Chevy..

The swaying trees cast shadows over Billy, sitting on the ground next to the wheel of the truck, his head on his knees wet with his tears. Meanwhile, Geronimo, sweat dampening the back of his shirt, heaved the kennel with the two cubs into the truck. The cubs growled and crouched at the back of the plastic container. They watched Geronimo with a wary look but made no move to cause him any harm.

The dogs locked in the cab panted and pressed their noses to the rear window. The bloodhound opened his mouth to howl, stopping short when Billy rapped his knuckles against the glass. The two men tied shut the tailgate of the truck and tied the kennels in place. They opened the doors to the cab and pushed the dogs to the center of the seat.

Geronimo started the engine as Billy wept again. He spread his hands on his knees. His jeans were covered with the blood of the female wolverine. He turned to look out the back window. In the reflecting glass, he saw Geronimo lying in a coffin, the lining yellow silk. Billy closed his eyes as the truck headed up the road toward the ranch at Tarrington.

Geronimo drove the entire trip. Billy finally fell into an exhausted sleep as the road slipped behind them and they crossed into Kansas. Night had long since fallen as Geronimo drove east into the flat, wheat-covered plains. He had stopped only to let the dogs out, to check the wolverines in their cages, to give all the animals food, and to take a pee into the roadside dirt. Billy stirred and mumbled, but his snoring continued even when the motion of the vehicle had ceased, the cab light came on, and the snuffling of the restless dogs surrounded him. Geronimo did not worry about Billy as the old man's snores rattled the windows, keeping time to the luscious tones of Glen Campbell singing "Gentle on My Mind" as they drove through the starry night.

Finally, Geronimo spied a dimly lit roadside motel, its flickering "Rise and Shine" sign illuminating the squat orange building. Geronimo shook Billy awake and then climbed down from the truck's cab. The three dogs followed him. He entered the wood paneled office of the aging motel. The clerk was a man of indeterminate age, his teeth brown from nicotine and rotted in the middle. He was pleasant, though, asking Geronimo whether he would be paying by cash or credit card and, sure, he allowed pets although the owner frowned on it.

"Take the end room to the back," the night clerk suggested. "Not many in the hotel tonight, just some trucker named Henry going to the Twin Cities from Tucumcari. See you all in the morning. Just leave the key in the drop box. Goodnight."

The night's silence sounded loud against Billy's eardrums as he watched Geronimo return to the truck. The ticking of the motor seemed to be ticking away Billy's life, tick by tick by tick. He turned and slid out of the truck, sliding his hand along the side until he reached the tailgate.

He untied the rope that held the piece of metal in place and climbed up onto the bed, laboring with the effort. Billy reached forward and pulled the kennels containing the wolverines toward him, inch by inch. The male wolverine, startled by the sudden movement, commenced a low growling, his teeth bared, and his hackles standing on end. The little female whimpered to her mate and he grew quiet, but his watchful eye gave Billy the onceover as he was lifted out of the truck and placed on the ground. Geronimo hurried to where Billy was straining to tug the two other cages off the edge of the tailgate. One by one, the old gentlemen pushed the cages over the threshold and into the dingy motel room. Geronimo hit the light switch and a sickly yellow glow filled the room. The three dogs sniffed the cages of the wolverines; the male growled and hissed in reply until, irritated due to his lack of sleep, Geronimo placed his fingers between his lips and let loose a long, high-pitched whistle. All of the other living creatures in the room froze in surprise.

"Abe, George and Thomas, go lie down. Pierre, Danielle, Andre and Renee, quiet down. Billy, get in bed!" Geronimo commanded. "I've had enough and you are all getting on my last nerve."

"Damn, Geronimo! You scared the piss out of me," Billy responded. "And who in God's name are Pierre, Danielle, Andre and Renee? I knew you were crazy, you old coot. But this time, you have really gone round the bend. And I *am* going to bed. You can sleep on the floor! Scaring me like that! Damn it, Geronimo, I'm ninety-two years old. You just took ten years off my life. If I die tonight, it's your fault!"

'Billy, I swear you never pay attention. Turn up your hearing aid, Old Man. I told you miles back that I named the wolverines. Guess you couldn't hear me over all that snoring you were doing. Never did listen to me, you old fool! Turn up your hearing aids. Now, hand me that phone. I want to call Jerome."

Billy stepped into the tiny bathroom, his naked rear peeking out of the door as he stood by the cracked and leaking toilet, hoping that his kidneys and prostrate would cooperate and allow him some relief. He could hear Geronimo dialing the operator and asking to be put through to "Geronimo Barse in Tarrington, Oklahoma. Reverse the charges, please." He smiled as he listened to the conversation. Geronimo was calm but emphatic in his comments to Jerome.

"We'll be home in the late afternoon, Jerome. I have a wounded animal with me and I need you to bring as many medical supplies as you can. I really need you to bring some animal tranquilizers and pain killers. No, it's not Billy! Don't be absurd! Of course he's in one piece. Yes, the dogs are in one piece. What kind of a fool do you take me for?

"Jerome, hush up, will you, boy? This is important. Now, this is what I need. Call Doc Dreiser, and give him this list. What? Never mind what kind of animal. Hush, boy. Don't vex me. Now, get what I need and make sure there are clean sheets on the guest bed. Yes, I know that's where you're sleeping. You can sleep in my bed, Jerome, don't argue with me.

"Tell Doc Dreiser this is what I need: Four packages of vet wrap. No, I don't care what color it is; pink is fine. Eight packages of six-by-six gauze squares. Two vials of morphine. Just make it for a large dog. No, Jerome, not one of my dogs. Four tubes of antibiotic cream and two vials of penicillin."

There was a brief pause as Geronimo listened and then responded. "Jerome, your father is blowing off steam. Don't take it personally. He's mad at me because you left New York. Jerome, it's up to you. If you could please stay three more days...

"No, I'm not mad at him or your mother. Yes, I would love to see your brothers. Of course I'll be there for your graduation but, boy, that is two years from now. You can fight it out with your father later. Jerome, it's midnight. I need to go to bed. Billy is right here, trying to squeeze some pee out of his kidneys. I can see his bare butt.

"What? Of course I love you. Look, don't worry about it. Yes, I know you fed the horses. Jerome, they don't care what song you sing. Jerome, go back to bed. Just make sure you have everything set up. Yes, Jerome, I love you, too. Yes, Billy loves you, too. No, I didn't cut his braids off. Jerome, you are a nut. I love you, go to bed!"

Billy flushed the toilet and dropped the lid with a thump. He flicked the light switch off, then paced out of the motel room door, ignoring Geronimo's questioning look. He was back in a minute, two duffel bags over his shoulders. He tossed them on the bed and plunked his body down on the edge.

"Geronimo, go brush your teeth and go to bed. I don't want any old man's breath in my face. You can tell me your grand scheme about them French wolverines in the morning. Poor Agatha, putting up with you all those years! French wolverines. For God's sake! If I didn't know better, I'd swear you'd been drinking."

The night was short; the noise in the room was an odd combination of dog, wolverine and old men snoring. Geronimo awoke with a start; the pain in his chest pushing against his ribs again, his left arm aching. He rolled onto his side and took a deep, slow breath.

"Huh, what?" Billy moved under the starched thin sheets of the queen-size bed. Geronimo groaned in response, rubbing his chest and arm.

"I'm getting up, Billy. We need to get these animals some food and get them on the road. Let me up and I'll find a way to clean out those cages. I swear, Billy, no more chili dogs on the run. My indigestion is killing me. This morning, you can buy me breakfast at the Denny's next door. Sure is hot in here. Man, I'm sweatin' up a storm."

Billy yawned and took a close look at Geronimo's face. It was pale and drawn.

"Geronimo, are you okay? What's wrong? Do you need a doctor?"

"I'm fine, Billy. Let's just get things taken care of and get home. Too many hours on the road and too much awake time. Let's go. I'll take a quick shower and help you load up the wolverines. Ah, Billy, I'm fine."

After his shower, Geronimo dressed in a flaming orange NASCAR tee shirt and black jeans. He seemed to have more color in his face but Billy wasn't sure if it was simply the reflection of the bright shirt. Singing Kiowa songs to the wolverines, Geronimo gently reached inside and wiped up the feces and urine in the kennels. Billy loaded the dogs in the cab of the truck and returned to help his old friend. The female wolverine, now christened Renee, seemed a little stronger. She tolerated the disturbance, her black eyes still filled with pain. The two cubs were more concerned with the dog kibble while the male paced the small space of his carrier, pressing his nose to the vents in the cage, whining at his mate.

Standing at the entrance to the room, Billy began crying again. He could feel the tears running down his chin and neck, wetting his green ribbon shirt. He had another flash of Geronimo laid out in a brown casket, dressed in a black suit, white shirt, and black string tie. He turned away so Geronimo could not see him. He wiped his eyes on his sleeve and then bent down to help Geronimo carry the kennels back out to the truck. Two hours later, breakfast eaten, animals fed and watered, and wolverine cages cautiously cleaned, the two men were on the road.

Geronimo crossed from Kansas into Oklahoma late in the afternoon and finally down the dirt lane to the white ranch house just as the sun began its descent into the west. A brand-new yellow Ford F-150 was parked next to the paddocks and a slender young man of average height stood on the porch. His hair was black and pulled into a ponytail at the back of his neck. He was dressed in an orange tee shirt, identical to the one Geronimo wore.

He ran to the truck as Geronimo pulled to a stop and opened the door of the cab. Three dogs tumbled out, jumping around the young man, licking his hand, tails wagging in welcome.

"Hey, Jerome! Come and help this old man out. He's older than dirt and creakier than a rusty pump!" Geronimo grinned. "Did you get what I asked for? Is the room set up? Come on, give us a hand. Billy, get out and let's get to work. Hold on, Old Man, let Jerome help you down."

"Hey, Billy!" Jerome ran around to the back of the truck, stopping short as he spotted the three kennels in the truck bed.

"Geronimo, what are you thinking? Damn, you two! You brought home a pack of wolverines. You know the law. How the hell did you sneak these into the state? Geronimo, is this what you were so cagey about? Billy, have you two lost your minds? Never mind. Geronimo, where do you want me to put these kennels? You need to sit down. You look like death warmed over."

"Jerome, take the one with the two cubs to the far end of the barn, the one with the full gate on it. Throw some hay down on the mat, put some food and water in a pan, and let the two little ones out. Be careful to close the gate all but for a few inches and put the kennel up against it. Open the door and when the cubs run out, close the gate. You can come back and get the male and put him in the next stall. Hurry up. I'm going to need your help." Geronimo coughed, a deep hacking cough that shook his body and bent him over. He waved Billy and Jerome away, taking another deep breath and placing his gnarled hands on his knees.

"I'm fine. Come on, Billy, let's get this little girl into the house."

That night, as the male wolverine and his cubs spent their first night on the ranch, Jerome, Billy and Geronimo worked their loving magic on the little female now known as Renee. To Jerome's amazement, the female lay still and silent as Geronimo soothed her and Billy cleaned and wrapped her torn paw. She stared into Jerome's eyes, her fear fading as the morphine took hold and, for a while, eased her pain. She lay on the clean sheets of the bed, falling into a pain-free sleep, dreaming of the gentle hands of the old men.

A pink-streaked dawn, laced with yellow and burgundy clouds, crept across the wide Oklahoma sky. Geronimo and Billy had fallen asleep at four in the morning, lying on the floor alongside the bed where Renee dozed. Jerome found them there when he rose to do the morning chores, feed the animals, and check on the small family of wolverines in the barn. He had left the horses out the previous night, giving them hay and grain in the paddock, keeping them away from the smell of the wolverines.

"No wonder you scare Dad, Old Man. You talk to animals, heal their pain, believe in treating all creatures as equal, and love beyond comprehension," Jerome whispered as he gazed at the scene, the colors of the prairie sky reflecting into the small bedroom. "Billy Hawk, you, too."

The female wolverine opened her eyes, her paw wrapped in bright pink vet wrap, a calm look spread across her face. She followed Jerome's movements, her nose quivering as he came closer.

I never would have believed it if I hadn't seen it with my own eyes. Dad, you were so wrong. You can keep your own counsel, Dad. I'm not leaving Oklahoma unless it's a matter of life and death, he said to himself. "Okay, Renee, let's see if I can get you into a kennel and back out to your babies and Andre. My God, French wolverines! Old men, crazy, wonderful old men."

Stepping carefully over the sleeping bodies of Geronimo and Billy, Jerome placed the kennel on the bed and put a bowl of kibble in the back of the cage. Renee raised her head and then scooted her way into the carrier. She sighed and began to eat, oblivious to the wire door closing, before Jerome carried her out to the barn and slid the metal stall gate open, placing Renee's carrier to the opening. He released the springs of the door and, as he stood in awe at the sight, Renee tentatively placed weight on her right paw and then limped to greet her babies. He shut the metal gate and peered through the metal bars at the four silver and black guests. He shook his head, shrugged his shoulders and sighed.

If I hadn't seen it, I would never have believed it. St. Jerome pulling a thorn from the lion's paw. There's the lesson from God, Dad. Geronimo Barse, our own St. Jerome. Dad, how could you have ever doubted the goodness of this man?

Jerome quietly went about his chores and as the clock reached ten o'clock, he carried a tray of bacon, eggs, ham, milk and coffee into the bedroom where Billy and Geronimo still slept. He placed the tray on the battered old dresser in the room that was once his father's. He pulled the sheets off the bed and turned to leave the room, calling out the names of the old men. He left the house and climbed into the yellow pickup, heading west across the ranch.

It was not until five that afternoon that Jerome returned once more to the ranch house. He stomped the dirt off his boots and made his way to the kitchen where Billy and Geronimo sat at the old table, a deck of cards laid out between the two of them, a pot of coffee wafting its aroma into the air. They halted their game as Jerome came into the room, wiping his hands on his blue work shirt, pulling it out of his jeans. The old men seemed tired in the dim light of the kitchen, the wrinkles and old age spots marking their hands and faces. Two sets of hearing aids lay on the counter; a tangible sign of the long-lingering effects of World War II but one commonly ignored by both Billy and Geronimo. The tray with the breakfast dishes sat on the counter next to the sink, with the still-strong smell of bacon and rancid grease.

"Hey, Jerome, where you been? Your brother Gary has called five times, looking for you. Guess he has big news." Geronimo nudged Billy's leg with his foot. Billy ignored him and picked up the cards to shuffle them.

"Geronimo, Gary is getting married. He wants me to be one of his groomsmen. I told him to come out here to meet you and bring his girl. You won't believe this, Billy; my brother's marrying a Mohawk girl from St. Regis. No matter how hard Dad tries, he's stuck with Indians! I'll call Gary later. I want to take you two for a drive. I've got the truck loaded. Leave the dogs here and come on. You two aren't the only ones who can keep a secret."

The two old men glanced at each other and shrugged their shoulders. They pulled on their cowboy boots left at the screen door the previous night. They followed Jerome out to the pickup and slid onto the bench seat, Billy scrunched into the middle. Jerome whistled the theme song to "Dallas" as he drove down the road and onto a dirt track that led across the ranch. Two miles out, Geronimo could see several piles of rocks rising up from the flat prairie. He frowned, trying to discern what had grown up out of his pasture over the course of the past week.

Jerome shut off the engine and silently rolled the truck to a stop. He sat in the cab, his arms folded across the steering wheel. As Geronimo began to open the door, Jerome reached an arm out to stop him. Geronimo started to speak, his question dying on his lips as four wolverines appeared in front of the odd stacks of rocks, a neon pink bandage wrapped around the leg of the small female. The carcasses of four dead chickens lay in front of the rock piles, feathers scattered in a large circle across the grass of the prairie.

"Hold on, Geronimo. Watch this!" Jerome slid the window of the cab down and leaned out, whistling through his teeth, much the way Geronimo had done in the hotel the last night on the road. The small female lifted her head and ran towards the truck. Jerome laughed and opened the door, squatting down on the ground, his hand held out in welcome. The female limped as she ran but was clearly nowhere near in as much pain as she had been three days earlier when Billy and Geronimo had rescued her from the torturous rusty trap.

Geronimo sat in contented silence as the beautiful black and silver wolverine licked Jerome's fingers and allowed him to feel her paw. She growled once and then calmed, turning to run back to her mate and cubs when Jerome stood up. Muffled sobs came from Billy's lips and he turned to hug Geronimo. The sun slipped down below the line of silver clouds that lined the horizon. Night settled in, providing the wolverine family the protection of dark as the yellow pickup made its way back to the ranch house.

The next day dawned overcast with the first fall rainstorm sweeping in from the west. Billy left early for Parmalee with his dogs sitting beside him, upright and attentive as they stared out the windshield. Jerome and Geronimo waved good-bye from the porch of the farmhouse.

"I have to go back to New York City tonight, Geronimo," Jerome said, looking off into the distance where the sheets of rain could be seen.

"Gary's wedding is next week. Come with me, Geronimo. You have two great-grandsons you've never met. Come with me. I have to be back in Norman shortly after that for the start of the quarter. I'll buy the ticket, Geronimo, please come."

Geronimo shook his head and leaned against the large post that had supported the overhanging roof for well over a century. "Thanks, boy. But, I'm too old to get on an airplane and I have animals to tend. By the way, Jerome, just out of curiosity, were those laying hens alive or dead when you took them out to those wolverine mansions you built yesterday? Ah, never mind, boy. Go on home. Thanks for your help. Call me as soon as you get back from New York City. I'll heat a stack of rocks for you and you can sweat off the dirt of the city. Give your mom and brothers my best and tell them to come and see me. Get along, boy. I've got work to do."

Jerome grabbed his great-grandfather around his chest and pulled him close.

"I love you, Geronimo Barse." Jerome kissed Geronimo's wrinkled cheek and then climbed into his truck. He drove down the road, waving his hand out the window, smiling as the herd of horses galloped alongside the fence, their whinnying accompanying him as he headed east to Norman.

Jerome grinned as he looked in the mirror and saw Geronimo waving him down the road. He inserted a CD into the player, turned up the sound, and sang at the top of his voice as the dust from the wheels of the truck whirled into a light cloud behind him. The words he sang were a fitting tribute to the grace and love of his beloved great-grandfather and Billy Hawk.

> *"One Love, One Heart!*
> *Let's get together and feel all right:*
> *Hear the children cryin' (One Love)*
> *Hear the children cryin' (One Heart),*
> *Sayin': Give thanks and praise to the Lord and I will feel all right:*
> Sayin': Let's get together and feel all right!"

⊰ 7 ⊱

The Red Pony

The frozen grass crackled and groaned under the weight of the trotting herd. They were headed west, toward the shelter of the barn and the warming face of the old man. The bay mare struggled to keep up with the others, her breath coming in sharp, painful bursts. She could see the wind plucking at the black stallion's mane as the horses moved through the sleet and rain. A ripple of pain cut through her belly, crushing her ribs and pulling her off her feet. She whinnied into the swirling air, calling to the others. Another spasm shook her, pushing her to her side. She nickered and called to the black stallion. He turned back to the bay mare; the others closed ranks, staying near in the looming dusk.

The mare lay on the cold ground, sweat shining on her neck mixing with the frozen precipitation as it began to cover her shaggy coated body. She tried to struggle to her feet but the pain washed over her again, holding her down. A mighty heave rolled from her neck to her hind legs. As it passed, a tiny face and two legs appeared between the mare's legs. Within a few seconds, a shiny body and two more legs, followed by a tail and umbilical cord, slid out onto the roughness of the frozen grass. Surrounded by the herd nudging and nuzzling the tiny body, the mare gave a final shudder, releasing the afterbirth from her body, its red bleeding into the frozen field. Off in the distance, two coyotes howled, hooting with joy over their kill.

The stallion, keenly aware of the nearby predators, pushed at the bay mare with his nose and then his hoof. He shook his head and nickered at her, urging her to her feet. The tiny colt, his body steaming from the cold and the effort of being born, wobbled to his feet. He stood spread-eagled, trying to find his balance in the cold, new world. The bay mare, exhausted by her effort, closed her eyes. The black stallion urgently continued to nudge her. After many minutes, the sound of the coyotes came closer. The bay mare rolled to her chest and, with one tremendous push, came to her feet. She stood over the tiny colt, rubbing her muzzle all over his body. He was hungry and wanted to feed but the bay mare, too, wanted to move to safety.

The herd also included a blue roan gelding, a chestnut gelding, a dappled mare, and a sorrel mare. The bay mare and the black stallion nuzzling and encouraging the colt, resumed their journey across the barren, frozen landscape. A short distance behind them, the coyotes reached the afterbirth, tearing into it with their teeth, yipping and screaming over the prize they had found.

Within an hour of the colt's birth, the herd slowly walked into the paddock next to the barn where the old man, Geronimo Barse, stood waiting. He had been there for hours, wrapped in a huge parka with a bright red scarf around his neck. He had been calling to the herd, peering with his rheumy and cataract-coated eyes into the sleet, straining for a glimpse of them.

The horses and the old man had been together longer than anyone had a right to be alive. They were used to one another, counting on one another for comfort and love. Geronimo could no longer lift a leg to ride any of the horses and passed his evenings now reading to the horses in their stalls and telling them stories of the Old Ones, the Ones who had been on this land in the past. He told them stories of the Kiowa and the Shawnee, of their beautiful ponies and the buffalo herds. He sang to them, told them of the events of the world, and discussed politics as if they were a crowd following a campaign train at whistle stops.

The familiar smell of hay and horses provided both solace and concern to him as he faced his mortality. He worried who would care for his beloved animals when he passed on to the next world. He sat on an old oak chair in the aisle between the barn stalls, snug against the screeching winds of winter and the scorching heat of the prairies in summer. The barn cats would sit with him, washing their matching black-and-white faces. At times, they would rub against his legs and jump up on his lap, patting his stubbled chin. Geronimo would laugh and gently place the cats back on the matted concrete floor of the barn and resume his recitation of the day's events to the horses as they munched their dinners of orchard grass and alfalfa.

Regardless of the season, every night Geronimo would stand at the gate to the paddocks, calling the horses home by singing a Kiowa warrior song and then slapping his hands on the metal of the gate. Every night, regardless of where on the ranch they were, the horses would form a single line and make their way back to the safety of the barn and their stalls. The old man, after making sure the door to each stall was ajar, hay was on the floor, and grain was in each animal's feed trough, would hold open the gate. It had been this way for Geronimo for seventy years, through hundreds of horses. The ranch was the last big property in the region in the hands and care of an individual. The surrounding lands had been sold for housing tracts or purchased by enormous corporations. Geronimo stubbornly refused to move, saying simply that the Kiowa did not own the land, therefore it was not his to sell.

The night the colt was born, he waited for the members of the herd. He heard the coyotes' howl and knew the old horses were particularly vulnerable to the circling pack. He counted them one by one as they trotted into the barn, their rank and order long established. When the bay mare entered her stall, a tiny red form wobbled behind. Mother and foal entered the stall together. The bay mare gratefully took a bite of hay and then sank to her knees.

"Damn!" said Geronimo. "Damn, Sarah, you was early. That baby weren't expected here for weeks. Damn, ain't he one pretty boy? Didn't know that old bastard stallion had it in him anymore."

Geronimo grabbed a rag off the wall and stepped into the stall. He squatted down next to the bay mare and picked up her baby. He rubbed the colt all over, pausing only to feel the legs and admire their black socks. The mane and tail were black as well; a white star marked the tiny face.

"Sarah, you have a pretty boy, looks just like you. Another pretty Indian pony, one of the last."

Geronimo turned to leave, rubbing his eyes with the dirty rag, smelling the horse smell and the sweet aroma of the new colt.

That night he dreamed of the herd running, tails high, across the prairies, scattering the prairie chickens and the meadowlarks in their path. He could see tall men and women on the backs of the ponies, black hair shining in the light of the moon. The herd ran on forever into the distant mist. He dreamed of his grandfather, a stately man who was one of the few ancient tribesmen left, a man who talked of the horses, the birds, the water, the people. Geronimo stirred in his sleep, listening to the voices of the horses in the barn and the ghosts of the ones who had gone before.

In the warmth of the barn, safely out of the cold and away from the night prowlers, the red pony spent his first night dreaming shapeless dreams of running ponies, flying geese, smoky meadows, and the old man.

Geronimo and the horses lived in their long-standing comfortable companionship until the fifth fall of the red pony's life. On that day, as usual, the horses made their nightly trek to the paddock, waiting for the old man to come and let them into the warmth and light of the barn. The night passed, the herd stomped and sniffed, waiting impatiently. The next day and night passed without a sign of him. The herd grew more restless and agitated with the passing of each sun and each moon.

At mid-morning of the third day, the herd still remained outside the paddock, knowing something was amiss. A white truck drove up the driveway to the house. It stopped and a man got out and went into the barn. A few minutes later, he reappeared, holding a handkerchief to his nose and shaking his head.

Three days later, standing where the old man had always stood, were three humans—a tall man, a thin, stooped man, and a woman with a head of hair as long and black as the bay mare's tail.

"I don't like them. I don't plan to keep any of them." The tall man spoke in a gruff, unkind voice, each sentence ending with a snort of disdain.

"Crazy old man. Damn him, leaving me with this old place. Glory of the Kiowa? There's no damn glory in being a Kiowa or any other Indian in this God-forsaken country." The tall man's voice rose with each statement.

"I'm finally selling this place. That crazy old man trying to make us believe that the old ways would be our salvation. Crazy old man, thinking those thoughts. I'm done. My father and sisters drank themselves to death. That's the real legacy of our past. Shit! Crazy old man."

Displaying his impatience and anger, he turned to the thin man and black-haired woman. He had been on a tirade about the old man for nearly an hour now. Neither the thin man nor the black-haired woman offered a word, standing silently with their eyes running over the herd.

"How the hell did you know the old man anyway? He never went any damn place. He never came to see us or his great-grandchildren. Wouldn't leave this piece of dirt. How the hell did you know him?"

The thin man, Dusty Plesent, began to answer his questions. He wanted to tell him of the kind old man who had offered him and his wife, Sarah, a room on a cold, stormy January night ten years ago when their truck had broken down on the dark country road. He wanted to tell of the trailer full of horses they were pulling and their fear of the horses freezing in the night. He wanted to speak of the venison stew, sliced apples, and hot coffee the old man had fed them. He wanted to tell this angry man of the breakfast of home-cured ham and fresh eggs with endless hot coffee. He wanted to speak of the old man's repairing the broken fan belt on the truck, refusing any payment except a promise from them to write him and tell him of their safe arrival home.

Dusty and Sarah had made many trips to visit the gentle-spirited old man named Geronimo Barse. The Plesents owned a small spread, Buffalo Springs Ranch, tucked in a far corner of eastern Wyoming, just twenty miles from Devils Tower. They sometimes brought a horse to Geronimo to add to his existing herd. The horses were the older ones, ones that would go to auction if not for the refuge provided by the old man. Many nights the couple sat with him, out in the barn with the horses, as Geronimo sang his Kiowa songs telling tales of the women, children and men of the prairie.

The young couple grew to love this gracious friend. They heard of his death from a trucker, a mutual friend. The trucker spoke of Geronimo's passing, falling in the aisle of the barn, hands clutched to the top of a spilled grain bag.

"It took three days before the mailman found him. He hadn't picked up his mail. There was a letter from you two in the bunch. I figured you would want to know."

The trucker, a thin man whose pants rode low on his hips and a greasy baseball cap always perched on his bald pate, shook his head and cleared his throat.

"Talked to his great-grandson. He intends to sell the ranch and put the horses to auction as soon as he can. I'm on my way to Great Falls and have to get on the road. Be a shame to send that herd to auction, way that old man loved them animals."

The trucker shot a glance at the couple standing in silent grief. The black-haired woman spoke in a soft, kind voice. "Wait a bit, Henry. Let me get you some food. We appreciate the news. Do you know how to reach the grandson? If nothing else, we want to pay our respects to the old man's family." She turned on the heel of her boot, walking with her head down to the cabin that they shared with two small dogs and four aging cats.

The trucker looked to the west across the hills where the clouds rose in brilliant white towers. A silence hung in the air between the two men. Finally, the trucker nodded and spoke.

"You know, Dusty, it really is a shame, not just about the old man, but about them horses. You know, he's got a really pretty young one out there that would make a really good cow pony. It looks just like that bay mare."

Sarah reached the side of the truck with a basket of food just as the trucker finished his statement. Catching hold and lifting the basket into the cab of the truck, he said:

"Ya know, it's only twelve hours drive from here. Could be there by midnight if you leave now. I'm outta here. See you in a week. Maybe I'll see some horses in that empty corral over by the pond."

The Plesents drove south that afternoon. Neither of them doubting if they would go, and knowing that the trucker had driven two *hundred* miles out of his way to bring them the news. Sarah drove, while her husband spat the cracked shells of sunflower seeds out the window. The big pickup was pulling an empty stock trailer; its metal creaking with age as the wheels encountered ruts in the highway.

"How are we going to do this? You know the cost of hay and grain. It's been a dry year. You'll have to go back to work. There were at least six horses in the herd when we were there three years ago. We must be out of our minds!" Dusty muttered.

"We'll find a way," said Sarah. "The old man sent us a message the way Henry found out. Dusty, we will find a way. I promise you. Just let's get there and see what's going on."

Her mind was already made up. Now as she listened to Geronimo's grandson's rant, she looked into the face of the red pony. It only confirmed what she had suspected: Geronimo had sent them a sign to come south.

"Look," she said to the tall man. "Let's me and Dusty get them all loaded. We will be gone and have them out of your hair and mind within ten minutes."

As the last of the seven horses were loaded into the yellow stock trailer, she turned to the tall man who now stood silently.

"Your grandfather was a good man. He wanted only the best for his family. You shame him with your anger and greed. He was a very good man."

The red pony stood next to his mother in the stock trailer as he felt the earth begin to move under him. He stomped fearfully until the black stallion nickered, sending a message of reassurance to the younger horse. The black stallion and the rest of the herd well remembered the thin man and the black-haired woman. So, they moved north as they had in previous days, not on the old Indian trails or through the weather but in a yellow trailer speeding up the highway.

Three years passed at the herd's new home. The Plesents' ranch proved to be as comfortable and safe for them as the old man's had been. The black stallion died, as did the roan gelding. They were buried on the hill above the ranch house, Dusty singing a Kiowa warrior song over their graves, one that had been taught to him by Geronimo.

The red pony grew taller but not as tall as his bay mother or black stallion father. He became Dusty's favorite mount, good at chasing cattle with his black tail in the air as if he was a purebred Arabian. Every night, Dusty stood by the gate of the corral as the small herd, now numbering five, came home to the warmth and safety of the barn. Every night, Dusty sang Kiowa songs to the herd. Every night, Sarah fed them hay and grain.

Night after night, the red pony dreamed of the old man, of loping across the dusty ground with hundreds of other horses galloping with him. Every night, he dreamed of full moons and the howls of the wolves, rising in octaves of sound. Every night, the old man came to him in his dreams and sang Kiowa warrior songs. The red pony dreamed his misty dreams every night until a year to the day after the Towers fell.

The red and gold of the shivering birch trees reflected the autumn coolness in the air. In the distance, Devils Tower could be seen from the high points of the ranch, more as a ghost than a solid monolith of volcanic rock. That night, Dusty brought two people with him to the barn. These strangers had come to spend a week as guests on the ranch. The woman was middle-aged with green eyes, high cheekbones, and a pale face. Next to her stood a younger man, shy in demeanor with gray touching his temples, belying his youth. He held a green bandana in his left hand and wiped his blue eyes every few seconds, a nervous tic he'd acquired in the past year.

"Jones, the bay mare is yours for the week you are here. Lola, the red pony is the best mount we have. He's a gentle pony. Be kind to him and he will take you anywhere you want to go. I'll say goodnight now."

Dusty started to walk away and then turned back as an afterthought crossed his mind.

"Breakfast is at eight o'clock sharp. We'll ride at nine o'clock and be back at noon for lunch at one. I'll leave the house light on but don't take too long. We're locking up soon. Sarah has your rooms ready. You'll find fresh towels in the bathroom. See you in the morning."

Lola and Jones—an odd name but the only one the young man gave—stood in an awkward silence, staring at the horses.

"Do you want to sit here alone?" Lola asked, uncomfortable as the young man wiped his eyes again.

"No, no, stay for awhile. It's fine." Jones moved to sit on a bale of hay, the lowest of a stack awaiting consumption by the herd. "Please, stay. I don't want to be alone tonight."

Lola looked at the man curiously. His face, half in darkness, held sadness and an ancient wisdom that made Lola catch her breath. Jones wiped his eyes yet again.

"Do you mind?" he said. "I really can't be alone now."

"Sure," Lola replied, her voice questioning. "But why don't you want to be alone?"

"I saw her fall that day." Jones's voice broke. "She held her hands to her skirt, holding it against her legs. I saw her fall. We'd only been married a month. I saw her fall. She was wearing the skirt I bought her for our one-month wedding anniversary. I saw her fall."

Lola looked at him in horror, her own eyes meeting the reddened tear-filled eyes of the young man. Her mind leapt to the picture of the woman from the South tower, falling forever, silhouetted against the silver and blue building as smoke billowed endlessly into the blue sky..

"I saw her fall. I was on the street below. You see, she'd forgotten her address book. It was a small thing but I wanted to hug her. I loved her. I just wanted her to have her address book."

Lola flashed back to that terrible day in Minot, the day she and Auntie Louella stood with their gaze fixed on the sight of the plane crashing into the silver and blue building. She began to shake, grabbing the top of a stall gate to keep her balance. She felt the fear and smelled the burning ashes as clear as the day she had leaned into the heated rock of Devils Tower and felt the cascade of rocks falling over her. Her breath caught in her throat as she stared, horrified, at the young man.

"I saw the second plane hit her building. Her office was above the floors where the plane hit. She called me, you see. She called and told me she couldn't get down the stairs; that there was nothing left. I could hear screams in the background. No one around me seemed to understand. I couldn't get to her. I couldn't get to her."

The young man wiped his eyes with his flannel shirt sleeve and shifted his weight on the bale of hay. Lola sucked in a long breath as quietly as possible, not wanting to interrupt the man's words.

"I told her to hold on. I could hear the screams. I just wanted to give her the address book. Her phone cut off and I couldn't get her to answer it. I waited for her and, finally, there she was, floating down to me. I saw her fall."

Lola reached out to touch the young man's face but he coughed and turned away, wiping his eyes again on his shirt sleeve. With a slow sigh he said, "I am going to bed now. I can't stand the night but I hate sunny days even more. I saw her fall, you know. I saw her fall."

He wiped his eyes again and rose to his feet. Turning to Lola he added, "You see, that's why I came here. I wanted to see Devils Tower. It won't fall. I came here because I heard you could see the Tower from the ranch. I don't leave New York much anymore. That's where she is. I saw her fall. I can't get it out of my mind. She's been gone a year and twelve hours. I don't sleep anymore. When I close my eyes, I see her fall."

Lola stared silently as the young man left the barn, thinking he must have been drunk as he staggered to the right. She did not recall the pungent smell of alcohol and realized he *was* drunk, but not from alcohol, from grief. She turned to look around the stall where she stood. Her hands were still braced against its door. The red pony stood quietly looking at her as if he had understood every word. She reached over and ran her hand down his soft nose, feeling his warm breath on her hand.

That night, the pony dreamed of falling towers and ash-filled skies.

⊰ ⊱

In the early hours of the next morning, Lola heard the barking coyotes in the distance and the unnerving call of the screech owl. A light rain welcomed the morning dawn, bringing with it a cool breeze. The smell of dampness wafted through the open window in Lola's small knotty pine-paneled room. She had slept on the bottom bunk in the corner of

the room. A small cabinet with a chipped sink stood to the right of the door. The windows were framed with filmy white curtains and a hand-braided rug covered the well-worn wooden plank floor.

She sat up, tugging the star quilt across her chest. She pulled her graying hair back from her face and then placed her hands palm up in her lap and studied them as if her future could be read from the unique configuration of creases and lines. She heard a cough in the hallway and then the click of a light switch as a beam of light passed under the crack of her door. As she listened she heard a door close and then the flush of a toilet. A few moments later, the sound of the bathroom door being opened echoed down the hall. Lola heard a soft sob and then another cough. She waited for the footsteps to retreat back down the hallway but only heard soft sobs coming from the bathroom.

She sat there on the narrow bed in the dark. The thought that had been troubling her led her to reach over to the bedside table for her purse. It lay propped against a lamp shaped like a running horse and oddly topped with a green plaid shade. She opened the purse and dumped the contents onto the quilt between her blanket-covered legs. In the midst of the hairbrush, pens, overstuffed wallet and, somewhat bizarre, a yellow dental night guard case, was a brown wallet, the edges curled and the leather spotted with water stains.

Lola opened the wallet and gazed down at the picture of the smiling couple, the young woman's brown hair cascading around her neck. Rubbing her hand searchingly over the face in the picture as she had done hundreds of times throughout the past eight months, Lola suddenly felt that at long last she had stumbled on an answer. She'd never been able to bring herself to let go of the brown wallet. She had never told anyone of its existence. Changing the subject as quickly as possible, she had deflected any inquiries Istie had made about the wallet since their trip to the sacred ground of the fallen towers.

Pushing aside the covers, Lola groaned, swung her legs over the side of the lower bunk and then slowly stood. She grabbed her faded gray robe and shrugged into it. Tying it with a frayed belt, she dropped the wallet into the pocket. She padded to the door and peered out into the lighted hallway where she could see Jones standing framed in the light spilling from the bathroom. He was dressed only in a pair of faded jeans, his feet and chest bare, his hair mussed. He was clutching the sink cabinet and his shoulders were heaving. He held a green bandana in his left hand and swabbed his eyes as he continued to sob.

"I heard you out here, Jones. I don't mean to intrude but I need to ask you a question and to show you something." Lola's voice was hesitant as she softly touched the brown wallet hidden in her robe.

"It's really important to me that I ask you this. Can we sit in the kitchen for a moment? It won't take much time but it really is important to me."

Jones looked up, startled at Lola's voice. He dropped the green bandana and then bent over to retrieve it. He looked into Lola's eyes as he nodded. Stepping sideways out of the bathroom and with the stooped walk of an old man, Jones made his way down the hall. They passed through the great room and down the stairs to the kitchen. A dim light over the stove threw a soft glow onto the wooden table where plates and silverware were laid out for breakfast.

Without a word, Lola and Jones tugged the bench out from under the edge of the table. They sat side by side, not saying a word for several moments. Slowly, Lola took the wallet out of its hiding place and slid it down the table in front of Jones. He looked at her in surprise and then tentatively flipped it open. A gasp escaped from his lips, his eyes filled with tears, and his hands dropped to his lap. Without looking at Lola, he spoke in a quivering voice as he stared at the picture.

"Where did you get this? How?..." His voice trailed off as he wiped his eyes with his bandana.

As he gently touched the face of the smiling woman, Jones's shoulders began to shake again. "Jones," Lola whispered, "I want to know. Is this your Annie? Please, I have to know. Last January, I was in New York and I found this in the snow at Ground Zero. It was empty except for this picture. Is this your Annie?"

Jones did not reply. With the most tender of touches, he closed the wallet and placed his hand over Lola's. He pushed back his side of the bench, slid his legs from under the table and, with a sigh, stood up. He left Lola sitting on the bench and quietly climbed the stairs. Then, stopping at the top, he gazed back at her for a few seconds. With the tiniest of nods, he disappeared from Lola's view. The only sound that echoed back to Lola was the gentle closing of his bedroom door.

Now, all alone in the quiet kitchen, Lola rubbed her hands together and thought of Istie and Auntie Louella. She thought of the elderly couple on the train and the picture of the woman floating forever against a beautifully clear blue sky. Lola opened the wallet Jones left behind. A smiling young woman looked back at her, caught forever in time and space. Sighing heavily, Lola stood up and turned to go back to her own room but left the wallet open on the table. She stepped inside her bedroom and quietly closed the door. An hour later, when Lola came down to the kitchen to join Jones, Sarah and Dusty for breakfast, the wallet was gone.

By the end of the week, Lola, Jones and Dusty had covered the hills of the ranch and the surrounding Bureau of Land Management land on the backs of their respective horses. Jones never spoke of that morning again. One late afternoon, as they sat on the bay mare and the red pony, atop the highest rise on the ranch, Lola saw Jones wipe his eyes again. In the distance, Devils Tower stood in the slanting sunlight of the day. Behind them, the sky was turning black with flashes of heat lightning sparking through the dry air.

Neither Lola nor Jones visited the Tower that week although it was less than twenty miles from the gate of the ranch. Lola did not know his reasons for staying away from the Tower. She just could not bear to think of what she had felt the day of Auntie Louella's and her visit the year before. She did not want to hear the screams and cries of pain or smell the ashes. She could not forget the words Jones said to her that night in the barn. When she closed her eyes, she saw over and over the woman falling through the sky, holding her skirt to her legs.

Lola spent most of her time stretched out in the grass in front of the ranch house reading and, at night, sitting in front of the red pony's stall, singing Cowlitz songs and telling him stories of the Taidnapam people, the horse people. When she was a child her grandmother always told her she was a stick Indian. She imagined a stick figure, feathers on its head, holding the halter of a stick figure horse. It was not until Lola was an adult and her grandmother had passed that Auntie told her the meaning of Taidnapam—those who lived in the woods.

Over the time of her stay on the ranch, Lola came to love the red pony. He was, as Dusty had said, a pony that could take her wherever she wanted to go. Her final morning at the ranch, she sat at the table, the remnants of a ranch breakfast still littering the wooden planks. Dusty and Sarah joined their two guests for this last meal. When Jones had finished his breakfast, he pushed his chair back from the table.

"I appreciate your kindness." He directed his remarks toward Dusty and Sarah, wiping his eyes. "I won't be back next year but I am glad I came."

He picked up the packed bag he'd left earlier by the door. Pushing open the screen, his slender frame filled the doorway. He turned back to look at the three sitting at the table.

"I saw her fall, you know." The stretched spring rattled against the screen door as it closed and the young man was gone.

No one spoke for several minutes. Breaking the silence, Sarah coughed and cleared her throat.

"Lola," she said, "Dusty and I have been talking this week. If you like the red pony, we want you to have him. We didn't pay anything for him but if you could pay us for some of his feed and keep, we would like you to take him home with you. You two belong together."

The next week, the red pony climbed into a trailer far more elegant and comfortable than the one that had taken him from Geronimo's ranch. As the trailer drove north and west, through the night, the pony dreamed of high mountains, an enormous body of water, the smell of salt, and white-topped eagles soaring into the sky.

Lola, who had returned to the coast earlier, awaited the arrival of her red pony. He finally came on a Wednesday and Lola rushed to the red barn that was to be his new home. He came off the trailer, calm and steady, more concerned with the grain Lola held in the pan than of his strange new surroundings or the fact that he had been in a fast-moving stall for thirty-six hours. That weekend, she and the pony had their first of countless rides, up into the foothills of the Cascades where the air was cool and clean and the Rufous-sided Towhees chirped.

Lola loved the red pony. Her only times of peace and comfort came in the barn next to his stall as he ate his dinner of hay and grain, or when they were galloping over the trails that ran across the mountains and in the sage of the high desert.

At night, the red pony dreamed of the thin man and the black-haired woman. He dreamed of the bay mare and the black stallion. He dreamed of hundreds of ponies, thousands of ponies trotting down dusty trails and over wild-running streams. He dreamed of figures dressed in blue, sitting tall on the backs of enormous black steeds.

Lola wrote often to Dusty and Sarah, asking about the ranch and thanking them endlessly in every letter for the blessing of her red pony. She promised to bring him back someday and looked forward to times to come. During their second year together, she took the red pony into the high desert for an endurance race. They found dozens of other trailers carrying horses parked by a nearly dry lake. As the red pony stepped out of the white slant load trailer, he tilted his ears forward and sniffed the air. A thrill ran through him as he quivered and snorted. Lola ran her hand over his neck, trying to calm him. His behavior was nothing she'd ever seen before. Lola ran a highline from her truck to the white trailer and tied the red pony to the line. She placed ample water and a large stack of hay well within his reach. Once she was satisfied, she strode off to stretch her legs.

The pony paced the length of the high line. He pawed the ground and neighed, the sound carrying over that of the other horses. He snorted and shook his head, showing little interest in the hay Lola had provided him. Lola returned and watched him as she pitched her tent and prepared camp. As darkness fell, she lit her lanterns and sat reading a book. The red pony, exhausted from his hours of pacing, finally stood at rest. Lola checked the highline, the water and feed and then crawled into her sleeping bag for a well-deserved sleep. Within minutes she was dreaming of Auntie Louella, Istie and Devils Tower shining in the sun. Outside, the red pony settled down on the ground. He dreamed of figures in blue on the back of black horses with rods of light in their hands.

The next morning dawned wet and gray; a fine mist filled the gaps between the trailers. Lola could hear the sounds of hoofs and nickering horses and voices calling in the distance. The first riders were already leaving the camp as Lola pulled on her cold jeans and made her way into the damp air. The red pony called to her softly, his hay gone and water bucket empty. He rubbed his soft nose on her shoulder and gently pulled her hair, a gesture he had learned would always get Lola's attention.

An hour later, Lola mounted the red pony and they trotted to where the ride would start. The rain began to fall, obscuring the view of the black cliffs to the west. Lola felt the pony's excitement as he neighed and crow hopped, his rapid breath blowing streams of vapor into the Spring morning. As Lola loosened her reins, he sprang forward and ran along the narrow trail. The rain pelted Lola's face and she winced against the sting. As the pony continued forward up the trail he shifted into a fast trot, snorting profusely. Relentlessly he went on, trotting to the west below the black cliffs and across the sage.

Lola felt the pony tense. As he ran, he turned his head from side to side, but never lost his gait. She sat at ease, yet alert, feeling his every movement. He could see hundreds of ponies running beside him, spread out across the sagebrush. Behind him was the camp, children running between the teepees made of deerskin and buffalo hide. He saw figures in blue, perched high on their black horses atop the side of the cliff.

The pony ran on, accompanied by hundreds of other ponies with men mounted on their backs, bows of wood and sinews held tight in their hands. On the ponies ran. The figures in blue perched on the black horses, rods of light in their hands, started their own descent down the cliffs. The red pony saw the black horses coming towards him. He saw the flashes of red and heard the sound of thunder rolling toward him. Lola felt the red pony break into a gallop. She could not pull him to a trot or to a stop as he raced across the wet ground. On he ran, the camp disappearing into the mist. He galloped in concert with hundreds of ponies with men on their backs. He ran with the figures in blue on the huge black horses. The noise of the battle rose around him. The smell of blood and gunpowder filled his nostrils. He could see the men and ponies falling to the ground. He felt the fear and smelled the burning gun powder He could hear the screams and the sounds of death and pain. Lola leaned forward on his back, holding tightly to his mane. Her fear of falling was the only thing that kept her on his back.

Suddenly, the mist and rain cleared and the sun broke through the gloomy clouds. The red pony slowed to a trot and then to a walk. Sweat coated his chest and neck. His breath was ragged. No more could he see the hundreds of ponies. The figures in blue on the black horses were gone. The smell of fear and gun powder was gone. He lowered his head, as Lola pulled on his reins. Ahead, dozens of trailers could be seen, the sun glinting off their steel and aluminum sides. The red pony walked the final mile back to the camp. Lola was trembling as she sat slumped on top of her exhausted horse.

When she dismounted in front of their trailer, her eye caught the sight of a piece of wood lying on the ground. She tied the red pony to the highline and squatted down to retrieve what she had seen. Before her lay broken pieces of a bow made of sinew and wood. As she stood, shaking her head in puzzlement, the red pony nuzzled her neck and gently pulled her hair.

⇥ 8 ⇤

The Spectacled Mice

Seattle, Washington   **February 7, 2004**

Lola pulled her turquoise parka tightly around her chest. Her graying hair was tucked up under a black knit fisherman's cap and a fluffy white scarf was wrapped around her neck. Her hands were encased in the fuzzy gloves that Istie had purchased on the frigid streets of New York two years before. The morning was cold and overcast with a biting wind blowing across the lake from the southeast. A thin crust of ice covered the dead remnants of lily pads and cattails. In the shallows, a disgruntled great blue heron stood appearing like a grumpy old man with his hands jammed into his pockets fighting to stay warm.

It was Lola's habit to walk the lake every morning from six to seven. Rain or shine, she made the three-mile trek. Through the seasons Lola tracked the inhabitants of the lake and the surrounding park. She loved the trill of the Red-winged Blackbirds, the majesty of the bald eagles, the squawks of the Steller's Jay, and the chickadee calls of the tiny birds of the same name. She watched the sunrise and the days grow longer with the approaching Spring and mourned the sun's disappearance in late fall. She dreaded the ceaseless dull of the northwest winters. It always felt like God had betrayed her with the constant drip of rain and the never-ending grey layers of murky clouds.

Her morning ritual began before she set foot out the red front door to start her brisk walk down the steep hill. Stepping out on the back porch, clad only in her nightshirt and sweater, she would hold four pieces of bread and three slices of cheese in her right hand and grasp the railing as she made her way down the slick stairs. She scurried across the flagstones of the patio, whistling as she moved towards the ivy-covered southeast corner of the back yard. A curved pink bench stood at the far side of the patio, ivy and moss creeping up its squatty legs. Lola shivered in the cold and bent down to place the bread and cheese on the bench.

As always, she backed away and waited to see what would happen. As it had happened every morning for the past eighty-seven years, a tiny brown mouse with pink feet and white facial markings ran out from the ivy, whiskers twitching and shiny black eyes focused on the scraps of food. As she had for all but a few years of her life, Lola held her hand over her mouth and giggled as the little rodent darted up the legs of the bench, grabbed the bread and a bit of cheese and dashed back into the ivy. The markings on the face of the mouse were white and circled the mouse's eyes, giving it the appearance of wearing spectacles. The odd facial coloring had marked hundreds of generations of mice living in the ivy that curled around the edges of the patio and lawn of the small city lot.

The green house where Lola lived perched near the top of one of the hills of the city on the Sound. Her grandmother, Lucinda LeFleur, built the house in 1911 after being widowed at the age of twenty-one. Lucinda was one of twins born to LeVie LeFleur and Chinook Granger. Her twin brother, Lamont, died only a day after entering the world. Chinook was a small, slender man with the high cheekbones of his Cowlitz mother and the green eyes of his French-Canadian/Metie father. He had blamed LeVie for the death of his son, refusing to divorce her—given his Catholic background—but also refusing to touch her again, declaring her a bride of the devil.

LeVie and Chinook had been married twenty-two years with no children gracing their lives. When LeVie became pregnant at the astonishing age of forty-one, Chinook was suspicious of his paternity, a doubt put to rest when Lucinda was born with his green eyes and the small, perfectly formed fingers of her Metie father. Chinook alternated between adoring his daughter and resenting her having survived when his only son had died. The nature of Chinook's interactions depended solely on his level of sobriety.

On the occasions he did work, Chinook was a laborer in the new hamlet of Toledo. LeVie and her daughter made a separate life. They had a small cabin tucked into the edge of the woods on the prairie opposite the Catholic Mission just four miles out of town. The cabin was built along the lines of the old Salish longhouses though of smaller dimensions. A sweat lodge stood behind the house, used daily by LeVie and Lucinda. Drying racks full of sockeye salmon and venison stood to the south of the cabin and held a year's worth of food provided by the abundance of fish and game in the forests and streams of the Cascade Mountains. The river ran along the west side of the property, cedars and firs standing branch to branch, forming a wall of protection and a measure of privacy to the small lodge. Deer trails ran through the woods and, down on the river, fishing nets hung on the branches, drying in the winds that blew across the small prairie to the north of the house.

Many of the LeFleur family had taken allotments on the Yakima reservation but LeVie had refused to leave the west side of the mountains. She fed her daughter with deer she hunted and salmon she caught. She was a tiny woman who desired only to be loved by her disdainful Metie husband. Abandoned by him, she became old before her time. Life on the prairie was filled with the abundance of summer and the cold rain of winter. At times, the harshness of life for a woman alone in the middle of the nineteenth century was almost more than she could bear.

LeVie vacillated between missing her husband and cursing him for abandoning her for the small town bars. She coddled her only child. She refused to allow the government or the Catholic Church to abduct Lucinda and send her to the Chemawa boarding school to the south in, Salem, Oregon, or north to Cushman Indian School in Tacoma. LeVie kept her only child close to her, singing traditional Cowlitz songs and speaking the language of the Taidnapam people. On his weekend trips from Toledo to the cabin, Chinook would sit on the shaky front porch and speak French to Lucinda. He would always remind her that he shared blood with the bold and courageous Ojibwa of Quebec and the glorious French-Canadian trappers and explorers who came west along the rivers, gathering furs as they went.

After a particularly bad bout of wintertime drinking and years of an absent marriage, Chinook finally left the cabin for the last time. He chose to move to the rugged Oregon coast with a blonde woman who had five children. LeVie had muttered the words "old fool" as her husband packed what meager belongings he had left in the cabin. The light from the cabin fire backlit her as she stood in the doorway. She threw an empty whiskey bottle at her departing husband's head, catching him squarely in the back of the neck. Chinook slowly turned to scowl at his wife and only child. Without a word, he walked down the road and never looked back. He strolled down the muddy path beneath a row of cedars, holding a large brown bottle to his lips. He tipped his head back as far as possible, as though he had no cares, no responsibilities, and no wife and child.

Lucinda was only nine years old when her father left the log cabin for the last time. Her mother was in a desperate financial situation so she chose to take her to San Francisco, away from the Cowlitz River, the misty mountains, and the brown prairies. But the city felt alien to LeVie. The only work she could find at the age of fifty was as a nanny to the two small children of a widowed fisherman who was gone much of the year. The fisherman was kind and demanded little of LeVie, only that she care for his children, clean his neat house on the flats of the city, and be frugal with the money he gave her on his return. The relationship between LeVie and her employer was one of politeness and appreciation for what the other offered, and sharing a bed together on the limited occasions he was home.

After awhile, attending school in San Francisco with the fisherman's children, Lucinda began to lose her Taidnapam language and her knowledge of the forest and prairie. LeVie withdrew into her own private world. She had only the memories of the grand cedar forests to the north and her now-deceased mother and father. She swore to return home every summer but summer never seemed to arrive and so Lucinda became an urbanite, no longer a child of the woods and prairie.

The house on the city flats did not survive the great earthquake of 1906. LeVie and the fisherman had to build another small house, this one in the Oakland hills. Shortly after its completion, LeVie died from measles. Lucinda accompanied her mother's body home to bury her in the family cemetery at the mission.

On that journey home, Lucinda had searched for her father but no one seemed to know what had happened to Chinook. She stood beside her mother's grave under gray skies, with only a few of her aunts, uncles and cousins left to stand with her in the faint shadows of the cedar trees. She returned to San Francisco within a day of the funeral unwilling to face the alcoholism and death that had come to the Taidnapam people. In her luggage, she carried a picture of her grandmother and grandfather. The woman was small in stature and dressed in a form-fitting dress, black hair pulled back in a bun. She was sitting beside an enormous man, Louie LeFleur. Katomski, her grandmother, had been full-blooded Taidnapam or Upper Cowlitz, as they were called by the government agents; her grandfather, a traditional chief. Now, two generations had passed, and the LeFleur family had only their memories of the horse people and their ways, of the salmon and elk, bear and coyote, of life on the prairie.

Lucinda left the mission cemetery with her mother's rosary, cedar skirt and a pair of beaded moccasins in her luggage. She knew in her heart that her tribal people were vanishing. The train wheels' screeching shredded her grief with each passing mile southward. Her bitterness over her mother's death and her father's desertion molded her young face with a coldness that startled people, closing off conversations and building a wall that even the most determined suitor could not breach. She vowed to marry rich and return to the north with as much money as she could. She was determined to regain the lost land of her people and to raise any children she might have as Taidnapam. No boarding schools for them but educated they would be.

Lucinda was sixteen, petite with the elegant nose and the green eyes of her Metie father. Jackson Greil was twenty-seven years Lucinda's elder. Lucinda met Jackson on the corner of Divisadero and California streets in Pacific Heights where she had taken a job as a teacher after her return to the city. Jackson, a wealthy silk merchant had spied the young woman on one of her trips to the piers to buy fresh crab and bread. He had hurried out of his pink mansion to introduce himself to the young teacher, taking her hand in both of his. Within hours, Lucinda was ensconced in the mansion and within months she was pregnant and married.

Lucinda was Jackson's third wife. He was twice widowed with no known children prior to his marriage to Lucinda. Their oldest child, Lily, was born in San Francisco in 1908, six months after her parents married. Their younger daughter, Louella, was born not quite four years later, seven months after her father died of alcoholism and tuberculosis, raising eyebrows and doubt in more than a few of Jackson's rich friends. Lucinda never felt the need to explain any aspect of her life to anyone and simply ignored any comments or suggestions questioning Louella's paternity.

After Jackson's shortly mourned death, Lucinda sold the pink mansion and her interest in his silk business. His business partners had pegged Lucinda an easy mark. They learned a rueful lesson when the young widow refused to sign for anything less than the full value of her late husband's estate, leaving her extremely wealthy and freeing her to return home to the Northwest.

Lucinda, in the company of Lily and Louella's nanny—a firm young woman by the name of Gretchen Haufstetter—returned to the north by train. Her family, once numbering parents, aunts, uncles and countless cousins, was now decimated by alcoholism, epidemics and sorrow. The house on the prairie was gone, seedlings growing where it had once stood. There were only rotting blankets to mark where the sacred lodge had been. The majority of the Taidnapam people were scattered, with only the hope of the reclamation of their land holding the survivors together.

Still, Lucinda was determined that her daughters would know of their Taidnapam roots and the little she remembered of her language. She told them of the legends of the horse people and, several times over the years, took them to the magical place of Ohanapecosh and to the falls that ran the Cowlitz River. Lucinda taught Gretchen how to do the intricate beadwork and weaving of her tribal people and evenings, as the girls grew older and entered school, the house on the hill became strewn with cut buckskin and silky threads waiting to be made into shawls.

Lucinda raised her daughters with a fierce independence, which struck her neighbors as decidedly odd. Her wealth set her apart from her neighbors and few dared approach her about her single life and obvious lack of male companionship. She had told Gretchen that men were too demanding and one husband had been more than enough. She did not regret the births of her daughters but winced when she thought of her infatuation and rapid marriage to a man whose main interests were fancy carriage horses and equally fancy women.

At the time Lucinda built the house, she planted a white lilac tree and a dogwood in the back yard. At the north side of the house, she added a maple and several birches. On the south side, she planted dozens of rose bushes; pink and white climbing roses that smelled of cinnamon, and red roses, a scent reminiscent of a deep, fine wine. At the back of the small lot, along a chicken wire fence, she planted wisteria and ivy. Odd pieces of art filled the back yard. Spinning cats, cats holding carrying trays, hummingbird feeders, and stone benches were everywhere. A favorite piece, a birdbath with two mermaids swimming in an endless circle, stood near the gate while three more birdbaths on pedestals lined the north fence.

The yard was a peaceful oasis smack in the middle of the noisy, growing city. Daily, Lucinda and Gretchen walked the path around the lake at the foot of the hill. White-headed eagles, hawks and ospreys still lived in the majestic cedars and hemlocks but, over time, most of the remaining pieces of nature disappeared. Lucinda mourned the loss of the trees, thinking of her mother and father and her long-lost grandparents. The only remnants she possessed of those graceful people were a cedar bark skirt and a photograph of her mother and aunt taken when they were fourteen years old in the middle of the nineteenth century. Lucinda guarded these treasures with the same ferocity that she protected and loved her children.

It was five-year-old Louella who had first discovered the spectacled mice. Spring had returned to the city. White blooms graced the lilac tree in the back yard. The daffodils and tulips, so lovingly planted by Gretchen the fall before, danced in all their glorious colors in the breeze.

Louella, as different from her older sister as was possible, loved being outside, regardless of the weather. She had rolled her yellow ball into the ivy that was threaded among the chicken wire fence at the back of the property. Her small child's hands had pulled at the tangled leaves and stems revealing, not the yellow ball, but a small nest of mice, babies so tiny they were barely longer than her own small pinky. The mother mouse stood on her hind legs, chattering her teeth at her in warning. Louella had screamed for her mother and Gretchen, pointing in joy at the mice and begging for cheese and bread to feed them. Lily had given her sister a disgusted look and a sneer, disdainful of anyone who would find the lives of mice worthwhile. Nonetheless, from the day they were discovered, Lucinda and Gretchen protected and fed the family of mice. The black cats of the household were banned from the yard, so they could only peer with their eager eyes out the kitchen window, tails twitching as the tiny brown and white mice ate their meals.

The small family passed the years in the green house, insulated from much of the chaos of the world but not completely immune to the events of the day. Lucinda lost several male relatives to the ravages of influenza and to the horrors of the First World War. She had managed to save much of Jackson's fortune, investing in land, hotels, and the coal fields that honeycombed the countryside south of the city. Gretchen had grown stouter with the passing of time but Lucinda, apparently owing to the genetics of her Cowlitz blood, retained her dark hair and elegant bearing.

Trouble came to the green house when Lily turned fifteen. On a hot summer night, she climbed down the roof, across the porch, and out into the dark. As she dressed herself in a fuchsia suit, rolled her hair, and lined her eyes in black, she had warned Louella of dire consequences if she told. Louella had sat in her bed tucked into the alcove and studied the long fingers of her own hands, saying nothing in words but with her eyes beseeching her sister to please make a different choice.

The room the two girls shared was small, a door opening out onto a deck and an equally small bathroom crowding half of the space. The walls were painted in an Easter purple, the beds covered in matching star

quilts lovingly crafted by Lucinda and Gretchen. The last sight Louella had of her black-haired sister was the hand that held a pair of fuchsia pumps, tiny anklet straps covered with rhinestones blinking a farewell as Lily disappeared through the window and into the foggy night

⤙ ⤚

Lola, deep in thought of the LeFleur women, shivered in the cold. Her sweater was fuchsia, the same color as her mother's suit the night she left the green house on the hill. She rarely thought of her mother who had returned home at the age of thirty-seven just long enough to give birth to her older sister, Lila, disappear, and then return a year later, eight months pregnant with Lola. Lucinda and Gretchen had pleaded with Lily to remain in the city on the Sound but, within days of giving birth to each of her daughters, she disappeared again.

Postcards her mother had sent over the years were hidden in the cedar chest at the foot of Lola's bed. They were spaced out over the course of months and years, each one detailing a new city, a new man, a new husband, and a bright new life. At the bottom of the chest was a long envelope, postmarked Havana, Cuba.

The letter had arrived on New Year's Eve 1951, the mailman's footprints clearly etched in the snow covering the yard. Alongside the boot prints were miniature imprints of birds' feet from the robins that had chosen to winter in the LeFleur yard. Louella, still single at the age of thirty-nine, and still living in the green house, stood with Lola in her arms as Gretchen picked up the letter dropped through the mail slot. Lila, a delicate child with midnight black hair and turquoise eyes, had leaned against her grandmother's skirt with a tiny black cat in her arms.

Lola had heard the story from Auntie so many times over the years that she was never sure where her memory left off and the tales began. She envisioned her grandmother taking the letter from Gretchen's hand. She carefully slit the top of the envelope with the letter opener whose handle was in the shape of a sitting cat. She believed she could remember Lucinda's anguished cry.

The letter detailed Lily's death. She had died in bed with a married man, shot by her jealous husband, a not-so-distant Cowlitz relative by the name of Matthew Bouchard. Matthew had written the letter from jail, relating the tragic story of Lily's trip across the country with him. He ended by asking Lucinda to bring his daughters to see him. Lucinda and Gretchen had hugged each other that long night, reading the letter over and over, hoping each time that it would say something different.

The next morning, as dawn brought in 1952 , Lucinda prepared for yet another train ride, a journey of grief, to bring another LeFleur woman back to the cemetery at the mission. As they had done forty years before, Gretchen and Lucinda took the train together. As the train left the station, Louella stood with her two young nieces, knowing in her heart that she would be burying not just one but three women in the days to come. Within a month, her prophecy came true. Lucinda and Gretchen both died in their sleep, refusing to be parted in death after so many years as companions in life.

Louella, as her grandmother and great-grandmother before her, chose to live her life with only her two nieces. She had earned a degree from the University of Washington, only four miles east of their house on the hill. She worked for the Port Authority and lived off her own salary. The money Lucinda had inherited from Jackson was invested in a variety of businesses, including automobile companies and huge parcels of land downtown. Louella, a curious woman with a quick intellect and even quicker wit, had retained only a few customs of the Taidnapam and Cowlitz people but she, too, took her nieces down to the mission, the river, and the remaining prairie. She taught her nieces the coyote legends and about the generations that had come before.

Lila, much to Louella's dismay, discovered early the joys of alcohol and young men. She left the perpetually green house on the hill for San Francisco in the summer of love. She had the grace to finish high school, but life on the street seemed more engaging than the mundane and quaint notion of education. Louella, in silent horror, watched her niece grow into the same woman Lily had been, making equally poor choices in men and returning to the green house at the age of twenty-nine with a long-limbed, black-eyed daughter and no man in sight.

Lola, a younger version of Louella, had begun to see gray hair amongst the black at the age of sixteen. She was determined to break the curse of the LeFleur women and never marry. However, she also left the green house on the hill and moved to Sacramento to attend college. Louella, now in her late fifties, had taken Lola to the airport, kissed her goodbye, and handed her a cage that contained a small black cat. She stood beside the gold Ford Mustang she had purchased for her fifty-seventh birthday and prayed a Taidnapam prayer that her baby would come safely home.

Louella drove home via the now-old highway on the west side of the city, across the concrete viaduct, and past the zoo. The forests that had once surrounded the lake and the green house on the hill were long gone; the neighborhood was now filled with Craftsman bungalows and small stores. The community where Lucinda had come to live so many years before was changed and reshaped and not in ways she would have liked. The green house now held only one woman, but the population of tiny black cats never diminished, with new black kittens appearing as others passed over to cat heaven. Mornings, Louella made her way down the stairs and across the yard, leaving bread and cheese for yet one more generation of spectacled mice.

⇥ ⇤

In 1967, Lola met and married James, a handsome man of thirty. The couple lived in Sacramento. Lola attended college and James worked in construction on the rare occasions that the mood struck him. Louella had no use for him. She was angry that the one LeFleur woman (besides herself) that she thought had any sense would fall for a pretty face and a good pickup line.

Louella would receive the weekly phone calls Lola made from California, nodding into the phone and staring out at the now-giant trees and rose bushes her mother had planted in the second decade of the twentieth century.

Lola returned with James to live in the green house in 1970, finishing her undergraduate degree while James roamed the bars of Pioneer Square. With her aunt the only member of her family in the audience, Lola received her master's degree in fine arts. Her thesis was on the history of Taidnapam art and beadwork, two of her abiding passions.

James did not make it to the ceremony nor did he make it home that night, disappearing into oblivion for the next seven years. It came as a relief when his body was finally found in Lake Washington. His death was the result of drunken driving and poor aim, missing the off-ramp and plunging into the cold and murky water of Lake Washington, east of the burgeoning city on the Sound.

As several generations of LeFleur women before her, Lola now made her residence with Auntie Louella in the green house on the hill—one more LeFleur widow. The two women greatly resembled each other: graying hair, sharp eyes, high cheekbones, and a sarcastic wit born of grief and loss. Lola took a job as a commercial artist for an architectural firm downtown and Louella moved into retirement. Four years of quietness graced the green house with only the occasional mention of the mysterious disappearance of James. Louella believed he had returned to Kansas to his Osage relatives but Lola, feeding the spectacled mice every morning, knew in her heart that her handsome, beloved husband was dead.

Lila returned to the green house in December 1977, bringing with her a little girl with the strange name of Wisteria and the odder nickname of Istie. She informed her Auntie Louella that as she went into labor, the only thing she could think of was the wisteria that climbed the back fence and mingled with the ivy. She described how she had imagined the faces of the spectacled mice mothers, distorted in pain as they pushed their brood of pups into the world. It seemed to Lola that Lila had lost none of her flamboyance but had lost the last of her common sense.

Lila, as her own mother had done, often left the green house for extended periods of time, dressed in a fuchsia coat and pants, but at least having the grace to walk down the front steps rather than escaping over the roof and down the porch. On the frequent occasions that Lila was gone, Auntie Louella and Lola would take Istie to feed the ducks and Canadian geese that waddled across the asphalt path encircling the lake. On rare occasions, the white-headed eagles were glimpsed but, in general, crows and sea gulls ruled the skies, their harsh cries muffled by the heavy gray clouds that hung over the ever-growing city.

It was in late 1978 that Lila dressed her daughter in a lilac and white pinafore and dropped her off at Lola's office. She waited until Auntie had gone shopping and then dressed herself in the yellowed wedding gown of her grandmother, Lucinda. She counted out a large number of Seconal, tore open a bag of pretzels, and drank a full bottle of Moët & Chandon. Auntie had discovered her body several hours later. When she called Lola at work, the plans for a funeral at the mission cemetery were already in place.

Three-year-old Istie stood beside the open grave and threw clumps of dirt down onto her mother's coffin, her tiny white glove stained with the brown earth. A cold wind had blown that day, despite the hot sun of July, and Auntie had sung an honoring song, her voice cracking with the loss of one more LeFleur. Istie, Lola and Auntie Louella had driven home in the lime green Camaro Auntie had purchased in anticipation of her upcoming sixty-fifth birthday. Little was said as the three generations of LeFleur women drove north to Seattle from the tiny cemetery on Cowlitz Prairie. The unspoken understanding was that Istie would, of course, remain in the green house and there would be no effort made to find the black-eyed man who had fathered her somewhere between San Francisco and Seattle.

Auntie Louella and Lola loved Istie. They passed on to her the few traditions left of the Taidnapam people, the blood now diluted by several generations of intermarriage or "interracial breeding" as Auntie so bluntly put it. Istie brought newness and joy back to the green house, a lightness of spirit that was lacking from the practical but loving natures of Louella and Lola.

Over the years, the inside of the house had been remodeled, updated, enlarged and freshened but the outside was always repainted green with red and white trim. In the back yard, Lola and Istie added more birdbaths and cut back the wisteria. They pruned the rose bushes as Auntie sat on the back steps, directing their every move. Every morning, Istie would stand by the kitchen window with three tiny black cats peering out to watch the spectacled mice snatch their daily treats of bread and cheese.

The routine remained as constant as the rain until 1979 when Lola married again, bringing Andrew home to the green house on the hill.

The arrangement in the house had been odd as Andrew was only the second man to live in the house since it had been built in 1911. Istie adored her uncle but Auntie had little use for a forty-two-year-old man who never appeared able to keep a job and who always reeked of marijuana smoke. Lola sat on the sidelines as Andrew and Auntie fought their silent battles over the rosewood table every night at dinner. Andrew held Istie on his lap, running his hands over her wavy auburn hair, a covert rebuke to the barrenness of Auntie and Lola. He would make Istie laugh and, at night, tuck her into bed, his actions the only proof of his value that Louella could see in him.

Lola constantly went from being glad Istie had a father figure in her life to being irritated that she had chosen a man who was irresponsible and disengaged. When Andrew died suddenly in a car accident in 1982, Istie was heartbroken, one more loss to absorb in her young life. Lola and Istie mourned Andrew's passing for years. Auntie, however, only sniffed, showing disdain for this ill-placed sadness for a man who had been willing to be supported by his wife, and reinforcing her less-than-stellar opinion of the male gender.

In a fit of melancholy one Spring evening, while sitting on the dun-colored front steps, Lola recounted the whole history of the LeFleur women to Istie and Auntie. None of them were able to maintain a marriage, several were born out of wedlock, and there wasn't a son in the lot. The only true LeFleur families around, Lola declared, were the endless generations of spectacled mice that continued to live in the southwest corner of the yard, hidden among the ivy.

Istie and Auntie Louella had laughed at Lola. The three wore identical denim overalls, fuchsia shirts and strappy sandals. The elegant Japanese maple that filled the front yard was slowly unfurling its red leaves tinged with silver. The white blooms of the lilac tree sent an intoxicating aroma over the yard and the multicolored tulips danced again in the warming air of early May.

Twenty-one years later, on a frigid February day in 2004, Lola was on the deck overlooking the lake below. The wind blew in from the south, its biting edge tossing the gray clouds around, allowing faint glimpses of the mountains to the east. She sat with a cup of hot mint tea and once again recounted the history of the LeFleur women. She and Istie had mourned Auntie Louella's death in September 2001. Her ashes resided in a black box on the hearth along with at least two dozen other boxes containing the ashes of small black cats. Istie was home for a visit from San Luis Obispo where she had been attending college for an indeterminate number of years, forever changing majors and boyfriends.

Lola continued working at the firm downtown but found the work dull, repetitive, and lacking in inspiration. Her respite from her life of ruts was her time at the lodge with Krissie and Rona and her rides on the red pony with Forrest, her riding partner of many years. She deeply missed both Auntie and Istie, feeling at times that she would just disappear into the earth, one last LeFleur woman being buried in the small cemetery by the mission.

It was on that cold February day in 2004 that Istie saw her aunt tucked in the blue parka, the white scarf wrapped around her neck, a pair of sandals pulled over striped wool socks. Istie had finally completed her degree at Cal Poly in the fall of 2003. She had taken a part-time job at a local theatre in Santa Barbara where she designed costumes and elaborate sets for simple plays. She had become very secretive about her personal life, ignoring Lola's not-so-subtle questions about who the flavor of the month boyfriend might be. She came back to Seattle on a monthly basis, primarily to assure Lola she was fine and to attend whatever musical was playing at the 5th Avenue Theatre.

"Auntie Lola," Istie's voice startled Lola out of her reverie. "I need to talk to you. It's really important. Can we go inside? It's freezing out here. I swear, old lady, you have lost your mind."

"Istie, come look, over the edge of the deck. Look, down on the bench! Hurry up while they are still there."

Istie peered over the edge of the deck into the back yard. Three brown mice, spectacles of white around their eyes, stuffed their cheeks with bread and cheese. They paused in their task and looked up, eyes like shiny black pools meeting Istie's equally black ones.

Istie laughed in delight, clapping her hands. "I can't believe it. They're still here. Oh, my lord, Auntie, how many hundreds of them have lived back there? Come here, pussycat! Look, down there! "

Istie picked up the small plush black cat that had followed her out onto the deck. "Don't those little guys look tasty?" She rubbed her face on the thick coat of the little cat and nudged Lola's leg with her booted foot.

"Auntie Lola, go take a shower and get dressed in some decent clothes. I want to go shopping downtown and pick up some salmon at the Pike Place Market. Come on!"

Lola gave in to Istie's demands, no different now than it had been twenty-eight years earlier when the long-legged child with the huge eyes had first climbed into her lap and buried her face in Lola's neck. She followed Istie inside, closing the door that led from the bedroom to the deck. She pulled her clothes over her head, once more marveling at the fine-lined and slowly sagging flesh of her thighs, firm to the touch only days before, or so she imagined. She stood in the flow of the hot water, trying to discern the words that Istie threw at her through the glass door.

"… London….six months…. Internship….he's… playwright…. fifty-four." was all Lola could understand through the pounding of the water.

"Will you wait a minute? Let me dry my hair." Lola grabbed a towel, wrapping it around her thickening body. "What are you talking about? I couldn't hear a thing."

"Auntie Lola," Istie sat on the bed still covered in the star quilts Lucinda and Gretchen had crafted more than a half-century before. "I need my trust fund signed over to me. I'm nearly thirty and I want to take over the responsibility for my own life. Don't start on how you and Auntie Louella scrimped and saved for me to go to college. I am fully aware of how much money the LeFleurs have and the size of my inheritance. I know exactly how much you spent on my education and the cost of gasoline and airplane tickets. I know what this house is worth and I know how much you got when you sold the restaurants and coal mines so spare me the "below the poverty line" speech. Now, dress in something nice and let's go!"

Lola shook her head for it was clear Istie had both the demanding nature of Auntie and the impatience and flightiness of her mother, Lila. Lola sighed in resignation and pulled a fuchsia sweater over her head. She stepped into black slacks and slipped her feet into black boots identical to Istie's. She started to grab for the blue parka, stopped by Istie's hand holding a blue pea coat and a pair of expensive leather gloves.

"I'm driving," Istie declared, opening the door to Lola's Tahoe. "Get in and don't say a word. I want to talk to you!"

"Talk *to* me or *at* me?" Lola asked. "Istie, the last time I saw someone as nervous as you was the day your dear-departed mother dropped you off at my office and took a bottle of pills. You aren't thinking of doing something like that, are you?"

Lola looked at her niece in sudden fear. But Istie seemed to have a glow to her and an excitement that Lola could not quite fathom.

"Hold tight, old lady. Of course I wouldn't kill myself. What, do you think I am melodramatic or something? It's been twenty-eight years since Mom died. Don't you think I am over it by now? And speaking of which, Auntie Lola, don't you think it's time you told me who my father was?"

"Istie, we've been over this a dozen times. Auntie Louella told you the same thing. We have no idea who he was. I hate to say this, but in all honesty, I don't think your mother knew either. So, where are we going? And stop driving like a maniac. You're scaring me."

Istie laughed again and pulled the Tahoe in front of a small bistro tucked under the edge of the Market.

"Come on, Auntie Lola. We're going to be late. Hurry up!"

Istie led the way into the bistro, heading for a table where a man sat. He was dressed in neat gray slacks and a matching gray turtleneck sweater. His long black hair was pulled into a braid that lay halfway down his back. His hair was touched with gray at the temples and, with a start, Lola realized he was her age or older. Her heart began to sink as Istie slid into the chair next to him and kissed him on the cheek.

Lola sank into the bench across the table from Istie. Istie's hands were entwined with the man's. In a sudden flash of understanding, Lola stared down at Istie's hand, a platinum band with inlaid diamonds gracing the ring finger of her left hand.

"Auntie Lola," Istie said, "this is Sean Bull. He's Nez Perce and he's a playwright. We got married six months ago and we are moving to London tomorrow. I've wanted to tell you but I knew how furious you would be and I'd have to hear the legacy of the LeFleur women and the mistakes of marrying a Native man and the nasty comments about a cradle robber, but I wanted to tell you before we left the country."

"Oh, Istie! Tell me you didn't. No wonder you wanted your trust fund. Are you going to make the same mistake I did, support some old man, ruining your life?

"And you," Lola nearly yelled, pointing at the tall, handsome man who watched in amusement, "don't you have something better to do than have a mid-life crisis and act it out with my niece? I don't really care if you are Mohawk or Nez Perce or Quinault for that matter. The last thing we need in this family is another unemployed mooch. Oh, God, Istie, why didn't you talk to me first? And how in Creator's name did you meet?"

The man sitting next to Istie smiled, showing gleaming white teeth. He coughed and turned his head, glancing out the window to the water where a ferry made its way to one of the islands in the Puget Sound. He shifted back in his seat to meet Lola's eyes. Staring directly into them, the man flashed a wide grin:

"Lola, let me introduce myself. My name is Sean Bull. I'm from Lapwai, Idaho, and I met Istie in New York two years ago when you took her to see *The Lion King*. I was sitting behind you two. We started talking when you went to the lobby at intermission. I'm based in New York but travel to California for business. I have a show opening in London. That's why we are moving. Well, Istie, you told me how she'd react. I can't say I am disappointed!"

Lola could feel her irritation growing. She seemed to be mocked by this man who had stolen her niece. Angry words sat on her lips but the look of love on Istie's face stopped her. She sighed and took Istie's hand, the one wearing the platinum ring.

"Istie," Lola asked, "do you love him?"

"I do," Istie replied. "I do."

Lola watched the next morning as the British Airways 747 pushed back and began to taxi down the runway. She, Istie and Sean had driven down to the Cowlitz River the afternoon before. The trio had stood on the banks of the river, watching the green water flow past the old cedar log. Istie had lit a fire and, in the glow of the light, had told Lola of their plans. Lola, helpless in the face of Istie's love for Sean, had given her blessing. She had watched the shadows dance across Istie's face and knew, in her heart, that Istie was no longer hers.

Lola returned that morning to the green house on the hill. An empty Starbucks coffee cup was sitting on the rosewood dining table. The room seemed old and shabby. The white carpet was dingy and the chairs worn. Lola picked up the smallest of the three black cats and, as Istie had done the day before, buried her face in its plush fur. She gently placed the cat on the floor and picked up a dull black box from the table.

"I am truly alone now. Auntie Louella, our girl is gone." Lola patted the top of the black box that held Auntie's ashes. "I know you can hear what I'm saying, old lady. I know you approve of Istie's life but I always thought she would come home."

Time passed in the green house on the hill. As the trees bloomed and the aromas of Spring once again filled the air, Lola re-painted the inside of the house, re-covered the upholstery, and tore up the carpet to polish the hardwood floors underneath. She rode the trails in the tree-covered hills on the back of the red pony and sat in lodge with Rona and Krissie. She listened to Krissie's ongoing laments of the cold bastard and to the details of the honeymoon Rona and Xavier had in China. Rona spoke in hushed tones of the rows of terra cotta warriors and rolling panoramas of the ancient country.

Rummaging through the cedar chest at the foot of her bed on a summer morning, Lola had found the old pictures and the letter mailed form Havana fifty years earlier, announcing Lily's death. She touched the white buckskin dresses so lovingly made by her grandmother and the shawls stitched by Gretchen. She sank down on her knees and prayed for Istie's happiness, praying with all her heart that Istie's life would be different, that Sean would care for her and that Istie would, someday, come home to the green house on the hill.

On September 11, 2004, three years after the attacks on the World Trade Center, Lola once again sat on the upstairs deck of the green house. As was her custom, she had fed the spectacled mice and read the morning paper, now full of the horror of Iraq and hundreds, if not thousands, of deaths. She thought of the Taidnapam people, now mainly memories, the few words she knew of the lost language running through her mind. As she shuffled through the pages of print, a small article flanked by a picture of a petite blonde woman caught her eye.

"9/11 Pentagon Attack survivor found dead" the headline read. Lola, in stunned disbelief, read the article, another missing piece of 9/11 falling into place.

> *"Jeannine Muir, age 47, was found dead in her Whidbey Island home on Tuesday, September 7th. Ms. Muir, a former civilian contractor for the Navy, survived the attack on the Pentagon two and a half years ago. Ms. Muir was severely wounded in the attack, losing her left leg at the hip. She was one of the last survivors to leave the hospital and returned to her home on the island 18 months after the attacks. Ms. Muir was an avid lover of nature, her older brother, Solis Muir said. In fact, at the time Ms. Muir was found on the patio of her home, a crow was sitting on the back of Ms. Muir's wheelchair and a small green garter snake was sleeping in her lap. Ms. Muir is survived by her mother, Hannah Carnes, four brothers, Thomas, Eric, Peter and Solis Muir, and five nieces and nephews. Ms. Muir apparently died from natural causes unrelated to the injuries she suffered in the Pentagon attack. Funeral services will be held at Our Lady of the Island Lutheran Church in Clinton on Sunday, September 12th. Donations can be sent to the 9/11 Children's Fund."*

Lola folded the paper, tucked it under her arm and sat staring into the ivy at the back of the yard. Memories of that last train trip with Auntie Louella came slowly into focus. She remembered the classic blonde woman in the pinstriped suit and her fear of flying. She saw Auntie nudging the toes of Jeannine Muir and thought of the car on the track. She, once again, saw planes crashing into the silver and blue buildings and the picture of Annie Jones. She thought of Sarah and Dusty and of Devils Tower standing in all its majesty. She thought about the cedar forests and how they had fallen and the land that was taken from the Taidnapam people. She thought of her long-dead sister and the mother and father she had never known.

Lola stared down at her hands, acknowledging again the signs of age. She reached down to stroke the small black cat that meowed for food and, with a sigh, closed her eyes.

"Too much, too much," Lola muttered to herself. "It's too much."

That afternoon, Lola sat at the rosewood table and sent an email to Istie and Sean, including the link for the article about Jeannine Muir and a brief explanation of how she and Auntie had met the woman on the train to Minot. Lola found herself exhausted that day, her heart beating with an irregular rhythm and her fingers tingling. She lay on the couch and watched the shadows lengthening across the living room. At midnight, she made her way up the stairs, carrying the box of Auntie's ashes with her. Her old lady cat lay on the blanket at the foot of the bed, her baby cat—the tiny black one—dashing up the stairs behind Lola and jumping onto the pillow.

Lola placed the black box by the side of the bed, slid between the sheets and held them open for the little black cat to crawl underneath. Lola felt the smoothness of the cat's fur and rolled over onto her side. She shifted her weight and then bunched up her pillow. The diffuse lights of a car on the street moved across the ceiling of the room. She sighed and closed her eyes, the images of a burning tower imposed on her eyelids.

Fall moved into Winter and then into Spring. Lola was becoming more and more depressed. She was unable to function well and finally took a leave of absence from work. She sat on the deck after her morning walk and feeding the mice. She missed Auntie Louella and Istie with every fiber of her being. Every day there were long emails from London, telling of the flat she and Sean shared at King's Crossing, the latest exhibit at the Tate Museum, the wonders of the London underground, and the excitement of Sean's latest play opening to rave reviews. Pictures of the couple at the castle in Edinburgh and at historic Gretna Green in Scotland, as well as in England's Lake District, arrived via Lola's laptop. Istie seemed happy in a way that was foreign to Lola, and she regretted her angry words that day at the bistro in the Market.

Istie begged Lola to come to London for a visit in the summer but Lola would not commit. She spent more time at the barn and down by the Cowlitz River, and sat in lodge, alone, and contemplated her rapidly approaching old age. Her depression persisted and, a year after Istie left for London, Lola finally resigned her position at the firm, thirty years of work signed away with the stroke of a pen. She planned a trip to Devils Tower for September, and wrote Dusty and Sarah she was going to bring the red pony home and stay a month at the ranch.

Dusty and Sarah wrote back immediately expressing their welcome. Still, Lola could not shake the feelings of foreboding that caused her heart to race and her chest to tighten. In the long nights, she could hear the voices of Lucinda, Lila, and Auntie Louella calling to her.

On the night of July 6, 2005, Lola climbed into bed, a large manuscript accompanying her. The manuscript was enclosed in a black three-ring binder, a note on a post-it stuck on the back of the binder with "I love you" in Istie's handwriting. Lola sat propped against the headboard, her knees bent under the quilt. She opened the binder and ran her fingers over the crisp paper and bold black printing:

Baghdad, South Dakota

A Play By Sean Bull

Narrator: *Look across the valley and listen to the wind. Watch the grass wave and feel the heat of the sun. Look, there in the distance. You can see them falling, you can hear them crying. Look, look closely and listen even more closely for this is the place of broken hearts and lost lives.*

The snow was deep that day and the people were starving. Hope was no longer present among the people, lost to the invaders who stole and killed and took what had belonged on and to the land for thousands of years.

Listen, for you can hear the ghosts.

Look, for on the grass you can see the blood rising from the ground and staining the grass.

Look to the East. See the swirling clouds of dust, clearing just enough for you to see the tanks and soldiers and guns. See the flashes of light and the people falling to the ground.

Listen, for you can hear the ghosts.

Look, for you can see the blood rising from the earth and staining the sand.

Come and join me and learn the story of Baghdad, South Dakota"

Lola could read no further than the opening paragraphs, a sickness filling her heart and a knot cramping her bowels. She thought of Istie so far away and of Sean, a man of many words, filled with the love of Lola's niece. It had been difficult for Lola to share Istie with Sean, a man she did not know but, as time progressed, the happiness Istie spoke of softened the loss and made the pain in Lola's heart a tiny bit more bearable.

Istie had sent the manuscript of Sean's new play to Lola along with a round-trip ticket to London. She begged Lola to read the play and to come to England for the opening night. Lola had deferred giving a response. She could not sort out her emotions and was confused as to why she did not want to go when she longed to see Istie's face and to stroke her soft brown hair. Lola sighed and ran her thumb over the plastic cover of the black binder. She laid the binder on the floor, dropping her glasses on it. She turned off the light. Lola drifted off to sleep, but was a spectator to disturbing images of frozen bodies on the prairie and wrecked and burned Humvees on the dusty streets of Baghdad.

The call came from Istie in the early hours of July 7th, 2005. Lola picked up the phone to hear Istie's screams.

"He's dead, Auntie Lola. He's dead. Turn on the television. Sean's dead!"

"Istie, calm down. What are you talking about? Let me wake up. Istie, calm down." Lola grabbed her glasses and swung her feet out of bed. She groped her way down the stairs and hit the ON button of the remote, turning to CNN. She held the cordless phone in her hand as horrific images of people running and covered in blood filled the screen.

"Oh God, Istie, not Sean. Tell me you're okay." Lola could feel the bile rising in her throat as she watched the television in horror. "Not again, please not again. Istie, where's Sean?"

"Auntie, they just took him away. He was just coming up from the subway. Auntie, I can't believe it. People are running everywhere. He was covered with blood. Auntie, what am I going to do? They took my love. Oh, Auntie, he's gone. They killed him."

Istie's voice disappeared into gasping sobs as Lola watched the carnage on the television. She saw a young woman being escorted down the street by a London policeman, a cloth covered in blood held to her face. Lola felt a fist push up under her ribs. She had a flash of the World Trade Center towers in flame superimposed over the sight of the London streets covered in debris.

"Istie, what happened? Were you hurt?" Lola struggled to stay calm as the realization of yet another terrorist attack sank in.

"Istie, are you alone? Who's there with you? Istie, you need to tell me where you are! Istie, what happened?"

"Auntie Lola, I am at the Hilton. We were going to have breakfast. I heard the explosion. A bomb went off. Auntie, it is terrible. They brought the wounded here and some of the dead. The police won't tell us anything more. They don't know how many are dead or hurt. Auntie, I have to go with the police. They're taking Sean's body. I have to go. I will call you as soon as I can. Auntie, oh, my God. My Sean's gone!"

Lola heard the phone disconnect.. She sat on the couch in front of the television screen, her tiny black cat purring and winding its way between her legs. She held the remote in one hand and the dead phone in the other, unable to withdraw her gaze from the scene of horror on the London streets. She dropped the remote and phone to the floor and picked up the little cat, rubbing her chin in the thick coal-colored fur. She put the cat on the couch beside her and lay her hands in her lap, staring at her palms and then turning them over.

Lola sat on the couch for most of that day, watching CNN's talking heads filling the screen in front of the pictures of the destroyed double-decker bus. Flashes of the wounded were interspersed with images of smoke and politicians speculating and posturing. The day passed with no call back from Istie. A call to the US embassy yielded no information but increased Lola's fear and frustration.

At five that afternoon, Istie's call came. Sean was, indeed, dead and Istie was bringing him home at the end of the week. No, she did not want Lola to come. Sean's mother and sister were on their way and his agent was making all the funeral arrangements with his family in Idaho.

Istie accompanied Sean's body back to the city on the Sound. She stood on the tarmac at the airport with Lola's arm around her as the coffin came off the plane and was loaded into the black hearse to make the journey across the state to Lapwai, Idaho. Istie's face now bore the same stain of grief that Lola had seen on Jones's face that first night at the ranch. Overnight, gray had crept into the lush brown waves of hair that Lola had lovingly brushed when Istie was small. Lola was overwhelmed by sadness.

"Oh, my God," she whispered, "another LeFleur widow. Oh, my poor baby."

Istie stood with Lola and Sean's family in the heat of the Idaho sun. Her black slacks slapped against her legs and her fuchsia maternity top billowed in gentle waves over her pregnant belly. She and Sean had planned to tell Lola of Istie's pregnancy the day of the bombings, celebrating the ultrasound that confirmed another LeFleur girl would come into the world. Istie had had the pictures from the ultrasound in her hand at the moment the bomb exploded. She never had the chance to show Sean the first pictures of his unborn daughter and now he would never see her.

Sean's mother and sister, graceful and gracious, hugged Istie and Lola as Sean's coffin was lowered into the ground. The words of the Lord's Prayer, spoken in the language of the Nez Perce, floated over the heads of the small crowd gathered in the cemetery.

Sean's mother, a statuesque gray-haired woman, moved to stand at the head of Sean's grave. She held a single typed page in her hand and, in the hot summer breeze, began to read:

> "The horse's black coat was slicked with rain. The young woman who held his bridle walked with slow steps across the muddy grass, her destination a small brown house surrounded by a split-rail fence. From inside the house, the man smiled as the horse and woman picked their way towards him. The woman's head was bent against the sharp pellets of rain and the black horse shook

his mane. The man gazed out the window and felt the love in his heart encompass him until he could hardly breathe. He knew he would die if she ever left him , for in her eyes and touch were the resurrection of his soul and the knowledge that any obstacle in life could be overcome if her hand was in his."

Sean's mother gently folded the page and moved to face Istie. She wrapped her arms around Istie's shoulders and pulled her around to face her.

"Istie, my son waited for over fifty years for you. Istie, this was what Sean felt for you. He loved you. We would like you to stay here with us, if you choose. But, if you choose to go with your people, you and your child will always have a home with us. You are all we have left of Sean. He loved you and we do, too."

Istie nodded and hugged her mother-in-law. Her face was lined and a fine trail of salt from Istie's shared dried tears shone in the sun. She quietly stepped away from the older woman and bent down to touch the dirt lying next to Sean's grave. She patted the earth and then picked up a handful of the Lapwai ground. A golden eagle flew silently overhead as Istie dropped a clump of dirt on the coffin and then stood and faced Lola.

"Let's go home, Auntie Lola. I want to go home."

Two months later, as the anniversary of 9/11 approached again, Lola fed the mice their breakfast. Istie sat in the kitchen watching the morning scene and rubbing her belly, feeling the baby kick in anticipation of release into the world. She had decided to name the baby Liliana after her mother. Istie had been quiet over the weeks since Sean's death, finally telling Lola of that awful day in July in London. She spoke of the kind police who had gently questioned her after the bombings. She told Lola of reading Sean's name among the list of dead. She spoke of the endless reporters and held her hands to her face as she described Sean's broken body but his expression serene even in the face of violent death.

She had been waiting for Sean at the Hilton Hotel near the Edgware Station. They had planned to meet for breakfast before heading across the city to visit Sean's agent about his new play. An explosion had shaken the hotel and within moments sirens began screaming. Sean's body had been one of the first carried into the lobby of the hotel. He had been climbing the stairs when the bomb went off, slamming his body to the ground. Istie described the scene that day as one of total chaos mixed with intense terror. She told her aunt how excited Sean had been when she told him of her pregnancy and how pleased he was with the plans for Lola to come and visit. They both wanted to surprise Lola with a new baby.

Lola listened in silence, her hands clasped around Istie's. Sean's family had begged Istie to come to Lapwai and have the baby in Idaho, but Istie refused to leave the green house on the hill. She sat for hours at the kitchen table, the tiny black cat on her lap, patting Istie's chin with one paw. Istie called Lola to her side one rainy afternoon.

"Look, Auntie Lola. I've been watching them. Look, on the bench." Istie pointed out the window and there, in the darkening light, a brown mouse sat on its hind feet, staring into the lighted kitchen window. Three miniature mice were huddled against their mother, pieces of cheese in their almost unseen mouths. Rain spattered against the window, the ivy shifting in the wind.

"New babies, Auntie. Aren't they cute? New babies. She brought her babies to show me." Istie smiled and rubbed her belly. Lola laid her hands on Istie's hair and kissed the top of her head.

"Istie, I think that is the first time I have ever seen babies in the fall. They've come to keep you company. Istie, Sean knows you are here. I'll take care of you. Istie, I am so sorry. My precious baby, I am so sorry."

Lola reached into Istie's lap and picked up the arm with the little black cat tattooed on it. She kissed the tattoo and murmured, "*Mon petite chat noir.* My little black cat."

Istie grew bigger as fall approached with its cold rain and dreary days. The green house was filled with a mixture of grief and anticipation. Lola brought home the smoked salmon Istie craved and, once a week, Rona and Krissie came to keep the women company. Lola raked leaves and trimmed bushes, cleaned the birdbaths and filled the birdfeeders. She listened to the chickadees and, on several occasions, saw a large crow sitting on the branches of the lilac tree.

At Istie's insistence, Lola made her annual late summer trip to the ranch, this time with Forrest and the red pony. She knew that Forrest had just lost his son in Iraq and she wanted to share Lola with him. Lola was too concerned about Istie to stay the whole month so she shortened her trip and returned to Seattle after only two weeks.

Istie chose to stay behind with Sean's mother to keep her company, deeming it the perfect time to get to know each other. The evening before Lola and Forrest left for Wyoming, Lola came down the carpet-covered stairs to see Istie and Sean's mother sitting on the couch, Istie running her hands over a photo of Sean. Lola turned away, not wanting to interrupt the intimacy of the two women, knowing that Sean's mother was the only one who could tell Istie the stories of Sean's life.

That night, Lola sat upright in bed, her back pressed against the headboard, studying her hands in the faint light that came from the window. She thought of Auntie Louella's passing on the train and of the woman falling from the tower. She thought of Sean's death and of the war that had now claimed so many, including Forrest's beloved son, Reed, and the Baines's twins, Curt and Todd. She remembered the stories of the glory days of the Taidnapam and Cowlitz people and the parents she never knew. She mourned the loss of all of the souls and prayed for the sleep that now eluded her on so many nights, ghosts chasing around in her mind and filling the small room with their moans and cries. She prayed that the Creator would forgive her for her selfishness in wishing for Istie to come home, never dreaming that her niece's terrible loss would be the cause of that longed-for reunion.

Two days after Lola and Forrest returned from the ranch to the gray city, Istie gave birth to a daughter in the bedroom tucked under the eaves. Sean's mother stood in the doorway of the room, shoulder to shoulder with Lola as the doula and midwife brought Istie's daughter into the world. A candle burned in the window, casting shadows across Istie's exhausted face. A tapping on the window glass caught Lola's attention. Sitting on the window ledge was a tiny brown mouse, its white markings giving it the appearance of spectacles. It peered into the room, whiskers twitching and tail moving in quick movements.

Lola turned back toward Istie, now with her daughter cuddled in a white blanket on her chest. She smiled at Lola and nodded as Lola picked up her great-niece, another LeFleur generation. Lola held the baby in wonder, smiling peacefully as Istie, exhausted from the delivery, cried tears of joy mixed with sorrow.

"Liliana Sean LeFleur," Istie whispered. She closed her eyes, and could see Sean's face floating above her, his brown eyes smiling as his daughter smiled back and reached her hands toward her father's face.

⇥ 9 ⇤

The Last Wolf

The she-wolf had lived in the shadow of the Tower for fifteen years. She and her mate migrated west from the Black Hills, when their fear of humans and loss of the food supply forced them from their birthplace. After successfully traveling across the mountains and prairies with the pups to their new home, they dug a den in the nooks and crannies of the rocks that had tumbled to the base of Devils Tower. There they and their pups fed on the ground squirrels and rabbits that populated the fields and bushes in the park. Occasionally, the she-wolf brought home the leg of a sheep or a calf but those treats were rare and acquired only on the coldest winter nights and with the greatest danger.

The she-wolf was a small, sleek animal, whose courage and determination belied her diminutive size. Her black coat was thick and her feet matched the ruff of silver around her neck. Curiously, she had one blue eye and one black eye and an extra toe on her left rear paw. The anomaly of the toe was passed down to her babies, but most of them had the tan and black markings of her mate.

The wolves lived peacefully in a growing pack at the foot of the Tower for many years. As the pups grew older and the pack grew larger, several of the younger wolves were sent out on their own. Many migrated back into the Black Hills while others journeyed west to the grandeur of the Grand Teton Mountains. Few survived their journeys. The ranchers and hunters in the area prided themselves on obliterating the noble predator and, eventually, only the she-wolf, her mate, and three of their pups were left on the land once owned by the wolf and the bear.

Still, over the years, through the persistence of the she-wolf and her mate, the pack managed to survive. Their self-preserving fear of humans dictated the need to hunt only at night. Often, they were fortunate to feast on deer that lived in among the cattle and sheep. The den was cool in the heat of summer, the smell of pinesap rising in the air, and snugly warm in the midst of the numbing cold of winter.

On one of the most frigid of winter nights, as the ground squirrels disappeared into their tunnels and the rabbits hunkered down from the cold, the she-wolf ventured out to the surrounding woods and fields. After hours of futile hunting, she smelled blood in the air. Following the scent, she discovered the frozen carcass of a dead sheep, eviscerated by the pack of coyotes that still remained in the area. She tore at the haunches of the sheep and managed to secure a piece large enough to feed her hungry family. She gave a loud howl that carried over the cold air and echoed in the hollows of the rolling hills.

Her mate and pups barked back in reply, their yips increasing in velocity and frequency as they heard her approach. Just as the she-wolf neared the den, a figure appeared at the opening. Four sharp cracks were heard, followed immediately by the screams of dying animals. Full of trepidation, the she-wolf vacillated between running to save her family and hiding to save herself. Frantically, she dropped the haunch of the sheep and crept forward towards the den. As she approached, she saw a tall human turn and walk away from the den's opening. Since he never looked back, he never saw the cringing small animal among the boulders and bushes.

A few last whimpers came from the den and then only silence. She moved slowly forward, crawling on her belly until she finally reached the den's opening. Her mate and all three pups were dead. The smell of their blood brought horror to her heart. Stricken with grief, she went from body to body, nudging each one, trying to lick life back into her slaughtered family. She threw her head back to howl her pain to the world, but a sense of danger stilled her voice. Instead, she lay down next to her dead mate and pups and waited for night to pass into day.

When the morning light came at last, the she-wolf crawled back out into the day and stood at the entry to the den. Taking a final look at her slain family, she began to dig. All through that first lonely day, she dug and dug. By the time the sun was setting and the temperature had dropped to a teeth-chilling cold, the she-wolf was exhausted. The entry to the den could no longer be seen and the dead wolf family was buried at the base of the Tower. That night, the she-wolf began her solitary life. She wanted to howl in grief and call to any of her kind that might be in the area, yet she knew her only hope of survival was to mourn her loss in deep silence.

Alone and lonely, the years of the she-wolf passed and the time came when she knew her end was near. She understood she would die in solitude and without ever being able to cry her loss to the moon. During the summer of what she felt would be her last, she gave up the safety of her hidden den and her furtive meals of ground squirrels. She grew bolder and took to lying on the rocks that were scattered in a jumbled mass around the indifferent monolith. She watched the humans that came to the Tower and, on occasion, one of them would spy what appeared to be a large black dog warming itself in the dying light as she dozed, dreaming of her dead mate and pups. She could feel them near her and hear them calling her to join them. As the summer days gave up their heat and the moon moved toward fall, the she-wolf prepared for her death in the coming winter.

To the west, the summer was fast coming to a close. The frost began to appear on the lawns and cars of the city. The rains came and the leaves turned brown and fell into the houses' gutters, clogging the drains and irritating the homeowners. Farther to the west, across oceans and mountains, in a faraway land, the summer's heat blazed as the desert dust swirled around the mottled tan and brown pants of the young women and men patrolling the dangerous streets of Baghdad. The electrical power had long since been shut off and clean running water was hard to find for the ancient city's millions of inhabitants.

Small cars full of dark-skinned and dark-eyed people drove the dusty streets interspersed with oversized threatening Humvees carrying American soldiers. Ever vigilant and tense, soldiers peered out from under their helmets. They maintained a trained awareness as they searched cars for hidden incendiary devices like the ones that maimed or murdered so many of their comrades. They were mystified by the carved stone wolf heads that adorned the narrow bridge over the dirty water of the Tigris. They were unaware of the power and strength the wolves symbolized. Most were very young soldiers who had been dropped as aliens from a spaceship into a strange and hostile world they did not understand.

A battered jeep pockmarked by bullet holes and shrapnel brought up the rear of the convoy. In it was the young captain in command of the platoon assigned to patrol that particular part of the teeming and shattered metropolis. He wore the "stare" that so often marked the face of combat veterans, a wariness and weariness borne of too many deaths, too many losses, and from witnessing the madness of war on too many occasions.

Reed Francis Kingston had joined the Army in 1999. This was his third tour of Iraq. This most recent military assignment was to the Stryker Brigade out of Fort Lewis, Washington, near his hometown of Seattle. He had been shipped back to Iraq after only forty-five days at Fort Lewis. His deployment was part of the "stop-loss" program intended to ensure continued troop strength to support the invasion and to carry out the ever-increasingly vague mission in the desert.

Reed despised the killing and the utter destruction of the city and lives of the people through "shock and awe," the words simply propaganda to disguise the very human toll the bombs took. He believed in diplomacy and thoughtful discourse. The unilateral preemptive strike into sovereign nations was a notion foreign to his view of the ideals of his beloved country. He pondered his choice of the military as a career, wondering how he had ever thought he could be part of what he believed was an unnecessary war. He had requested a posting to Afghanistan to fight against the brutality of the Taliban and its support of Bin Laden. This became an ongoing debate with his superiors who believed the US Army was best served if Reed remained in Baghdad.

Reed was the only son of Marie and Forrest Kingston. The couple was now in their sixties and while their visages were wrinkled with time and weathered from life's toils, their hearts were kind and their actions belied the gray on their head. Forrest stood ramrod straight, the bearing of an old soldier. Marie was the grandmotherly type, like the ones featured on the boxes of cookies and in Christmas commercials.

Reed was thirty-two years old and had been single until the age of twenty-six. His mother often despaired of him ever marrying or having children, but Forrest reminded his wife of their own marriage in their thirties and finally being gifted by their wonderful son long after they had given up the dream of a child.

In his parents' eyes, Reed was the most extraordinary child. He was born with black hair tinged with silver. He had one blue eye and one black eye, an oddity that never ceased to startle his parents. Reed was as tall and slender as his name and had been a star athlete in high school. He also ignored the niceties of following directions or turning class work in on time. Nonetheless, he was awarded a swimming scholarship to the local university. He also managed to earn an engineering degree *summa cum laude*, which astonished his father but simply fulfilled the faithful dream of his doting mother.

Upon graduation, Reed took a position with Raytheon in Tucson, Arizona. He loved the desert and dry heat, which was so different from his childhood's northwestern home climate. He laughed at the Gila monsters that lived in his back yard and drank from his pool. He was fascinated at the males who bobbed their heads as they challenged each other for supremacy of their small world. At work, he rose quickly through the ranks and, within four years, had become an assistant director. He accomplished this while completing an MBA. The work he was responsible for was contracted through the Department of Defense. Reed had an endless budget for seventy-dollar hammers and two hundred-dollar toilet seats. He would often complain in long letters to his father about this wastefulness; and his father would reply with agreeing consternation in staccato emails.

On his twenty-sixth birthday, Reed put his pink adobe house up for rent and went down to the Army recruiting station. He had walked past the office many times with fleeting thoughts of the innate nobility of warriors. Each time he strolled past the Army recruiting posters, the stronger became his desire to participate as part of a greater good. Explaining his decision to his parents, he simply said, "I love my country." Within a few short weeks, he was sent to Fort Benning, Georgia, for Officer Candidate School. Through the weeks of training, his body grew more muscular and his mind sharper.

Reed loathed the cloying humidity of the south and resented the caste system that separated officers from enlisted troops. He isolated himself from the coarse humor and language of his campmates, preferring instead to read poems or the history of China in the semi-quiet of the mess hall. He became known as "Odd-Eyes" and, eventually, was left alone by the rest of the squad. The camp's noise would slowly recede into the background as he immersed himself in tales of far-flung lands and southern heroes.

His only relief from the misery of his life in the camp came from his occasional trip to the gentle city of Savannah with its mossy cemeteries. He purchased the book *Midnight in the Garden of Good and Evil* and retraced the footsteps of the book's characters, imagining the parties and gossip of the endearing ensemble. Occasionally, he made the short drive to Hilton Head Island where he sat at the edge of the ocean and walked the golf courses filled with water hazards inhabited by indolent alligators.

On one of his trips to the Island, he stopped to have lunch at the local Mexican restaurant. His accompanying book that cool fall day was a fitting one for the time and place, *A Stained White Radiance*, by one of his favorite authors, James Lee Burke. Reed absently nibbled the chips placed on the table by the young redheaded waitress. He stopped and looked up only when the shadow of a woman fell across the pages of the book. The tiny woman was dressed in white with a black velvet ribbon around her throat. Another black ribbon pulled her black hair back from her long neck. Reed took in her turquoise eyes, small hands with no jewelry, and the black velvet dancing slippers.

"Out of my dreams and out of my league," murmured Reed. "And what exactly can I do for you?" he asked, addressing his question to the woman.

"I don't mean to impose," the young woman said, "but do you mind if I sit with you? I don't really like to eat alone and I love James Lee Burke." She held up a tattered copy of *In the Electric Mist with the Confederate Dead.*

"I've seen you here before," she said. "I'm Jamie Dupree. And, no, I am not French. My ex-husband was Cajun and I just liked the name."

She pulled out a chair across from Reed and, as the waitress passed, raised her hand to get the waitress' attention. "I'd like a mint julep," Jamie said, "and if you don't have that, a banana daiquiri will suffice."

"As to what you can do for me," Jamie laughed, turning back to Reed, "you can tell me what a northern boy like you is doing down here. No, wait! You're a rich businessman from California. No, that's not right. You're a lawyer from Kansas City. No, actually, you're an officer in training from Fort Benning."

Reed scowled at her, "Yes, on the last count, but how would you know that?"

"Because," Jamie replied, "my father is your drill instructor and he always talks about your astonishing eyes; and I've seen you on base."

After a pause she continued, "Savannah is one of my favorite towns. I especially like the cemeteries."

"I take it," Reed said, "that we are having lunch together. But then, I am leaving for camp. So, I will say it now, it's been nice to meet you and I will wish you a good day."

Jamie laughed; tendrils of hair beginning to escape from her ribbon. A banana daiquiri was placed on the table and, as she picked it up, she toasted Reed.

"Cheers," she said, "and here is my phone number. I hope to see you back at the base."

Reed watched as she drained the glass and licked the rim. She wrote a number on the napkin and slid it across the table. Pushing back her chair, she stood up and picked up his book.

"Call me when you want this back."

That afternoon, on the drive back to the base, Jamie's dark eyes and white dress lingered in his mind and his hand caressed the napkin as if it was her skin. He pulled over at a gas station and went to the battered phone booth, an oddity in this time of cell phones. He dialed the ten digits that had been his parents' phone number for four decades.

His mother answered with her usual crisp "Hello."

"Mom, get Dad on the extension, please." Reed waited in silence despite the repeated questions from his mother asking what was so important he could not tell her alone.

"Hi Reed, it's Dad. What can I do for you?"

"Mom, Dad, sit down. I have something important to tell you. Are you and Dad doing anything next Saturday night? Can you come to Georgia? I'm getting married and I would really like you to be here."

The memory of that day and their intimate wedding in the Savannah cemetery replayed through Reed's mind as he climbed out of the jeep and stepped onto the dusty road. He approached his sergeant and as he did, he could smell the yellow roses that had graced Jamie's hair. He thought of his father in a black tuxedo adorned with a yellow boutonniere, his mother smiling in relief as she watched her son marry the beautiful woman he had obviously been waiting for.

Reed pulled his sergeant away from the rest of the company. "I think we should go back to base. I have a bad feeling about this spot. Tell the crew we are turning around and make sure everyone has their flack jackets buttoned up and helmets on."

The sergeant nodded and waved at the lead driver. He knew of Reed's previous two tours in Iraq and implicitly trusted his captain's judgment. Reed's leadership and quiet confidence inspired a sense of safety in his troops. The convoy turned around and moved off toward the setting sun. Heat waves rose from the pavement, causing waxing and waning images of the large vehicles.

As the convoy moved away, Reed climbed into his jeep and drove down to the bank of the river. He sat for a moment with his arms folded across the steering wheel, staring into the water. War debris littered the filthy stream of the Tigris. This cradle of civilization was now ravaged by death and destruction of a culture, a people, and a country.

His three tours in Iraq were measured in increasing horror and cynicism. He had shaken his head in disgust at Abu Ghraib and the graft of some of the military contractors. He was appalled at the banner of

"Mission Accomplished" that waved from the decks of the USS Abraham Lincoln, knowing the truth of the long struggle still to come and the enormous costs of the invasion, the economic drain, the environmental destruction, and the loss of human life that would forever mark this era of history.

He was bereft at the sight of an Iraqi child, maimed by a weapon he had helped design, wondering why he had never comprehended the reality of what such armament could do. He grew to believe, as his father had before him in Vietnam, that the war was for the ego and greed of small- minded men and an evil, cold-hearted lunatic. He questioned whether this was the "right" war. Was this war worth the American lives? Only the future would tell. But he was tired, and disillusioned and heartsick. He longed for the peace of his home in Tucson and the hearty laugh of his petite wife.

Reed and Jamie had four years together before he was sent to Iraq for his first tour of duty. She was now living in Tucson in their adobe house, sending daily emails with pictures of the Gila monsters and dragonflies that still lived around the pool. She sent him boxes of cactus, an ironic but loving gesture to a man who now lived in the most ancient of deserts. She reminisced over their first encounter, the very short courtship that led to this path to nirvana, and how she missed his face, his body and his touch.

Every week on Sunday mornings, without fail, Reed wrote a long letter to his father. He used the time he had previously spent attending mass. Now he refused to go. Instead he wrote long missives to his father expressing his doubt in the existence of a God that could allow men of such evil into positions of power and ignore the pain and suffering of the American soldiers and the Iraqi people.

Over and over, as he struggled through his letters to his father, he would ask himself, "Why?" Again and again, he puzzled over why he had not connected the manufacturing of weapons to their actual use against a country that posed no obvious threat to his.

"How?" he wondered, watching the children of the battered city scooping up drinking water from the filth of the Tigris.

"What am I doing here?" was the endless refrain that pulsed through his mind. Never finding acceptable answers to his questions, he would put pen to paper and begin to write.

Every letter started the same way: *Dear Dad, love you. Tell mom I am okay and do not show her this letter.* He then went on to tell of the palaces being looted and the loss of Persia and Baghdad's priceless treasures. He told of trips to the Anbar province and the angry glares from the people they were freeing. He shared his memories of the World Trade Center towers falling and his belief in the goodness of his country. He wrote of his time with Jamie and the longing he felt each day they were apart.

Reed told his father of people dying from starvation and thirst; how they stood in the disease-ridden waters of the Tigris to cool themselves in the blistering heat. He told of the men and women, American and Iraqi, and their screams of pain as the bombs exploded and their loved ones died. He mourned over the sight of one of his platoon dying in the arms of a weeping medic. With each passing week, he became bitter, angry and spoke with a more pronounced longing for home.

That hot night on the Tigris, Reed composed a letter to his father in his head. The day had been long and the tension of looking for IEDs and waiting for battle had become unbearable. He turned and swung his legs over the side of the jeep, wiping the dust from his hands and slapping it from the legs of his pants. The convoy had long since disappeared down the road. He gazed off across the river and, in the distance, could see flashes of light and hear the sound of thunder.

"Is it war or nature?" Reed asked himself.

He pulled a blanket from the jeep and spread it on the ground. From his pocket, he took a notepad and pen. He sat on the blanket on the still, heated ground and started to write. His service revolver lay next to him, well within reach. He thought of Jamie and the sun setting over the mountains of his homes. He thought of his childhood home in the Northwest and the adobe home in the Southwest where Jamie waited. He ran his hand over the revolver, its smooth feel as familiar to him as Jamie's face. He heard her voice and felt the wash of her long black hair over his hand. He could feel her tiny feet against his leg and hear her laughter as they lay entwined and the sun sent shafts of dancing light over their faces.

He picked up the pen and began to write: *Dear Dad, I love you. Tell Mom I am fine and do not show her this letter...*

◄ ►

Three weeks later and thousands of miles west across the oceans, mountains and deserts of the world, Lola and Forrest readied their horses for the long journey to Devils Tower.

Lola and Forrest had met at the barn after the red pony came west from the Buffalo Springs Ranch. They enjoyed weekly rides through the three winters and summers the red pony had been with her. Often they would trailer the horses to the mountains or the ocean, sharing meals and stories. Marie always gave her blessing to the outings, knowing it was her husband's outlet for the anger he harbored in his heart about Reed's three tours in Iraq and the never-ending war for an elusive goal.

Forrest rode a big red roan quarter horse gelding named Roxie. A large Siberian husky dog named Henrietta always accompanied them. Henrietta had a thick white coat tinged with silver tips. His feet were enormous and his tail seemed as long as his body. He had the one blue eye and one black eye common in his breed. Henrietta loved to chase balls and Lola found him attempting to retrieve a large blue ball from the field where the red pony was grazing with the herd. The pony kicked the ball away every time Henrietta got close. Lola laughed at the antics of the two animals and went into the pasture to retrieve the ball. She tossed it back to Henrietta who pushed it over to Forrest, then lay down with his head firmly on top of the ball. Forrest was Henrietta's source of joy and his loyalty never wavered.

Lola, on several occasions, had asked Forrest why his male animals had female names but he would never answer and ignored the question each time it was asked. Forrest loved his animals with a passion. Henrietta never left Forrest's side on the long rides Forrest and Lola made each weekend.

Marie sighed when Lola questioned her about the odd names. They were, Marie said, the nicknames of the two men who had carried Forrest to the medevac helicopter when he was shot in the neck during his 1969 tour in Vietnam. "Every animal we have ever had is male and they were named either Roxie or Henrietta. Even when Reed was young, his gerbils had the same names. Forrest hates to give credit where credit is due but, next time you're here, I'll show you the shrine he built for those men."

"Where are they now?" Lola asked.

"Well, Roxie died in 1972 in a plane crash on his way home from San Francisco. Henrietta died last year of a stroke. Their deaths broke Forrest's heart. That's why your rides are so important to him. It takes him away from his grief and from the fears he has for Reed. I have a new picture of the house in Tucson. I love that Jamie girl. I talk to her every day. She's promised a visit when her job will allow. I know Forrest would never show it, but he is pleased as all get out that Jamie wants to come and spend time with us. She truly is the daughter we always wanted and never had!"

"Huh," Lola mused. She had suspected Forrest was really a tender-hearted man but getting past his rough exterior was difficult. "Is Jamie coming before or after our trip to Wyoming?"

"She's coming the last week of September, after you two get back. I think this tour has been very difficult for her. So, Lola, tell me, why do you go to the Tower every year? This must be your fourth or fifth trip. What do you do while you're there? I know that's where the pony came from and that you love Dusty and Sarah, but why every year?"

Lola thought for a moment and then replied in a quiet voice, "I go because that Tower never falls."

≕ ≔

On their rides, Forrest would tell Lola about the steamy, rancid jungles around Saigon. He had been a second lieutenant with the 199th Light Infantry Brigade and was drafted straight out of college in 1968. He also had been in Officer Candidate School at Fort Benning and was discharged from the Army in 1971, a year after he finished his tour in Vietnam. During his tour he was shot twice; once in the left calf and once in the side of his neck. The neck wound merited a month-long stay in the Army hospital in Japan. After an additional two-week R&R in

Bangkok, drinking in the bars, and having indiscriminate sex with the prostitutes, he returned to his squad and finished out his year of duty.

Forrest told Lola of how he despised war and the men who create it. He believed Lyndon Johnson was a bastard and Richard Nixon a paranoid crook. He took Ford to task for the installation of Rumsfeld and Cheney; and labeled Carter as a Georgia cracker but a good man.

He scoffed at Reagan's claim of destroying the Soviet Union, declaring the man had been senile and asleep at the wheel during his entire administration. He labeled Bush Sr. an elitist but adored Barbara, adamant that she should have run for president. Clinton was a man who could not keep his britches around his waist. Forrest held him personally responsible for allowing Bush 43 to ever be considered for office.

Lola listened to Forrest's vitriolic rants against the various presidents and politicians who had taken the country to what he perceived as an unnecessary war and the war before. He sneered at the notion of Saddam Hussein ever having weapons of mass destruction. He scoffed at the implications that Al-Qaeda was in Iraq, proclaiming it was the Saudis that had flown the planes into the towers, and that the government of his country had made a deal with the devil for oil. His anger masked the fear he felt for his son—a fear that overwhelmed him in the dark morning hours.

Lola learned not to respond to Forrest's endless lectures and rants, much as Marie had done over their thirty-plus years of marriage. In time, Lola understood that while Forrest could express anger, he was unable to articulate the deep love and admiration he had for his son and daughter-in-law.

One morning over a cup of coffee, Marie told Lola about the nightmares Forrest still had from his time as a soldier and his fear of losing his only son in Iraq. She described how Forrest cried for hours the day Reed had told his parents he was joining the Army and again on the day Reed shipped out to Iraq. Lola listened in silence, accepting but not fully grasping the level of Forrest's anguish.

Marie was a descendant of Holocaust survivors and firmly believed that Reed would survive the Iraqi war just as her parents had survived the internment camp at Bergen-Belsen. She refused to believe that a loving God would take her only child from her and knew in her heart and soul that Reed would return home to them and Jamie. She was unwavering in her stance that Reed and Jamie would have a child and that child would know nothing but love and the smell of chocolate chip cookies in her kitchen.

On every ride over the course of Reed's three deployments, when Forrest and Lola stopped to rest the horses, Forrest would pull a letter from his pocket. Each letter was creased and folded, some worn thin from the dozens of times it had been opened, read, and re-folded, and then tucked back into Forrest's breast pocket. Each letter began: *Dear Dad, I love you. Tell Mom I am fine and do not show her this letter.*

The letters grew more angry and hopeless over time, each one detailing life in the war zone. Reed viewed the generals hiding in the Green Zone as cowards, and the pomposity of the government officials who "dropped in" to visit the soldiers as insulting. He could no longer view war as a means to an abstract ideal. Rather, as Merlin had succinctly noted so many generations before, the current war was being sold to the world as "might being right." He told of the beautiful children he saw every day and of his hope he and Jamie would someday have a child of their own. He wished for a girl, one that shared Jamie's black hair, petite hands and tiny feet. He spoke of the fear of his soul being damned for his participation in killing, no longer able to convince himself of the nobleness of his actions. At the end of each day of his third tour, he grew more and more bitter and more and more disheartened and depressed, convinced he would never again see Jamie or his parents.

⇥ ⇤

It was a cool Friday morning before Labor Day as Lola took the wheel of the Tahoe, pulled out of the barn driveway onto the narrow road and headed east. She picked up the eight-lane highway and traveled toward the sun. She and Forrest had planned to camp with the horses in the high country of the national forest. Lola could see the noses of the horses sticking out the trailer windows, making her laugh. On the back seat, Henrietta lay with his nose nuzzled in Forrest's hand.

"Lola," Forrest said, "don't forget to take that side trip we talked about. It's really important, you know. It should be coming up before we hit the freeway."

"I know, Forrest," Lola replied. "The turn is just ahead. How could I possibly forget? We've talked about this for the past three weeks. I know, Forrest, I know."

Lola turned the Tahoe into a wide, blacktop road that led through an arch and then past two brick pillars that marked the Tahoma National Cemetery in Maple Valley. A few moments later, she pulled over and reached behind her for the lead ropes for the horses. With Henrietta following, they slowly walked to the back of the trailer. Simultaneously, they unlatched the doors. Lola climbed into the trailer, led the red pony out, and then Roxie, Forrest's big gelding. Forrest held the lead ropes while Lola closed up the trailer.

With a horse close behind each of them, they walked into the cemetery. The graves lay in neat rows, an American flag marking the resting spot of each gallant man or woman. Halfway down the last row was a grave covered in yellow roses. Forrest and Lola stopped and Lola took Roxie's rope. Forrest bent down and did something Lola had never seen. He kissed his fingers and pressed them to the stone, running them across the name engraved in the black marble:

Reed Francis Kingston
Captain, US Army
1973-2005
Beloved Son and Husband

Lola could barely see as tears crowded her eyes. She stood in silence waiting for Forrest to finish his homage. Finally, Forrest rose to his feet and together they returned to the truck and trailer and loaded the horses inside. Neither said a word as Lola circled the truck and trailer, pulling out of the cemetery and back onto the highway heading east.

Their journey to the Tower took three days. Each afternoon, they made camp down one of the logging roads that zigzagged through the mountains. Each night, as the sun set, they saddled the horses and rode until the dark encircled them and Forrest could barely see. Every night, by firelight, he pulled out a stack of Reed's letters and read them one by one into the night: *Dear Dad, I love you. Tell Mom I am fine and don't show her this letter.*

Forrest was driving when they finally came around the ridge and Devils Tower came into view. As the Tahoe started up the incline, Lola smelled the trees and the moist earth. Although she had been to the Buffalo Springs Ranch several times since 2001, she had not returned to Devils Tower. Memories of the past four years flooded her mind, the feel of heated rock under her hand and the sight of Auntie Louella sleeping in the white rental car in the parking lot. She saw the prairie dog village and the trading post. She recalled climbing higher and feeling the heat radiating off the rocks. She remembered watching the clouds racing over the top of the Tower. The Tahoe hit a bump, bringing Lola out of her reverie and into the present. She sighed deeply as Forrest maneuvered the truck and trailer up the narrow road.

They drove to the parking lot and opened the doors of the trailer to let the horses feel the fresh air. The red pony stood at the back of the slant-load trailer and, as Lola opened the door, he turned to look at her, nickering softly. Towards the front of the trailer, Roxie stamped his feet and snorted impatiently. Lola gently walked the horses out of the cramped trailer and tied them to its side.

After the horses were secured and provided fresh water, Lola turned to Forrest. "Do you mind if I just take a few minutes and walk up the path? I won't be gone long."

"I'm fine, Lola," Forrest replied. "I'll keep the horses company and make sure they get to stretch their legs."

Lola nodded and started off at a quick pace up the path towards the altar. She rushed past the other visitors on the trail, her eyes drawn to the top of the Tower. She could see the climbers on its sides. As before, the sun glinted off their helmets and their calls echoed down to Lola. She thought back to her previous visit and imagined she could hear Auntie's endless chatter as they traveled from Minot to the Tower. She remembered the endless blue sky and the smoke billowing from the stricken twin towers in Manhattan. She recalled the tiny figure of a woman, endlessly falling. Lola dropped to her knees and touched the earth.

"Creator, if you are there, please give Forrest and Marie peace. Please, Creator, bring peace to this troubled world. Please, Creator, bring peace to this world."

After a reverent pause, Lola rose and slowly walked back down the path. A Red-tailed Hawk screamed as Lola reached the Tahoe. Forrest was patting the red pony on the rump as he repositioned the horses in the trailer and secured the padlocks. Lola quietly climbed back into the passenger's seat. Forrest joined her behind the wheel and continued their journey to the ranch. They stopped at the same stop sign where Lola and Auntie had been four years before. Forrest turned the Tahoe to the north and headed up the highway.

They reached the ranch just before dinner. Dusty and Sarah appeared from behind the barn. Their smiles welcomed Lola and Forrest as they pulled into the yard, the end of the long journey from the rainy Northwest.

"Sarah! Dusty! We're back!" Lola called as she ran to give and receive welcoming hugs. "This is my dear friend, Forrest. This is his horse Roxie and, look, here's your pony. We're back!" Lola hugged Sarah and Dusty again, and then turned toward Forrest.

"Forrest, these people will take great care of us. Come say 'Hello!'"

Forrest held Henrietta by the collar as he got out of the vehicle. He let the Husky loose and Henrietta bounded across the lawn, sniffing as he ran. He circled the yard where the Tahoe was parked and then came back to stand by Forrest's side, following closely as they unloaded the horses and guided them to the barn.

The red pony began to neigh and snort, prancing as he tugged at the end of the lead rope Lola held in her hand. He continued to call to the other horses, who came to the fence responding with welcoming greetings.

"Look, Lola. He remembers them!" Dusty pointed to the horses. "Turn him out and let him go see them. I think he's glad to be home! We have dinner ready. Let's go and eat. We're so glad you're both here!"

"I can't believe another year has gone by!" Sarah smiled. "Wait until you see what we've done to the house. You won't recognize it."

They walked the horses into the pasture and laughed in delight as the animals ran freely around the field and performed their welcome home rituals. They slowly strolled across the grass to unload the Tahoe, casually chatting and catching up on news. The easiness of the late summer day continued until after dinner.

As Sarah poured coffee and Dusty cleaned his boots, Forrest began to speak. In a grief-filled voice, he shared with Dusty and Sarah the story of the loss of his son. He described the Army chaplains coming to the house, how he heard the knock at the door, and then Marie's scream as she crumpled to the ground. His hands shook as he re-lived his call to Jamie and the uncontrollable sobs on the other end of the line.

"They told us he died when a bomb exploded near his jeep. He was by the Tigris River. For some reason, he was alone but no one knows why. Reed had sent the rest of the convoy back to camp. He told his sergeant that he did not think the area was safe. The sergeant got worried when Reed did not return to base and they sent two Humvees back to look for him. They found him beside his jeep, dead. The military told us he died of an IED and told Marie and me it would be better if we did not see the body. I talked to his sergeant and he told me how much Reed was admired and loved by all of his men.

"When he enlisted, Reed told me how much he believed in the ideals of this country and how serving as a warrior was the best way he could give back to it. Now he's dead. They gave him a Purple Heart and a Silver Star. They sent him back to us in a box and now he's in the ground. The funeral was horrible. Jamie and Marie were inconsolable. I tell you, I did not think they would be able to make it through that day."

Tears welled in Forrest's eyes as he continued: "I can't believe he's gone. I keep checking the mail for another letter. I got the last one a week after he died. Marie just sits in her chair. She doesn't talk or cook or anything. And Jamie, well, she calls every day and cries.

"Jamie is talking about selling the house in Tucson and moving back in with her parents in Georgia. I think we are going to lose her, too. No grandchildren. We have nothing left. I am afraid Marie is giving up on life. I hated to leave her at home but she insisted I come. I think she just wanted to be left alone for a while."

The room grew silent except for the thumping of Henrietta's tail on the floor as he lay his head on Forrest's lap. Outside, the wind rustled the leaves through the trees and softly whistled around the corners of the house. Dusty, Sarah and Lola sat without comment as Forrest shared his story of grief. This was the first time Lola had heard him talk about Reed's death. All she had known was that Reed had died on August 9, 2005. Forrest had called her the night he got the news and asked her to meet him at the stable. There, in the midst of the smell of horses and hay, he told her: "My boy is dead. His body will be coming home in a few days. I would like you to come to the funeral. I have to go take care of Marie now."

Lola had watched him walk away that night, Henrietta at his heels. Roxie nickered softly as Forrest climbed into his truck and drove away.

Lola snapped back to the cozy room where the four of them sat, the last of the aromas of Sarah's cooking fading into memory. The room was growing cold and with a last nod and a final sip of his coffee, Forrest stood.

"Well, I'm going to bed. Goodnight everyone and thanks for listening. Sorry to have burdened you."

"No burden, Forrest. We're glad you're here." Sarah's voice was soft and gentle. "Goodnight."

The camaraderie and warmth that drew Lola to the ranch was wrapped around Forrest like a Pendleton blanket. The ranch was truly a place of healing for all who came. During the next few days, each morning and evening, Dusty, Lola and Forrest rode the ranch. Some evenings, Sarah joined them and the four would watch the sun set over the hills. Henrietta accompanied them, often bounding ahead in search of forest treasures.

Lola and Forrest good-naturedly grumbled that the excellent meals Sarah put on the rough-hewn table thrice daily had added ten pounds. Day by day, the summer edged toward the autumnal equinox and they spoke of the coming snow. Many times they saw deer, wild turkeys, and hawks going about their daily rituals. As the sun set over the ridge of hills, a golden eagle was often seen gliding over the terrain and sailing on the air currents down into the valley.

On their horseback excursions around the ranch, Dusty rode his Indian pony, a recent acquisition from the ranch next door. The pony was only a generation removed from the mustangs that had roamed the area. He was sturdy and calm but ever alert to sounds and events only he was aware of. The red pony, returned to his origins, stepped out at a fast pace on the trails up the hills. He remembered well the old paths and snorted as he climbed the mountains, looking for cattle as he went.

Dusty often amused Forrest and Lola with his tales of missed shots while hunting, recalcitrant cattle, and tiny chickadees that sang in the bushes outside his bedroom window. He knew the healing power of companionship and listened compassionately to Forrest's stories of his son and of the shattered dreams he and his wife had had for their only child.

At night all four of them shared the swing on the back porch and swatted away the mosquitoes. Their idle chatter, simple discussions of the day's events, and the price of alfalfa was intermingled with soft laughter. The moon would rise and the coyotes would bark. Sometimes, as they waited for one of them to call an end to the day, a small bat would fly by. Its eyes shone in the mist that rose from the pond in the pasture where, by day, the horses grazed.

On the final morning of their trip, Forrest, Dusty and Lola took one last ride out across the ranch. They trotted over the hills to where Devils Tower could be seen in the distance. To the west, a rainbow glowed against the backdrop of black clouds while to the east, the sun shone brightly. The tall golden grass of late summer rippled in waves around the horses' legs. The three horses shifted on their feet and the red pony bent down to scratch his face on his leg. Roxie shook his head and, as the storm blew off to the north, Forrest reached into his pocket. He pulled out a letter that was folded into tiny squares. With great care, he opened the letter and began to read:

Dear Dad,

I love you. Tell Mom I am fine and, please, don't show her this letter.

Dad, I cannot take it any more. I miss you and Mom and Jamie so much. I cannot believe the pain I see every day, the loss of life. I cannot believe I am part of this. Dad, I can't go on. I want to come home. Please, don't be angry with me and don't tell Mom. I love you. Kiss Jamie for me and, no matter what, tell her and Mom I love them.

Your son,

Reed

P.S. Forgive me, Dad. This is the only way I can think of to get home for good.

Lola and Dusty turned toward Forrest with looks of shock on their faces. The bottom of the letter was covered with rust-colored splatters. Forrest looked across to the Tower, his face hidden. For a month he had kept this secret. As they watched, Forrest pulled a lighter from the front pocket of his jeans. He climbed off Roxie and squatted on the ground. As he held the letter aloft in the air, he set it on fire. It turned from paper to ash as the storm swept over the ranch and began to spill out rain in sheets. The wind increased in velocity and, as the last of the letter burned, the embers and remnants spiraled upward into the sky.

Forrest's face crumbled as the letter burned. "Maybe if he had held on, things might have gotten better."

A few hours later, it was time to load the horses into their trailer and begin the long trip back to the coast. The red pony gazed around him one last time as he entered the trailer. Softly he nickered his farewell to the other horses and the ranch, and then plunged his face into the hay bag that hung at the front of his stall. Lola gave long hugs to Sarah and Dusty and then opened the back door of the Tahoe for Henrietta to settle into his makeshift bed. He jumped onto the back seat, his eyes following Forrest's' every movement. Forrest leaned against the Tahoe and absently wiped the ever-present dust off the mirror.

"We are going home but I think I'll be back soon. Dusty, you save a spot for me on your next elk hunt. I wish Reed could have seen this place. I think he and Jamie would have loved the peacefulness you have here and would have never wanted to leave. I know I sure don't. Well, it's sad to leave, but come on, Lola. If we don't get going, we never will. We have one more stop to make. Dusty and Sarah, thanks again for your hospitality. I'll bring Marie next time even if I have to drag her kicking and screaming. I know she will love it as much as I do."

Lola and Forrest waved to the couple. Lola navigated the Tahoe and trailer down the gravel road and vanished from sight in a thick cloud of dust. Dusty and Sarah waved back and, as their guests disappeared, they walked back towards the fence beside the pasture, arms entwined around each other's waist.

"Do you think he will ever come to accept Reed's loss?" Sarah asked her husband, who stood with his arm on the railing that encircled the corral. "Do you think he will come back? Dusty, we've known so many who have either gone before us or have lost ones they love. What do you make of it all?"

"I don't know," Dusty replied. "I still wonder what became of Jones. He never answered the card you sent out to all of our previous guests. As for Forrest and what he told us. Well, all I can say is, I am hoping these wars will end soon and everyone can come home. Come on, Sarah, let's get these horses watered. I have fences to mend and I want to get to town this afternoon before the bank closes."

Forty-five minutes later and twenty miles down the road, Lola once again turned up the lane that led to the Tower. It stood as it always had—eternal, peaceful and majestic. As always, the prairie dogs whistled and time seemed suspended. Lola pulled into the parking lot much as she had when she and Auntie had come to visit so many years before.

Without a word, the two friends climbed out of the Tahoe. The smell of dust and pinesap drifted to Lola's nostrils and she could feel the smooth asphalt path beneath her feet. In the woods, Lola could see visions of faint figures of the ones that had come before, of the men and women who had lived in these woods and the animals that had roamed in freedom around the monolith. She could see a large wolf running among the trees, its eyes a peculiar unmatched pair of blue and black. Lola shook her head, certain it had been a trick of light or a ghost come to visit.

Behind her, Forrest and Henrietta slowly walked up the trail. The day's heat had sapped their energy and made them sleepy. As they continued their walk, the trio reached the bench where Lola had rested on her previous visits. They watched the river running through the green valley beneath the Tower as it made its journey to bigger rivers and, ultimately, to the Atlantic Ocean two thousand miles to the east.

"Forrest," Lola said, "I am so glad you came with me. I wish I could take your pain away. Are you ever going to tell Marie and Jamie what happened with Reed?"

Forrest shook his head and wiped the sweat from his forehead with a swipe of the blue bandana he kept tucked in his shirt pocket. He reached forward to pat Henrietta's thick coat.

"No, no. I think that is one pain they don't need. I think he was counting on me to know the truth. If he had wanted his mother and Jamie to know, he would have told me to tell them. Better that they think he died at someone else's hands rather than his own. Henrietta, what are you doing? Sit still, you old hound."

Lola looked over to see what was causing Henrietta to be so restless. She saw that he had his ears cocked forward and she heard him begin to whine. His fur stood on end as he growled low in his throat. Suddenly, with a loud bark followed by a howl, Henrietta leaped forward and sped down the rocky slope towards the valley floor. He bounded from boulder to boulder, barking furiously, his tail waving like a furry plume.

Forrest and Lola jumped to their feet. Forrest called over and over again for Henrietta to come back. As the dog raced down the hill, another figure appeared from the woods. Two howls of joy merged into one and, in that moment, Lola knew it was not a ghost but a wolf she'd seen in the woods by the Tower. As Lola and Forrest watched, the she-wolf jumped towards Henrietta's face, licking him and rubbing her head against his ruff. The Husky, his eyes questioning, looked back toward Forrest who stood, gasping in wonder, and then sat back down on the bench, his movements heavy with understanding. He realized it was time to bid Henrietta good-bye. Forrest nodded his head in farewell. Giving a 'good-bye' yip, Henrietta turned back to the she-wolf.

The sun's glowing rays lit the animals' way into the forest. The climbers' voices high up on the Tower reverberated down to Lola and Forrest. Still sitting with his sun-chapped hands loosely clasped between his legs, Forrest absorbed one more loss in his life as he stared at the spot where Henrietta had disappeared into the thick underbrush. A small brown rabbit sniffed at Lola's sneakers and, in that time and in that space, she knew a circle had been completed.

For the she-wolf, hope had risen in her heart that this winter, in her new den, with her new mate, in the shadow of the Tower, she would again bear pups. She would teach them to hunt and to stay away from humans. She would teach them the power of silence and, in the end, she would treasure the pups born with one blue and one black eye. And in the end, life would go on. The Tower would eternally guard the wolves and all of the life that lived within its domain.

⇥ 10 ⇤

The Snow Raven

Cook Lake, Wyoming   **September 22, 1999**

Four miles from Cook Lake, a lonely white bird lived deep in the piney woods. He had watched the comings and goings of the old men for decades. Every year, without them noticing, he would steal something from their camp. One rich year, he absconded four round silver buttons embossed with a buffalo head. The buttons had been sewn on the front of a blue denim shirt lying on the back bumper of a black, step-sided pickup. He had cawed with delight, wheeling off to the tip of a crooked-topped snag, and dropped each of his treasures, one by one, into the hole in the top. He neatly arranged them in a row; decaying pinecones lying next to shoelaces, a leatherman's tool, and the grandest prize of all—a metal cup that he had snatched from the campsite when the old men turned their back.

He was larger than most of the coal-colored ravens that lived around the lake. His humped beak was strong enough to crack open even the most stubborn objects he found. He cackled and crackled over his treasure trove, daily counting the items. He was ever vigilant against the black squirrels that were as brazen as he, little furry thieves who scolded the raven from the backsides of the trees.

The raven spied on the old men as they built their sweat lodges and cooked their bacon. He harassed the hound dogs that traveled with the men, swooping down to pull at their leather-studded collars. The dogs would bay as the raven dove towards them, pulling up at the last moment, laughing in unconcealed hysteria at the frustrated hounds. One or the other of the old men would come running to see what their dogs had treed, only to see them pacing in circles leaping at a wisp of white disappearing into the sky.

He was there the day the old men rescued the wolverines. He had spent the night perched on a branch just above the trapped female. He had sung to her, trying to comfort her, as the male wolverine hunted through the night, bringing food to his dying mate and to the pups that lay hidden in the den. The raven had been the first to hear and see the old truck pull down the dirt road, and he called to the wolverines that the old men had finally returned to the forest for another year.

His white feathers glistening in the Fall sunlight, the white raven watched as the old men gently released the female wolverine from the deadly snare and loaded the three crates carrying the four black and silver animals into the back of their old pickup. Unnoticed, the snow raven had flown down to the wooden bed of the truck and hidden between the crates. Not knowing of their feathery stowaway, the old men drove from the woods and down onto the plains of Kansas and Oklahoma. He had perched on the roof of the rundown motel where the old men spent the night on the long journey back to the ranch at Tarrington. He waited patiently through the night, looking for morsels of food left by uncaring and oblivious humans.

When the truck was reloaded with its endangered cargo, a snowy shadow hopped up on top of the crate carrying the little female wolverine. He poked pieces of chicken and beef into the cage, bits and bites he had salvaged from the trash bins at the back of the rundown motel. The wounded wolverine slowly munched the tidbits of food, her pain weakening her with each passing moment.

The step-side pickup rattled off the highway down the gravel road and finally rolled to a stop in front of an old faded white ranch house. The raven flew to the peak of the house, where he could observe the unusual scene below as the old men unloaded the cages carrying the wolverines. A younger man helped lift one of the plastic containers into the house, closing the door behind them. He returned to the truck and carried the other crates into the barn, disappearing for several minutes before coming back into the autumn sunlight.

One of the old men wiped the sweat from the back of his neck as he lifted the female wolverine to the bed in his bedroom. The old man caught just a flutter of white through the window as the raven flew into the air. He sailed through the barn window in the stall that held the male wolverine. As soon as night closed in, the white raven jumped to the edge of a food bin and filched a few pieces of grain before settling in the loft of the barn to get some sleep.

The ranch awoke to the cackle of the white raven. The crows that owned the trees around the ranch house screeched their indignation at the pale intruder in their midst. The black crows laughed their disdain at the raven, mocking him, and chasing him from tree to bush. Ignoring their taunts, the raven followed the young man out to the center of the ranch, watching him curiously as he built stone cairns for the wolverines. The raven flew from the open prairie back to the tree in front of the house to spy on the old men as they cared for the little female wolverine. Watched by the unseen spy, the old friends ate their breakfast, then played hand after hand of cards, all the while spinning tales of wild ponies and huge buffalo herds that had run across the unfenced fields of Oklahoma in the long ago days.

Under the watchful gaze of the white raven, one of the old men, Billy Hawk, left the next morning for Parmalee. He watched the young man, Jerome, hugging the second old man, Geronimo, good-bye. Then he followed the yellow pickup until it turned onto the highway and headed back towards Norman in the first leg of Jerome's trip home to New York for a visit. He soared over the heads of Geronimo's herd as they trotted out to pasture in the misty morning and back to the barn that night where Geronimo waited with the grain bag, singing Kiowa songs to the horses as they settled into their stalls.

The raven was the only witness to Geronimo's death two days later, cawing in distress as the old man fell to the barn floor, clutching the

cloth bag in his hands. He saw the last smile come to Geronimo's face and heard the words "deliver me from evil" as the old man died.

The white ghost stood sentinel over the old man's body for three days, ensuring that none of the marauding mice and rats that prowled the barn disturbed Geronimo's peace. On the morning of the third day, a white vehicle drove into the yard and a man in a blue uniform came into the barn. He knelt beside the body of the old man and felt for a pulse. He rose to his feet and left the barn, calling softly to the horses waiting in the paddock. With the door ajar, the old bloodhound and the three black-and-white cats came in to pay their last respects to the old man who had loved them and cared for them over the years.

The call came to the ranch at Parmalee seven days after Billy Hawk had left the ranch at Tarrington. Janice picked up the phone to hear Jerome's teary voice.

"Janice, this is Jerome, can you put Billy on the phone? I really need to talk to him. Get on the extension, Janice. I can't say this more than once. Where's Jake? You need to get him, too."

"Oh God, Jerome. He's dead, isn't he? He died right after Billy left, didn't he? Billy knew it. Billy's done nothing but cry since he came back from Tarrington. Oh, Jerome, I am so sorry. Where are you? Billy, pick up the line in the kitchen."

Janice sank into the couch cushions, her heart starting to break as she listened to Jerome tell the story. Geronimo had been found by the postman in the aisle of the barn, an open grain bag clutched in his hands. He had been dead for three days; the herd of horses Geronimo loved so much was waiting patiently in the paddock, the house unlocked and the dog and cats unfed.

The pastor's hoarse voice passed the news to Geronimo's grandson, Frank, at his brownstone in New York City. Frank listened in detached silence as the old pastor gave him the sad information. Muttering a brief "Thank you," he hung up the phone noting the information about the funeral home director on a pink tablet lying by the phone. He stared out the window into a rain-spattered night, remembering the old man who had loved him so dearly and then turned him out into the cold, cruel and bitter world.

"Jerome," Frank called to his youngest son who was standing in the dining room listening to his father's side of the conversation. "Pack your bags. Your great-grandfather is dead and we're leaving for Tulsa in the morning. I guess this will be a short visit home for you. It figures the old man would die right in the middle of your time at home with your family. Go on, get ready."

Frank's voice held the bitterness of fifty years of anger at his grandfather. He refused to look at his son, staring instead at the towers of light that marked the unforgettable skyline of New York City on an early fall day.

Jerome flew from New York to Tulsa with his father, driving the last miles to Tarrington in an unbroken silence. Frank was furious at the timing of Geronimo's death. Once more, the old man had shown a lack of consideration and concern, dying at such a time as to cause the delay of Frank's middle son's wedding. The white ranch house and red barn stood empty save the horses, cats, and hound dog that mourned the old man's passing as surely as did Jerome.

Jerome, sitting on Geronimo's bed, responded to the questions that came over the phone line from the ranch in Parmalee.

"No," he said, his mother and brothers had not come to Tarrington.

"Yes", he said, his father was at the ranch with him. Frank had already gotten rid of the horses and Jerome was going to take the dogs and cats back to Norman with him. The pastor from the church in Tarrington had been caring for the animals since Geronimo's body had been found.

"No," he said, his father was not going to have a memorial service. He was too anxious to get back to New York City and his business as soon as possible.

"Yes," Jerome said, Geronimo had been buried the day before. The attendees at the funeral included only himself and a preacher as old as Geronimo saying the 23rd Psalm as his great-grandfather was laid to rest.

Up on the ranch in Parmalee, Billy leaned his head back over the chair on which he sat. He remembered the young boy who had spoken to him in Kiowa all those long years ago. He placed the phone back into the cradle and made his way to the small bedroom that had been his for nearly three quarters of a century. He lay down on the bed and watched as the room spun around him.

"Good-bye, Geronimo Barse," Billy whispered. "Fly with the eagle. Good-bye, my friend. Say hello to all of those in the spirit world, Geronimo Barse, and tell Creator thanks for sending you to me."

Later that day, Jerome sat on the wooden floor of Geronimo's bedroom. He heard his father pacing through the house, pulling drawers open and banging doors closed. A dark blue footlocker stood at the end of Geronimo's bed, its latches closed but the lock hanging open. Jerome opened the footlocker and there, in front of his eyes, was the history of his great-grandfather's life. A tray lay over the clothes packed in neat stacks in the bottom of the footlocker. Envelopes with the ranch's address on them filled the tray along with large folders neatly marked, detailing the years on the ranch. They contained photographs, report cards, horse and cattle registrations, dental records and pads of numbers noting every cent of income and expenses for each day since 1925, the year Geronimo had come home to the ranch from Genoa.

Under the tray were wool uniforms in a variety of sizes; buffalo head nickels sewn onto the flaps on the shoulders. Four white baptismal gowns were tucked into a corner of the trunk, neatly labeled "Frank," "Ruby," "Margaret," and "Belinda." On top of the baptismal gowns was a pale blue sheet of parchment paper. Beautifully inscribed on the parchment were the words, "A good name is to be chosen rather than great riches, and loving favor is better than silver or gold." Jerome, entranced by his finds, did not hear his father come into the bedroom.

"What are you doing, Jerome? Get this garbage picked up. The appraiser will be here in a few minutes. This place can't be sold soon enough for me. What is that you're holding?"

Frank grabbed angrily at a long white envelope, embossed with the words "Final Will and Testament of Geronimo Yi Pay Barse." He pulled the pages of the will out of the envelop and quickly scanned them, his tortoise shell glasses perched on his aquiline nose, the sleeve of the Ralph Lauren shirt sliding back to reveal his gold Rolex.

Jerome continued his search through the trunk, finding next a photograph of a small boy leaning against the tall legs of an older man, a somber and pensive expression on the boy's face. Long black braids framing the child's face appeared to blow in the wind. A new grave was clearly visible in the background of the picture, a rounded mound of dirt heaped to the side. He raised his head in surprise as his father gave a snort of disgust and threw the pages of the will into Jerome's lap.

"Damn that old man. He turned me out again. Well, congratulations, Jerome, the ranch and everything on it are yours. He left me a dollar, damn that old man. Here, this is yours. Damn him. He did it to me again."

"Dad, what are you talking about? What do you mean he left the ranch to me? What about Gary and Gerald? What do they get?" Jerome stood up in alarm, his voice rising as his father punched the door jamb with a fist and stalked out of the room, the sound of the screen door slamming and the expensive rental car engine turning over. A few seconds later, the screech of tires and the gunning of the engine told Jerome his father was gone.

Jerome bent down and picked up Geronimo's will, the pages fluttering in a small breeze blowing through the window. He could see the empty paddocks where only hours before there had been a herd of horses. He had overheard his father ranting about Geronimo to a woman with long black hair and a thin man who stood at her side. A yellow trailer pulled by a large diesel truck had creaked under the weight of the horses being loaded. The black-haired woman had said only a few words to Frank before climbing into the truck along with the thin man. The truck and trailer pulled away, the horses so beloved by Geronimo were gone from the ranch in a matter of minutes.

The snow raven chortled in glee as the wheels of Frank's rental car squealed in the dust heading to Tulsa and then on to New York City. Ignoring the taunts of the black crows that lived in the cottonwood trees near the ranch house, the raven rode the air currents over the ranch, finally landing on a branch of a tree hanging out over a cool lazy creek, a hundred yards from the rock homes of the wolverines of Tarrington.

Just above the branch where the raven perched was a hollow filled with bits of shiny metal gleaned from the farrier's trailer, along with a few rusty nails, a yellow streamer from one of Geronimo's ribbon shirts, and his most beloved possession, a three-piece Mylar horse bit stolen from the tack room in the barn. It had taken all of the raven's strength to carry the bit to the hollow in the tree but the sight of the metal and brass bit brought joy to the bird's heart. It was a joy he rarely knew. His sorrow was caused by the rejection of his kind due to his pure white feathers and his odd love of humans.

He stood guard over the wolverines, smiling as the little female limped down to the creek to drink, her pups bounding behind. He spied on the other animals living on the ranch, noting their movements and activities the way a surveillance camera monitored a shopping mall.

Back at the ranch house, Jerome wandered the empty rooms, reading the words of the will one by one. It was as his father said—everything on the ranch and the ten thousand acres now belonged to Jerome Frank Barse. Ten thousand dollars was bequeathed to both Gary and Gerald Barse, with a gift of one hundred thousand dollars to be provided to his mother for "her sainthood in staying married to Frank Jerome Barse" for so many years. Should Jerome Frank Barse die without issue, he read on, the ranch was to pass to Jake George of Parmalee, South Dakota. An inheritance of five hundred thousand dollars was left to Billy Hawk, and one of equal size to both Janice Leary and Jake George.

A trust fund of one hundred sixty thousand dollars was to provide care to Andre and Renee Barse and any issue for "their natural lives." Two final bequeaths were listed at the end of the will; one was a grant of two million dollars to the Kiowa Warrior Society and one to the Nature Conservancy specifically for the purchase of lands to foster the restoration of the endangered wolverine in the mountains of the West. All told, Geronimo's estate was worth well over forty million dollars, a staggering and unfathomable amount for a simple man who never dressed more elegantly than in an orange NASCAR tee-shirt and a faded pair of black jeans.

The will was signed and dated the day Billy had left for Parmalee and Jerome had departed for Norman and then on to New York City. The executor was one Pastor Huston Brown; the attorney one Wesley Leonard Manderson of Tarrington, Oklahoma. As he finished reading the will, Jerome went to stand by the bedroom window. Sun-streaked clouds slid across the wide sky of the Oklahoma prairies. The tall grass bent in front of a gust of wind, a fairy dust of dandelions seeds floating through the air.

A flapping sound caught Jerome's attention. A tattered blue ribbon shirt hung from a post marking the edge of the paddock. A small brown coyote trotted across the yard in front of the house, his head turning as he eyed Jerome.

A profound silence echoed through the halls of the old house, whispers and sighs speaking of those who had lived there across the century. A single drop of water fell into the steel kitchen sink, the metallic sound as musical as the pluck of a harp. The screen door creaked and a light step crossed the porch. A rattle of a chain against the wooden floor of the living room followed the closing of the front door. The old bloodhound, followed by the three cats, padded into the room where Geronimo had spent his nights. The old hound placed his cold nose against Jerome's hand and nudged him. Jerome looked down at the four animals sitting on the floor in front of him.

"Come on, guys, let's get you some food. I guess I'll be moving down to live with you. That wonderful old man. I can't believe this is mine. Come on, George, let's go take a walk and figure out how we're going to get some horses back in that paddock.

Parmalee, South Dakota   **September 11, 2001**

The day had dawned a bit overcast with a light rain predicted for morning and a sunny afternoon to follow. Billy sat on his yoga mat in front of the television tuned, as it was every morning, to CNN. Janice stood between the kitchen and the living room, her hands on her slim hips, turquoise rings flashing, as she asked Billy for the hundredth time how he could do either down dog or up dog watching the never-ending gloom that spat from the talking heads of the news channels. Billy ignored her and continued his practice, moving smoothly into a sun salutation. He had taken up yoga after Geronimo's death, his morning practice now occupying the time previously reserved for Geronimo's phone calls.

Janice rolled her eyes and began to step through the door to call Jake for breakfast when she heard Billy's gasp. She swung back to make sure the old man; now sitting on the green mat with his legs stretched out in front of him, was all right. A look of horror swept over Billy's face as he watched the small screen. Janice looked to where Billy's eyes were fixed and there it was, a tall silver and blue building in flames. A second plane sped across the screen careening into the other silver and blue tower, a fireball shooting out the side of the building, the shape of the jet appearing in the flames that shot into the air.

Janice stared transfixed at the television screen as Billy started to weep, tears of grief streaking his sad and ancient face. He pulled his thin knees into his chest and reached out for Janice's hand. She kissed it and lowered herself to the floor beside her beloved great-uncle.

"It's war, Janice," Billy said, his voice resigned and hushed. "Call Jake, tell him to come inside."

Janice nodded and stepped outside to the front yard. She shivered as if the day was in the middle of winter instead of the end of a warm and dry summer. Around her a faint mist rose from the ground and a thousand eyes appeared. In unison, the eyes closed and vanished. Janice, feeling sick to her stomach, called for Jake across the front pasture, preparing herself to tell him the horrendous events of the past twenty minutes.

⇥ ⇤

In the ranch house at Tarrington, Jerome sat at the kitchen table finishing his third cup of coffee. The small television on top of the bookshelf next to the stove held his attention. His eyes took in the horrific scene in New York City, black smoke billowing from the buildings where he once believed God lived and the weather was made, the buildings that had grown up with him, the ones that graced the view from his parents' brownstone. The old bloodhound roused from the braided rug at Jerome's feet. He shook himself, turned in a circle and lay back down on the floor, the three black-and-white cats pushing against him, oblivious to the catastrophe unfolding a thousand miles to the east.

The cordless phone Jerome had purchased when he moved to the ranch two years earlier rang, the caller ID telling him it was Frank Barse calling. Without taking his eyes from the television, Jerome picked up the phone and spoke into the receiver:

"I'll be home as soon as I can, Mom. Is Dad okay? I saw it, Mom. Where are Gerald and Gary? Okay, good. No, Mom, of course I didn't know Dad was in Florida visiting the boys. How would I know that? Mom, I don't think this is the right time to discuss Dad's anger at Geronimo. Yes, I know he was hurt but, Mom, it's not my fault. Mom, look out the window. Do you see what's happening? No, I don't know who it was. Okay, Mom. I am fine. Tell Dad and the boys I will be home as soon as I can get someone to take care of the ranch. Yes, Mom, I love you, too."

The phone rang a second time. He pushed the talk button and it was Janice's voice, low and tense.

"Jerome, is your family okay? Are they safe? Are you going home? If you want to go, Jake is willing to come and take care of the ranch."

"Thanks, Janice. I am going to take you up on your offer. I was going to fly home from Tulsa but it looks like things will be shut down for some time. Oh, God, Janice. God, help us. Did you see that? The towers are coming down. Oh, my God, all those people. I have to go, Janice. I need to try to reach my family again. I will call you back."

Jerome stared in disbelief as the top of one of the silver and blue towers tilted to the left and then, as if it was the proverbial stack of cards, the building collapsed, story upon story upon story. An encompassing cloud of black dust, debris, smoke and ash rolled through the streets of New York City. Screaming people ran in front of it as if trying to escape from the hot lava of a volcanic eruption. Jerome shuddered and stood, reaching over the oblivious animals to touch the screen. A sense of doom and the world changing washed over him. He tapped in the numbers of his father's brownstone in New York City as if in a dream, praying for his mother's voice to answer at the other end. Jerome's body shook and his teeth chattered as he listened to the ringing of the phone.

The phone rang two more times and then cut off into a metallic voice announcing that all circuits were busy. He tried the call again. Once more, the disembodied voice told him to try his call later. He cried out in physical pain as the second tower fell into oblivion, voices from the dust and ashes screaming the names of their loved ones as millions of tons of rubble stole away their breath and stopped their hearts.

In the old house outside of Parmalee, Jake sat on the floor next to Billy listening to television voices attempting to explain a reality that none could accept. Billy sat totally still, his back to Jake, his gray unbraided hair spread over his shoulders. Janice stood in the doorway. All eyes were locked on the tiny television screen in the small living room. The pandemonium crowding the screen seemed too enormous to be contained within the square black box. Janice held the white telephone receiver in her hand, her turquoise and silver bracelets catching and shredding the light into shards of color on the white wall over Billy's head.

"Billy," Janice said, "Jerome's on the phone. His father and brothers are safe for now but he can't reach any of his family. He says their house is only a mile from the towers. He wants Jake to come down to Tarrington but he says he needs to talk to you first, something about Renee and Andre. He says he's worried about their safety if he should leave. What's he talking about, Billy?"

"Hand me the phone, Janice. I'll talk to him. I know who he is concerned about, let me talk to him."

Billy struggled to stand, stumbling over Jake's legs as he reached across his great-grandson and took the receiver from Janice's hand. He listened in silence as Jerome spoke:

"Billy, the wolverines are doing well. Renee barely limps and Andre is fine. The little ones are grown now. I've made them new homes a half a mile from their parents and there are three new cubs. You need to tell Jake about the wolverines, Billy. I don't want them hurt or neglected. I know how much you and Geronimo loved them. "

"Jerome," Billy replied, "don't worry about anything on the ranch. Jake will be down in the next day or so. Go ahead and pack and get ready to hit the road. Call us as soon as you can reach your family again." Billy's voice trembled as he said good-bye and handed the phone back to Janice. Billy broke into deep, soul-shaking sobs, his heart shattering as the towers fell, cutting short the lives of thousands of innocent souls. Only a few other times in his entire life had he succumbed to such raw grief.

Two confusing days passed after the towers crumbled to the ground. They were a blur of cross-country calls, mixed with confusion, sorrow, anger, fear and despair. Once the phone lines cleared, Jerome's mother called him nearly every hour, crying nonstop as she recounted the events of September 11, 2001 that had unfolded outside the windows of the brownstone. The dust and debris of the destroyed silver buildings coated the city, making the air difficult to breathe, and clogging the mind with horror. She begged Jerome to come home as quickly as he could, declaring that only the knowledge of her youngest son's safety could ease her grief over the terror that had occurred outside the windows of her formerly safe and unsullied house.

Jake arrived at the ranch late on the evening of Thursday, September 13, 2001, a long stock trailer following behind the old Chevy Cheyenne. Jerome heard the neighing and whinnying of horses and the stamping of feet against the wood floor of the trailer. The radio of the old truck, a Bose stereo system recently installed by Jerome, blared an old Merle Haggard song:

> "*I'm proud to be an Okie from Muskogee;*
> *A place where even squares can have a ball...*"

The music cut off as Jake shifted the old truck into Park and shut off the engine.

"Hey, George!" Jake's voice called to the old hound dog on the porch from beside the dusty paddock. "Where are your cat buddies? Jerome, hey Jerome! Come on out and see what Billy and Janice sent down to you."

The bloodhound and the three black-and-white cats scooted themselves out from the cool space beneath the front porch. The ancient bloodhound waddled on arthritic legs and stood in front of Jake, panting and smiling as his long tail wagged. The three cats milled around, rubbing Jake's ankles in feline welcome. It was a serene and homey scene dropped down into the scary world of 9/11, a "Wizard of Oz" moment of color and surprise between the howling tornadoes of the events of September 2001.

Jerome pushed through the screen door of the ranch house, his hair long and braided, and a pair of jeans riding low on his hips, a leather belt with a beaded buckle shining from his waist. His shirt was blue with a running horse over the pocket. Embroidery under the pocket read "G-J Ranch." A dusty pair of work boots, beaten and battered from the elements of the earth, waited on the wooden porch for his feet.

"Glad to see you, Jake. I've got the truck packed and ready to go. Let me show you around and what I need to have taken care of. Jake, what are those horses doing here?" Jerome pulled on his boots, the hollow thud of heels as he stepped down to where Jake stood grinning by the big stock trailer.

""Well, Billy heard about what your dad did with the horses after Geronimo died. Billy knows Dusty Plesent so we know they are in a good place but a real ranch needs horses. Help me get the gate open and take a look."

Jake lifted the handle and pulled open the swinging gate. The head of a large roan Appaloosa was turned towards the open light. The horse's eyes were huge and brown, and gazed at him with a curious look. Behind the Appaloosa gelding was a small bay gelding, mane and tail black, black stockings running up his legs. He was nearly identical to the red pony that had gone from the ranch years earlier. Yet one more horse stood shifting its weight at the front of the trailer. A chestnut mare whinnied and stepped back, pulling on her halter.

"Oh, Lordy, Jake. He sent me horses, quarter horses and an Appaloosa at that. Ah, Jake, that blessed old man. Where's the bill and I'll give you a check. Man, those are pretty horses. Let's get them out."

Jerome climbed into the trailer and, one by one, led the horses out into the light of the Oklahoma afternoon and into the paddock that had stood empty and lonely for so long.

"There's some alfalfa and grass hay in the back of the truck, Jerome. Didn't know what you'd have here, if anything, to feed them. I talked to Ferris at the grange in town. He's hauling a truck of hay out here tomorrow and we'll stock the loft. Billy said something about your dad hating the horses and wanting to sell the ranch. Billy was pretty damn thrilled to hear Geronimo had left it to you. Bet your dad was furious. Billy also said to tell you not to bother writing a check. These are presents for you from him."

"Ah, Billy!" Jerome said: "What a wonderful old man you are! Yep, Jake. That about sums it up in terms of my father. Anyway, what are their names?" Jerome asked, his foot on the bottom slat of the fence that had been newly replaced, watching the horses explore their new homes.

Jake's eyes took in the fresh coat of white paint on the ranch house, the floor of the porch stained and shiny. A weather vane in the shape of a shooting star topped the chimney, spinning in a slow circle in the breeze. He turned slowly noting the barn had a fresh coat of red paint. The fields of grain and hay had been harvested and golden stubble covered the brown earth. A huge green swinging gate hung to the side of the fence lining the dirt road into the ranch. A sign hung over the gate with the letters "G-J Ranch" hanging from the crossbeam.

"So you finally named the ranch?" Jake pursed his lip, nodded his head and looked around. "This place looks great. Geronimo would be proud. He knew you'd take good care of the ranch. Billy said I'm supposed to ask you about Andre and Renee. Said it was some kind of secret and that it was my job while you're gone to check on them. Wouldn't tell me a thing about them but Janice knew. She was smirking about them when I left the ranch."

Jerome grinned: "Let's get the horses settled and I'll take you out to meet Renee and Andre.

Half an hour later, with George sitting between them on the bench seat of the pickup truck, Jerome pulled up near where six odd stacks of stones stood. A creek ran in through the field in back of the stone mounds. Small alder, birch and willow trees were planted along the creek and at the sides of the man-made caves. Though small, they offered a measure of shade to both the fish in the creek and the wolverines living on the prairie.

Jerome opened his door, telling George to "stay," and climbed out of the truck. He reached behind the seat and pulled out a bag of soup bones and one of dog food. He winked at Jake's confusion and put his fingers to his lips, whistling as loudly as possible. A wolverine of medium size, limping slightly, appeared at the entrance to one of the stone mounds. She sniffed the air and looked around. A second wolverine, this one larger, ran towards Jerome from the creek. Behind the female, three juvenile wolverines appeared and, with one last whistle, two more adult wolverines ran towards the truck.

The bloodhound began baying when he saw the wolverine but remained in the truck, licking Jake's hand as Jake stared out the windshield in disbelief. Jerome laughed as he shook the bag of dog food and slung the plastic sack of bones down to the ground. The ground around the dens had been planted in the tall yellow prairie grass. Jake looked closer past the wolverines, finally noticing large silver dog bowls placed in front of the mounds.

"Jerome, are you kidding me? You have a pack of wolverines living on the ranch? Holy cow! That's what Billy was so mysterious about."

Jerome grinned. "Come on out. They don't bite. Just stand by the truck and watch. George, stay in the truck!"

"Jerome, how did a pack of wolverines get here? Does anyone around here know?" Jake shook his head at the strangeness of watching seven wolverines eating out of dog bowls in the middle of a ranch in the middle of Oklahoma. The sight was so bizarre he felt he had dropped through the rabbit's hole or crawled through the looking glass.

The bloodhound shook his head and whined, pawing the dashboard. He panted and then licked the inside of the window. Jake rapped on the glass, turning back to watch the wolverines. He noticed one had a wide stripe of scar tissue around her right front paw. She growled every time one of the other wolverines looked her way. The two smallest wolverines finished their meals long before the larger ones, scampered away and disappeared into one of the rock dens.

"Geez, Jerome. Tell me the story." Jake laughed at the antics of the gorgeous black and silver animals. "How do you keep them alive? Man, I know an awful lot of people around here that would want them dead."

Jerome walked around the front of the yellow pickup. He wiped the dust off the headlights and dropped the bag of dog food in the dust, kicking it with his foot.

"I wonder why Billy didn't tell you, Jake. Didn't think there were any secrets up in Parmalee."

"That's no answer. Come on, give it up, Jerome."

Jerome laughed as, one by one, the wolverines licked their bowls and returned to their dens.

"Billy and Geronimo found the first four up in the mountains past Cook Lake. They went up to camp and do ceremony, you know, like they did every summer. The female, the one with the scar on her paw, was caught in a trap. The male was guarding her and there were two little ones in a den. Billy and Geronimo, somehow, I never knew how, got them back to the ranch. They've been here for two years. I made the dens and I feed them every day. The pretty one with the scar, I guess she knew we were going to help her. She never fought the old men or tried to bite us when Geronimo changed her dressing.

"We had them in the barn when they first got here. Geronimo named them Renee, Andre, Danielle, and Pierre. When the three smallest were born, I named them Suzette, Yvette, and Yves.

"There's no one else who lives on the ranch, Jake. When I need help, I hire some of the high school kids out of Tarrington High School. No one is allowed out to this part of the ranch. This is the part of the ranch Geronimo kept in its natural state. I'm planning on them remaining here forever. This is a secret from the rest of the world, Jake, but I don't know why Billy didn't tell you. Those two old men, I don't know, Jake. You know, Geronimo died the week the wolverines came home with them. I think it was his last act of kindness."

Jerome leaned against the hot metal of the hood of the yellow pickup. "Jake, I tell you. It was strange. I was surfing the net one night and came across a painting of Saint Jerome pulling a thorn out of a lion's paw. I just about fell over, Jake. There's the evidence. My great-grandfather, named for Saint Geronimo, saving the life of a wolverine. I broke down and cried, Jake. I truly loved that old man."

Jerome sighed, slapped the hood of the truck, and picked up the bag of dog food, scattering a handful across the prairie grass. Two Rhode Island Reds and two Leghorn chickens strutted at the edge of the creek behind the rock dens. Chicken feathers floated on the bit of a blue breeze that ruffled the hair of the two men.

"Meat on the leg, huh, Jerome?" Jake grunted.

"Well, I figure if they can catch them, they can have them." Jerome pulled open the door on the driver's side of the truck and tucked the dog food back behind the seat.

"Move over, George!" He pushed the bloodhound across the seat and slid under the wheel. He paused before turning over the engine, his hands flat on the dashboard. He stared out the window as the falling sun cast an orange tinged light across the wildness of the Oklahoma landscape, the rock dens the only structures of any size for as far as the eye could see.

"You know, Jake, I grew up in sight of those towers. My dad used to take us there every time my aunts came to visit New York City. My dad never got over losing his sisters or his mom and dad. He was furious when I moved to Norman to go to school. I didn't think he would ever talk to me again. We were okay for a while but now he's so angry about Geronimo leaving me the ranch.

"He blamed me for turning Geronimo against him again. Says I grew my braids just to spite him. I guess he forgot how he wore them as a child. Geronimo never cut his braids that I know of once he was discharged from the Army. He was going to cut them when my aunts died. He said it was a sacrifice of love to honor them. But, I think Billy talked him out of it. I wrapped Geronimo's braids in white when we buried him.

"I'm leaving for New York in the morning. Two reasons. I need to see my family and my hometown but I also know they need rescue workers up there. I have such a bad feeling about all of this, Jake. I think there will be a war. You know the worst part? My dad will make billions off of any war. I don't know if Mom has told him I will be staying at their house. Jake, when we get back to the house, there are some things I need to show you. I don't know why, but I have this feeling that some things in this world will never be the same."

Jake said nothing, his eyes taking in the raw beauty of the country. A hawk flew overhead and then landed ten feet in front of the truck. *Remember this moment,* Jake thought to himself. *It won't come again.*

Jerome started the truck as the female wolverine peeked out of her den, winking and smiling at Jake, her head lying on the paw Geronimo had healed.

Back at the house, Jake sat at the foot of Geronimo's bed, packets of pictures in his lap, a can of Miller Lite on the floor next to him, a bag of Ruffles open on the pillow. Jake ate one chip and handed the next one to George. The lamp next to Geronimo's bed cast a pool of illumination across the room, the night breeze teasing the curtains. The young men had been reading through the faded letters and studying the pictures that covered a span of nearly ninety years. Tears ran silently down Jake's cheeks. He wiped them off with the cool beer can, the condensation on the can soothing the skin that had been burned under the late summer Oklahoma sun. He cleared his throat and nudged Jerome's leg with his foot.

"Look at this one, Jerome. It's Billy and Geronimo during their first week at the boarding school. Look at those faces. Here's one of them in the Army. They've seen it all. Hey, if you are going to leave early in the morning, you should get to bed. I can pick all this up. Jerome, did you ever think Billy and Geronimo knew some special magic, something, I don't know what, that kept them from going crazy? I mean, look what they lost. It's a miracle they could still love. I wish Billy would teach me Sioux. He says I will learn if I just listen to him talk to the cows."

"Wait one minute, Jake, there is one more thing I want you to see." Jerome pulled out a long white envelope and handed it to Jake. Jake pulled out the folded pages and began to read. He reached the third page of the packet of heavy paper and a look of shock passed over his face. In the pages of the will was another envelope.

"Open it up, Jake. There's something for you, Janice and Billy in there. We closed probate last week. I'll see you in the morning." Jerome stood up and snapped his fingers. "Come on, George. Let's go get the cats and go to bed."

Jerome's footsteps faded as he walked through the rooms of the house, the front door opening and then closing again. A second door closed and Jake was alone in the room of the old Kiowa man, a sheet of paper in his hand and three checks fluttering to the floor. Tenderly, with the spirits of the old men around him, he laid the will on the trunk. He pulled off his shirt, socks and pants and climbed in between the soft sheets of the bed. He reached over and shut off the lamp, the only light in the room now from the ambient light outside the window. A moon shadow of the elm tree outside appeared on the wall of the bedroom, and then disappeared. Jake stared at the ceiling for a moment, turning on his side. He became startled as a ghost in the form of a large white raven flew in front of the window, a low chuckle reaching Jake's ear as he fell asleep.

Jake awoke to the sound of the yellow pickup pulling away from the house. The noise of the engine was accompanied by the howl of the bloodhound and the running beats of horses' hooves. The three black-and-white cats sat on Jake's chest, staring at him with their unblinking green eyes. He laughed and pushed them off his chest, flipping back the covers and standing up, his strong young body a reflection of Billy Hawk's at the age of twenty. He stood by the window watching Jerome drive away, a spattering of gravel flung up as the truck spun its wheels and rolled away in a whirlwind of Oklahoma dust.

"You crazy old men. Look where we are now, Geronimo Barse and Billy Hawk. Three generations later, here we are now. Drive safe, Jerome. Give my best to New York City. Maybe this time, your Dad will stop being so angry. Drive safe."

Unseen, the raven crouched in the back of Jerome's pickup, hitching a ride to unknown places much the same as two years earlier when the old men drove from Cook Lake to Tarrington. It took two days for Jerome to make his way to New York City. He drove through the countryside of Pennsylvania, detouring on a side trip to Shanksville. At the edge of a forest, in a field of green, a crater opened into the earth, a burial site where lay the heroes of United Flight 93. He stood a mile away from the crash site, a white raven flying overhead, a piece of ragged clothing held in its beak. Jerome linked his fingers behind his head, stretching his shoulders stiff and aching from the long drive.

Jerome felt the soil give way under his feet and with it, a sighing of the earth as it accepted the forty passengers and crew of Flight 93, the shadow of the giant plane speeding across the landscape, forever marking the changing of the world.

The highway seemed endless as Jerome pushed through the final miles to his hometown. He had been deeply shaken by his moments at Shanksville, a dawning in his core of what was to come when he finally reached the brownstone.

He entered the city through the Holland Tunnel; coming into the solemn metropolis at seven o'clock on the evening of Saturday, September 15, 2001. An oppressive cloud of smoke and ash hung in the air. The two enormous silver and blue buildings that had defined Jerome's childhood were gone, the cityscape empty, the roads littered with the aftermath of the collapsed towers. An eerie silence hovered like a toxic cloud over the city. The low clouds were lit from below by the kliegs that illuminated the stacks of steaming and still-burning twisted rubble. Jerome drove slowly through the streets, the pavement glistening in front of him. The only traffic on the usual bustling streets was official police, rescuers, and excavation equipment.

"Armageddon, Revelations, or just plain evil," Jerome whispered into the air. The lights of the dashboard washed his face in sapphire blue. The family brownstone with its wide steps, elegant wrought iron railings, and hanging baskets of flowers, seemed surreal to Jerome. He stopped the truck in front of the house, leaving the engine running, wondering if he had the courage to climb the stairs and face his father.

As he surveyed the wooden front door topped by a frosted window engraved with the initials "FJB," a feminine face peered out the window. Andie Barse had been impatiently waiting for her prodigal son. The face disappeared from the glass. When she reappeared she was captured in the light of the opened front door, a pinkish hue framing her face. She stood under the same hanging lamp in the shape of a flower that Jerome had always feared would drop on his head. The odd thought passed through his weary brain as he shut off the engine and climbed out, pulling a battered army green duffel bag from the passenger's seat. He faced his mother, her eyes hooded from the indirect light. She wore a white silk blouse and pink slacks, matching perfectly the color of the flowered lamp.

Jerome's black eyes met the blue ones of his mother who, at fifty-five, retained an elegance and grace rarely seen in women half her age. She stepped to the side as Jerome, carrying the heavy duffel bag, climbed the granite stairs and entered the foyer. He dropped the bag on the white marble floor with its ribbons of green and black. Andie closed the door and hugged her missing son; holding him at arm's length to inspect every inch of him and then pulling him close again. Neither she nor Jerome saw the pale shadow of the raven fly to the iron lamppost in front of the brownstone; his flawless white a stark contrast to the black and blowing dust that covered the crying city.

A deep voice called from the living room for Andie and there was his father. Frank, strangely, appeared smaller and shorter than Jerome remembered.

"So, you finally left the ranch and Geronimo? Left him in the ground where he belongs, did you? Did you come here for something other than to gloat over his rejecting me one more time? I've always wondered, Jerome, just exactly how did you convince him to leave the ranch to you? What was it you said against me? Damn that old bastard. And why are you wearing those damn braids and what the hell is that on your shirt? NASCAR? Do you think we're some rednecks living out in the wilds of the west or deep in the heart of Dixie?" Frank's voice was harsh and unforgiving as he swirled the ice in his fine crystal tumbler, the brown liquid sloshing up over the side of the glass and spilling on the marble floor

Jerome wearily shook his head; "Nice to see you, too, Dad. As loving and charming as ever. Haven't seen you since you squealed out of the driveway at the ranch. No flies on you, huh, Dad? I'm home because, Dad, you forget, I'm an EMT. You know, a person who tries to help in emergencies. Look out the window, Dad, has it escaped your notice that there's a disaster out there? Oh, jeez, Dad. This is not right. Look out there, can't you, just once, stop hating? Don't you get it? Look at what hate has brought to all of us, Dad! It's time for some healing, here, now and in your heart, Dad. Jesus, Dad, stop it, just for once."

The air in the room grew hotter with tension and anger and the smell of rejection. The pink light from the flower lamp hanging from the ceiling seemed an odd accompaniment to the standoff below. Andie, in her role as the peacemaker of the family, wrung her hands, breaking the heavy silence with a nervous laugh. She picked up a silver bell on the high rosewood table that stood across from the front door. She shook it lightly and a petite Hispanic woman appeared dressed in a pink uniform with a white apron tied around her waist.

"Rosella, this is my youngest son, Jerome. He'll be with us for a while. His room is the one at the top of the staircase and to the left. It's too late for dinner but I'm sure you can find something for him to eat."

Andie looked pleadingly at her husband and son, so alike in their faces and so different in their hearts and souls. "Please, you two, it's been so long. Let's be a family, at least for now."

Jerome held up his hands in surrender.

"Dad, Geronimo did not hate you. He loved you. He hated your rejection of his ways and the kindness he gave you, but he loved you and missed you. I never asked for the ranch and I never asked for the money. I didn't even know he had it. Listen, the only reason I am here is because I heard they needed rescue workers at the towers. I'm just going to be here until the cleanup is done. I'm not fighting with you, Dad. I'm not here for any more family drama. This time, Dad, it's not about us."

Jerome, dressed in his black jeans and orange NASCAR shirt, was clearly out of place in the refined and rarified atmosphere of his parents' home. Shaking his head in frustration, he shrugged his shoulders, walked into the cavernous living room, and went to look out the picture window. His gaze was fixed on the tragedy that continued to unfold, second, after minute, after hour, into a black eternity. He could see his father and mother's reflections in the thick glass, one standing to either side of him, looking for all the world like the happy family that had once lived in the shadow of the majestic silver and blue buildings.

Jerome stepped away from the window and back into the foyer. He picked up his duffel bag and climbed yet one more set of marbled stairs, the mahogany railing smooth beneath his hand, Rosella's pink-clad back leading the way. Pink ribbons had been wound between the dark wood of the supports. *No doubt*, Jerome thought, *another one of Mom's decorating schemes!*

Through the windows facing the street, Jerome could see the hell of 9/11, thousands of ghosts calling out to him; their voices shrill with the coming of death. He saw the images of people jumping from a height of a thousand feet, the air streaming past them in their last seconds of life. A young woman floated down in front of Jerome's eyes, brown hair streaming, her hands holding a blue skirt against her legs. He closed his eyes tightly against the images, imposed now on his eyelids for all eternity. The horror shown on the television in Tarrington seemed insignificant in comparison to the real-life scenes of destruction so close to his home. Below him, in the living room, his mother and father stood, posed as if they were life-size dolls, waiting for the hand of Frank's God to bring them back to life.

Rosella, a somber woman near Andie's age, gently pushed open the door to Jerome's room. She switched on the light, stepped to the side, nodded and started back down the marble staircase. Jerome's room was exactly as he had left it eight years before. The bed was neatly made, covered by a striped black-and-white bedspread, matching pillows at the head of the bed, and a black wool blanket at the foot. A picture window made up one wall and through the window Jerome could see the smoldering agony of Ground Zero. He dropped his duffel bag and pressed his body up against the glass. "I'll be with you in the morning. Please wait for me before you leave this earth," he whispered.

As he spoke, a snow white raven jumped from a branch of a tree to the ledge of Jerome's window. The raven's eyes were midnight black instead of the red of the true albino. The bird turned his head from side to side as if trying to converse with Jerome. In his beak, he held a bottle cap. As Jerome watched in puzzlement, the raven carefully laid the bottle cap on the ledge; Jerome noticed half a dozen caps already lined up on the ledge outside the dark window. Finished with his duty, the raven flew back to the branch of the tree, staring at Jerome, who slowly closed the blinds and turned to ready himself for bed.

Next morning, the dining room table was covered with an embroidered pink tablecloth; pink seeming to be the color of the day, of every day. Chills prickled Jerome's spine as he sat down at the huge table Frank had purchased in Milan and shipped to New York City, as if there weren't equally large tables to be had close by. The ghastly scene of the previous night was minimal in its ability to shock compared to the reality of 9/11 in daylight. Andie sat at the head of the table, her left hand with its enormous pink diamond catching the light from the windows and throwing prisms onto the light pink walls. Her hands were folded primly in her lap, her hair neatly curled, white pearls circling her still-smooth neck. She beamed, for a fleeting moment, at her youngest son, her smile fading as he spoke:

"Mom, I'm going down to Ground Zero to work. I've already been in contact with the relief agencies. I'll be back sometime this afternoon or tonight." Jerome's voice echoed into the quiet room, a pink napkin clutched in his right hand under the edge of the table.

"Where's Dad? I thought he'd want to be here for his morning lecture? Oh, yeah, church in the morning to erase your sins before screwing millions out of money. Yep, that's my old man. And you can tell him for me, Mom, I'm not cutting my braids."

Andie sighed in resignation and slipped into a chair across the table from Jerome, the seat of the chair newly upholstered in pink with tiny white flowers embroidered into the fabric. The whole room seemed ludicrous to Jerome, a fancy breakfast in a pink room with crystal juice glasses while outside the world died. He shook his head and placed a small bite of scrambled egg into his mouth, chewing it as if it was dried shoe leather. The clink of silverware against china was Jerome's undoing. He pushed back his chair, sliding it over the pink carpet, and stood up. He made his way around the table, kissed his mother on the cheek, and opened the front door.

A thought came to Jerome's mind and then to his lips before he could halt the words:

"Mom, Geronimo was right. Dad is an ungrateful bastard. He had the best of everything and he destroyed it. I'll pay for my room and board while I'm here. Jesus, Mom, look at the world around you. Does anyone in this house even get it? It's not you, Mom. I just can't believe Dad can still cultivate hate when all it does is kill. Never mind, Mom. I'll see you tonight."

The walk to the rescue and recovery center took about fifteen minutes from the brownstone. Jerome, in the milling crowd of workers, found the police lieutenant in charge of sifting through the tons of rubble in the northeast corner of where the South tower once stood.

"No," the lieutenant said, they had not found any survivors beyond the few that had been rescued that first day.

"No", he said, they did not know if anyone could have survived the collapse of the towers.

"Yes, tools will be provided, talk to the man in the black coat with the FDNY on the back, the one with the thick moustache. No, there are no surgical masks available yet but there should be a supply by noon. Thanks for coming and let's get started." The lieutenant shook his head at the grim and never-ending task ahead of him and pointed Jerome towards the other police officer.

Wearing another pair of black jeans and a green long-sleeved shirt, Jerome joined the line of rescue and recovery workers, carefully moving bits of metal, paper, ceiling tiles, and ash. The work was grueling, the dust choking off the breath of the workers.

"This must have been what they felt, "Jerome shuddered, grasping a shovel in his hand and moving the first pile of debris. Nothing could have prepared Jerome for the scene that surrounded him. The wind off the Hudson River moaned through the tattered, defiantly standing remnants of the tower, the twisted iron destined to become the symbol of the awfulness of September 11, 2001.

Day by day, shovel-by-shovel, Jerome toiled along with hundreds of others. Late autumn arrived and with it came cold rains and moisture-laden ash filling the sky. The pictures of the missing lined wooden walls, candles flickered in the dusk and dawn as the sad year of 2001 came to an end and the invasion and war in Afghanistan began. Jerome, on the rare breaks he took, ate his lunch or a quick snack leaning against a piece of wall or a gigantic earthmover that had been turned off for a brief few minutes by its weary operator. Few words passed between the men and women on the line, hope turning to a hard acceptance that their goal was no longer rescue but recovery of the remains of those who died; remains that would bring a family inconsolable grief mixed with the relief of having something tangible to bury.

Jerome returned to the elegant spotless brownstone well after night-fall, walking down the emptying streets of Manhattan as the hookers took up their places for the nighttime trade. The pink flower lamp was always on and a place was set at the table. Regardless of the time of day, Andie sat at the dining room table waiting to share dinner with her youngest son, her hands folded and her wedding rings gleaming. Jerome, his body cramping and fatigued, would methodically move his hand to his mouth, nodding at whatever comment his mother would make.

The only sighting Jerome usually had of his father was the back of Frank's head above the back of a pink recliner, his black hair neatly groomed, the daily issue of the *Wall Street Journal* rattling like a rattle-snake. After eating, Jerome would walk quietly into the living room; kiss his father on the top of his head, and head up the marble staircase. In his bedroom he had installed a private phone line and a laptop computer. Each night he would call Jake, asking about the condition of the ranch and the welfare of the wolverines. He would open his email as Jake recounted the events of the day and the antics of the much-loved silver and black animals. Yes, Jake admitted, George and the cats had taken to sleeping with him on Geronimo's bed. Yes, he added, Janice and Billy were fine and wanted Jerome to call them.

Each email contained photos of the horses, cattle, birds, cats, and wolverines that resided on the ranch. Jerome longed for the peace and solitude of the ranch, sniffing back tears as he clicked on each photo. He opened his email after a particularly bad day at Ground Zero, a day where dozens of bits of bones and scraps of clothing had been found. Jake had sent a picture of the female wolverine taken at ground level, peering into the camera's lens, her scarred right paw crossed over her left. Her eyes shone with a light of resiliency and hope, a poignant reminder of survival in a brutal world.

A river of grief, loss, sorrow and pain finally flooded Jerome's heart and soul, crashing over the barriers of restraint that had contained his emotions since he had set foot in his father's home. A sorrowful cry escaped his lips and he sank to the plush white carpet that covered the floor. The dirt and ash of Ground Zero left brown and gray smudges on the immaculate carpet, staining the spotless surface as the falling towers had stained the souls of millions.

A faint knock on the door brought Jerome back to the present moment, his back stiffening as Frank pushed open the door and stepped into the space crowded with the sound of Jerome's pain. Jerome looked up at his father, his black eyes filled with dread and the deep knowledge of death that had come from his time in the grim remnants of the once-magnificent towers. A floorboard creaked under the thick carpet as Frank walked across the floor and stood over his grieving son. He squatted next to Jerome and placed his hand on his son's neck.

"I am sorry, Jerome. I'm not saying I was wrong, Jerome, but I am sorry about Geronimo's death. I'm sorry for my mother and father's death and I am sorry for the deaths of my sisters. Every night, before you come home, Jerome, I stare out that window and think of what you used to tell me as a child. Do you remember, Jerome? You would sit on my lap and tell me that God lived at the top of the towers and that's where He created the weather. I am sorry, Jerome, every day I am sorry."

Frank's voice turned wistful, the first glimpse of vulnerability Jerome had ever seen his father display. "Your brothers called tonight from Palm Beach. They are staying home for the holidays this year but both send you their love. Your sisters-in-law are fine Christian women a lot like your mother. Maybe next year we can all be together, Jerome, I'm glad you came home and I am sorry. Okay, that's it. Goodnight, son. I am proud of you."

Jerome stared up in confusion at his father. Frank nodded once and then shook his head. He pushed to his feet, gently touched his son's cheek, then let himself out of the room.

Outside on the ledge, in his usual perch, the white raven stared at the scene between Jerome and his father. The ghostly bird seemed more ghostly than ever, tendrils of white mist swirling around his body, appearing and disappearing in the ribbons of fog. The raven's treasure trove had grown to include pieces of bones and material from Ground Zero and, evermore, he defended his booty from the curious squirrels of New York City.

Thanksgiving and Christmas came and went in the brownstone, a pink wreath hanging from the front door. A silver artificial tree, covered in pink ribbons, ornaments and lights, stood in full holiday glory shining into the city night through the picture window in the front room. Presents wrapped in silver with perfectly tied pink ribbons and bows leaned in stacks against the tree stand. The tree, with an embarrassment of riches underneath its branches, was a jarring sight to Jerome each night as he entered the house, covered in soot and sorrow. Rosella would welcome him in to the warmth of the pristine rooms, taking his coat and handing him a hot towel.

Jerome had refused Andie's plea to stay home from Ground Zero with her and Frank on Christmas Day. It was his first Christmas home in eight years, she said. It was important that he attend services with his father and, really, it was the only gift Frank wanted. Please, she asked, couldn't he just take this one day of all days off?

Jerome sat on the floor in the foyer, pulling on his work boots, tying and retying them as he listened to his mother's plea. No, he responded, he would not take the day off. Didn't she understand, all of those families on this day without their loved ones? Yes, he would come home early for Christmas dinner, but truth be told, it was excruciating for him to celebrate when so many mourned.

Andie sighed and opened the door for her youngest son, ignoring the biting cold and wind that rattled her teeth and chilled her thin body in its pink cashmere dress. A wisp of her frosted blonde hair fell across her eyes, blurring her vision as Jerome, huddled in a black quilted coat, disappeared down the block.

The holidays passed in the elegant brownstone, snow falling on some days, cold winter sun shining on others. Freezing rain spat down on the recovery workers as their bitter tasks continued. A squad of relief workers from Baton Rogue, Louisiana, joined the crews in January. Two of the crew were Seminole Indians, transplanted Floridians whose mother was Creole. Their names, oddly enough, were Alexander (Alex) and Alexandra (Alley) Dupree. They were two years apart in age. Both were forensic scientists who had learned their skills working for the New Orleans Police Department for four years after college before returning to the town so oddly named after a "red stick."

The Duprees were wiry and strong, meticulous in their work and gregarious in their manner. Under her coveralls, Alexandra wore a polka dot blouse and blue jeans. Her brother inevitably dressed in a Michigan Wolverines sweatshirt, a thick banded steel watch wrapped around his right wrist. The connection between Jerome and the Duprees was instantaneous and deep. It was based on the shared heritage of their

Native roots and their confessions of fear that were so often worn under the stoicism of getting through each day at Ground Zero.

The friendship of the three young people grew as they combed the rubble for something, anything, to give the families and friends of the ones who died. A fine dust, grainy as the ashes of cremated bodies, choked their throats and nostrils and burned their eyes. Over time, Jerome and the Duprees shared tales of their families; their joys and pains, their hopes and their anxieties. One cold, snowy, winter day, Alley bent over the delicate task of cleaning off a small piece that had been uncovered during that day's recovery efforts.

The bone was partially wrapped in a blue skirt stained with the sacred earth of Ground Zero. Jerome and Alex carefully cleared the space around the remains of a young woman. A high-pitched whistle sounded overhead as two peregrine falcons dove from inside the swirling winter clouds and raced towards the hallowed ground. The graceful raptors came within inches of where Jerome and the Duprees stood, pulling up as the earth came to meet them and then racing back into the New York City sky.

Alley, snowflakes spotting her blue coveralls, reached her hand toward the heavens, called a farewell to the guardians of the souls of 9/11. Jerome, moved to tears, reached for the cold hands of his companions, squeezed them tightly, and sang a Kiowa prayer Geronimo had taught him many years before. He looked up to where the chain link fence enclosed the graves of three thousand men, women and children. Two female figures stood at the fence, one leaning against it holding the links as the other, wrapped in a gray coat, watched the work going on beneath them in the deep pit of Ground Zero. The shorter woman dropped to the ground, the taller woman crouching beside her companion, cuddling her close in the dim light of a winter's day.

The women huddled together for a few moments and then came to their feet, sliding in the snow as they left the site of such an epic tragedy Seconds later, the smaller of the two women came to an abrupt halt, bending down to pick up something lying on the ground. The two women leaned in toward each other, their gray coats giving the impression of two New York City doves snuggled together for protection against the cruel bite of winter.

"Come on, Jerome," Alley called, "we need some help here. See if you can grab that piece of metal and slide it to the right. Alex, turn the blade of your shovel just half an inch. Okay, let's move her."

As delicately as a mother laying her baby in a bassinet, the three friends pulled the femur and skirt onto a blue plastic tarp. The material crinkled, giving off a whisper of sound and a smell of decay. Together, in a coordinated movement gleaned from the never-ending hours of labor at the gravesite of three thousand souls, the three friends carried the tarp to a recovery vehicle, headlights shining into the murky atmosphere of Ground Zero.

Jerome leaned against the black hearse, his head down and his arms wrapped around his shaking body. He coughed, wiped his face on the sleeve of his coat, and bent over at the waist. The smell of smoke and death filled his lungs and he coughed again, his lungs straining for air.

"I'm going home, you two. I don't feel good; think I'm getting a cold or something. Let me tell the Captain and I'll get someone to cover for me." Jerome coughed again, his face suddenly pale and sweaty. "I'll see you in the morning."

"Hey, Jerome!" Alley called as Jerome coughed again, leaning against the cold metal of the black station wagon for support. "Let me walk you home, you look terrible. Come on. Hey, Alex, I'll catch up with you back at the apartment. Come on Jerome, let's get you out of the cold."

The two young people slowly made their way over the sad remains of the buildings. The klieg lights gave the landscape a bizarre appearance, worse than Dante's *Inferno* and his circles of hell. Behind the couple, a voice yelled, "Look out!" as a pile of rubble shifted and slid down to the floor of the crater. A crackling of glass and a pile of metal rolled in a small avalanche down the north side of the pit, rescue workers scrambling to escape the falling debris. Jerome and Alley stuttered in their steps and whirled around to see where Alex was as the last of the ash and mud, burned papers and shards of metal rained from the sky once again. Alex was crouched in the protection of the black station wagon. He waved his hand at Jerome and Alex, motioning that he was safe and for them to go on. Grit and grime coated the winter streets, red banners in the store windows announcing "50% off" sales for everything from lingerie to washers and dryers. Once again, Jerome was shocked by the juxtaposition of the gaudiness of New York City commercialism and the bloodstained earth of Ground Zero.

The couple hurried through the icy darkness of the January evening, reaching the brownstone in record time. Andie stood in the entry to the living room, the curved arch giving her the appearance of a Madonna statue placed in a niche of a stucco wall. Jerome began to cough, blood foaming on his lips as he stepped over the threshold into the softly lit foyer. He coughed one last time, fell to the floor, and rolled onto his face.

"Frank! Call 9-1-1," Andie screamed as Alley knelt beside Jerome, his blood staining Alley's jacket and overalls. Jerome's eyes were unfocused and his breathing became increasingly shallow, sounding more as if it was the last efforts of a dying man than the young and vital man who had left the brownstone earlier that morning.

Andie, Frank and Alley followed the white ambulance, riding to the hospital in the black stretch limo that Frank kept at the ready. Andie twisted her large pink diamond on her left ring finger, reached to take her husband's hand, age spots faintly showing on the back of his hands that were softer than the cashmere of Andie's pinstriped pink suit. She had asked Alley what happened that day and withdrew in horror at the graphic description of the dirty piece of bone wrapped in the remnants of a blue skirt.

Frank's mind re-played the sight of his son's limp body in the foyer, Jerome's blood slowly spreading across the marble floor. He thought back to the day he stood beside his grandmother Agatha's grave and wondered if he would soon be standing in a black suit next to Jerome's. He stared through the window of the limousine. The windshield seemed to be blocks ahead of the back seat where he sat with his wife of thirty-plus years and a young woman who seemed to know his son better than he could possibly imagine.

Frank traced the lines of the blue veins on Andie's hand, feeling the blood pulse through them. He remembered Jerome leaning against his legs as a child, staring out the huge plate glass window at the wondrous blue and silver buildings that now lay in smoking ruins..

"God, my God," Frank whispered, "please, don't take my boy. I acknowledge my sins and my anger. I give over my will to you. God, please don't take my son. Grant me this prayer, God, and I will dedicate my life to you."

The lights of the New York streets and the red and blue pulsing strobe lights of the ambulance invaded the darkness of the sleek limousine following behind the emergency vehicle. The ride to Lenox Hill Hospital seemed to last an agonizing eternity.

Finally, the rear door was banged open against the sides as the two female attendants removed the stretcher with Jerome strapped at the chest and feet. The sheet covering him was blood-stained and a thin line of red dribbled down his chin. A cannula was placed in his nostrils and an IV hung from a steel pole, the needle in the back of Jerome's left hand. No one noticed the pale shadow raven who had silently flown behind the ambulance through the wet streets of New York.

The attendants brushed aside any questions as they rushed into the emergency room, two smock-clad nurses at their sides. Jerome and the medical personnel disappeared from sight into the treating rooms, an admissions clerk asking Andie, Frank and Alley questions as to what had happened. The clerk suggested they take seats in the sickly yellow waiting room. The fluorescent lights made the starkness of the overly crowded room even more claustrophobic.

Thirty minutes passed before a white-coated physician appeared. His skin was dark, a long black braid lying neatly along the back of his coat. His hands were strong, the fingers elegant but ending in raggedly chewed and tobacco-stained nails. He held a clipboard in his hand and absent-mindedly flipped through the yellow, green, white and pink papers clipped to the plastic. Deep lines ran from the corners of his mouth as he finally raised his head to speak.

"It's a good thing your son was healthy. He's bleeding from both lungs and is being transfused. As soon as he is stable, we'll send him for a chest x-ray but my best guess is he's got pneumonia and pulmonary obstructions. He was able to talk some. He told me he is a recovery worker at Ground Zero. My best guess is he's inhaled too much of the toxic chemicals, dust and pulverized glass at the site. We've started seeing this problem in the last few months.

"Are you Alley? He said you were a close friend and he wanted you to come in when we get him more stable and back from x-rays. Give me another hour and when we get him upstairs to a room, you can all visit."

The doctor, a man in his early fifties, rolled his head on his shoulders, easing the muscle tension that came with the often grim task of sewing bodies, removing bullets, and explaining that there was nothing more the medical profession could offer an old man in the last throes of emphysema.

The long night passed. The ER physician or an exhausted nurse in blue cotton pants and a smock with dancing bears on it would step into the waiting room to provide updates to the three exhausted people sitting in the spine-aching gray plastic chairs. It was not until early in the hours of January 12, 2002, twelve hours after Jerome's collapse, that a definitive word finally came.

This time, the physician who came to speak with them was a petite blonde woman, no more than thirty years old, with tortoise-shell glasses hanging from a beaded cord around her neck. She wore green scrubs, the crimson of dried blood leaving a macabre Rorschach on her sleeves.

Alley, Andie and Frank blinked and stared into the eyes of the young woman. Andie sprang to her feet in alarm. Before Andie could utter a word, the young woman held up a hand:

"I'm Dr. Tangley, your son's physician for his stay here at Lenox. He's fine, sleeping and sedated. His lungs, as Dr. Aranui told you, were bleeding. He's got pneumonia and an enlarged heart. The bleeding from his lungs has stopped. We gave him three units of blood and his vitals are back in the normal range. We're going to keep him for a few days and, hopefully, send him home. His lungs are pretty damaged and it looks like he's got a good start on COPD. His days as a recovery worker are done. You all can go in but don't plan on staying too long. You can come back later this afternoon. He's lucky you got him here when you did.

"You know," she said sadly, "this is only the beginning of what is happening at Ground Zero. I don't think we'll ever know the total loss from September 11th. By the way, Ms. Barse, get to the New York City Department of Labor and Industries and get the paperwork to file a medical claim on behalf of your son. His working days are pretty much a thing of the past."

Three days into Jerome's confinement at Lenox, Andie arrived at the hospital early in the morning. She was dressed in a pink linen blouse and cream linen slacks. Fresh flowers, a *People* magazine, and *The New York Times*, peeked from under the cover of a woven basket. Her frosted blonde hair was perfectly coiffed and her makeup, as always, freshly applied. She wore immaculate cream-colored pumps, a fashion faux pas that Andie had, astonishingly, ignored.

Jerome's room overlooked Park Avenue, his window situated in such a way as to allow him an expansive view of some of the priciest real estate in New York City. Andie was scandalized by the skimpy gowns in which Jerome was dressed. She had brought him new dark blue satin pajamas piped in sky blue. A matching robe lay on the top of the woven basket along with expensive brown slippers lined in sheep's wool. That third day she had also brought shampoo and demanded a male assistant help her ailing son into the shower, to wash the dust, debris and stench of Ground Zero from his body. Jerome, his lungs painful and compressed, allowed his mother to dress him, ministering to him as if he was the small child she had once washed and held.

Jerome, his IV line held tight to his arm with a plastic board and mesh wrap, sat limply on the edge of the bed in his pajamas. His mother brushed his long black hair, a few stray grays showing at the part. Andie plucked the white strands from her youngest son's scalp and gently brushed his long hair, braiding it with loving care and tying it in red silk cloth. Jerome closed his eyes as his mother tended to him. Images of Geronimo in his NASCAR tee shirt and black jeans burned inside his eyelids, the old man's voice calling directions out to him as Jerome rounded up horses and set sprinklers in the hay fields.

Images of him on the hood of the yellow pickup truck flickered through his exhausted mind; pictures of the wolverines scampering to their silver bowls and then down to the crisp clear creek eased his fear. He had believed he was dying the first night he had been brought to the hospital, a gush of blood coming from his lungs, Alley's horrified face bent over him. He had seen her black eyes crinkled at the corners, a small diamond stud sparkling on the left side of her nose as she held his head up. The smell of iron gagged Jerome that night, his panic increasing when he realized it was from his own body. The memories of the good and the sad, the hopeful and the bad, fought for space in his mind.

"Mom," Jerome finally asked his third day at Lenox, "where's Dad? Why hasn't he been here? Why hasn't he called? Is he angry with me? Gary and Gerald called. Jake's called and so have Billy and Janice. Why isn't Dad here?"

Andie, her back turned to her son, paused in her task of arranging the pink carnations and white roses she had brought. Unseen, her smooth brow furrowed. She shook her head, the loose curls at the back of her neck fluttering with the almost imperceptible movement of her head.

"He's in Florida with your brothers, Jerome. He had a business trip and decided to stay a few extra days. He'll be home in a week. I'm sorry, my darling, he was here the night they brought you in. He spent the whole night waiting to find out you were okay. The doctors told him you were fine so he left. I thought that Gary or Gerald might have told you."

A hydraulic drill sounded outside on the street, the *clack clack clack* of the blade covering up the thunder thumping through Jerome's heart. He could see the smoke of Ground Zero curling through canyons and valleys of the great city. A grainy mist obscured the tops of the buildings. Pigeons cooing and strutting on the ledge seemed remarkably calm and undisturbed by the noise, congestion and confusion of the city.

"Mom, Alley was here last night. She and Alex are leaving for Baton Rogue tomorrow. Mom, why do you think they would name a town after a red baton? Does that make any sense to you? Huh, you know, Mom? I mean, are we all crazy?"

Jerome's sobs cluttered the room, bouncing off the yellow walls and curling through the broken pieces of Andie's heart.

"I'm in love with Alley, Mom. I know Dad will never accept her because she's not white enough for him and she believes in her traditions. It doesn't matter that she is smart and sweet, and loving. No, he is so busy denying who he is and being angry. Mom, I love you but I'm going home to Tarrington as soon as I get out of here. Mom, did you ever read Geronimo's will? You know, the part where he left you the hundred thousand dollars? Remember what it said? Because you stayed with Dad for so long. It should have been a million dollars, Mom.

"I know why he hates me, Mom. I remind him of Geronimo. He thinks I stole his money from him. Mom, all he had to do was love Geronimo and accept him. Now, look at us. Mom, I'm going back to Oklahoma. I'm not sure I will ever come back to New York again."

Jerome leaned back against the pillows of his hospital bed, the satin of his robe and pajamas a stark contrast to the starched and crumpled sheets. He dug the heels of his palms into his bleary eyes and gasped for breath. His lungs wheezed and crackled, a thin line of blood trickling from his right nostril.

"Go home, Mom. I'm tired. Please pack up all of my things at the house. I'm going home when they let me out of here. I know what they told you, Mom. All of you thinking you're hiding things from me. Mom, I'm not stupid. I'm an EMT. I know what's going on. I know my lungs are trashed. They won't let me back to work at Ground Zero. I can't be an EMT anymore. I'm going back to Tarrington, Mom. Please go home and pack my things. I'm going back to the ranch."

A shadow passed outside the window, the pigeons scattering into the mist as a white raven landed on the window ledge, a small gold ring held in his beak. Andie picked up the now-empty basket and left the room, her head bent beneath the pain of her son's words. Alley stood on the outside of the door, a facemask dangling from her hand, and a backpack with the initials "BRFD" on the flap hanging from one shoulder. Alley started to speak but the words died as she saw the grief-stricken mask on Andie's porcelain face.

As Andie rushed past her, Alley confronted Jerome. "What did you say to your mother? She looks like the world ended. What did you say? Where is your dad? Jerome, say something, please, say something!"

"Alley, you know, I love you. I want to marry you and take you home to the ranch. You know, after Geronimo died, he left me the ranch. It had never been named. Now I call it the 'G-J Ranch.' Alley, come home with me. Please, I love you, come home with me."

Jerome searched Alley's face, her cheeks wind-burned, her hands cracked from the cold. He reached out his hand to her. Alley slowly pulled one of the pink carnations from the crystal vase that sat on the serving tray. Her fingers caressed the fragile pink petals, feeling the lacy edges. She lowered herself onto the bed and dropped the carnation onto the pillow and took hold of Jerome's hand, carefully avoiding the plastic IV tubing.

"Jerome, Alex left for home today. He said he needed some time on the bayous and some jambalaya and boudin. He thinks we're Creole.. Makes me laugh. Although, you know, Jerome, maybe he's right. We do have a French last name."

"Alley, stop it. I'm not kidding. Marry me. Come home and meet the wolverines and Jake and Janice and Billy. Come home to Tarrington with me, please."

"Jerome, I just saw your doctor. She looked like an angry mother bear when I asked how you were. She said you need to be here for another week or more and then you could go home. She says you were bleeding from both of your lungs. Your mom filled out all of the papers for the City to pay for your care. The lieutenant knows you're not coming back. He said to tell you everyone misses you. Jerome, if you really love me, tell me tomorrow and the day after that and the day after that. If you still want me to marry you when you leave the hospital, then I'll marry you."

Alley shoved off the bed, pulling her ever-present backpack over her shoulder. Her black hair was cut short, a maroon scarf tied around her neck. She untied the wool scarf and wrapped it around Jerome's neck, her fingers caressing the rough beard on his cheeks and chin. Her black work boots squeaked as she stepped on the linoleum floor and disappeared out the door.

Unfortunately, days stretched into weeks as Jerome's lungs and heart slowly repaired themselves. His breathing gradually improved and the wheezing that had filled the small space of his sterile room lessened. Valentine's Day dawned bright and sunny. Andie brought red, pink and white carnations to Jerome's room, and had a small square blue Tiffany's box tucked inside her pink Stella McCarthy bag. A slender, black-haired woman peered over Andie's shoulder, a taller man with Alley's black eyes brought up the rear. A hospital attendant, pushing a chair in front of him, whistled a mindless tune. The blonde physician who had been caring for Jerome the past month bustled in through the door, her white coat swishing around her.

Jerome smiled at the procession filling the yellow hospital room. He stood at the window, his back to the pigeons that had kept him company for over a month. He was dressed in a pair of black jeans and a Tulane sweatshirt. His body was far thinner than on January 11th, his face gaunt but happy as the doctor handed him his discharge papers and gestured to the silver wheelchair, its seat swayed from the myriad of bodies it had transported over the years.

"You're released from prison, Jerome. Time to go home." Dr. Tangley smiled.

Jerome cleared his throat and took a deep breath into his scarred lungs. "Could you wait a minute, Dr. Tangley? I want to introduce you to everyone and I have something I want to say. Dr. Tangley, this is my mother, Andie Barse. I know you've met her already, but this is important. This is Alexander Dupree and this is my soon-to-be fiancée, Alexandra Dupree. Mom, can you hand me that blue box?" Andie beamed with an unmasked joy as she passed the small blue box to her youngest son.

"Alley, you promised to marry me if I still wanted to marry you when I went home. I'm going home and I still want to marry you. In front of all these people, I'm asking you to come home to Tarrington with me, as my wife. We can get married at Mom's. Please, Alley, tell me yes, in front of all these people and all these pigeons, marry me. I'd get down on my knees but I'd never get up again. Alley, please, marry me."

Andie, Alex, Dr. Tangley, and the hospital attendant clapped and cheered as Jerome opened the Tiffany box and slipped a star sapphire ring onto Alley's left hand. No one mentioned Frank's absence as the impromptu celebration came to an end. Then Jerome, sitting in the wheelchair with Alley on his lap, was pushed by the attendant down the hall, into the elevator and, finally, to the door of the waiting limousine.

A simple wedding was held at the brownstone four days later, the presiding judge a friend of Andie's. Andie had informed Frank of the nuptials. She begged him to come home from Florida where he had been for the month since Jerome was hospitalized, reminding him of his presence at the weddings of his two older sons. Frank had refused, insisting his work prevented his return to New York City. He had left the hospital the morning after Jerome's admission, never calling Jerome but getting twice-daily updates from Andie.

Alley, dressed in a simple white strapless gown and Jerome in a matching white tuxedo, exchanged wedding vows in front of the plate glass window. The smoldering wreckage of the World Trade Center provided a tragic background in stark and startling contrast to the joyous scene inside the luxurious brownstone. Andie poured champagne into pink crystal glasses, J and A etched into the fine crystal.

"A salute," Alex proclaimed, raising his glass to the couple "A toast to my sister and new brother. May your lives be long and blessed with joy. And, little sister, may your marriage last a lot longer than the three months I was hitched, bless Jamie's little Georgia Peach soul!"

"Mom, Alex, we have some news," Jerome grinned, tipping his champagne glass back to Alex. "Alley's pregnant. We found out this morning. Mom, you're going to be a grandmother. We were going to wait to tell you, but we're leaving for Tarrington in the morning and we wanted to tell you in person. We wanted to see the shock on your face when you counted backwards on your fingers!"

His expression changed to one of wistful longing: "I was hoping Dad would be here before we left but you can tell him the good news. Really, I do understand he's upset but I wish he had been here. He is so angry with Geronimo but Mom, that anger is misdirected at me. I hope that, someday, he'll talk to me and someday he'll come back to the ranch to see us and his grandchild."

Andie stepped between Jerome and Alley. She wrapped an arm around each of their waists and squeezed them tightly.

"Alley, welcome to the Barse family. Come back and spend time with us. You can meet Gary and Gerald. Take good care of that baby. Thank you for being there for my son. Okay, enough of all of this emotional to do. Let's get that wedding cake cut!"

The dining room table was covered in a lacy cloth, elegant dessert plates lying between silver forks and knives. The cake was two-tiered, covered with pink roses and pink ribbons. A bride and groom stood on top of the cake, a scene so stereotypically bridal that Jerome could only laugh. He placed his hand on Alley's, cutting through the soft white sponge cake, frosting clinging to the edges of the silver knife.

An hour later, the judge and Alex left the brownstone. The judge headed home to New Rochelle and Alex to JFK airport for a flight back to Baton Rogue via New Orleans. Andie and Alley lingered over the cake and coffee on the table, an easy camaraderie filling the room. A light rain fell outside, delicious dinnertime aromas wafting through the gracious rooms of the brownstone. The grandfather clock standing against the wall in the pink-hued living room chimed out the quarter hour. Jerome sat on the plush white carpet of his bedroom, faint streaks of gray marring the impeccable surface. A black laptop, its Apple logo glowing white, perched between Jerome's crossed legs, his face and long braids reflected in its screen.

"Dear Billy, Jake and Janice, check out this picture. Yep, that's me! I'm the groom and that's my new wife. Her name is Alexandra (Alley) Dupree and the good-looking guy standing behind me is her brother, Alexander (Alex) Dupree. No, they're not twins.

"Alex and Alley worked with me at Ground Zero. They're forensic scientists, like on *CSI*. You will also like this: They're Seminole and a lot of their family is from the Tarrington area. I think Geronimo would have been pleased.

"Ok, so here is the deal, Jake. We're leaving for Tarrington tomorrow. Don't laugh but we're going to Niagara Falls for a two-day honeymoon and then on down that ribbon of highway. So, figure five days and we'll be home.

"One more thing! I'm going to be a daddy in about eight months! See ya'll soon. And Jake, tell George he'll have to make room for another person in the bed!"

A familiar tip tap at the window caught Jerome's attention, pulling him up off the floor and to the window. In his usual place on the concrete ledge, the snow raven peered in through the frosty glass. For the first time, the blackness of the raven's eyes registered on Jerome's mind.

"You are my guardian angel, aren't you ghost bird? You've been with me on this journey. All those treasures on the ledge, you brought them for me. Oh bird, I know who you are. You're Geronimo come to watch over me."

Jerome pushed the window sash up and reached his hand out into the icy night. The raven rubbed his face against Jerome's fingers, gently nibbling them. He gave a small caw and flew off into the gloom. Left behind on the ledge were four white tail feathers, a gift to Jerome on his wedding night. Jerome gently lifted the feathers from the ledge, closed the window and sat back down at the computer. The unsent email waited patiently on the screen, the cursor blinking in time to the beat of Jerome's heart.

The front door creaked open and then closed as Jerome hit the SEND button. The sound of a dropped suitcase echoed off the floor in the foyer, followed by a heavy step. The feminine chatter that had been a pleasant backdrop to Jerome's laptop composing ceased. Quietly, Jerome closed the lid of the laptop, laid it on the floor, and pushed himself to his feet. A small cough made him catch his breath and then cleared. He inhaled deeply and then exhaled through his mouth, preparing himself for the confrontation sure to come as his father realized there was a new member of the family.

Jerome linked his hands behind his back and stretched his arms over his head, cracking his knuckles. He slipped his feet across the white carpet and stepped out of the room, slowly walking down the marble staircase. He blocked his father's path as Frank entered the living room, a stack of mail in his hands. He became startled as Jerome spoke his name.

"Dad, can we sit for a minute? There are some things I need to talk to you about and some questions I want to ask. I don't want to fight with you. Dad, this isn't a confrontation. We're both men now. I just want to talk to you, man to man. Please, can't we talk?"

Frank stared at his son, indeed a young man, albeit much thinner than the one he had last seen the night of January 11. Finding whatever it was he was searching for in his son's face, Frank nodded and sat down on the plush pink Louis XV couch. Jerome pulled a matching ottoman close to his father's legs, determination etched on his handsome face.

Jerome's braids were wrapped in white, a small difference that had initially escaped Frank's notice. Father and son sat in silence, their profiles and postures identical. So intent were the men on studying each other that neither noticed Andie and Alley standing at the curved entry.

"Dad, I do understand your business is important. Really, I get it. Really, I do. But, I needed you here for me. Dad, the doctors tell me I am pretty sick. Get this, Dad. I have advanced emphysema at the age of twenty-six. Isn't that a hoot? Dr. Tangley says it's from working at Ground Zero. How about that, Dad? I've got a terminal disease from air that Ms. Christine Todd Whitman herself told us was safe. Makes you want to laugh, doesn't it?

"Well, you always told me not to trust the government! Anyway, Dad, that's not the point. I needed you. Do you remember when I was a little boy and you and I would look out the windows at the Trade Center? Do you remember? I always thought God lived at the top of those buildings, Dad. Where do you think He lives now? Who makes the weather now, Dad?"

Frank leaned forward, his clasped hands dropped between his knees, a wary and confused look on his face. A knot clenched in his stomach and a flutter of fear bumped his heart. He started to speak but the expression on Jerome's face stopped the words of defensive explanation from crossing his lips.

"Dad, Alley's pregnant. We both thought I was going to die and we decided to have a baby. She got pregnant while I was in the hospital. We made love, Dad, and I watched the pigeons on the window ledge. You see, Dad, I always thought the pigeons were messengers of God, coming to our window to tell us of His love. But I just figured it out. I was wrong. White ravens are the birds that bring God's word. Pigeons are just coyote bait.

"So, Dad, here's what I want to say. Alley and I got married today. We're moving home to Tarrington. We're having a baby. I want you to know; I have never spoken a word against you, Dad, not one word. See, Dad, I loved you and Geronimo loved you, too. I have horses on the ranch again, a small herd. One of them is a big Appaloosa, Dad. I want to show you something. I was going to leave it on the table for you. But, since you're home, I'll give it to you now."

Jerome reached out and took his father's hand, once again astonished at its softness, the nails buffed, the cuticles immaculate. He turned Frank's hand over and slid a faded photograph into it. In the photo, a small boy nestled against the black-clad legs of a tall, slender man, long braids blowing in the unseen breeze, a fresh grave visible in the background.

Frank stared at the photograph taken nearly a half-century before. The look of grief on the face of his former self broke the dam of anger and sorrow that Frank had held in his core for fifty years. His eyes, red-rimmed and suddenly old, were raised to meet those of his beloved youngest son. The knot in his gut tightened and he sank to his knees, a groan of irreconcilable pain escaping from his lips. Andie started moving towards Frank, her instinct to console and comfort her husband. She felt a light touch on her sleeve. A compassionate look from Alley and a shake of her head halted Andie's forward motion, preventing any interruption of the scene in the living room.

Jerome, his young face serious and solemn, continued: "Dad, really, I do understand. I just want you to know that. The doctors told me that they don't know how long I will live, maybe a year, maybe a lifetime. In some ways, Dad, it doesn't matter."

Jerome placed his strong but scarred hands on his father's elbows. He leaned forward and laid his head on his father's shoulder.

"When I die, I want you to bury me next to Geronimo in the cemetery at Tarrington. Say the 23rd Psalm over me. Dad, Geronimo and I…well, we always loved you. I love you, Dad."

Jerome sighed, his black eyes closed, the images of the dying towers imposed on his eyelids. Without looking, he reached his hand out towards Alley and his mother, his outstretched fingers a plea for love and solace against the terrible loss in his heart and soul as his father wept.

⇥ ⇤

Neither Frank nor Andie heard the light footsteps that marked the early-morning departure of Jerome and Alley. A sepia-tinged dream full of running horses and flying doves floated around Frank's tormented mind, a familiar laugh bringing him to the edge of consciousness. Andie's petite body barely made a dent in the pillow top mattress cushioning her body, a pink wool blanket tucked under her chin. The grandfather clock announced seven o'clock to the house, breaking into Frank's sleep and pulling him into the dawn.

The house seemed to hold its breath as Frank stumbled from the bedroom to the bathroom and then down the hallway towards the luscious morning smell of coffee. The remains of the wedding party from the night before had been neatly stacked at one end of the table, the white cake missing its top layer, a half-empty bottle of champagne raising its lone head in salute.

And there, at the place where Frank had presided over the large table for thirty years, was a pristine white dessert plate, a pink napkin laid open over the fine china. A gasp of sadness escaped Frank's lips as he realized what he was seeing. In the simple pattern of a cross, their ends wrapped in white silk and their blackness a stark contrast to the joy of the scene, lay Jerome's braids on top of four long white feathers. At the sight of his son's final sacrifice, Frank's soul emptied itself of anger in a flood of tears and hope.

⇜ ⇝

Tarrington, Oklahoma   **February 23, 2002**

The moon was a silver crescent, the winter stars glowing against the black heavens as Jerome pulled into the lane leading to the small white ranch house five nights later. He shut off the engine and gently shook Alley awake.

"We're home, Baby."

A light blinked on in the house and the front door banged open, the screen door screeching in protest as it scraped across the frozen boards of the porch. A grizzled bloodhound ran stiff-legged towards Jerome, smiling as he greeted his master. Jake, his chest bare and hair mussed, waved from the front door, calling them into the house. Alley sat up, blinking her eyes and pushing her hair back from her face. A look of wonder came across her eyes as she took in the scene, a quiet joy encompassing her soul as she anticipated the life she, Jerome, and their unborn child would have on this ranch.

A quick motion, a flash of silver and a shine of eyes appeared at the corner of the barn and, there, in the faint light from the winter's moon, sat a beautiful female wolverine, a small scar of pink tissue a bracelet around her right paw.

"Jerome," Alley murmured, 'look, just like you told me, there she is. She's come to say 'Hello.' Oh, Jerome, look. I love you, and I'll love you until the day I die. Thank you, little lady, for welcoming us home."

Perched up on the roof, next to a weathervane in the shape of a shooting star, the snow raven smiled as Jerome helped Alley from the truck. He chuckled as the door to the white ranch house closed. His job done, he lifted off into the sky, in pursuit of the shooting star and in search of the waiting souls.

⇜ 11 ⇝

The Guardian Elk

Cook Lake, Wyoming   November   1843

The soft footfalls of the woman's moccasin-clad feet were barely audible over the murmur of the raindrops slipping between the needles of the ponderosa pines. A slight breeze shook droplets from the pines wetting the woman's long black hair. She was young, in her twenties at most, long in the legs and arms, and slender through the waist and hips. Her shoulders were broad and square under the white buffalo skin robe. Her face was unlined and tanned from the mountain sun. A bow of white pine hung over her shoulder and she held a quiver of arrows tipped in red stone and graced with turkey feathers for true flight.

The temperature began to drop, turning the rain to sleet and then to snow. As the snow accumulated, the woman's feet left a trail quickly covered as the wet white flakes continued to fall. She entered a hidden glade in the heart of the forest but stopped still at the sound of breaking branches. She detected feet shuffling to the right of the clearing. Suddenly a bull elk broke through the bushes. His coat matched the crystal-white snow. A majestic rack crowned his noble head. He stared at the woman with serene brown eyes. Slowly he bent his head to scratch his muzzle against his knee.

The woman stood silently as a tiny zephyr lifted the tips of her hair. She faced the elk, waiting to see what he would do. Behind her, a coyote, its belly low to the ground, timidly slunk across the wet grass. He eyed the elk and the woman before he continued into the woods. The tall grass beneath the pines gave way then closed behind the coyote, erasing any trace of his path. From the trees surrounding the woman and the elk came a cacophony of peeps and calls. Chickadees, nuthatches and brown creepers joined the chorus, their songs loudly resounding in the quiet of the forest.

Suddenly, a total silence draped the enormous bull elk and the black-haired woman. As if choreographed, the two stepped towards each other. The woman dropped the quiver of arrows to the ground and reached out both hands, tenderly stroking the elk's soft nose. She reached up and ran her fingers over his thick, muscular neck, touching her cheek to the side of his face.

The snow began falling more heavily, obscuring the trees and muting the birdcalls. A fluffy white mantle covered the buffalo robe on the woman's shoulders and the ridge of the elk's back. Sinking to his knees in the snow, the elk placed its head on the woman's moccasins. She leaned forward to touch his antlers as the elk closed his eyes and eased into the woman's soft caress. A mule deer and its yearling gingerly entered the clearing and lay down next to the elk. The coyote that had followed the woman on her trek slowly crept forward from his hiding place in the long grass and, with a soft sigh, placed his brown and black muzzle on the woman's other moccasin, his face touching the elk's.

As if called by an unheard voice, more animals slowly came forward into the clearing. A wolverine, badger, raven, black bear, and large gray wolf appeared, followed by a woodpecker, vole and beaver. As more heavy wet snowflakes fell, covering the odd assembly, a rabbit, owl and red fox stepped into the opening in the pines. Soon the clearing was full of creatures that lived in the forest. As they appeared they came closer to the woman and the elk and found their places in the circle.

A final flurry of crystallized flakes covered the landscape. As the sky began to clear, the silver moonlight illuminated the distant mountains. Frosty clouds sliced the light cast by the moon, glowed softly then disappeared into the darkness of the night sky. The snow lay in thick mounds around the inhabitants of the forest now crowded tightly together in the clearing. The animals paused in silence, waiting for the ancient signal. The tall young woman dropped her pine bow to the ground and wrapped her arms around the neck of the elk. The diminutive brown and black coyote lifted his head alertly to watch the woman. With a soft sigh, she pulled her buffalo robe around her and then knelt down in the snow, stretching her body the length of the elk's torso.

She pressed her body close against the giant animal and closed her eyes. The denizens of the forest gathered around the woman and the elk. The coyote inched closer, pushing his nose under the woman's hand. The snow began to fall again within minutes, gained in strength, and left only white mounds where once the woman, elk, coyote and forest animals lay.

Afghanistan   **January 22, 2002**

To the Far East, the snow fell in the Hindu Kush Mountains of Afghanistan and Pakistan. The timeless peaks were beautiful, blue and white in the cold winter air. A small band of men dressed in heavy coats, boots and gloves pushed through the cold plains beneath the mountains, their packs filled with dried food and clothing. Three of the men carried M-16 rifles while the man in the front of the line and the one in the rear carried sniper rifles. The men were clearly American although they were dressed in the garb of the local inhabitants. Their faces were unshaven and their hair long. They had been out on patrol for ten days, miles away from their unit and base, searching for the Taliban and the most prized of all targets, Osama Bin Laden.

Three hundred yards ahead of the Americans was another small band of men also clothed in the traditional dress of the Pashtun tribe. The trio was huddled underneath a rugged outcropping of rocks, shielding themselves from the cold and snow. They spoke quietly, arguing over the wisdom of aiding the five Americans who had been with them for nearly two weeks. The eldest of the Pashtun tribesmen gestured towards the Americans and shook his head.

"Let them go on their own. We need to return to our families. This is not our battle. We have already lost seven of our people this week. I no longer want any part of this madness."

The youngest of the three Pashtun men nodded in agreement. "I have children waiting for me in Kabul. They want to return to the village. I see no reason to continue in this battle. I think we should take them to the pass and then return to our homes. I have no argument with Bin Laden. This is not our fight. One more day, then we're going home."

The third man looked back over his shoulder as the Americans drew closer.

"You tell them, Mairanay. You speak their language. One more day."

The men shivered as the snow blew in whirls across the frozen ground. The Americans reached the spot where the Pashtun men squatted, huddled together against the biting wind. The two men carrying the sniper rifles, in identical movements, shifted their weapons from one hand to the other. The American leader, a thirty-one-year-old captain, squatted by the Pashtun men and began to speak rapidly in their dialect.

"We have to find the Canadian or American soldiers as soon as possible. Have you seen any signs of them? I don't want to be out here on our own much longer. It looks like a storm is coming in and we must find shelter. I am sorry for the loss of your comrades but we have to continue our mission."

The eldest of the three Pashtun men pulled his scarf tighter around his neck and scraped the snow away on a patch of frozen earth. He picked up a stone and carved a map into the ground. He spoke in response to the American, gesturing with his left hand, indicating to the other two Pashtun men that squatted by him and then the towering mountains to the east.

"The pass is forty-five kilometers away. We'll make camp here. The Canadians should be twenty-five kilometers ahead of us but it is hard to be sure. We need to get out of the open. There are Taliban fighters in this area. They know this area better because they live here. We want to go home and are leaving you tomorrow. We have had enough of your war. This is your battle, not ours."

The youngest of the Pashtun men spat into the snow as he stood up and wiped particles of ice from his legs. He picked up his Russian AK-47, swung it over his shoulder, and lit a cigarette. He had no use for either the Americans or the Canadians. He saw them as occupiers, as intrusive and irrelevant as the Russian invaders twenty years before. *They too, will fail in their endeavors*, he thought to himself. He and his two comrades were survivors of the Russian invasion and had, initially, agreed to aid the Americans in exchange for enough money to feed their families for a year. But, as time passed, they had become disillusioned and angry by the arrogance of the Americans and their ignorance of the Pashtun and other tribal people's cultures. The gust of wind that blew his scarf around his face exposed an opening to a small cave ahead.

"There! Let's go inside and get out of the storm. I have had enough of this nonsense. I am going home tomorrow. I am not waiting any longer. I miss my children and my wife. The Americans had the chance to take Bin Laden months ago. They want this war for their own purposes." The youngest Pashtun man was speaking sharply to the eldest.

The third Pashtun had been silent throughout the exchange. They were his seven relatives who had been killed in an avalanche five days earlier. He had buried them in the cold ground far from their family and their homes. Although the Americans helped dig the graves, they clearly did not understand the bitterness fermenting in his heart. He had had enough of the invaders and planned to leave early in the morning no matter what his companions chose to do. He was simply tired and wanted to go home.

The five Americans were part of the early contingency of Americans and Canadians who had been placed in Afghanistan in the first of many futile attempts to capture or kill Bin Laden. They had fought in parts of Tora Bora and watched the bombs fall on Kabul. The Americans, four army privates and a captain, believed passionately in the "cause." They were enraged over the September 11th attacks and vowed to get rid of the Taliban who protected and supported Bin Laden.

Two of the young soldiers were identical twins, average height but stocky. They had sandy hair and eyelashes so pale they were almost invisible. Their freckled faces made them look like Iowa corn fed boys, healthy and hearty. Curt and Todd Baines were actually from Springfield, Virginia, the sons of Marshall and Katherine Baines. Their father was a retired Army colonel who had served over thirty years with the 82nd Airborne. Their mother was a small, plump woman who adored her sons and husband, acceding to her husband's command of the house. She was a staunch evangelical Christian who attended church three times a week, raising her boys to fear the Lord even more than they feared their father.

She believed in headship and the superiority of men, giving thanks every day that she had given birth to sons. She believed that it was the duty of Christians to convert the masses to glorify Jesus, and she feared the "unwashed" would not know the glory of Heaven's salvation. Katherine did not believe in dancing, slacks for women, or drinking. When the boys were small, she read them stories of the Crusades and the search for the Holy Grail. She was utterly convinced that universities, other than Bible colleges, were bastions of evil. She was greatly relieved when her sons finished their secular education and joined the military, following in their father's path and validating the righteousness of the colonel's life.

Katherine's husband was also seen as a representative of God's Word. He had worked tirelessly to purge his units of homosexuals and anyone not demonstrating his definition of proper allegiance to America. He wept at the sight of the Towers' destruction and, at the age of sixty-one, tried to return to active duty. He was deeply disappointed when he was refused, fuming at the thought that his leadership skills would not be of value in this epic battle of good over evil.

Colonel Baines was thrilled when his sons volunteered for service in Afghanistan in response to the audacious brutality of Bin Laden. He did not differentiate between the Sunni or Shiite, Iraqi or Arab. He believed in the Bible and that the rifle was the emissary of Christ, and killing for Christ was the pathway to Heaven. He read the Greek legends of Odysseus and Homer as well as the stories of Troy and the legions of Alexander the Great. He believed God was on his side and had no doubts of the ultimate glory of victory and the American way of life.

The colonel had been a brilliant military tactician, and retired right after the first Gulf War and the Bush Administration's refusal to march into Baghdad. Colonel Baines viewed himself as a fair-minded man. He held himself and others to a high standard, brooking neither incompetence nor excuses. He viewed soldiers as pawns, and understood that in the process of war, pawns sometimes had to be sacrificed. He would go so far as to say that, at times, even rooks, knights, and bishops were expendable. However, he concluded, the king must always be protected. He loved his twin sons as deeply as any father could, and held them to the same high standards he set for himself. He was slow to praise his sons but in private spoke to his wife of his deep pride and admiration for the young men he had sired.

When the twins were fourteen years of age, the colonel and Katherine took the boys on a cross-country trip to the hills of South Dakota. They drove through the deciduous forests of the Appalachian Mountains, across open prairies, and through the Badlands, then spent several days hiking around Mount Rushmore and soaking up the history of the tiny town of Custer, South Dakota

They stayed at a small spread called the Buffalo Springs Ranch at the base of the Black Hills owned by Sarah and Dusty Plesent. The corrals of the ranch were empty, the paddock in disarray and inhabited primarily by wild turkeys and white-tailed deer. The only livable building on the property was a small yellow bunkhouse with a tiny kitchen. A half-finished shell of a large house stood on a small rise, overlooking an enormous red barn.

The colonel and his family were provided rooms at the back of the barn. Originally built for ranch hands in a bygone day, they were small but clean and warm against the encroaching autumn. The twins shared a room across a narrow hallway from their parents. A tiny bathroom with a metal sink was at the end of the hall. The aroma of hay and horses filled the area.

The first day at the ranch, Dusty refused the offers of help from the colonel and his boys. However, it was soon apparent that the colonel took this refusal as an affront to his values and, as Dusty and Sarah could not pay for ranch hands, they accepted the unexpected help with gratitude.

Every day after breakfast, the colonel, Curt, and Todd spent their time repairing fences with Dusty and listening to his stories of a huge elk that lived up in the hills. An enormous rack of antlers, light reflecting off their bony protrusions, was usually the only glimpse that the hundreds of hunters who swarmed the hills were ever privileged to see.

Katherine, in her usual way, left her men to their masculine endeavors. She chose, instead, to help Sarah with the cleaning, laundry, cooking and, at the end of the day, delighting in serving enormous meals that were devoured by the four ravenous men. Katherine sang hymns as she worked and questioned Sarah about her religious beliefs and her rate of attendance at the local Christian church.

Sarah took the questioning in a good-natured manner, assuring Katherine that her immortal soul had been saved and that she was close friends with the pastor and his wife. She redirected Katherine back to stories of her husband and sons, which Katherine was willing to share. She told Sarah about the identical twins being born twenty-two minutes apart; Todd was first and the larger of the two.

She described the closeness of the boys, a bond bred of sharing a womb and, Katherine believed, a response to her prayers for her growing belly. She shared how she read the gospels and psalms to her unborn babies, glorying in every kick, roll, and movement. Katherine smiled as she recalled the identical shirts, bicycles, shoes, baseball uniforms, slacks and shirts.

Sarah listened and nodded as Katherine spoke of her dreams of her boys graduating from high school and their father's desire for them to attend Georgetown University. She admitted to Sarah she was concerned about the Catholic religion upon which the university had been founded. However, she also confided, the colonel had spent much of his career at the Pentagon so was well versed in how to deflect the dangers of the city and the evil that resided on every corner.

Besides, Katherine added, the colonel felt Georgetown University had a solid curriculum in political science and, eventually, should the twins take their father's sage advice, an excellent law school. Personally, Katherine did not believe in lawyers but staunchly believed in God's law. However, if the colonel wanted them to go to Georgetown and become lawyers in order to work against the evil present in so much of the country, well then, he knew best and the boys would abide.

Katherine did not have any particular field of endeavor she felt her sons should pursue although she would be happy if they followed in their father's footsteps and made a career of the Army. The Army was all she had known all her married life. It had been good to her family. Even if the separations were hard, they simply tempered the steel of which her sons were made. She was looking forward to their retirement years, even more than her husband was.

Katherine confided to Sarah that she felt she had four years left to shape the boys and to ensure the salvation of their souls. Her husband encouraged a belief in one's self and an adherence to discipline. Admirable qualities, Katherine acknowledged, but she also believed Christ wanted her children to love and care for the weak and the vulnerable. Every month she took the boys to a mission to feed the poor and to teach them the value of the gifts God had bestowed on the Baines family.

For the most part, Sarah listened quietly as she went about her work. She would murmur a polite "uh-huh" at the appropriate place and "that's nice" at other times. Katherine did not seem to notice, feeling she was filled with the Glory of Jesus' spirit. Katherine was not overbearing with her faith but it was clear that her priorities in life were God first, the colonel second, and her sons third.

The last day the family was at the ranch, Sarah and Katherine finished their work and took their lunch to the yard swing on the slope below the unfinished shell of the large ranch house. Red squirrels chased around the base of the oak trees, grabbing acorns and carrying them up into their nests. Sarah laughed at the antics of the squirrels and sat down on the wood swing, patting the spot beside her as an invitation for Katherine to join her.

"Sarah," Katherine asked, "how did you and Dusty come to own the ranch? It is so peaceful here. I am such a city person but this place is wonderful. I can tell your husband is a good Christian man. Every day, I pray for my sons to meet good Christian girls. I want them to have the type of marriage you and Dusty have, one blessed by the Lord and one to last for eternity."

"Well, Katherine," Sarah replied, "it looks like you and the colonel also have a wonderful marriage and you have two handsome and good sons. It appears to me your Lord has blessed you just as he has blessed us.

"We bought this ranch with a small inheritance Dusty received from his parents. We looked for months and finally found the place. It was an absolute mess, totally in disrepair. We've worked for years to get it to this point and we still have years to go. But, we love it, and completion will come in time." Sarah sighed deeply and looked around her. She smiled to herself, thinking of the day she and Dusty first drove down the road and pulled into the dirt driveway. They had immediately christened the small spread the "Buffalo Springs Ranch." Not a day went by without the Plesents pinching themselves over their good fortune. It was Dusty's idea to start a guest ranch and, amazingly, the guests did begin to arrive, simply with word-of-mouth advertising.

Sarah's reverie was disrupted when Katherine took a deep sigh and leaned down to watch a ladybug crawling through the blades of grass in front of them. It spread its dotted wings and lifted off into the slight summer breeze. Katherine smiled and bent double, grasping the bottom of her tennis shoes with her well-manicured hands. Without looking at Sarah, her expression grew somber and she murmured, "The colonel is not an easy man to live with. He treats me with little respect and views me as part of the furniture. Oh, don't get me wrong. I love him but I am not sure he would notice my departure as long as I sent a maid in to take care of the house. He loves his sons, but mostly as extensions of himself. I have to laugh; for years he could not tell the boys apart. I am really glad he is here with the boys on this trip. I hope and pray every day that he will recognize the fine young men they are becoming, not as a reflection of him but in their own right."

Taken aback by these comments, Sarah couldn't think of how to reply. The two women sat in silence as the heavy summer air pressed down upon them. The red squirrels began to scold in the branches above them. Acorns dropped into the grass and the squirrels scurried down the tree trunk, sitting in front of Sarah and Katherine, causing both women to laugh.

"Katherine, sometimes people show their love in different ways. Maybe this time together can be the start of a better way of life. The colonel is a good man and the boys are wonderful."

Katherine shook her head and plucked several blades of grass, tearing them into small pieces and tossing them into the air. She whistled a few notes and sat back in the swing. She lightly touched Sarah on the arm.

"Sarah, do you know why I go to church so much? I don't tell people this but I feel I can trust you. The colonel has done things that are against God's Word. He has been responsible for deaths and he is unrepentant. Do you remember that movie *The Godfather*? The one where Diane Keaton goes to Mass every day to pray for the soul of her evil husband? That is the same reason I go. I pray every day and go to church to save my husband's soul. I don't want to be alone when I go to Heaven."

Katherine placed her hands back on her lap. She whistled a few more notes and then sat quietly in the swing. Sarah sat staring up into the hills that surrounded the ranch, absorbing Katherine's words. She felt the wind lightly brushing the back of her neck, lifting strands of hair and cooling her heated skin. She looked over at Katherine, noting the delicate profile, the skin soft and lined, the lashes long, and the lips curved in a gentle smile. Sarah turned back to look upon the hills, wondering how long it would be before Dusty returned with the Baines men.

Earlier that day, Dusty had asked the colonel and the boys to hike with him into the hills. There were places on the ranch from which Devils Tower could be seen, a sight well worth the walk. Dusty was also going to scout out hunting locations for the outfitters that would come that winter to stalk the mysterious elk that had eluded even the most avid of hunters. After a strenuous climb, the four men came to a clearing in the forest. A patch of grass grew in the glade nearly covering the outcropping of gray stone. The area was shaded from the late morning sun by the ponderosa pines.

Todd noticed one of the pines with scratch marks of a bear and scat at its base. Dusty shook his head, declaring that the last bear in the Black Hills had been killed years ago and that it was not likely one had wandered back into the territory. At one side of the glade, a large patch of grass had been flattened and faint tracks of an elk could be seen. Dusty squatted on his haunches and studied the tracks. He brushed his hands on his pants and nodded.

"Yes," he told his three companions. It did appear to be the hoof prints of the bull elk. Maybe, he said, the colonel and the twins could come back to the ranch in the winter someday to hunt the elk.

The weather that summer day was hot and dry. A slight wind blew through the pines, creating an eerie creaking noise. Curt, more interested in hunting than idle chatter, had wandered away from the rest of the group into the edge of the forest. The air rattling through the trees was cool and soothing. A mottled, Duskywing butterfly sat on a small twig on the forest floor, fluttering its wings in a lazy manner. Above Curt's head, a tiny barred tiger salamander scooted up a branch and bopped up and down as if to challenge Curt's intrusion.

Curt squatted down on his haunches, his hands resting on his knees. He could hear the voices of his father, brother and Dusty in the clearing. He felt a strange stirring deep in his soul, almost a calling of his spirit. For the first time in his life, he had an appreciation of his mother's deep faith. He tilted his head up and blinked his eyes at the bright light appearing through the leaves of the oaks. He lay down on the cool earth, stretched his hands above his head, and crumbled the leaves under his fingers.

Red spots peppered the inside of his eyelids as he peacefully closed his eyes. Giving way to a deep sigh, he relaxed into the ground and eased into slumber in this protective forest glen. A leaf crackled. He awoke startled, opening his eyes. A tall, slender woman with long black hair in a white buckskin dress stood above him. She held a quiver of arrows in one hand, a white bow over her shoulder, and a wide red beaded belt circled her waist. She knelt down and began stroking Curt's forehead. Leaning down, she kissed his cheek.

At the touch of her lips, Curt bolted to a sitting position; sweat running down his forehead and onto his neck. He wiped his face with the back of his hand and pushed himself to his feet. He looked around but no one was present. Once more, he could discern the voices of the three other men in the distance. He glanced about again and wiped his hands on his pants. Trembling, he thrust them deep into his pockets.

He slowly walked back to the clearing. His father, Todd and Dusty stood in a circle, laughing at a comment the colonel had made.

Dusty smiled at Curt as he joined the others. Still clouded with the memory of the woman standing over him, Curt had difficulty trying to stay focused on Dusty's words. He shook his head and pulled his hands from his pockets, crossing them on his chest.

"Well, let's go back to the ranch," Dusty suggested. "If we leave now, I can show you the eagle's nest on the bluff. They have babies every year and sometimes we can see the fledglings flying with their mama and papa. Last week, I saw the female eagle bringing a rabbit back to the nest. Go ahead of me, colonel, but watch the log!"

The colonel nodded and led the way down the path. Dusty stepped to the side, allowing Curt and Todd to move past him, as they fell in behind the straight back of their father.

"Where did you go?" Todd asked his brother as they traversed the path. "You have dirt and leaves all over your back. Did you fall?"

"Don't even ask," Curt replied, the kiss of the woman still warm on his cheek. "I just want to go home. I'm going to tell Dad I'm ready to leave. Mom's probably doing her usual thing with Sarah, telling her how wonderful we are and what a bastard dad is. You know, Todd, next time we come here, I'm going to kill that bull elk."

Curt's voice was shaky as he raised his hand in a "stop" motion. Todd stopped , then pulled away and stared at his brother. . For a moment, the twins stood silent, staring at each other, neither moving as Dusty stepped around them and followed the colonel down the trail. The moment passed and without a further word, the boys resumed their journey back to the ranch, neither of them looking at the other during the return trip.

◄ ►

Four years later, after they had started their classes at Georgetown University, the colonel took the boys to the forests of West Virginia. They stayed at the historic Hilltop Hotel, gazing across the Shenandoah Valley. Prior to the trip, the colonel bought the boys bolt-action 7 mm magnum rifles, carrying cases, binoculars, camouflage pants, jackets, vests, and hats.

Curt loved the thrill of the hunt, the gathering of camping gear, cleaning the rifles, rolling the sleeping bags, and the meticulous packing of required accoutrements. On the first hunt, he bagged a white-tailed deer, killing it with a single shot. He had no fear of the rifle and felt no revulsion over the loss of the deer's life. In keeping with the colonel's values, the deer was dressed and quartered, every edible piece wrapped and frozen for the family's consumption over the next year. The colonel did not tolerate people who hunted for trophies. He had no use for hunters who displayed their kills as proof of their manhood, believing that to be a sign of egotism and stupidity.

Todd, on the other hand, found the sport of killing intolerable. He loved the outdoors and the smell of the crisp cold air. He adored the company of his father and brother but wept uncontrollably at the sight of the dead deer hanging upside down from a notched board tied to the trees. In their senior year of college, he had refused to attend the hunt, incurring the colonel's derision and the open-palmed shrug of his brother.

The twins enlisted in the Army immediately upon their graduation from Georgetown University in 2000. The colonel and Katherine sat in the front row of the auditorium, beaming with pride as their sons were handed their diplomas. Katherine stood up from her seat, clapping her hands in joy as her sons stepped over the threshold into manhood.

The colonel believed strongly in working one's way up from ground level, so at their father's direction Curt and Todd entered the Army as privates. They were posted at various bases around the country and completed Special Forces training, eventually assigned to their current platoon under Captain Henry Wadsworth.

Henry endured the unending comments about being a poet. His own focus was on the safety of his country and eradicating evil in the world. He believed in his men and viewed his role as a procurer of the best possible equipment and, when needed, time for his soldiers away from the battlefield.

⇥ ⇤

So now the twins found themselves-in the mountains of Afghanistan. The other members of the small American band were two eighteen-year-olds, Dell Martin and Hal Obertin from Los Angeles. They had the blond good looks of southern California surfers and complained constantly about the snow and being so cold. They had enlisted immediately after the September 11th attacks and were shipped to Afghanistan just as soon as their training was completed.

The five Americans were part of a forward patrol for a company of soldiers intended to mop up the allegedly minute number of Taliban survivors left in the region. They had been on patrol with another small band of Canadian soldiers but in the storm the groups had become separated. The ten Afghani men viewed the Canadians and Americans as interlopers. The young Californians had been trigger-happy and, spying what they believed to be Taliban fighters, they had let off volleys of bullets into the cold winter air. The gun blasts that filled the valley and echoed off the peaks of the Blue Mountains loosened the ice and snow. The resulting avalanche had killed seven of the Afghani men.

Curt and Todd stood off by themselves watching the exchange between the captain and the oldest of the Pashtun men. The Afghanis shook their heads in disgust and kicked through the snow to the entrance of the cave. It was dark but dry with room to stand and space to lay out their packs and set up camp. Icicles hung from the entrance and frozen moss shone from the walls. The floor of the cave was packed dirt and stone. Outside, the snow began to fall again, blocking light and obscuring the view of the countryside.

The American soldiers sat apart from the Pashtun men; their mutual dislike and distrust hung thick in the air. The loss of seven men days earlier had induced a rage in the Pashtun men. They were angry over the perceived callousness of the Americans and the indifference to the destruction of their beloved country. The frigid day finally slipped into dusk. The wind increased as the temperature continued to drop. At the instruction of their captain, a West Point graduate born in Barrow, Alaska, and well-versed in the survival of cold and snow, Curt and Todd set up camp and heated food on their portable stoves.

The Americans' attempts to contact their company and the Canadians were thwarted by the storm and distance between the groups. The isolation from their own troops forced the Americans into an uneasy dependence on these Pashtun men. The ensuing alliance was as fragile as the strands of a spider's web.

Again, the eldest began speaking to the captain in a loud and irritated voice. The other four Americans listened to the exchange, unable to understand the tirade. The conversation between the two men became more heated and after exhausting their words, the two Pashtun men turned their backs on the captain and muttered among themselves.

The four privates leaned against the rough stone walls of the cave. They could cut the tension between the captain and the Afghani men with a knife. The captain's voice was again raised in anger. The Pashtun man was gesturing to the outside and banged his rifle butt on the floor to make his point. In a simultaneous movement, the young soldiers reached for their rifles and pulled them across their laps, hands at the ready. The captain finally held up his hand and stopped speaking, pointing to the entrance of the cave and then to his four soldiers.

"They're leaving us," the captain reported to his men. "They do not feel it is safe for them to stay with us any longer and they are going back to Kabul to get their families. They have to tell their families of the deaths of their seven kin. We have to find the rest of our company and the Canadians tomorrow on our own."

Curt and Todd looked at their comrades in concern. Dell and Hal shook their heads in irritation. They had constantly derided the Afghani men, angry that the Pashtun guides did not appear to share their commitment to the war on Bin Laden and the Taliban. The friction between the Americans and Pashtuns had grown over the dark days to the point that trust had totally evaporated into the strong winds.

The captain sat down by his four privates, shaking his head as the Pashtuns eased themselves onto the ground at the end of the cave, pulling dried meat and fruit from their own packs. Their uneasiness grew with the intensity of the storm raging outside. Slowly the cold night passed. At dawn, the three Pashtuns slipped out of the cave and began their trek down the mountains back through the valley and towards Kabul.

The Americans, sleeping in their warm bags, did not stir at the departure of their guides. A sudden movement outside the cave startled Todd awake. Just as suddenly, a flash of orange light and an ear-deafening noise filled the cave. Taliban fighters fired AK-47's, raking the cave with bullets. Chips of stones fell in cascades, covering the trapped soldiers.

After what seemed an eternity, the shooting stopped followed by loud voices. Todd lay as still as he could, his heart racing, afraid to look around or move. He waited for death, for the Taliban fighters to come inside and spray the cave with more bullets.

Agonizing minutes later the voices outside faded. Todd slowly eased his way from his sleeping bag and crawled over to his four comrades. The captain lay curled on his side, blood running from his mouth, blank eyes staring back into Todd's. Todd rolled Captain Wadsworth onto his back and pulled the shredded sleeping bag up over the captain's face. He heard moans coming from another bag; tufts of lining marked the bullet holes' entrances.

Afraid to stand, Todd inched his way across to Curt who was still wrapped in his bag. Curt was on his back, gasping for breath. Shaking with fear, Todd felt around the top of Curt's bag and then inside. He felt a warm stickiness as he ran his hand down Curt's arm. Curt winced and then pulled his brother's face close to his.

"It's only my arm. I was afraid to say anything. I was afraid they would keep shooting. I think Dell and Hal are dead. I heard their breaths rattle. Neither of them has moved. What about the captain?"

Todd gently pulled back the top of Curt's bullet-ravaged bag. The wound was small, a line of crimson inching across the bicep where the bullet had grazed the skin. Todd was astonished that Curt was alive given the number of bullet holes that split the bag. Fear kept Curt from moving as Todd slipped across him to the ripped sleeping bags of Hal and Dell. Just as Curt had feared, both men were dead. Stunned, Todd leaned back on his heels, burying his face in his hands. As blood pounded through his ears, silent screams of pain and the sound of gunshots gripped his mind.

"They are all dead, Curt. Those Afghanis set us up. That's why they left. They knew the Taliban were in the area. We've gotta get out of here.

We have to find our company. Oh, God, Curt. I'm afraid the Canadian soldiers are probably all dead. That's why we couldn't find them. Oh, God, Curt. We gotta get out of here." Todd's voice held a hushed urgency as he pulled his brother out of the remnants of his sleeping bag.

Todd went about inspecting the wound on Curt's arm and reached behind him for a first-aid kit. His hands were shaking from shock making it nearly impossible for him to loosen the clasps of the small red box of antiseptics and bandages.

"Don't look at them, Curt. They're all dead. We have to leave them here. It's too dangerous to stay."

Curt pushed his brother aside and crawled to each of the sleeping bags. Tears ran down his face as he stared into the empty eyes of his three dead comrades. He dropped to his stomach and rolled into a ball, rocking back and forth, moaning and sobbing.

"Todd, they are all gone. It was those guides. They hated us. I know they set us up. How did they know to leave this morning? How did they know? What are we going to do? We don't even know where we are. We don't have enough food or water to stay here but I'm afraid to leave. We're going to die. Todd, what are we going to do?"

"Be quiet for a minute, Curt. Let me clean up your arm and then we can figure out what we're going to do. Shhh! I know you're scared, so am I. You've got to hold on. Let me get you bandaged and then we'll talk."

Todd sat down and grabbed Curt's hand, pulling him close to his chest. The smell of gunpowder filled the small space of the cave, the ringing from the gunfire seeming to continue to echo off the walls. The icicles that had hung from the entrance of the cave lay shattered in the snow, reflecting back the gray light from the winter sky.

Todd pulled a large roll of gauze and tape from the first-aid box and then gently rolled up his brother's sleeve to bandage the wound. As he clung to his brother, Todd crooned, "We'll get out and get back to our unit. Shhh!. Come on, Curt, let me fix your arm."

Curt turned to face his brother, his eyes large and the pupils dilated. "Todd, did I ever tell you what happened that day on the ranch by Devils Tower? Do you remember when I walked off from you guys? Did I tell you what I saw? I was lying on the ground and this beautiful black-haired woman came and sat with me. She gave me a kiss. She was the most beautiful person I had ever seen. Then, she was gone."

"Shhh, Curt. Sit up and let's figure out what we're going to do. Come on, we need to think about what we're going to do."

Todd looked at his watch and then around him at the three dead men wrapped in their bedrolls. Slowly, he got to his feet and surveyed the horrific scene. Taking a deep breath, he bent down, picked up the rifles and pistols of all three dead men. As Curt watched from his place against the wall, Todd pulled each of the three bedrolls containing the corpses into a far corner of the cave. He prayed the Lord's Prayer, kissed his thumb and pressed it to the forehead of each. He asked God for their salvation and then, as he had been taught by his mother, he began to sing "Amazing Grace," his voice low and trembling.

Curt watched his brother tend to their fallen comrades. He saw a shadow pass by the entrance of the cave and gasped as the tall black-haired woman stepped inside. She walked lightly towards Curt. Bending down, she wiped the tears from his face, kissing each check and then his lips. She backed away from Curt, smiled, and then ducked back out of the cave's entrance, disappearing into the blowing snow.

A deep fatigue came over Curt. He slumped over, his eyes closed and his breath deepened as he slept. As soon as he finished his grim task, Todd crawled across the uneven floor of the cave to his brother. Leaning against him, Todd wrapped his coat-clad arm around Curt's shoulder. He nestled his face into his brother's neck and, just as his brother had, he fell into a deep slumber.

Day faded into night. The sickening smell of blood and death hung in the close air. The cooling air caused Todd to stir. He looked around and, in a second, the ghastliness of the scene pressed in on him. The three fallen soldiers had grown rigid, causing the sleeping bags to assume odd positions. The temperature had fallen and, once again, icicles hung from the entrance of the cave. Todd grimaced and pulled away from his brother, shaking Curt's shoulder.

"Come on, Curt. Let's go. The snow's stopped falling. We've gotta go. We can mark the location of the cave and cover up the entrance. I know what Dad says about never leaving your dead, but we can't take them with us. Get the radio and I'll get our packs. We can't be that far away from our unit." Curt climbed to his feet and took a deep breath as he reached for his bedroll. His voice was shaky, his eyes averted from the frozen bodies as the iron smell of blood clogged his nostrils.

Curt nodded and started to gather up the items needed to ensure their survival in the cold. He avoided looking at the three dead soldiers at the back of the cave. The smell was fetid and overwhelming. Trying not to take a deep breath, the twins finished their tasks. In unison, they ducked out the entrance of the cave, taking care not to break the icicles hanging down, and pulled their packs out after them. Outside, the dark air was crisp, turning their breaths into clouds of ice as they shrugged into their packs and began their lonely journey to the southwest. The twins hiked in silence, alternating who led, breaking a trail through the snow for the other. The only sounds were the crunch of the icy crusted snow and the occasional blast of wind that cut through their clothing.

Todd timed his pulse, trying to escape the memory of the three dead American soldiers, the Pashtun men killed in the earlier avalanche and their blue faces when they were pulled from beneath the tons of snow. A headache began behind his left eye, the pain growing with each throbbing beat of his saddened heart.

"So much death, dear God, what are we all thinking? I hope Dad forgives us for not taking their bodies with us. I just don't know how we could have managed. Dad, do you ever think you were wrong? What if there is no God? Mom, pray for us. I have had enough. I'm only twenty-four. God, I can still smell their blood, all of them. I wonder if the Pashtuns did set us up. Maybe they just had good timing, leaving when they did. They lost seven people trying to help us. What if I am wrong? Poor Curt. He looks so dejected. Look at him. I don't know what to say. God, help me get through this. That is all I am asking. Let me make it through and make sure Curt does too. Dad, Mom, I let you down. I was supposed to take care of him. Now see where we are."

Off in the distance, dim lights blinked, brightened, and blinked again. Through the night the twins trudged on, stopping only to urinate, drink water, or eat a quick snack. They stayed as low to the ground as they could, alert to any movement or sound in the inky darkness. Curt could feel the tightness of the bandage on his arm. He welcomed the pain as it helped him stay alert. He thought he could smell death on the thick muffler protecting his neck from the bitter wind blowing between the indifferent frozen mountain peaks.

Todd sighed deeply and slightly shifted his path, heading for the twinkling lights ahead. He was tempted to pull the Maglite out of his pack but was afraid to reveal their existence. He thought back to how they had gotten lost in the snow and the coincidence of finding the cave.

Or was *it a coincidence?* he thought. *Stop it. Just focus on walking. Stop thinking!*

Deep into the night, the twins approached the source of the lights they had seen from the cave. It was a small village. Both of them swung their rifles to the front, pausing in mid-step as a dog began to bark. A tall, shadowy figure wrapped in a thick coat moved cautiously towards them, two other figures close behind.

"Stop!" Curt commanded as the three figures came closer. Behind the shadows was a yellow lamp affixed to a pink painted concrete house: "Stop, or I'll shoot. Stay where you are! Stand back!"

The three figures, identified now as men wrapped in thick pants and coats with headdresses and scarves covering their faces, all held rifles pointed at Curt and Todd. The man in front shouted something to the other two, raised his rifle, and held out his hand in a stop signal. The three Afghani men and the two Americans stood stock still; Todd and the lead Afghani man screamed at each other to drop their rifles.

"Todd," Curt said from the corner of his mouth, "those are the three Afghanis that set us up. Hold your rifle on them. I'm going to try to talk to them. If they make a move, shoot them. "

Todd held his gun in a ready position as his brother slowly approached the men. The scene appeared surreal to Todd. What little light there was caused the snow to glisten and threw the houses of the small village into bas-relief. Thin streams of smoke rose from the distant houses. An eerie thought crossed Todd's mind that the smoke was the breath of the village, misting into the air just as his own breath surrounded him. Faint popping sounds could be heard as the snow froze and expanded.

Ten feet ahead of Todd, his brother approached the lead Pashtun man. The two men stood rifle-to-rifle, and nearly face-to-face. Suddenly, the Pashtun man lowered his rifle and waved his two companions forward. He turned to them and spoke rapidly, gesturing to the two Americans. The two other men nodded and stepped forward, lowering their AK-47's, and reaching out their hands toward Curt.

They were the three men who had left the Americans prior to the fatal attack. The oldest of the Pashtun men raised his hand in greeting and as he did, Curt opened fire. The scream of dozens of bullets filled the air. The odd pop of the bullets hitting the Pashtuns made a bizarre accompaniment to the horrendous noise of the firing rifle.

Behind Curt, Todd screamed to stop! But the noise went on and on. Todd dropped his rifle to the ground, covering his ears and continuing to scream for his brother to stop! He could see the men's bodies jerking back and forth in slow motion as they crumbled to the ground where they finally came to rest in the icy snow. Blood ran from the noses and mouths of the three Pashtuns, staining the white snow. Curt sobbed and screamed obscenities as he emptied his rifle into their bodies. Behind him, Todd begged his brother to stop! He hit his fists on his thighs, sobbing and pleading over and over for his brother to stop! The smell of cordite filled the air, mixed with the iron aroma of blood and the clean bite of the icy air.

In the village, lights came on inside the shattered brick houses. Puddles of illumination showed the devastation from coalition bombs and RPGs of the retreating Taliban. The furious barking of the village dogs added to the chaos of the winter night. A small child dressed in a nightshirt and sheepskin coat ran forward to where one of the dead Pashtun men lay on the ground. A woman dressed in a black burqa pushed past the child and cradled one of the men in her arms. She ran her hands over his face. His blood left glistening wet spots on the black cloth covering her body.

Curt stood in the road leading into the small town, his rifle dangling from his now limp hand. His mind was filled with the images of his dead comrades and a deep rage came over him. He felt the bitterness and bile clutching his throat as he raised his rifle and aimed it at the woman and child crouching over the dead man.

The woman in the burqa raised her arms towards Curt, crying and yelling, her words indecipherable to the Americans but her feelings and intent very clear. As if in a daze, Curt turned to his brother who stood with his mouth hanging open; his eyes wide and frightened. Todd, motionless in the light from the village, waited for the bullets of the angry Afghanis to pierce his body. He readied himself in anticipation of the hot lead pellets. His brother's voice seemed to echo in his head with portent and disaster. His body was frozen in place.

"I had to shoot them, Todd. You know that!" Curt exclaimed. "They were the ones that betrayed us. You understand. I had to kill them. Don't look at me like that. Look at these people; they would kill us if they could. Come on, Todd, you understand."

Todd could not look at his brother; his gaze fixed on the small child and the woman huddled over the broken body of the dead husband and father. More people began to emerge from their homes, running towards the Americans. The few bare-limbed trees stood as sentinels to the tragedy unfolding below.

The colors of the villagers' clothes were like bright lights against the dark night and the white snow. A tiny girl dressed only in a yellow Sponge Bob tee shirt toddled towards Curt, sucking her thumb. She tugged at his pants, bracing herself against his legs, and smiled up at him, reaching out her arms for Curt to pick her up.

Todd slowly backed away from the horrific scene. He turned and began to run, not caring what direction, not waiting to see what his brother was going to do. He ran from the dead men and the villagers. He could feel sobs shaking his chest. Behind him, he could hear other running feet, a shrill voice calling his name, a tiny voice shrieking into the biting air.

Nearly a mile from the village, Todd tripped over a stone and fell to the icy ground, his flak jacket caught on a broken tree branch as he slid to a stop. He rolled over onto his back, sobbing and moaning. He tried to bring into focus an image of his mother kneeling by his bed, saying prayers with him and kissing him goodnight. He closed his eyes and flung his arms out to his sides, a bloodied Christ-like figure lying on the cold ground of a disdainful land. The black heavens above him were filled with white stars, whirling around in an eternal pattern, the little bear climbing forever while Orion shot his arrows into infinity.

A pair of black-clad legs stepped over Todd's body, a voice from afar calling his name. Todd looked up into the small face of a green-eyed angel in a yellow tee shirt with dark brown hair gently flowing around her delicate face. She smiled at him and then waved over Curt's shoulder to where her mother was calling for her daughter to return. Curt's voice was demanding as he held the little girl and stared at his brother. "Get up!"

Todd shook his head, refusing to meet his brother's eyes.

"Todd, I had to kill those men. They were the ones that betrayed us. We have to get back to Kabul. We're not safe here. Get up! Please, get up!" Curt's voice held a shrill edge of hysteria and a level of desperation that cut his brother to the bone.

Todd rolled to his side, tears sliding down his cheeks and into the corners of his mouth.

"What are you doing with her? Take her back. No more, Curt, no more. Take her back. Enough! Enough! We've taken enough from these people. Take her back. What do you imagine we are going to do with her? Curt, you're crazy. You killed all of those people. Why, Curt, why?"

A wind began to blow; frozen particles of ice pelted the brothers and the shivering child. As Curt stood over him, holding the little Afghan girl, Todd thought of the destroyed Buddhas of Bamiyan, the thoughtless destruction of ancient treasures by angry zealots. His brother appeared to him no less damaged than the serene faces of the Buddhas that had been blown into infinity by fanatics. "That's what we've become," Todd whispered into the ground, his left cheek resting on a stone. "Take her back, Curt."

He closed his eyes as tightly as he could, the memory of the Pashtun men falling, forever falling. Above him, Curt placed the little girl on the frozen ground, gently pointing her in the direction of the decaying village. Her yellow tee shirt was blown against her small body as she smiled and waved goodbye to the brothers and ran back towards the lights and the grieving village.

Curt knelt beside his brother, shaking Todd's shoulder. "Come on, Todd. We've gotta get out of here. They're going to be coming soon. We have to go. We have to get back to our unit. Get up, Todd. Get up or I'm going without you."

"Go on, Curt. I can't stand anymore. I don't care if they come. We deserve it. Mom was right, you can't break the commandments. Curt, just go." Todd's voice was subdued. "I'm not going anywhere."

"Todd," Curt pleaded, "you're coming with me. Mom and Dad would kill me if I left you here."

Todd swore as he came to his feet. "Never, ever talk to me about killing again. I'll come with you but as soon as we reach our unit, I'm telling them everything, everything, about the cave, about the village, about everything. I don't care what happens. Now, get out of my way. You want to go, let's go."

Behind the twins, angry voices could be heard, coming closer. To the east, a faint orange glow cut across the horizon. Without another word, the twins began to run again, their souls left somewhere behind them and the rugged angry land stretching out in front of them. The sun was a muted ball, trying to break through the gloom, the mercury-colored clouds dropping an occasional snow flurry, The temperature hovered just at freezing for most of the day, numbing the two young men's fingers holding their rifles. No further words had passed between the brothers. Todd refused to make eye contact with his brother as they painstakingly made their way towards their unit. They took care to avoid any villages and counted themselves fortunate for escaping the men that had come after them. The GPS's the twins carried told them they were moving to where their unit had been before the disastrous mission.

Later that afternoon, far from the village and the burial spot of their three fallen comrades, the twins rested against a huge slanted rock. Its surface was smooth and rounded from years of exposure to the elements. A half-mile to the south, a small convoy of armored vehicles made its way across the plain. A red maple leaf was clearly visible on the side of a jeep.

"Look, Todd!" Curt pointed across the valley floor towards the convoy with a tone of hopefulness in his voice. "We can make it to them. They'll take care of us."

Todd started to push his way past his brother but Curt grabbed him by the leg. "Todd, you can't tell anyone what happened. They'll arrest both of us. You know that. It was an accident. You know those men set us up. What could I do? Promise me you won't say anything."

Todd slowly pulled his leg away from his brother's grasp, plucking one finger at a time.

"Curt, why did you take that little girl? Just tell my why."

"Because they were chasing us. I took her so they wouldn't shoot me. I let her go. Did you want them to kill us? I had to shoot those men, I told you that. They betrayed us once and they would betray us again. You know that's what happened. You said so yourself."

"Curt, I can't talk to you about what you did. I'm not making any promises. Just don't talk to me anymore. Let's get down to the convoy before it's gone. When we get back to Kabul, I'm going to put in for a transfer. I cannot believe you shot them and took that little girl. My God, what were you thinking?"

Todd pulled his rifle off his shoulder and aimed it at a point a hundred yards down the hillside. He pulled the trigger, letting loose a stream of bullets, and then walked towards the closest Humvee with his hands in the air, his rifle abandoned on the ground.

Curt swore at his brother, the obscenities flowing from his lips like a stream running freely across stones. He angrily kicked at the wretched ground, convinced his brother would betray his secret to the Canadian soldiers who now stood at the ready, their guns trained on the two brothers as they made their cautious way down the rocky hillside.

Todd's face looked strained as the first Canadian infantryman reached him and then hugged him, welcoming them back to safety. He began to gasp and choke, realizing his brother's fate now lay squarely in his hands. He clutched the lapels of the Canadian soldier's coat, wiping his tears on his sleeve and then, bending at the waist, he vomited as the smell of blood came back to him. He stared at his feet, clearing the bile from his mouth as he saw his brother come up behind him. He closed his eyes to shut out the images of Curt firing into the chest of the Pashtun men, the little girl in the yellow tee shirt grinning and mouthing 'good-bye' as she floated across the snow, her bare feet leaving nearly invisible imprints on the ground.

Curt strode past his brother and saluted the ranking lieutenant, pulling himself up on the fender of the Humvee and shaking the proffered hand.

"There were five of us out on reconnaissance. We were betrayed and ambushed," Curt told the lieutenant. "We got separated from our unit and held up in a cave. There were ten Afghanis, but we lost seven of them in an avalanche and the other three set us up. We lost three members of our team. We've been hiking now for the past day. Do you know where our unit is? We figured we were close to them."

Curt pointed over his shoulder to where Todd stood, still bent at the waist, his hands on his thighs. "I think my brother is in shock. He hasn't said anything today. We need to go get the bodies of the rest of the team. They were all killed." Curt's voice increased in pitch and pressure, pushing to tell the story before Todd uttered a word. He gave his brother a warning look as Todd stared at him in cold anger. Turning away, Todd climbed into one of the dust-covered green Nyalas. A cup of hot coffee was placed in his hand and a tan blanket draped around his shoulders.

The Canadian lieutenant told Curt, "We're within an hour's distance of the American camp. Can you pinpoint the location of the cave?"

Turning to the troop, the lieutenant barked, "Sergeant, get some men and take one of the trucks. We've got a recovery mission that can't wait. Give the coordinates of the cave to the sergeant and let us take care of it. Night's coming and I want to get us all to safety." Looking back to Curt he asked, "What's your name, son? Come on, we'll take care of you."

The convoy moved off while a truck with four soldiers aboard sped off to the northeast. As the vehicles carrying Todd and Curt moved to the south, the gray clouds began to weep rain, snow and sleet closing off the mountains and the horror left behind.

The next day the Canadians arrived in Kabul with Todd and Curt. The two were to meet with the brigadier general overseeing the fight against Al-Qaeda and the Taliban. Sunlight sifted through the dust-streaked window of the cramped office as the general leaned across his plywood desk. His weight was propped on his wrists, his fingers tapping in a mindless rhythm as he listened to the story of the doomed reconnaissance team.

The general confirmed that they had recovered the bodies of the three dead Americans and brought them back to Bagram Airfield. The bodies would be on their way back to Dover and, eventually, to their families. The general said he understood the horror of the ambush and the subsequent hike across the bleak winter landscape. He also understood that Todd wanted a transfer to a unit separate from his brother. Staring into Todd's eyes, the general did not ask any questions but quietly signed the order, separating the brothers for the rest of their tours.

⇥ ⇤

Springfield, Virginia   July 4, 2003

The humidity hung heavily in the summer air, pasting the cotton shirts to the back of the two men sitting by the pool. The younger man sat on a wicker chair; his feet spread apart, his head tipped back, and a cold Tecate resting between his thighs. He held his fingers tightly over his eyes, pressing out the light of the sun. A blue jay screamed in the oak tree branch that hung over the swimming pool while a cardinal picked sunflower seeds from the bird feeder perched on a steel post.

The older man lay on a chaise lounge, his thinning legs crossed at the ankles; a green and white-striped towel draped over his feet. The colonel had welcomed his two sons home from Afghanistan on Memorial Day. In an odd twist of irony, after being apart for well over a year, and having no contact with each other, the twins were slated to fly on the same flight back to the United States. They asked for seats as far apart from each other as the 767 would allow.

The colonel and Katherine reunited with their boys in the baggage claim area at Dulles Airport. Both were overjoyed to see their beloved sons standing safely in front of them and each hugged both sons with overwhelming thankfulness.

"I've prayed for this day!" Katherine exclaimed. "I knew God would protect you. I am so happy my boys are home. Look at you, my handsome ones. Thank the good Lord, my boys are home."

The colonel shook hands with Curt, clasping his son's shoulder as he reached for Curt's bag. Todd barely nodded to his parents as he pushed through the crowd. Panic rose in his chest as he felt the pressure of fellow-travelers around him. His throat tightened, cutting off his breath. He rushed forward and literally fell out the door that opened onto the sidewalk. The busy sidewalk gave way to the street cluttered with waiting cars and more rushing people.

"Is something wrong with your brother?" Katherine asked Curt, who stared at Todd with a furious glare.

Curt deflected the question, taking his mother's arm as he walked her out of the terminal. "Come on, Mom. Let's go home. Don't worry about Todd. He's just tired from the flights."

The family left the airport and drove through the last remnants of the Virginia countryside. They headed to their large and comfortable home on the tree-lined cul-de-sac in Springfield. Curt sat in the back seat behind his father in the black LeSabre, his forearms resting on the top of his father's seat. Without a word, Todd climbed into the other rear passenger's seat, pausing only to kiss his mother's cheek as he ducked into the car. He slouched into the corner of the rear seat; head tilted to the right, his eyes closed against the bright lights reflecting off the passenger's side mirror. Once again, he smelled cordite and blood and saw the tiny barefoot figure in yellow running into the freezing night. He winced as he thought of the three Pashtun men, again seeing their bodies in slow motion dropping through space as the woman in the black burqa screamed.

Curt sat next to his brother, leaning forward over the center console to talk to his father. On occasion, Katherine patted her son's tanned arm, delighting in the nearness of her children. Her smile faded, though, as she noticed Todd sink further into his seat. His face was brooding and somber as he listened to his brother and father discuss the merits of "shock and awe" and the thrill of "Mission Accomplished."

Todd pulled his body upright and stretched, lacing his fingers behind his head as he squeezed his elbows together. The white line marking the division of the lanes blinked as the car sped down the freeway. Blurs of yellow, green, red, black, white and blue grazed the corner of Todd's consciousness. He barely registered the ebb and flow of the traffic and the rise and fall of the conversation in the car.

"I'm so proud of you boys," the colonel said as he negotiated the I-95 traffic around the ever-expanding metropolis of the nation's capital. "You know I tried to re-enlist but there doesn't appear to be a need for a sixty-three-year-old patriot. Todd, you've been sitting there for almost an hour and haven't said a word. What's your opinion of all this?"

His father's words brought Todd out of his reverie. He was startled into alertness, his knee jerking against the back of his mother's seat. He could see the pinkness of his father's scalp beneath the military haircut he had sported for as long as Todd could remember. Todd felt a tendril of anger creeping through his gut as he stared at his brother's smooth profile, the eyebrows so white they could barely be seen. Todd knew the freckles on his brother's face matched his own, a mirror reflection that had followed him throughout his life.

Curt twisted on the bench seat the twins shared, his hands sliding on the slick beige leather. His blue eyes narrowed and his lips twitched as he waited for Todd's response:

"Dad, I'm just tired. I don't feel like talking. I'm just glad to be home."

Curt smirked across the empty space of the back seat, a look of madness in his blue eyes. He relaxed back into his seat, sun-freckled and strong hands wrapping around the side of his father's headrest. Reaching over, he patted Katherine's shoulder. The rest of the ride passed in silence, the loud freeway noise bouncing off the windows of the LeSabre.

The Baines's house sat regally at the end of the cul-de-sac. Ancient oak trees circled the lot, interspersed with leatherwood and Christmas ferns. Fluorescent red, pink and purple lilies lined the smooth concrete walk that led from the driveway across the immaculate green lawn. The house was built in 1946 when lots were large. Trees still lined the two-lane roads of the housing development, shading the black top as they had the dirt lanes of the early 1900's.

The LeSabre glided into the driveway, a faint squeal of brakes signaling the end of the ride. Katherine pulled on the door handle, kicking the heavy door open. The loud ticking of the motor echoed in unison with the beating of Todd's heart. They were both counting away the seconds of his battered life.

The adjustment back to civilian life proved difficult for the twins. An unspoken, uneasy truce had been declared between them. Todd left the tidy house every morning at eight, taking a bus to the Springfield/Franconia Metro station, and then riding the Yellow Line to Gallery Place. He made his way through the rushing commuters, transferred to the Red Line and got off the train at the Woodley Park-Zoo/Adams Morgan stop. The anonymity of the Metro and the harsh streets of the city were an odd balm to the oozing rawness of Todd's soul. He watched the plastic bags and candy wrappers blowing into the gutters of the hot and muggy city.

Todd meandered through the streets of the city's northwest district. His first stop was always the national zoo where he spent hours at the red panda exhibit. The antics of the animals soothed his troubled spirit. He quickly became a fixture at the zoo. Every day, the staff smiled and welcomed the handsome young man with the sad and haunted eyes.

At noon, Todd would take the 30 series bus going south on Wisconsin Avenue. He would disembark at his usual bus stop. He strolled the mile and a half south, arriving at the National Cathedral at two p.m. He stared at his feet as, one after the other; they lifted him from step to step. The open doors beckoned him into the cool silence of the great building which became a place of healing for his bludgeoned heart and suffering soul.

Every day but Sunday, Todd quietly slipped into a back pew of the cathedral, his hands folded in front of his heart. He'd watch as the rainbow-colored light streamed from the stained-glass windows and made its way across the soaring walls. He began to understand the fear that drove his mother to her faith as he prayed for forgiveness of his brother's sins and for the sin of his silence. He whispered pleading words to God that the dark-haired, green-eyed child in the yellow tee shirt had been safely welcomed back into her mother's arms.

At three o'clock, Todd left the Cathedral. The peace and tranquility of the glorious church yielded to the jammed roads. Carbon fumes filled Todd's nose, as had the horrifying smell of cordite from the cold cave and on the frigid road leading to the Afghani village. Todd boarded the Red Line back to Metro Center and then on to home in the Springfield suburb. Each night, he ate at a small Afghani restaurant near the Springfield Mall, appreciatively observing the movements of the young, elegant, long-haired Afghani waitress.

One night, the waitress carried a small girl across the restaurant. The child smiled at Todd with a gap-toothed grin and gentle green eyes. That night he wept over his dinner, wiping his eyes and nose on his cloth napkin.

Evenings, Todd surfed the Internet, searching for jobs in hopes of finding a way back to the innocence he lost in the snowy mountains of Afghanistan. He applied for a teaching position in the stark mining town of Colstrip, Montana. The only requirement was a bachelor's degree and a willingness to work for a minimal salary in exchange for room and board in the company-owned house.

He avoided contact with his brother and parents, fearing the secrets that raged in his brain would spill from his lips and forever seal his brother's fate. His mother, evening after summer evening, would come to his room and smilingly invite him out to the pool or to the kitchen for a cold drink. Todd refused to meet her curious gaze, thanked her, and always refused the invitation. Katherine accepted his decline with quiet nods, as the abiding knot of fear in her heart grew larger and more painful with each passing day. She confided her worries to the colonel every night, convinced he could mend the tear in the fabric of the family. She knelt next to the bed; her hands on the colonel's pajama-clad shoulder and prayed for a means to re-create the joy of years gone by.

Curt's daily routine was the exact opposite of his brother. He always left the house upon Todd's return. He also took the Blue Line to Metro Center and the Red Line to the Tenleytown-AU stop. He prowled the streets below the National Cathedral wearing a knife in a black case threaded through his belt, hidden by blue denim shirts he wore over gray tee shirts. People on the streets shied away from the hostile demeanor of the young blond man, his hooded eyes bringing reptilian fear to any that came near.

Curt became a denizen of the dark, stalking the dirty city streets, preying on the baby prostitutes that paraded the streets in impossibly short skirts and revealing tops. Their young faces were aged and haggard, eyes hollow and full of hate as Curt lay over them on the stained sheets of shabby hotels and rundown apartments.

Curt was filled with malicious anger and uncontrollable brutality as the reddened lips of the young prostitutes mouthed mechanical words of encouragement. His sexual contact increased in violence, culminating with his fist punching the lips of the screaming victims who lay beneath him. On several occasions, he came home with blood on his denim shirt and around the waist of his pants.

One sultry June night, Katherine and the colonel were sitting in their white-carpeted living room. Katherine, dressed in a red-striped terry cloth robe, sat on the gold upholstery of the love seat embroidering a silk pillowcase. Her husband was stretched out on a matching recliner with the remote in his hand. The colonel flipped idly through the hundreds of channels that contained nothing of interest as the clock approached two a.m. Todd had come home early, kissed his mother on the cheek, ignored her questions, and retreated into his beige room, firmly closing the door and effectively shutting out his mother's constant questions.

Outside the living room window, fireflies blinked in Morse code to each other; cicadas buzzed in the trees, pausing occasionally as if an unseen conductor had lowered his baton. A scuffling sound came from the front steps followed by a fumbling noise and the sound of a key being inserted in the lock. Katherine and the colonel looked up to see Curt coming through the door.

"What are you doing up so late, Mom and Dad?" Curt asked as his parents stared in shock at his blood-stained clothing. His blond hair was mussed and the knife he wore was clearly visible on his belt.

"For God's sake, Curt," the colonel's voice trembled in shock at the sight of his son. "Where the hell have you been and what were you doing? Look at you. Were you in a fight? Should we call the police? What are you doing out all hours of the night? My God, look at you!"

"I'm going to bed," Curt retorted. "And, Dad, I'm not doing anything you haven't done hundreds of times. You created us. Mom, pray to your God for us. See if *He* can clean up this mess. See if *He* has the answers."

Curt gave a snort of ironic amusement as he turned his back and slammed the door to the room that mirrored his brother's. Back in the living room, Katherine shook out her pillowcase, her eyes focused on the smooth silk lying under her fingers. She dared not look at her husband. After a long, deep silence, she sighed and got up and left the colonel alone.

The tension of the household continued to mushroom until the afternoon of July 4th. As the sunlight filtered through the thick leaves of the oaks gracing the backyard, Curt and his father watched damselflies skim the water of the pool. Lines of sweat ran down their necks, mimicking the condensation on the bottle of Tecate Curt was drinking. It was his fourth beer of the afternoon and his dark mood was deepening with each one he drained.

Katherine stood on the inside of the screen door that led out to the crystalline pool. She steadied herself against the frame and surveyed the interplay between the two men. Both were people she loved beyond comprehension. The past six weeks had generated an anxiety in her chest, a fear never released even with hours of prayer. She had been unable to shake Curt's bitter statements that night. Those hateful, accusatory words confirmed her belief that, even though her sons had come home safely from the war, she was losing them to a hell she knew existed but remained unnamed.

A step sounded behind Katherine and Todd brushed lightly past her as he pulled open the screen door. As Todd emerged into the sun, she saw the blue duffel bag and a small black hard- sided case that he was carrying.

"Dad, Curt, I'm leaving for Colstrip today. My cab will be here any minute. Take care of Mom. I'll call when I get to wherever it is I'll be. Curt, don't think about it anymore. I'm as guilty as you are. Don't worry about it anymore."

Todd took a last look at his childhood home. The only emotion he felt was a deep sadness, knowing he would never set foot in this house again. He dropped his bags, stepped over Curt's legs and bent down to hug his father. His tears left wet splotches on his father's face. Todd sighed as he picked up his bags and disappeared around the corner of the house.

"Curt, what is your brother talking about? You two have avoided each other the entire time you've been home. You come home drunk every night reeking of sin. You won't talk to your mother or me. You sleep all day and are back out all night again. You don't look for work and you won't clean up after yourself. I'm not going to tolerate this much longer, Curt. Whatever it is that you and your brother are battling over, you need to resolve it and get on with your life. I'm giving you until Labor Day and then you're out. Consider this your notice!"

The colonel's voice was rough, the voice he had used to command hundreds of men, a voice that was instantly obeyed without question or comment.

Curt snorted at his father's words and popped the lid off another Tecate. "You're a real pompous ass, Dad; you, your morals and your righteousness. Don't ever talk to me about life again. You have as much blood on your hands as I do, probably more. You think you have such a corner on the right way to live. Well, I blame you for this, all of this."

Curt went on, "You talk about the glory of war and your exalted status as a veteran. You are so deluded. You practice deceit and deception. You are despicable, Dad. You are such a bastard. How dare you even, for one second, talk down to me? Shit! Does Mom know what a lying asshole you are? You want me to get on with my life? Yes sir, right away, sir! Let me tell you about my life. You're a liar, all my life you lied to me. I'll tell you about reality."

Curt's voice rose in anger, his beer bottle gripped tightly in his right hand, his left hand clenched into a white-knuckled fist. Spittle gathered at the corner of his lips as his eyes narrowed, the whites of them streaked with red. Above his head, the jays shrieked in the oak branches. A damselfly buzzed the top of the pool, dipping its proboscis into the warm water. A ripple spread across the pool causing the skimmer to rock back and forth. The humidity was heavy, lying like a leaded coat on the men sitting by the pool. Both men had strong, straight noses and sensuous lips, belying the rigidity of the personalities that had been battling for supremacy that summer.

Curt leaned forward to face his father. His veins in his neck bulged and his presence was so menacing that his father drew back in genuine fear. Curt sneered at his father's physical withdrawal.

"I'll tell you about bravery, Dad. Let me tell you about the glory of war. I killed the enemy, just like you taught me to. I aimed a gun and killed three men. No big deal. Shoot, kill, and walk away. That's what I did, Dad. I shot, killed and walked away. No, not quite true. I ran away. Shot, killed and ran away. I took a little girl with me. They wouldn't kill me if I had her, Dad. I shot those people, and then I ran away with a little girl as my shield.

"That's why Todd won't talk to me. He thinks I'm a murderer and a kidnapper. He doesn't have blood on his hands, just me, Dad. I shot those men and then I took that little girl. That's your glorious legacy, a son who is a murderer. Are you satisfied? You've succeeded. I killed those people. I did your 'eye for an eye.' They killed three of us, I killed three of them. Don't you think justice was done, Dad? Don't you think God is pleased?"

Katherine, unseen, listened to her son's horrifying confession. Her husband stared open- mouthed at Curt; the only sound the cicadas, cardinals and blue jays calling to each other in the oaks. A shiver of foreboding replaced the celebration of the day as even the damselfly ceased its motion, drifting to the surface of the blue water.

His tirade finished, Curt threw his beer bottle into the pool. "Happy Fourth of July, Dad. Welcome home the conquering hero. You're a liar, but don't you worry, I'll be out of here as soon as possible. I wouldn't want to taint your Christian home with Muslim blood. I took that little girl. I took her to protect me. There's your brave soldier, Dad. Aren't you proud of me?"

The colonel sagged into the chaise lounge, his towel falling unnoticed to the flagstone of the pool deck. His wounded eyes watched his son push to his feet and slam through the screen door, nearly knocking his mother into the wall.

"Give your hero son a kiss, Mom. I'm going to bed. I've had enough of celebration. Come on; give your hero son a kiss."

Katherine reached for Curt as he laughed and kept moving. His footsteps were heavy and menacing as he staggered toward his room, knocking several lights to the floor. She heard the bedroom door slam and listened to the harsh, rapid breathing of her husband slumped forward on the end of the chaise. She gently pushed open the screen door and, with slow steps, made her way around the pool until she reached him. He sat quietly, a devastated shell of the strong man she had loved for over thirty years. Kneeling down she placed her head on her husband's lap and whispered, "I love you and you will always be my hero."

Curt's deterioration continued over the next several months. His father's ultimatum was ignored as the deadline for his departure came and went. His midnight forays continued. His drinking increased until he was no longer sure when his last drink of the day ended and his first one began. His angry confession was never mentioned again. The television was never again tuned to the news on the continuing war in Afghanistan or the bloody battle in the desert of Iraq.

Katherine dreaded the sultry summer evenings, particularly after Todd's abrupt and detached disappearance from the family home. Like clockwork, every night at eight, Curt stumbled down the stairs to the basement where Katherine perched on the end of a red silk couch, endlessly painting her fingernails, layer upon layer upon layer. Lines from his bed sheets still creased his freckled cheeks. His bare torso was hairless and tanned as he reached under the couch for the sneakers he left there early each morning upon his return from his night's escapades.

Curt patted his mother's dyed brown curls and her rouged cheeks. Then he ran up the carpet-lined stairs, ignoring the beseeching look on his mother's rapidly aging face. Every night, in trepidation, she drew the front room's heavy gold curtains to the side and watched Curt's shadow stagger down the road. He held a bottle in his left hand as if it was a pistol aimed at the doors of the neighbor's houses. Behind her, the colonel shook his newspaper, his slipper-clad feet crossing and uncrossing on the gold and black-striped ottoman. A beam of light from the black reading lamp cast a dim light across his taut face that was masked in detachment. He refused to comment on Curt's behavior, ignoring his wife's distress and what he called Curt's "weakness."

Night after night, upon Curt's departure, Katherine would clean his room. The sheets on the twin bed were twisted and dank; the smell of night sweats filling the room. One night, while picking up Curt's discarded clothes, she found a picture of the twins at the age of eight dressed in blue and orange football jerseys. The boys grinned at her, arms around each other, with pure joy and innocence. Katherine fell onto the tussled bed, weeping in frustration and grief for her lost children. The colonel's slow footsteps went unnoticed as his tired face peered around the door. He paused for a moment, running his hands up and down the coolness of the painted door jamb.

The bed creaked under Katherine as she cleared her throat and shifted her dwindling weight. She noticed the top drawer of the dresser was ajar with socks and bright-colored muscle shirts hanging against the polished pine wood drawers. As her eyes shifted to the door, she saw the colonel watching her. She closed her hands over the picture, hiding the precious treasure from the man she had married so many years before, the man who had sired her precious sons.

Colstrip, Montana   **November 22, 2003**

Todd had begun his tenure as a first-grade teacher two days after Labor Day. The children of the Colstrip School were a mixture of races and cultures. Their parents all came to work in the open pit coal mine. The coal company owned the town, just like so many towns in the hills of Appalachia near his childhood home.

Todd loved the children's simplistic view of the world. Their words and laughter was the first softness his heart had felt since that tragic winter night in that faraway land called Afghanistan. He called his mother when he arrived in the bleak town, and told her about his tiny house, omitting the truth of how squalid his living quarters actually were. He did not ask about either his brother or father and hung up when she called the colonel to the phone.

One of the other teachers at the school was a tall woman from the Northern Cheyenne tribe named Madeline Wilson. Her hair was long and black and she held it back with a simple clasp covered in a beaded design of stars. Around her waist, she wore a red beaded belt. Her mother was from the Pine Ridge reservation and had been the superintendent of the school for most of Madeline's twenty-seven years.

Every day, Madeline dressed in white knee length moccasins and flowing skirts, topped by either white blouses or white sweaters. She had taken quickly to the young man from Virginia, sensing his broken soul but also seeing a kind and generous heart. Slowly, over the course of several months, Todd revealed his life's story to Madeline. He spoke of his mother and her faith, his father and his unwavering sense of right and wrong, and his twin brother's descent into rage and violence. He stopped short, however, of reciting the events of that terrible day in the cave filled with death and of the night on the road to the village. He kept Curt's secret, never revealing the abduction of the tiny Afghan child or his belief that the child had died in the icy clasp of winter.

He told of his time in the Army and his recent discharge. He shared how he planned to use his GI benefits to pay for the teaching certificate he would need to continue at the school. In turn, Madeline taught him her traditions, of the Sun Dance and the healing ceremonies for the warriors that bore the weight of fighting for their families and countries. She spoke to him with understanding of the difference between hating war and its destruction and the love of the warriors. She told him about the falling of eagle's feathers at the dances and that only a veteran could retrieve the lost feather. She taught him of the healing ceremonies and the welcoming of the wounded men back into the community. She spoke to him of his valor and his courage and of ceremony.

Twice a week, Madeline and her mother, Sheneen, invited Todd to their apartment above the company store. The small space the women occupied was full of blankets, medicine wheels, flowers, and woven baskets. Navajo rugs covered the worn carpets and crocheted doilies decorated the shabby arms of the green couch and chairs. The contrast to the elegant home in Springfield was insignificant to Todd as he relaxed into the laughter and love that made the cramped apartment warm and healing.

The dilapidated house in which he lived leaned to the west. Todd placed matchbooks under half the legs of the chairs and tables to hold them even. Over time he furnished the little house, purchasing kitchen towels with houses and flowers embroidered on them. He hung brilliant blue bath towels in the bathroom; matching sheets and quilts on the bed. A blue and white-striped rug was nudged up against the bed with a scratched dresser next to the small closet crammed with Todd's shirts, slacks, jeans, and shoes.

He had no television, no phone, and no computer. He lived austerely, painting the weather- beaten fence and the outside of the house a bright yellow; never realizing it mirrored the yellow of the cotton tee shirt of the Afghani child. Todd scrubbed the cracked and faded linoleum in the neon green kitchen, spending hours using Comet cleanser to make the old stainless steel sink shine. He prowled the thrift shops in Billings, finding a barely used set of pots and pans, buying a slightly chipped set of plates and cups and other mismatched tableware.

A solitary peace crept over Todd's life, the first one in nearly two years. His friendship with Madeline and Sheneen evolved into pillars of trust on which his salvation rested. At night, jazz beamed in from a radio station in Billings and accompanied him while he completed his daily tasks and prepared for the next day at school. He wrote curriculum plans and drew smiley faces on the papers turned in by his diminutive charges. Photos of the children he taught dangled from a thick piece of twine he hung from two green pushpins that adorned the rarely used fireplace.

The serenity Todd found in his new life came to an abrupt end with the first snow of the season. The storm hit at midnight, rattling the windows and blowing snow in through the cracks of the house. Todd woke up to pellets of ice being flung against the windows by the raging wind. Terror encompassed his soul as his mind filled with horrible images of his dead comrades and the tiny green-eyed girl running barefoot into the Afghani night. He spent the rest of the night leaning against the headboard with the blue and white quilt clutched in his hands. Sleep finally came at dawn. The snow continued to fall as the wind tapered to a low hum. Todd opened his eyes to frosted windows and bone-chilling cold in the little house. He rolled over to read the clock, the red numbers telling him it was 6:48, leaving him only twenty-seven minutes to shower and be at school.

He bolted upright. Sitting on the edge of the bed he rubbed his feet against the nap of the rug, creating heat with the friction warming his soles. The images of the nightmare faded as he started his morning routine. Yawning, he bent over, touching his toes, and then stood, stretching his back. He padded down the cold hallway and into the bathroom. Turning the shower on, he waited for rust to clear from the water that poured out of the showerhead.

Within fifteen minutes, Todd was dressed and out the door, wrapped in a heavy parka, orange scarf, jeans and woolen gloves. He entered his cold classroom and quickly turned on the radiator. Next he readied the classroom by placing a pink sheet of paper on the corner of each desk and a black crayon on the paper. He smiled at the neat child-friendly room as he walked towards the front to stand next to the ancient chalkboard.

Todd picked up the broken piece of chalk and started writing out the alphabet. He stared at the blackness of the board and the wisps of white chalk giving it a gray tinge. Outside, the day was dark from the storm, the wind gaining velocity and moaning across the prairie surrounding the small town. Feeling a chill creeping down his neck, Todd commenced writing on the chalkboard:

> A is for apple and agony
> B is for boy and battle
> C is for cat and crazy
> D is for dog and death
> E is for egg and enemy
> F is for frog and fighting
> G is for goat and gore

Todd began to weep, leaning against the board, smearing his blue and white sweater with the chalk. He slowly lowered himself, finally kneeling on the floor. His arms were wrapped around his knees and his face pressed against the rough wood.

Madeline found Todd still crouching on the floor as she walked into his classroom to say "good morning." She ran to his side and dropped beside him. She lifted his tear-stained face and gently cradled it in her hands.

"Todd, what are you doing? What's going on? You can tell me, nothing is so awful that it can't be spoken. Come on; let's get you up. Your children will be here in a few minutes. Mom can watch them while you come with me."

She pulled Todd to his feet, wrapping her arm tightly around his shoulder. She reached across him and using a worn eraser, she wiped the painful words from the board. He leaned into her, his tears now flowing freely as he and Madeline made their way through the school to a small office at the back of the cafeteria. Todd sank into a plastic chair, dropping his head to the table. His left cheek lay on the smooth surface and his eyes were shut tight against the image of the little girl in the yellow shirt disappearing into the night. Madeline closed the door to the office and flipped a "Do Not Disturb" sign in the window. She sat down next to Todd and gently placed her hand on the back of his neck.

"Todd, tell me what it is. We can figure it out together. Let me help."

He turned his face away from Madeline as his memories poured from the depths of his grieving heart.

"We lost our friends. They were killed in an ambush. We left their bodies in a cave. I don't know if the Afghanis set us up. I don't know. Curt and I left the cave at dusk and walked for hours. There was a village. Then three men, the Afghanis who deserted the team, came out of one of the houses and down the road towards us.

"Curt shot them. I stood there. I let him do it. I ran, Madeline, I just ran. I don't know how far. When I looked up, Curt was there. He was holding a little girl from the village in his arms. It was so cold, so terribly cold. She didn't have any shoes on and we were so far from the village. Madeline, he put her down and sent her out into the snow. I don't know why he took her. I could have taken her back. I could have saved her but I didn't.

"I could have told our general what we did. He would have understood, but I didn't. I can't talk to Curt anymore. I can't look at my mother and father. I can't hate my brother but I hate myself. I didn't do anything as she ran off into the night. I let her go and we were so far away from the village. I let her go."

Madeline was perched on the edge of her chair. She did not say a word but all the while her warm hand rested on Todd's neck until he was done. At last, his words trailed off. She gently pulled him around until he was facing her.

"Todd, call your brother and tell him to come and visit you. We'll go to Lame Deer and Mom will come with us. We will do ceremony for you. There is nothing so terrible that we can't help. Call your brother and tell him to come."

Madeline gently brushed Todd's blond hair from his forehead, lightly kissing his lips.

"Come on, we'll call your brother. I'll help."

The phone rang in the house on the cul-de-sac in Springfield. Todd's father's voice came through the line, answering the call as he always had:

"Colonel Baines."

"Dad! It's Todd. I want to talk to Curt. If he's asleep, wake him up. I want to talk to him."

The harshness in Todd's voice prevented the colonel from asking questions. Todd heard the sound of the phone dropping on the kitchen counter and footsteps going and coming.

"What do you want?" came Curt's irritated voice. "You got me out of bed. What do you want?"

"I told her, Curt. I told Madeline. She isn't angry, she doesn't hate me. She wants to help. Come to Colstrip. She wants to take us to her home and help us. Curt, please say you'll come. I haven't told anyone else. Curt, I'm asking you as your brother. Please come." Todd's voice cracked as the tears washed from his eyes. Madeline took the phone from his trembling hand.

"Curt, this is Madeline. I'm a teacher here in Colstrip and a friend of your brother. He needs you, Curt, and I think you need him. You can fly into Billings and I'll pick you up. Curt, will you come?"

A light rain misted the air of Springfield, blurring the view of the oaks now barren of leaves, and the pool, now covered with blue plastic. The phone seemed enormously heavy as Curt nodded and then cleared his throat.

"I'll catch a flight today. Give me a number to call. I'll be there this evening."

Hanging up the phone, Curt ignored his father's questioning gaze. He walked down the plush carpeted hall and into his bedroom. He started to shut the door and then turned to look at his father who stood at the other end of the hallway.

"You got your wish, Dad. I'm leaving. I 'm going to Montana to be with Todd. I'll be gone before Mom gets back from the store. I won't be back. You can go on with your life, just like you told me to. But Dad, I hold you responsible. You lied to us, you lied."

⇥ ⇤

The United jet from Denver pulled into the gate at the Billings airport. Snow swirled in furious clouds from the exhaust of the engines. Madeline and Todd waited for Curt in the baggage claim area, Todd's stomach twisted with fear and anguish. Madeline grabbed his hand and stood silently beside him. A young man, identical in height, weight and features to Todd entered the area and came towards her. As he reached them, Todd started to bawl. He threw his arms around Curt's neck and pulled him close.

"I'm so sorry, Curt. I am so sorry. Forgive me, please. I am so sorry."

Curt returned his brother's embrace, whispering in his ear, "It's okay. I know and I am sorry, too. I love you, Todd."

Madeline smiled as the twins hugged each other. Moving between them she took each by an arm, and spoke in her soft and calming voice: "We're so glad you are here, Curt. Grab your bags and we'll get going. The roads are icy so we'll have to take it easy. It will probably take us three or four hours to get back home."

"Which bags are yours, Curt?" Todd asked. His foot rested on the edge of the baggage mover, reminding him of their return to Dulles Airport six months earlier. He shook his head back to the present and reached forward as Curt pointed out his bags. Among them was a rifle case, its hard sides scuffed and dirty. Curt reached forward and swung it off the belt, turning to hand it to Todd. Todd slowly backed away from the dirty conveyor belt, a look of horror on his face.

"Curt, what is this? Are you crazy? Why did you bring this? Oh, God, are you out of your mind? How could you do this?"

"Todd, stop it. I'll tell you if you'll stop yelling. I thought that since I was here in Montana, we'd get a rental car and drive to the ranch we stayed at when we were kids. You remember, the Buffalo Springs Ranch? I called them before I left home and Dusty said he would take us. I have elk tags. I thought you could go with me and we'd go hunting after driving back to Lame Deer. I thought we could spend some time together before we meet Madeline's family."

Todd stood rigid and stared in disbelief at his brother. He exhaled a heavy breath and then nodded. "If you want me to come, I will. Madeline, I can't let him go alone. You understand?"

Madeline reached up to stroke Todd's face and nodded in agreement. "It's fine, Todd. Go on with your brother in the rental car. You can follow me back to Colstrip. Curt, I am delighted you have come. I think you will love Lame Deer. Let me show you where the rental car counter is. I think some time with your brother will do both of you good."

Todd and Curt followed Madeline through the airport, both carrying a bag in each hand. Outside, the wind chilled them as they made their way to the cars waiting in the parking lot. Madeline climbed into the battered Subaru station wagon she had driven to the airport. Pulling her seat belt over her shoulder she started the engine. It sputtered and caught as Madeline shifted into first and accelerated out of the lot. The twins sat bundled in their rented Explorer, Curt peering out of the small cleared patch on the windshield as they followed Madeline's small green vehicle.

The drive back to Colstrip was quiet. Neither brother was willing to start a conversation. Curt drove the entire trip, looking straight ahead and in his rearview mirror. Todd's gaze alternated between the view outside the front window and the profile of his brother's face. As they drove into Colstrip, Todd pointed out the two buildings that made up the school and then the freshly painted yellow house where he now resided.

"Pull up in the driveway, Curt. We'll see Madeline in a few days when we get back. It is too late for company tonight. Curt, I'm glad you came. Really, I am, I've missed you." He put his hand on his brother's arm, his touch saying more than his words ever could.

Curt nodded, squeezed his brother's hand and opened the door. A sudden flash of the three dead bodies buried in the confines of the cave crashed over him. He shook his head, reorienting himself to the tiny town of Colstrip. Its shabby houses and broken streets were reminiscent of the pock-marked road leading to the Afghani village. He followed Todd into the bright yellow house, the floorboards creaking with the weight of their steps. Todd's face was masked in the dim light as he pointed to the second-hand couch.

"There's a sleeping bag there. The house gets cold at night but there are plenty of Pendleton blankets on the chair. Curt, look, I'm really glad you're here. No matter what, you're my brother. I love you and I always will."

The next morning was Saturday. Curt busied himself reloading his bags into the back of the Explorer. Todd followed, his blue duffel bag bulging with clothes and boots. He tossed it into the open trunk and climbed into the passenger's seat.

"It will take about eight hours to get to Devils Tower and the ranch in this weather," said Curt. "Let me know if you want to drive. I am glad to be here and I am really sorry…"

"Curt," Todd's voice was low and distant, "I don't want to talk about it. It's done and over. I told you last night. I'm glad you're here. Forget it. I can't talk about it."

"Okay, Todd. We'll leave it at that. I am sorry." Curt gripped the wheel and drove onto the highway, heading east into the snow.

The brothers did not speak for the entire trip. Stopping only for gas and quick snacks, Curt drove across the breathtaking scenery of Wyoming. The mountains provided a backdrop of grandeur as they drove through Sheridan and finally into the hamlet of Moorcroft. As dusk fell, the Explorer left the highway and pulled onto State Route 14 and then to State Route 24. The sky cleared as they drove north. The faint outline of Devils Tower came into view as they peeked over the ridge. Its sides glistened with ice, feathery winter clouds scuttling across the summit.

The ranch lay ten miles off the main road. The dirt road was icy and slick even with the Explorer in four-wheel drive. An agonizing forty minutes later, the ranch came into view. The red barn sat on the right and a large lodge was directly ahead.

Sarah came out of the lodge with her arms wrapped around her body to keep the cold wind out. The twins stepped out of the Explorer, quickly reaching for their coats for warmth and protection. They pulled out their baggage and Curt's rifle case. Shivering in the wintry air, they ducked their heads and followed Sarah into the main part of the lodge.

Inside, they found a middle-aged woman with green eyes and graying hair seated in a wooden rocking chair, her feet propped up on the stone hearth. She looked up and smiled at the twins as she fingered a stone black owl fetish that hung on a cord around her neck. Her feet were encased in sheepskin slippers and a copy of *The Once and Future King* lay open on her lap.

"Don't get up, Lola. These are our guests for the week. Let's see if I can get it right." Sarah faced the twins with her hands on her hips. Her brow furrowed as she looked for clues to determine who was who. "This one is Curt and this is Todd," she said, pointing correctly to the two men.

"Curt has the mole on the left side of his neck and Todd's is on the right. Their mother told me they were mirror images and the mole was the easiest way to tell them apart. It's been years since the boys were here. I can't believe how big and handsome you both have become. Dusty will be so pleased to see you again. He's in Spearfish but should be back within an hour or two."

Todd and Curt laughed. Todd said he was impressed with Sarah's ability to recall the identifying detail from so long ago. Both boys remembered when the lodge was an empty shell with only the roof and walls in place.

"Are we sleeping in the barn again?" Curt asked.

Sarah laughed and shook her head. "No, we have plenty of rooms now. Lola is our only guest and we have three empty bedrooms here in the lodge. I've put you in separate quarters but you'll have to share a bathroom. I hear you were in Afghanistan after September 11th. I want you to know how much Dusty and I appreciate the work and sacrifice you and all our soldiers have made. It's a sad world now but soon maybe this madness will end. Anyway, welcome back to the Buffalo Springs Ranch. We're glad you're here.

"Todd, I understand you are playing hooky from school for a few extra days."

"Who told you that, Sarah?" Todd looked perplexed.

"A nice young woman by the name of Madeline called and said I was to tell you that they found a substitute for your class and to enjoy your time off with your brother. She sounds quite lovely, Todd. She also said to tell you she would be here on Wednesday to take you back to Colstrip. I think she wants to see the ranch and take a few days off herself. So, it looks like we'll have a full house for Thanksgiving dinner."

Lola watched the interplay between Sarah and the brothers from her place by the fire. She sensed a tension between the twins but could not tell its origin. Todd stood away from his brother. Curt's rifle case brushed Todd's leg as he followed Sarah down the hall. Todd jumped away as if the case had given him an electric shock. Curt was seemingly oblivious to Todd's actions but, on closer examination, Lola could see a hurt look on his face.

The boys trailed after Sarah and disappeared as they entered their respective rooms. Lola returned to her book. The story of Arthur, Merlin, Pellinore, and Kay interested her more than the obvious tension between the new guests. She dozed off for a moment but awoke as Sarah returned to the room and stirred the fire.

"You know, Lola, I think those boys have been through some rough times. I can't put my finger on it, but I feel the anger between them. I wonder what caused it or why they came up here together if they are so angry. Well, it's not my business. I'm sorry to disturb you, Lola, but I was wondering why you came out so late this year? You usually come in September."

"You didn't disturb me, Sarah. I've read this book a dozen times but I always find it thrilling and prescient. Its timelessness is kind of

like Tolkien and the *Lord of the Rings* or maybe even the Bible. I feel
like there is wisdom here that will somehow explain the world to me.
Anyway, I came later this year because of my work. I was trying to get a
project finished before I came, but I just wasn't motivated. After thirty
years I think I am bored with my job. Imagine that!"

Lola chuckled and placed her book on the table next to the rocker.

"Sarah, I felt the tension, too. Something is amiss between them.
Dusty asked me to ride to elk camp with them. I guess he is borrow-
ing some mules from the ranch down the road. Said that Marnie and
Mandy threw shoes and he could not get the farrier out here in time to
re-shoe them. I haven't ridden in the snow for a long time so I'm looking forward to it.

"So, it sounds like you are having another guest out this week. I
thought you were done with your guests by this time of the year. You're
working late this year. Look, Dusty just pulled up. I think I'll go see if
there is anything I can do to help him."

Lola stood up and stretched her legs. She gave Sarah a quick hug and
then trotted down the stairs towards the back door, calling to Dusty as
she left the warmth of the lodge. Sarah stirred the fire one more time,
listening for the twins before following Lola down the stairs.

Later that night, Sarah provided a simple dinner of cold cuts, cheese
and wheat bread on the red oilcloth tablecloth. Lola, wearing a sweater,
sat on the plank bench with her feet tucked under her thighs and her
arms wrapped around her knees. She studied the young faces of the
twins; an odd animosity filled the air, chilling the warmth of Sarah's
kitchen. During dinner, Dusty, Curt and Todd made their plans for the
trek up into the hills to the clearing Dusty had shown them so many
years before.

"No," Dusty said, as far as he was aware, the elk still roamed the woods
and had not been shot and killed. "Yes," most of the hunters had left
the forest but the trail was still clear enough for the horses to get up the
mountain. "Yes," he said, they now had a large herd of horses acquired
the year after the boys had been at the ranch. The weather was forecast
to remain clear and cold, perfect for hunting. "No," Dusty would not
stay for the entire four days that the boys would be up at the camp. He

and Lola would ride up with them and then return on Wednesday to help them pack out the equipment. "Yes," they had steady horses that were surefooted and easy to ride.

Towards midnight and finally yawning, the women excused themselves for the night. Lola climbed the stairs to her room and Sarah returned to the kitchen to prepare food for the three-night stay at elk camp. She muttered about the tension between the twins. Through dinner and into the evening, Todd sat as far from Curt as the bench allowed.

Upstairs, Lola dressed in a purple nightshirt covered with dancing bears. It had been a gift from Istie who knew that Lola loved oversized nightshirts. She did not allow anyone else to know of this peculiarity, including Kristin and Rona. As Lola climbed under the thick blankets and snuggled beneath the covers, she thought of her trip the previous year, and of Jones and Annie's wallet. She wondered where Jones was and if he still wiped his eyes on that green bandana. She reached out and turned off the lamp and rolled over. She was asleep before the image of the room left the inside of her eyelids.

The sun rose on a greeting card day, with a glorious display of red, yellow, gold and purple. Lola carried saddlebags of food, tents, ropes, boots, and flashlights, and even pillows down to the barn. Dusty systematically packed the bags, lashing them to the frames cinched on the two mules. The mules had been brought to the barn the previous night. They were sturdy, intelligent animals that spooked at nothing and knew the way to the campsite better than Dusty himself.

Lola pulled four horses from the herd as soon as they finished their breakfast of crimped oats and alfalfa. Steam rose from the horses, their breaths frosty in the cold air and their coats woolly and thick in preparation for the Wyoming winter. She tied the horses to rings in the lean-to and saddled them as Dusty finished packing the mules. They worked in companionable silence with only an occasional comment passing between them.

At seven-thirty, Sarah called everyone to a breakfast of hot pancakes and scrambled eggs already set on the oilcloth-covered table. Lola and Dusty were filling their plates as Curt and Todd clattered down the stairs. Curt carried the rifle case in his hand.

"Do you have a safe place to put this, Dusty?" Curt asked. "I want to make sure it is packed before we go. By the way, thanks for picking up the ammunition yesterday. I left a check for it on the table in the great room. Todd wouldn't let me stop to get it on our way up here yesterday."

"Sure," Dusty replied, wiping his hands and rising to take the case. "I'll put it outside next to the door and we can pack it when we get ready to leave. Where is your rifle, Todd?"

An awkward silence fell over the table as neither twin responded. After an uncomfortable pause, Todd cleared his throat: "I saw enough killing in Afghanistan, Dusty. I'm just along to keep Curt from shooting himself. Sarah, do you mind? I think I'll go out and meet my horse and finish loading my saddlebags. Dusty, which horse is mine?"

"It's the big buckskin Appaloosa gelding, Todd. His name is Pastor Ben. All he needs is a tightening of his cinch and his bridle. I can take care of that if you want."

"Thanks, I think I can do it. Sarah, thanks for everything. I'll see you in a few days. I'll wait for you three down at the barn." Todd grabbed a piece of hot cornbread and disappeared out the door.

Lola got up from the table. "I'm done with breakfast. Sarah, let me help you clean the dishes and then I'll get on the rest of my winter clothes. I'll be down to the barn in fifteen minutes, Dusty. Curt, I saddled the palomino mare for you. Give me a few minutes and I'll finish getting her ready. She can be testy at times when you are on the ground but once you are on her, you'll like her."

Lola picked up the plates and made her way to the kitchen. She piled the dishes on the table in the middle of the kitchen, pondering again the tension and simmering anger between the brothers. She heard Dusty go out the door, whistling as he made his way across the cold ground towards the waiting animals. She caught a few words of the conversation between Sarah and Curt before Curt left to join the others. Moments later, Sarah came into the kitchen.

"They're waiting for you, Lola, go ahead and get ready. I can take it from here. I tell you, the tension between those boys makes me feel like I'm choking. I hope they can settle their problem while they are up at elk camp. You and Dusty should be back around three this afternoon.

I've packed you lunches and thermoses of coffee and hot chocolate. Give me a hug and get on out there. I'll see you when you get back."

"Sarah, I am so glad I came back this year. You have no idea how important this place is to me. I bless you every day for the red pony you gave me last year. Someday I'll bring him back for a visit. He has been the love of my life, not that I would tell my niece that! Anyway, I'm out of here. See you this afternoon."

Lola grabbed her coat, scarf, hat and gloves, donning them as she headed out the door. Behind her, the door closed; ahead of her the three men huddled around the horses and mules, their breaths mingling and creating a cloud in the winter air. She made her way across the frozen grass to the paddock. Pulling open the gate, she slipped inside the corral where the men were finishing up readying the horses.

As the group headed out, Dusty led the way up the switchback trail, ponying a mule. Todd followed next on the big Appaloosa and then Curt on the Palomino. Lola brought up the rear, also ponying one of the mules. The trail from the ranch wound around the pond and disappeared up into the hills. After two hours of riding and climbing, the party came into the same clearing Dusty had led the twins and their father to so many years before. Within an hour, the camp was established, tent erected, and tarps laid out; Curt's rifle was pulled from the scabbard and placed alongside the tent under a tarp.

The packs were removed from the mules and secured on the boards nailed to the trees along the edges of the clearing. As the sun climbed higher, the day warmed a little but the air remained cool and crisp. Lola, Dusty and the boys shared a lunch of roast beef sandwiches, cheese and fruit. Dusty threw the crusts of his bread to the jays screaming overhead. The ponderosa pines seemed to lean toward the clearing, whisperings coming from deep inside the forest as a mild breeze blew the snow off the tree branches. The twins sat opposite each other, directing their questions at Dusty and Lola, avoiding eye contact. The sudden piercing cry of a Red-tailed Hawk caused the four to look skyward, where they could see clouds gathering to the southwest, foretelling of more snow despite the weatherman's proclamations.

"Let's go, Lola." Dusty said. "We'd better get back to the ranch. Curt and Todd, we'll be back around noon on Wednesday to help close up camp and bring you home. If anything happens, head straight south and you can raise us on the cell phones I put in your packs. Sometimes you can get a signal up here but if the weather is bad, it's more difficult. Be careful and we'll see you in three days."

Dusty and Lola mounted their horses, this time each ponying a second horse along with the mules. The twins stood in the center of the clearing, watching them disappear down the trail. Todd sat down, folding his arms over his knees and resting his chin on his arms as he stared across the valley to Devils Tower standing in the distance. From where Todd sat, the Tower seemed to float above the valley, clouds ringing its striated sides. He was entranced by the playful shadows on the hillsides; fine particles of snow misted the cliffs that marked the edge of the Black Hills.

Caught in the moment, Todd did not realize his brother was standing behind him. Finally, Todd looked up and squinted at his brother silhouetted against the winter sun.

"What are you doing, Curt? You startled me."

"I'm going to change my clothes and then go scout locations for hunting tomorrow. I'll be back soon." Curt wiped his nose on his sleeve and spit on the ground next to his brother's boot.

Curt went into the tent and emerged a few minutes later clothed in camouflage from head to toe. He had painted black under his eyes; a knife was strapped to his belt, and he held a riflescope in his left hand. He reached under the tarp and picked up his rifle. Affixing the scope, he set the sight. Swinging the rifle around, he pointed it at Todd's chest.

"It was easy, you know, Todd. I pointed my rifle just like this and pulled the trigger. I was surprised how easy it was. I didn't feel a thing. *Pop, pop, pop!* You left me there. And then, when we went back to Kabul, you begged for a transfer to get away from me. You left me there, Todd, all on my own.

"You know I had to do it, Todd. I had to take that little girl. She was my only hope of getting out alive. Then, you ran away from Mom and Dad's and left me there. Alone with that man, alone one more time. You left me there, alone, Todd. Now, you tell me to come here for healing and you won't even talk to me. You're leaving me alone one more time, Todd, aren't you. Why?"

Continuing to point the rifle at Todd's chest, Curt pulled the trigger into the cocked position. "*Pop, pop, pop.* Just like those Afghani men, Todd. *Pop* and you're dead. It would be so easy, a hunting accident. Don't trust me, brother? Well, I don't trust you! *Pop, pop, pop...*"

Todd stared at his brother, cold fury curling inside him. "I was there, Curt. I saw what happened. Those men weren't going to shoot us. And that little girl. Curt, what was she going to do? You let her go with no shoes and no coat. You knew she would die out there. You took her to save your skin and then you let her die. I didn't tell your secret. I didn't turn you in. I didn't tell anyone."

"You are as big a liar as Dad, Todd. You told that girl Madeline. You didn't bring me here for any healing ceremony, whatever that is. You brought me out here to tell me how you're going to turn me in. You're going to betray me again. You're just as guilty as me, Todd. You could have taken that girl back to the village. You let her run off into the cold and snow. You could have saved her, Todd. You didn't do anything different or better than I did. I'm just more honest about it. Do you see their ghosts, Todd? Do they visit you at night, too? Do you feel them around you? Do you hear them whispering to you? I do. I hear the captain, and Dell, and Hal calling me. I see that little girl. They talk to me, Todd. Do they talk to you?"

"Is that why you wanted to come up here, Curt? To tell me about your guilt and about your ghosts? I don't want to hear it! Go on, get out of here! Go hunt. Go find something else to kill. That's all you know. Go on, find your elk. Kill it, too. You've always wanted to. Go ahead. Go find something else innocent to murder. Leave me out of it. Go on! If this is what this trip is going to be about, I'm done. I'm hiking out of here. I'm going back to the ranch. You're on your own."

Todd stood up and turned his back on his brother and stepped forward to head down the trail Lola and Dusty had left only thirty minutes before. He had only a split second to hear the sound of the rifle fire before the bullet bit into his back below his left scapula. He was thrown forward onto the ground, blood already flowing from his nose and mouth. He felt numbness and cold beginning to spread throughout his body. He tried to raise his head but it was too heavy to lift. Coldness crawled up his back and into his chest. His face lay on the frozen ground with his left cheek resting on a stone. He saw the little girl with the green eyes running into the forest, her yellow tee shirt floating around her small body. She turned and waved at him, laughing as she disappeared among the trees.

The crack of the rifle echoed forever off the rocks and hills. The Red-tailed Hawk flew across the sky, crying for the dead man. Curt stood for a moment, once again the smell of cordite hanging in the air. He stepped forward to stand over his brother. He didn't say a word; he just waited for Todd to roll over and talk to him.

He nudged Todd's body with his foot. Then he reached down and shook his brother's shoulder. "Come on, Todd, get up. Don't you dare leave me again! You bastard, get up. Get up!" Curt began to scream, kicking Todd's body in a fury. His rage poured out of him as he hit Todd's head with the butt of the rifle.

"Get up, get up, get up! You are such a bastard. Come on, Todd. Get up."

His breath left his body as if he had been punched. As he sank to the ground by his brother's lifeless body, he looked at the dirty boot marks he left on Todd's back and legs and the gashes on the back of his brother's head from the rifle butt.

"Oh, God! Todd, don't leave me alone. I can't take being alone anymore. You have to wake up. Oh, God, Todd, I'm sorry. I didn't mean it. Come on, get up." Curt started to cry, his salty tears running down his cheeks into the corners of his mouth.

Speaking to himself, Curt began to ramble, "Okay, I remember what he did in the cave. I remember. Todd pulled the bodies into a corner and covered them up. I remember, he covered up their faces and said prayers over them. Okay, that's what I'll do. Come on, Todd. Come into the tent. I'll keep you warm. Just give me a minute. Okay, remember, keep your weapon dry. Okay, just give me a minute. Okay, Todd, now get up. Oh, God, Todd. I didn't mean it. Wake up."

A small whirlwind rolled through the glade where Curt sat, rocking hysterically. Todd's pants rippled with the breeze. A cloud passed overhead distracting Curt for a moment. He heard faint sounds drifting from the dark woods. Curt shivered in the cold and bent toward Todd's limp body. His face was twisted in fear as he once more pleaded with his brother. "Come on, brother. We've been through worse. Come on, let's go home."

Slowly Curt pulled himself to his feet, wiping his eyes with the back of his hand, smearing his brother's blood over his cheeks and chin. He grabbed his brother by the back of the coat, pulling him, inch by inch, towards the tent. Todd's blood left a crimson trail across the campsite. His limp body was almost too heavy for Curt. He began sobbing, this time the tears tasting of his brother's blood. He pulled at Todd's body again and finally got it onto the tarp in front of the tent.

Curt climbed over Todd's body and entered the tent. He unfolded one of the sleeping bags and zipped it open. Grunting and swearing, Curt took off his brother's clothes and rolled the body inside the bag. As he zipped the bag, he carefully avoided the empty stare of his brother's blue eyes.

He carefully folded Todd's clothes, placing them into a neat stack next to Todd's body. Sitting down again, he patted his brother on his shoulder as tears rolled down his cheek. Curt reached for his rifle and placed it across his knees with his legs stretched out in front of him. His back was propped up against a tree trunk, the pine tree a silent witness to the tragedy that had taken place in its domain.

Two miles down the trail, Lola and Dusty pulled the horses to a halt as they heard the retort of a rifle echoing across the hills and rolling down to the valley's floor.

"Dusty, what was that? It sounded like it came from the campsite. Do you think we should go back? We aren't that far away. Do you think Curt went hunting already? "

"Hold tight for a minute, Lola. Let's wait for a few minutes. If there aren't any more shots and no one comes down, we'll go on home. Let's see if we can get a signal on the cell phone. There's one in the cantle bag right behind you. Hand it to me and I'll call."

Lola turned in her saddle and unzipped the green bag tied to the cantle of the saddle. She pulled out the small phone and reached across her mount, handing it to Dusty. He flipped it open and dialed a number. The phone rang once and then cut off, "call failed" flashing across the screen.

"No signal. Well, let's sit for a few more minutes and see if anyone comes. If not, let's get on back down to the ranch. Those boys were in Afghanistan. They have survival training. Don't worry, Lola. I know you and Sarah share the particular hobby of worrying too much but, if there is a problem, one of them will come to get us."

In unison, Dusty and Lola swung their legs over their saddles and slid to the ground, causing the horses to shift their weight. They checked the cinches and bridles. They waited half an hour. No one came down the trail and they heard no further gunshots. Lola and Dusty remounted their horses and continued their way down the trail. The wind picked up. Large flakes of snow landed and melted as soon as they hit the warm bodies of the animals carefully picking their way down the steep trail.

Back at the camp, Curt sat next to Todd's body, watching the snow-flakes beginning to cover Todd's sleeping bag. He flashed back to the cave, seeing the icicles hanging from its entrance and listening to Hal talking to Dell in a hushed voice. The captain squatted beyond Hal and Dell talking to the Pashtun men, his voice rising in anger and frustration. He saw the wind blowing the frozen moisture around him as the light flashed from his rifle and the Pashtun men fell to the ground. The little girl stood in front of him, holding her arms up to him, asking him to pick her up.

The snow was falling heavier now, muffling the calls of the birds in the trees. Curt saw a sudden movement from the corner of his eye as a figure in white moved through the snow under the green trees. Again, a motion caught his eye, this time on the other side of the clearing. Curt clutched his rifle to his chest, his breathing ragged and harsh in his ears. All around him he sensed movement and a hushed murmuring. He sat next to his dead brother, jerking his head from side to side. The branches of the trees swayed in the wind and twigs snapped.

From the thicket a majestic elk stepped into the clearing. His rack of antlers was heavy as he lifted his head high into the air. He walked forward and stopped in front of Curt. His large, intelligent eyes mesmerized Curt as he stared back in disbelief. Across the glade, a tall woman dressed in a white buffalo skin cape glided forward. A red beaded belt cinched her small waist and she carried a quiver of arrows in her hand. A white bow was slung over her shoulder.

Simultaneously, the woman and the elk stepped towards each other, bowing as if beginning a waltz. Slowly, they turned towards Curt. The woman smiled and held out her left hand, reaching down and pulling Curt to his feet. She dropped the quiver to the ground and shrugged the bow off her shoulder. Placing her right hand on the neck of the elk she leaned towards the beautiful animal, rubbing her cheek against the fur of the enormous animal's neck.

A beaded clasp of shining stars pulled the woman's long hair from her forehead, as the ends swirled about her face. Tiny flecks of snow created a halo around her hair. She smiled at Curt as she held his hand and draped her arm around the neck of the elk.

Curt held tight to the woman's hand as other animals silently emerged from the snow-covered woods. A small black and brown coyote crept forward, laying its face on the moccasin-clad feet of the tall woman. Above her head, jays and crows, chickadees and nuthatches flew onto the nearby branches. A deer and its fawn moved on silent feet, followed by fox, vole, rabbit and bear. A small black she-wolf with one blue eye and one black eye lay down next to the coyote.

Faint figures flowed from the primal forest, their soft sighs filling the air. Shimmering lights shone in the small space where the animals waited. Down across the valley a clattering of rocks could be heard, echoing in waves to where Curt stood, paralyzed by fright and anticipation. He closed his eyes and clutched the woman's hand as tightly as he could. He felt something brush his shoulder, lighter than a leaf drifting down to the forest floor.

He opened his eyes to find the clearing ringed with thousands of spirits, beseeching arms reaching out to Curt. Shaking, he stared into the black eyes of the woman standing calmly in front of him. The

woman nodded and gently placed Curt's hand on her waist, his fingers feeling the smoothness of the belt tightly wrapped around her white buckskin dress. She looked into his eyes and began to speak, her voice low and soothing.

"Curt, we've come to help you. You were promised healing in this place and we are here to tend you. We know your pain. We know your thoughts. We know your heart. It's time to make a choice that will decide the fate of your soul.

"You can choose to return to your world of anger and revenge, or make your peace and allow healing in your heart and soul. Look around you. We have been waiting for you for so long. All around you are the ones who have died in wars or from anger and revenge. These gentle animals are the ones left after years of slaughter. They have suffered as you are suffering now. It can end here. You can stop the pain. We've come to help you, to bring you peace, to bring you home. It's time to come home. Hold my hand and walk with me. You can atone for your sins, Curt. Come with us, come home."

A great weariness engulfed him as he listened to the woman's voice. She leaned forward removing her arm from around the neck of the elk. Placing her hands on Curt's cheeks she leaned forward, kissing his lips and gently stroking his forehead.

"Come home, Curt. We are here to welcome you. Come with us, Curt, come home."

Curt looked into the woman's brown eyes filled with infinite forgiveness. She smiled as her long fingers helped Curt remove his clothes and fold them, piece by piece, placing them in a neat stack next to Todd's. As tears rolled freely from his eyes, Curt smiled and lay down, curled around his brother's body just as he had that awful day in the cave in Afghanistan.

He could feel the woman pressed up next to him, her body fitted into every curve and swell. The elk came to lie at Curt's feet, his head resting on the black bedroll that contained Todd's body. The coyote crept forward and placed his head on Curt's hand. The snow continued to fall heavier and heavier. Soon, the only things visible in the clearing were mounds of snow. The sky gradually slipped into indigo blue and the night came to pass.

On Wednesday morning, Lola and Dusty made their way back to the campsite. The journey was more difficult this time, the horses and mules breaking trail through the deep snow. The horses wheezed, their feet slipping as they made their way up the narrow path. . Lola and Dusty speculated on whether Curt got his elk. The day was spectacular, the sky a deep blue with no clouds to be seen. As Dusty led the way, the horses and mules made a final push up the ridge and the clearing came into view.

Lola heard Dusty's cry of shock as he dismounted from his horse. She saw him fall to the ground, his hands over his eyes. Climbing off her horse she ran to Dusty, stopping in horror at the scene in front of her. Curt lay in the nude, curled up against a black sleeping bag. From inside the bag, Todd's frozen eyes gazed forever into the blue sky. At their feet lay a huge elk, his brown eyes closely watching Lola and Dusty.

At their approach, the elk rose to his feet and stood guard over the brothers. He moved his huge head from side to side as Dusty and Lola carefully inched into the clearing. Keeping a cautious eye on the two humans, the elk lowered his head, scratched his face against his leg and shook his body. He nodded to Dusty and Lola and then bowed his enormous head. Straightening, he turned and stepped gracefully away from the bodies of the twins, moving to the side of the clearing as Dusty and Lola came forward.

Stunned, Dusty and Lola held onto each other. Lola peered over Dusty's shoulder, not believing what she saw. She pressed her head into Dusty's shoulder and then slid down to her knees. Crawling across the frozen, unforgiving ground to where the bodies lay entwined, she gingerly pulled down the zipper of the black bag that entombed Todd.

"Come on, Dusty. We have to get them home. We need to get them dressed and onto the mules. I don't know how long this weather will hold. We'll come back and clean up the camp later. Oh, my God, Dusty! Look! Todd's been shot. That's what we heard on Sunday, Dusty. Curt killed Todd."

Dusty knelt next to Lola and examined the bodies of the young men. "Lola, Curt must have shot Todd right after we left. Lordy, I wish we had returned that day. I will never forgive myself for not coming back. Lola, it looks like Curt took off his own clothes and lay down on the ground. Their bodies are frozen pretty solid. You're going to have to ride back to the ranch and get Doc Leighton and Sheriff Martz. Ah, Lordy, Lola. He killed his brother."

Dusty leaned away from the bodies, squatting on the ground. He took off his hat and placed it on the ground beside him. "Lola, we can't move the bodies. I know how upsetting this is but we have to leave the scene as undisturbed as possible. Aah, man. I can't believe this. What are we going to tell their parents? I think Todd's lady friend is supposed to be at the ranch today. Ah man, this is so bad."

Lola took a deep breath and let it out with a long sigh. She pushed herself away from the bodies, resting her gloved hands on her thighs. A puff of wind blew through the clearing, shaking tiny bits of snow from the overhanging branches. The horses and mules became startled and pulled back against the reins Dusty and Lola still held in their hands. The elk continued to stand in the clearing, quietly watching Lola and Dusty as they examined the twins' bodies.

"Dusty, I think that elk must have been protecting them. Why else would he be here? Curt was going to shoot that elk and the elk ended up watching over him. Dusty, none of this makes any sense. What do you think happened? Here, let me take the reins. I'll tie these guys to a tree and we can see what we need to do."

Lola shook her head in grief at the tragic scene. She took the horses' reins from Dusty. Carefully skirting the edge of the clearing, she tied the four horses and two mules to the lower branches of the pine trees that lined the forest. The animals shied away from the bodies of the two young men, snorting their concern. Lola stroked the white mane of the Palomino, soothing the nervous animal. She wiped her damp eyes against the warm fur of the big animal and then made her way back to Dusty who was now sitting on the ground. Lola placed her hands on Dusty's shoulder. He reached up and gently squeezed her hand.

"Lola, it looks like Curt shot Todd in the back. I don't know why. Take the Appaloosa and head back to the ranch. It will be dark by the time you get back if you don't leave now. Tell Sheriff Martz that we're on the Masterson Trail. He'll know where we are. Leave the mules and the rest of the horses. Go on, Lola. I'll stay here."

Lola nodded and went back to untie the big Appaloosa. As she led him to the edge of the clearing, she took a long look back at Dusty who was squatting by the dead bodies. She lifted herself into the saddle and started down the trail.

Alone on the mountain, Dusty rose. He pressed his right hand over his heart and thought of the straight-backed colonel and his wife. He worried what the news would do to the couple and wondered again what could have caused such a horrid tragedy. He listened to the retreating sound of the horse as Lola began her solemn journey back to the ranch.

"Okay, boys, I'm staying right here with you. We'll get you home as soon as we can."

A creaking branch pulled Dusty's attention to the trees where the horses and mules stood waiting, shaking and rubbing against each other. The elk that had guarded the twins was rubbing his antlers against the tree where the horses were tied. Dusty began to stand up but froze when the elk continued his stately walk across the clearing and back to stand by the dead bodies of the twins. The elk lowered his massive head and sniffed the ground next to Todd and Curt's feet. His front legs bent and his graceful body followed to the ground. Together, the elk and Dusty sat in vigilance while the day drew to a close.

Dusk was falling as Lola rode into the paddock. Sarah looked up at the clinking sound of the Appaloosa's bridle. Her welcoming smile changed to fear when she realized that Lola was alone. She ran across the hard-packed dirt and grabbed the gelding's bridle.

Before Sarah could speak, Lola leaned forward to grab Sarah's hand. "Sarah, they're dead; both of them. They've been dead since Sunday. Curt shot Todd. We've got to call Doc Leighton and the sheriff. Sarah, did Todd's friend arrive, the girl from Colstrip?"

Stunned into silence, Sarah nodded and held the gelding as Lola slid down onto the ground.

"Go on in, Lola. I'll tie him up. The numbers for Doc Leighton and the sheriff are on the wall by the phone. Lola, Madeline is here. She arrived just after you and Dusty set out this morning. Are you sure they're both dead? Oh Lord, this is going to devastate their parents. Madeline must have their phone number. If not, I've got it somewhere in my book of old numbers. Go on, Lola. I'll be in in a minute."

Lola sprinted to the lodge. A tall black-haired woman, dressed in white moccasins, jeans, and a white turtleneck sweater held the door open for Lola.

"Hi, you must be Lola. I'm Madeline, Todd's friend. Where are the boys? I thought they were coming back with you. Lola, what's wrong? Oh, my God, something's happened. They're dead, aren't they? I knew it. I felt it days ago. Oh, my God, Lola, they're dead, aren't they? Where are they?"

"Madeline, you're right. They're both dead. It looks as if Curt shot Todd. We think it happened right after we left them on Sunday. I've got to get the sheriff and the doctor out here. Sarah's coming in now. Let me make the calls and then I'll tell both of you everything I know."

The aroma of soup filled the kitchen, steaming the windows. Lola lifted the receiver of the red phone, the long cord twisting around itself as Lola punched in the sheriff's number. Her gaze focused on the pan of soup bubbling on the stove. Forty minutes later the sheriff and doctor arrived. They were dressed in winter clothing, scarves, gloves and woolen caps. They stood with the three women in the parking lot of the ranch. Night had fallen and with it the temperature dropped into the teens. Two SUV's, both pulling horse trailers, were parked beside two identical black hearses. The sheriff and two deputies listened intently as Lola told of the horrific scene on the lonely mountain. She relayed the message and directions as Dusty had instructed.

The sheriff, a gregarious man of sixty years, spat a wad of chewing tobacco into the snow, kicking it with the scuffed toe of his riding boots. He listened in silence and, at the end of Lola's recitation, motioned one of his deputies to his side.

"The lady with the white moccasins; she's a friend of one of the boys. Get as much information from her as possible and ask Sarah to call their parents. She knew the family from before and no one can give as much comfort during a hard time as her. Pete, Doc, Kyle, let's get going. Doesn't look like we'll get much light tonight but let's get ourselves up to the site."

Madeline stepped forward. Her lovely face was wreathed in sorrow and her shoulders were slumped. "Sheriff, I'm going with you. I know how to ride a horse and I'm not afraid of death. Todd was my friend. I have to go."

Sheriff Martz slapped his gloved hands together, the thick cloth muffling the sound. "Okay. Lola, are you up to more riding tonight? If so, saddle a horse and come along with us."

Lola nodded in agreement and took Madeline's hand. Hand in hand, they walked back across the frozen grass to the paddock where the horses had gathered, huddled against the cold of the winter night.

In the kitchen, the receiver of the red phone was lifted one more time. A pleasant female voice answering from across the country escalated into a scream in response to Sarah's soft-spoken words. The kitchen light cast a yellow glow out into the mountain night, barely illuminating the pasture as six horses carefully picked their way across the field and up the snow-covered trail.

It was nearly midnight when the recovery team reached the clearing. A fire cast a glow against the forest, repeating the glow of the kitchen miles below. An eerie scene greeted the small party. At the far side of the fire, Dusty sat peering towards the trail. Across from the fire lay the frozen bodies and at their feet lay an enormous elk. Mounds of snow were piled up against the bases of the ponderosa pines. The flicker of firelight bounced shadows up into the tree branches. The icy faces of the twins were staring forever into the night sky as the stars and planets whirled in an endless dance across the waiting heavens.

It wasn't until late Thanksgiving Day that the rescue party finally returned to the Buffalo Springs Ranch. Todd and Curt had been placed with loving care across the backs of the steady mules who never flinched from either the weight or smell of the frozen bodies.

When they were alone, Dusty told Sarah how unnerving it was that the elk had refused to move until Madeline approached and wrapped her arms around its neck. She spoke softly to it in the Cheyenne language. He swore the elk understood Madeline. It bowed down to her and then disappeared into the woods and never returned. Madeline then brushed the snow from the faces of the twins and sang a Cheyenne song of fare-well; the flames of the fire burned higher with each note. The dancing embers shone brightly and reflected off the beaded clasp that held her hair back from her forehead.

Dusty whispered in awe of how Madeline had lovingly run her hands over the bodies of the twins, melting the snow as she did. The boys' faces had actually turned red and flushed as if life had returned to them. Finally, the bodies of the brothers relaxed into a peaceful sleep instead of the frozen mold of death. As Madeline finished her ceremonial song, embers flew into the sky and the fire flickered and went out. Madeline then rose from beside the bodies, her black hair lifting gently as a tiny wind blew over the stunned group. She rubbed her hands together, her fingers chapped with the cold. She smiled at them, Dusty said, and a chickadee called from a bush and a crow stood guard over the prepared bodies. The sheriff, Doc Leighton, the deputies, and Dusty zipped Todd and Curt into their black sleeping bags and gently laid them onto the backs of the mules. The animals, Dusty murmured, stood motionless as steam billowed from their nostrils.

No one had said a word as tiny flakes of snow, each one as clear as crystal drifted down and landed gently on their heads. Madeline climbed onto her horse and took the lead rope of the mule carrying Todd. Dusty took the lead rope of the other mule carrying Curt's cold body and the party started their precarious journey down the steep trail. An eerie wind rose from the cliffs, sending a mournful moan across the valley. In the distance, the Tower, a fleeting guardian of the land, appeared and then vanished in the snowy skies.

In the great room of the lodge, the colonel and Katherine waited for their boys. They had arrived shortly after noon in a black rental car. They had refused the food and coffee Sarah offered. They spent the afternoon sitting rigidly on the overstuffed couch as heat from the fire flushed their cheeks. The hands of the clock moved tick by tick, each passing second bringing the death procession closer.

After hours of waiting, they heard the sheriff's heavy footsteps on the stairs. Hushed words floated down into the lodge just as the pale winter sun disappeared behind the mountains. Steamy clouds rose off the backs of the horses that gathered in the paddock. Up on the mountain peak, its brown eyes glowing, the elk stood with the small coyote at its feet staring down to the valley below.

In the welcoming warmth of the kitchen, Doc, Sarah, Dusty, and Lola laid out a meal on the planked table. It was not the joyous meal that had been anticipated on Sunday. Lola and Doc, contemplative and somber, verified the tale of the elk and Madeline's ceremony honoring the dead twins. When the rescuers went to move Todd, they found a beaded red belt laced between his fingers, the pattern matching exactly that of Madeline's hair clasp. After discussion among the four, it was decided that Katherine would be the appropriate recipient of the mysterious belt.

Madeline refused the offer of the warm kitchen, hot coffee, and a filling meal of venison stew. Instead, she unsaddled her horse, shook Dusty's hand, and kissed Sarah and Lola on their cheeks. No, she said, she did not want to meet the colonel and Katherine. No, thank you, she said, she did not think she would stay the night. She wanted to go home. Yes, she said she had sensed their deaths even before arriving at the ranch. No, she could not tell them why it happened. Yes, she said, the boys were at peace. Thank you, she said, but it was best that she leave.

As Madeline turned to climb into her old Subaru, she pulled the beaded clasp from her hair and pressed it into Sarah's hand. "Give this to their mother," Madeline whispered to Sarah. "Tell her that her boys are at peace and are with the Creator. Tell the colonel they forgive him."

Madeline backed her car around and started down the road. A gust of wind blew a small tornado of snow across the road, blocking the view of Madeline's retreat. When it cleared, Madeline was gone and the road was empty. Only the hair clasp now in Sarah's hand confirmed that Madeline had ever existed.

"If I didn't know better, I'd swear that woman must be a shape-shifter," commented Lola.

Sarah responded, "I don't understand what you mean by that."

"The best way I can explain it is that there are some beings who can physically transfer into another form. They tend to be wherever people need the help and the spiritual guidance."

The next day, the bodies of the beloved twins were loaded with care into matching black hearses that had waited at the ranch for their cargo. As they started their final journey back to Virginia, the colonel and his wife followed behind in the black rental car. The SUVs pulling the horse trailers made their way down the dirt road behind the others. The sorrowful procession then made its slow trek down the icy dirt road and onto the highway under the watchful eye of Devils Tower. The Red-tailed Hawk sang its mournful dirge as night closed in, a funeral song sung in honor of two soldiers whose lives were lost in a moment of madness in a cold and snowy faraway place.

The memorial service for the twins was held in the National Cathedral; the pallbearers were Army soldiers, veterans of the Iraqi and Afghani wars. Large photos of Curt and Todd dressed in US Army uniforms stood behind their matching coffins, their eyes tight and firm as they stared out onto the mourners. As she listened to the eulogy so eloquently delivered by the Army chaplain, Katherine clung to a picture of two boys, their arms around each other smiling into the camera. In her hair was a beaded clasp with stars shining into the hushed light and a beaded red belt wrapped the waist of her simple black coatdress.

The colonel sat rigid and contained next to his wife. He was lost in thought, counting the massive stones that lifted the Cathedral into spiritual grandeur. His eyes were drawn to the colored lights cast by the sun shining through the stained-glass windows. A soft stir of air brought his attention back to the words of the Army chaplain. Unnoticed by the mourning parents, a tall black- haired woman slid into the pew next to the colonel.

She took the colonel's hand and leaned towards him with her lips gently brushing his ear.

"Let them go, let them go. They are together now and at peace. Let them go."

The woman pressed a small package into the colonel's hand, closing his fingers around soft white buckskin. She lightly touched his hair and kissed his cheek. Quietly moving away from him, she slipped out into the aisle of the Cathedral and retreated. The colonel opened his hand and then the small square of white buckskin. There, shining in the blood-colored glow from the Cathedral's stained-glass windows, were the dog tags of his beloved sons.

⇥ 12 ⇤

The White Buffalo Calf

Buffalo Springs Ranch, Hulett, Wyoming April 14, 2006

"The summer heat had not yet filled the day as the white buffalo calf, Miracle, entered the world on the farm in Wisconsin. She was born on August 20, 1994, exactly sixty-one years after the last report of a white buffalo calf. The people of the plains and the Black Hills rejoiced and temporarily put aside the burden of hundreds of years of oppression and grief to celebrate the birth. The blessed people on whose ranch she was born created a website for her with the words 'She was seen by a vast number of people as a symbol of hope and renewal for humanity and for harmony between all peoples, all races, in our world today.' The white buffalo calf died in 2004 but the hope she had brought continued on in the hearts of the Native people."

Sarah dropped the magazine with the article about the white buffalo calf back into the rack. She looked around the tidy room and listened for the call of the crows. She could just hear a creak from the old rocking chair in the great room above her, along with the shake and rattle of the old brown dog's collar. She heard the dog's faint whimper and then, a moment later, his snores. Sarah stood up from the overstuffed couch and, moving stiffly, began to climb the stairs.

At the top of the stone-sided stairs, the great room opened onto a deck; its sliding door allowed the cold to seep into the house. The old man was sleeping in the wooden rocking chair, his feet propped on the back of the loyal old dog. His long hair was shot through with gray, neatly parted, braided and tied at the ends with red cloth. His hands on the arms of the chair seemed to twitch and tap in rhythm with an unheard drum. The red plaid wool blanket had slipped from his lap and was bunched around his feet and across the back of the brown dog.

Sarah patted the old man on the cheek and drew the blanket back up over his chest. He was clad in a pair of blue denim jeans with a rope belt holding them around his thin waist. A red plaid shirt that matched the material of the blanket covered his torso. His eyes fluttered open to gaze at Sarah and he grinned at the sight of her smile. He slipped back into slumber as Sarah gently slid the door closed and made her way back down the stairs.

By the calendar, Spring had arrived. But Winter was retaking its position, with great fury slinging snow against the windows of the ranch house with the same ferocity as a swarm of angry hornets. The Spring weather had been very odd; 20 degrees on Monday and, by Wednesday, the thermometer read a staggering 82. The horses in the large pasture shook their heads and flipped their tails as the flies that plagued them during the hot months of summer tentatively reappeared. By Thursday afternoon, the temperature had plunged again into the 20's. A freezing rainstorm blew in from Gillette which turned the rain to snow by early Good Friday morning.

The herd now flicked their tails and shook their heads against the hard particles of white. They had moved into the lean-to built against the side of the huge red barn, a B/S within a circle of running horses painted on the sides in white. Sarah had just rushed in from the laundry room, inconveniently located in the bunkhouse. The phone's ringing made her run faster to catch it before the caller gave up.

"Hello?" Sarah picked up the phone, holding the laundry basket under one arm and tucking the receiver under her chin. She wiped a clear spot on the window above the sink. "Buffalo Springs Ranch, this is Sarah."

An oddly familiar man's voice came crackling across the line. "Sarah, this is Jones. I got your card last week. I am in Gillette and will be at the ranch in ninety minutes. I'm sorry for the short notice but I wasn't sure until I got off the plane that I was actually coming. I hope it isn't too late to let you know."

"Jones, oh Jones! I am so happy to hear from you. We have been so worried about you all these years. Please, drive safely. The roads are getting bad. I have a fire lit and will have some hot rum waiting. We are so glad you decided to come. Your room is ready. We were so afraid you were gone, that something had happened to you." Sarah's voice held warmth and welcome as she gave Jones directions to the ranch. She hung up the phone, put the laundry basket down, leaned against the wall, crossed her arms over her chest, and smiled.

She was still lost in thought when the door banged open and the thin man came in, shaking the dusting of snow off his coat and beat-up cowboy hat. His mustache was caked with ice and began to drip as the heat of the kitchen wrapped around him.

"Sarah, what on earth are you doing? You didn't even hear me call. Hello? Earth to Sarah!" Dusty touched his wife's arm and gave it a tiny shake.

"Oh, Dusty! Jones is coming. Can you believe it? I was so afraid he was gone for good. He's on his way."

Sarah turned to face her husband as the snow from his coat and hat dripped onto the blue- and-white linoleum. "Dusty, he just called from the airport. That means all of them will be here. I am so pleased. Oh my! Look, it's already noon. I have to get ready."

Sarah gave her husband a quick kiss on the cheek and rubbed his arms through the thick material of his hunter green parka. She turned to look through the window into the swirling cloud of snow and shook her head at the condition of the road. Dusty opened the door to the kitchen to let a small black-and-white cat into the warmth of the room. He took off his coat and hung it next to the door and then sat on one of the benches tucked under the long plank table. His hands were pink from the cold and he studied them intently, noting the lines and crinkles of skin, marking the passing of the years.

Dusty thought of the old man sleeping upstairs, a guest in their house since the previous July when he and Sarah had gone to Cheyenne to the rodeo. Dusty and Sarah were adamantly against the "sport" of rodeo and often went to rescue horses that were no longer of use to the stock owners. The day had been hot and dusty with only a brief thundershower breaking the heat. Once again, the truck and old stock trailer had rumbled down the highway, creaking and groaning across the miles. The landscape became drier and flatter the farther the couple traveled. Out in the fields, the yellow and white antelope raised their heads for a quick look and then returned to their grazing among the cattle and horses that had taken the place of the enormous herds of bison.

The sky was deep blue with clouds an odd purple and gray. Sarah murmured that it looked like rain but none fell. Dusty, sitting in the passenger seat, waved his hand out the window, his fingers spread wide, the air rushing past them. He looked at the road disappearing in the side mirror and thought of his own life disappearing second by second.

Once at the rodeo grounds, Sarah had gone to sit in the grandstand to watch the competitions. Dusty walked out to the paddocks to see what horses he could purchase and bring home to the ranch. He thought of Geronimo Barse, now in the cemetery at Tarrington, and of the hundreds of horses that had graced the old man's life. He thought of the small herd to the north on the ranch and silently counted the space available for new members of the equine band.

Sarah had noticed the old Native American man sitting on the top bench of the grandstand. His back was stooped and his face was as wrinkled as a lime, long past its prime. Something about this old man brought memories of the old Kiowa man, Geronimo Barse, and his horses. She almost cried as the haunting images ran through her and she found herself climbing the steps of the grandstand to sit next to the old gentleman. He did not look up as Sarah took her seat but reached over to take her hand and held it to his chest.

"My name is Billy Hawk. I am from the Rosebud Reservation and I am on my way home. I saw you and your mate. I was hoping you would come to see me."

Billy's voice was as weathered as his face and his hand was cool and dry. He smiled and showed a gleaming set of dentures, as white as the sheets Sarah hung on the clothesline on summer mornings. Sarah blinked in surprise at the old man's words. She had felt drawn to him, his eyes magically calling her to his side. A small breeze blew dust sideways, stirring Sarah's black hair and the braids of the old man. Sarah could feel the rapid beat of the old man's heart as he held her hand. She felt the cool cotton of his ribbon shirt and the ribbons fluttering against her fingers. Sarah looked up into the old man's brown eyes, faded by time. The noise of the crowd disappeared into the blowing dust and Sarah felt herself transported back to Geronimo Barse's ranch. She could hear the nickering of horses and the stomping of their feet. She could feel the wood of the stalls underneath her hand and smell the sweetness of fresh hay and alfalfa. Oddly, the words of a Lynyrd Skynyrd song came to her mind.

> "If I leave here tomorrow
> Would you still remember me?
> For I must be traveling on, now,
> 'cause there's too many places I've got to see.
> But, if I stayed here with you, girl,
> Things just couldn't be the same.
> 'cause I'm as free as a bird now,
> And this bird you cannot change."

Sarah held the old man's hand as tightly as she could. "Are you leaving us, are you traveling on?" she asked him.

Billy nodded, and with the tenderness of a lover's touch, laid Sarah's hands in her lap. The announcer's voice suddenly broke the spell as he called the crowd to their feet to cheer the winner of the bull riders. A husky young man, dressed in jeans, a sweat-stained hat, and a well-worn blue cowboy shirt, spurs on his black snakeskin boots, strode into the center of the arena. He tipped his hat to the crowd and then raised his clasped hands in victory. Billy, watching the rider, laughed.

"Oh, he's a cocky one, that one. I've seen him in Reno, Ellensburg, Pendleton, and Sheridan. I've watched him thrown in one second. Only luck held him on for eight seconds today!"

Sarah shook her head in confusion. The heated metal of the grandstand seemed to burn through her pants and brand her thighs. As she turned her head toward the young bull rider, the wind wound her hair around her neck. Billy shook his head too and then leaned over to whisper in Sarah's ear.

"Your name is Sarah and your man is Dusty. I stood behind you in the ticket line. Your man is looking for horses. I know he is a good man. I know you, too, Sarah. You remind me of my grand-niece. I think I am ready to leave now. Can you help me get down?"

The bull rider bowed once more to the crowd and then, as he saw the old man begin to stand, he ran to the railing directly below them.

"Billy, you owe me twenty. I made it today. Do you hear me, old man?" the young rider threw his hat towards Billy who laughed and swatted it away.

"I'll pay you twenty when you learn to ride, Jake. Now, help me down and stop your swaggering. This lady is Sarah. I'm going home with her tonight and you have to help her man load the horses."

Sarah looked at the old man, puzzled, and started to speak. Before she could say anything, a roar broke from the crowd.

Jake chuckled at Sarah's confused look and bent over to pick up his hat. He placed it back on his head, tipped it to Sarah, and reached over to shake the hand of the old man.

"Billy, why aren't you home? All last year and this season you've been telling me you're going home. Just hanging out to pick up pretty married ladies, huh? You old goat! Come on. Let's go. Where's your bedroll and backpack? I'll take them for you. Miss Sarah, I hope you are prepared for a winter of tall tales and loud snores."

Sarah stood with one foot perched on the steel plank of the seat and the other on a concrete step. "What on earth are the two of you talking about? I don't even know this gentleman. And, you, sir, I have never laid eyes on you before and I don't believe that I invited either of you for dinner, let alone to stay for the winter. So, excuse me, but I have to meet my husband."

Sarah nodded to the old man and gave the young cowboy a cold look. She hurried down the steps of the grandstand, ignoring the calls of the two men behind her. She brushed past the people gathered around the arena and walked briskly to where she had left Dusty, the truck and trailer.

She found Dusty leaning against the side of the stock barn, his hands placed behind his hips on the worn side of his jeans. He was engrossed in a conversation with a tall, lanky woman in her fifties, a yellow bandana wrapped around her neck, her hands and wrists covered in exquisite turquoise jewelry.

"Take the little buckskin. I can't keep him and I don't want him to go to meat. He's a smart little boy but he's no good to me, as I can't ride him. He's bucked me a few times and I am too old to get hurt." She was holding the lead rope of the yellow buckskin, his mane and points black, with a sweet expression on his face. She turned in Sarah's direction and her face broke into an enormous smile, two gold teeth glinting on either side of her mouth. She looked past Sarah and her smile grew even wider.

"Billy Hawk and Jake George. As I live and breathe, what are you reprobates doing here? I thought you were both on your way home. Dusty, you know these two con artists. Does Sarah girl? If not, let me introduce you to two of the worst cowboys ever to sit a horse or bull for that matter. Sarah, this is Billy Hawk and Jake George. They're close neighbors of mine in Parmalee. Well, Jake is anyway. Where you living these days, old man?"

Sarah spun around and nearly bumped into Billy Hawk. He laughed and, gently taking her shoulders, turned her back to face Dusty and the tall woman.

"Sarah, you ran away so fast from Jake and me, I didn't have time to tell you I knew your man. Janice, how the heck are you? I'm almost home. Did you forget, South Dakota is just the next state over? Dusty, take that buckskin home with you. He is a great little horse. Jake, this is Dusty and Sarah Plesent. Sarah, I know your friend Henry, and I also knew Geronimo Barse."

Dusty pushed himself away from the side of the barn and moved over to put an arm around his wife. He brushed his hand over her face, trying to remove the confused look.

"Sit down on the truck seat and take a drink of water. You look like a tornado blew you in." Dusty opened the door to the truck and wiped off the grit from the bench seat. He bent down and slid the seat back as far as possible.

Sarah looked from Dusty to the old man to the tall woman and then to the young bull rider. They all seemed to share a joke of which she was the punch line. She could feel her irritation grow with each passing minute. She climbed into the truck and scowled at her husband and asked him in a grumpy voice, "Dusty, is there something going on you should tell me? You seem to know all of these people. Maybe you could fill me in on all this?" She pushed her hair back from her neck and blew out a long sigh.

Sarah," Dusty replied, "this is Janice Leary. She is here selling some of her horses. She runs Angus cattle out of Parmalee. This young man is Jake George. He rodeos and trains horses for Janice. And this gentleman? Why this is Billy Hawk. He is an elder out of Rosebud. Janice tells me he's on his 'farewell' journey but don't ask any specifics. I don't know the details. I met all of them last year when I went to Ellensburg to buy those Appys. They are all a bunch of reprobates but the nicest reprobates you could ever meet.

"And, Sarah, they all knew our old Kiowa friend, Geronimo Barse." Dusty's voice dropped lower and he wiped a smudge of dirt from below his wife's left eye.

Billy bowed to Sarah and then began to cough, a raspy sound that seemed to echo in the heat of the day. Jake reached into the truck across Sarah and handed the old man a bottle of water. His face was somber as he watched the old man drink. His green eyes darkened as Billy continued to cough. Tenderly, he put his hand on Billy's back, rubbing it until the old man was able to catch his breath.

The noise from the grandstand engulfed the five people sitting in and standing around the truck. The voice of the announcer excitedly proclaimed the start of the calf-roping competition. A scattering of clouds cast transient shadows over the crowd and the sun seemed to grow warmer. Sarah intently watched the scene between Billy and Jake. She sensed something was in the air but could not tell what it was from the expressions of the others' faces.

"Come on, old man." Janice said with tenderness. "Let me take you home. I have all of your stuff here in the barn. Dusty, are you taking this gelding or not? We have a long drive and Billy needs to go home. Jake, here are the keys. The truck is parked by the tree on the other side of the barn."

Jake gave Billy a final pat, grabbed the keys from Janice and ran off across the field. His hat blew off, he bent down to retrieve it, and held it against his side as he sprinted around the corner of the barn. In the late afternoon sun, Jake's shadow seemed to run ahead of him across the uneven dusty ground.

"Yes, Janice. I'm taking this one. Can we help?" Dusty's voice deepened in concern. "Let me load this little guy. Sarah, there's some fruit in that bag. Can you toss that to Billy? Billy, let's get you taken care of. Give me a moment here."

Dusty took the lead rope of the buckskin and walked him to the ramp of the stock trailer. The little buckskin looked around, pawed the ground and sniffed the sides of the trailer. He cautiously put one hoof into the trailer, sniffed again, snorted and then climbed in. Dusty closed the door to the trailer and reached through the slats to rub the horse's forehead. He sighed at the thought of the long drive home and of the horses he could not buy.

Sarah, sitting in the truck, rubbed her hands around the circle of the steering wheel. She stared straight out the windshield, squinting in the brightness of the sun. A flicker of heat lightning appeared and then disappeared over the line of trees that marked the boundary of the town. The grandstand winked a bright silver and the colors of the crowd seemed to be a gigantic rug waving in the summer wind.

"Janice, how did you know Geronimo? We miss him so much. We still have four horses left from the herd we brought north when he died. Do you ever hear from his family?" Sarah's eyes were filled with tears and her voice shook at the recollection of the now long-deceased old Kiowa man.

Janice squatted down on the ground and tenderly wiped the dust off Billy's worn moccasins. She then took Billy's hands and pulled herself to her feet. Billy smiled at her with a loving look and then raised his head to Sarah.

"Miss Sarah, Geronimo was well known to all of us old people. Knew that devil grandson of his, too. Janice here used to drive us down to visit Geronimo as often as she could." Billy began to cough again, bent over at the waist, trying to catch his breath.

Dusty walked up from the back of the trailer and took the old man by the arm. He walked him around to the passenger side of the truck and helped him into the vehicle. Billy continued to cough, his breath halting and raspy in his throat. At that moment, Jake drove up in the green Dodge truck, his concern showing in his eyes as he heard Billy cough. He parked next to the truck where Sarah and Billy sat. He opened his door and climbed down to stand by Janice, handing her the keys.

"Let me get our stuff packed, Janice. We need to get on the road and get him home. Sarah, nice to meet you. Dusty, good to see you again. Billy, let me help you out of here. Come on, old man, time to go home."

Sarah watched the scene in silence. Another roar came from the grandstand and a jay screamed from its perch on the barn roof above Sarah's head. She could hear the little buckskin stomping his feet on the floor of the trailer. The face of the old Kiowa man flickered across Sarah's mind as more heat lightning flickered across the late afternoon sky.

"Billy, stay in the truck, you're coming home with us. Jake, if you'll hand me his things, Dusty and I will get going. We have lots of room. Come on, Dusty. We won't be home until midnight if we leave now."

Three sets of eyes stared in surprise at Sarah but Billy just chuckled. He nodded and then started to cough, his head down between his knees. Dusty looked intently at Sarah and she nodded again, reaching over to touch the old man on his shoulder.

"Billy, we'll take you home. Jake, hand me his things. Janice, thanks for the little buckskin. We'll take good care of both of them. I'll be in Parmalee next month. Billy can stay with us until then."

Dusty shook hands with Janice and Jake and climbed into the passenger seat next to Billy.

That was nine months ago. August had come and gone. Dusty had driven to Parmalee with Billy beside him in the truck, the old stock trailer rattling behind. The trip had taken three days and, when Dusty pulled back into the driveway of the ranch, Billy was in the passenger seat and four horses filled the trailer. Sarah had laughed as she looked out from the deck and watched Dusty and Billy each lead two horses to the barn.

Billy had kept Sarah company through the long Wyoming winter. The snow came early and piled high. At times, Sarah would drive him into Spearfish and he would catch the Greyhound bus to Billings or Bismarck, Minot or Minneapolis. He would take his battered suitcase and load the bus, telling Sarah 'thank you' for her kindness and that he would call in a few days. Usually two to three weeks later, a car or truck or van or semi would come rattling down the long dirt road and stop at the ranch. Billy would tip his hat to whoever had driven him home and climb out of the vehicle. He always brought a gift for Sarah and Dusty and the old brown dog.

He seemed to know when Sarah and Dusty would have guests, for inevitably he would disappear just before the others were scheduled to arrive. Sarah was keenly disappointed when he left two hours before Lola and Forrest came to the ranch but she respected the old man far too much to question his actions.

Throughout the Fall, Winter and Spring, the old man's cough worsened and he grew visibly weaker. His trips from the ranch grew fewer and he spent most of his time dozing in the rocking chair in the great room, his feet resting on the back of the brown dog. Sarah and Dusty loved the old man, agreeing that the old Kiowa man had sent him to them, a reciprocity allowing them to repay the kindness Geronimo Barse had shown them over the years.

Sarah, without any discussion between the two of them, had started to brush and braid Billy's hair for him in the morning, wrapping the ends with red cloth. She fussed over him and checked on him every night after Dusty had helped him up the stairs from the kitchen. Over the winter, Sarah took him to Spearfish several times for medical care.

His cough was deepening and the pounds were disappearing from his bony frame.

Through the nine months he had been with Sarah and Dusty, Billy had many visitors. Without notice, Native people of all ages would appear at the door of the ranch house, each one bringing a gift of food, bags of beads, tanned hides and, on one occasion, fifty pounds of elk steaks and venison.

During the long winter nights, Billy would sit with Sarah and Dusty and work on exquisite beadwork. He was crafting a tiny pair of white moccasins with beaded lilies. He sewed a tiny white buckskin dress with leggings to match. As the winter moved into Spring, Billy finished the buckskin outfit and started working on a shawl and a beaded belt. The outfit was sized for an infant. Sarah asked several times whom the outfit was for but Billy would just smile and shake his head.

"You will know when you know!" Billy would chuckle, pulling the needle with the fringe through the edges of the shawl. In the middle of the shawl was a bunch of lilies, their bright green stems tied in a yellow ribbon.

Sarah would lay the tiny outfit on the table in the great room and run her hands over the beadwork. Billy never spoke of his family except to say he was raised on the Rosebud Reservation and had survived boarding school. In a moment of weakness, brought on by a particularly bad period of illness, Billy confessed he had been born in 1907 and could remember when his mother was finally given the right to vote.

Billy had been given the room closest to the bathroom where Dusty installed a handrail in the shower to ensure the old man's safety. One morning in mid-March, Sarah sat next to Billy on the edge of his bed. A winter thaw had started the day before and Sarah could hear the sound of the snow melting on the roof and dripping onto the ground outside the window. A narrow slice of light peeked through the plaid curtains, throwing a beam across Billy's face.

He was clearly weaker and Sarah feared he would not live out the week, so she had called the doctor, a neighbor who lived in the first house eight miles down the road. Dr. Leighton had come that night, bringing with him two surprise visitors, Janice Leary and Jake George.

"Dusty called this morning, Sarah." Janice said in a quiet voice as Sarah opened the door to the three. "Jake and I were on our way to Sheridan to look at some Angus bulls. We were afraid we would be too late. Can we see him?"

"Hello, Jake, Doc. Janice. Thanks so much for coming. He will be so glad to see you two. We were hoping he would make it to Spring but he is pretty weak. He's in the first bedroom. Let me give you some hot tea to take to him. Put your bags inside the door, Jake. I'll show you your rooms in a few minutes. I am assuming you and Janice are staying the night? Dusty is down feeding the horses; he'll be up in a minute."

Sarah gathered the coats from the three visitors and led Doc Leighton down the hall. Billy's room was lit by a small lamp. He lay in the bed with his hands on top of the blanket. His breathing was shallow and the sour smell of illness hung in the air.

"Billy, Billy," Sarah gently shook his shoulder and the old man opened his eyes, pushing himself up on one elbow.

"Hello, Doc. What are you doing here? Sarah, hand me my teeth! I'm not ready for a visitor. Doc, Sarah worries too much. I am fine." As the words left his dry and cracked lips, Billy began to cough, clutching the blanket with both hands.

"Give us a minute, Sarah, and tell the other two to wait. I'll be out soon." Doc Leighton's voice was quietly authoritative.

Sarah left the room and joined Jake and Janice at the long plank table downstairs. Dusty came in from the barn and stood by the sink looking out the window. The temperature had dropped again and icicles were starting to form from the water dripping off the roof. No one said a word. Sarah went to stand by Dusty. She stared into the sink and saw a tiny black spider trying to climb up the stainless steel of the basin. She reached over and took a spoon from the drawer in the cabinet. Sarah gently placed the spoon in front of the spider, sending silent messages encouraging it to climb to safety. She smiled as the black arachnid reached out a tentative leg and then scrambled onto the curved surface of the spoon. The other three watched her as she walked over to the door, stepped outside, and let the spider loose in the enclosed woodbin.

Sarah stood outside the door in the gathering dusk. She looked around her at the peaceful place where she and Dusty were so blessed to live. She could see the steam coming off the horses as they stomped their feet and ate the hay Dusty had spread for them. She could see the moon rising and its reflection on the ice forming on the pond. She thought of the guests that had come to stay with them over the years, Lola, Forrest, Jones, and the others. She thought of the horses buried up on the hill and the songs that Dusty sang over their graves. She thought of Geronimo Barse and his kindness. She thought of the old man inside and began to pray as light tears fell onto her cheeks.

"Dear God, if it is your will to take him, take him fast and don't make him suffer. If it is your will he stay, don't make him suffer. I can let him go if that is your will but God, please don't let him suffer."

Sarah heard the door open behind her and felt Dusty's hands on her shoulders. He leaned forward and spoke into Sarah's hair at the back of her neck. "Doc wants to talk to us. Come back in, honey."

Sarah looked up, nodded and led the way back into the house. Janice and Jake were still at the table, their faces in shadow from the light over the stove. Neither had moved to switch on more light. The four turned toward the stairs at the sound of Doc Leighton's footsteps.

Doc Leighton was a young man who had been raised in the valley and returned home to the land that he loved. He was deeply loved by the people of the area, not the least of reasons being his willingness to make house calls.

"Can I get a cup of coffee, Sarah?" Doc pulled out the bench opposite Janice and Jake and lowered himself. He looked around the room, comfortable, cozy and full of the love that flowed between Sarah and Dusty. He held his hand over the speckled blue cup Sarah silently passed him, feeling the steam warm his fingers. He sighed and took a sip of the scalding coffee, gathering the right words to tell the four people who loved Billy the news.

"Sarah, he has an enlarged heart, congestive heart failure, atrial fibrillation, and a pretty good case of pneumonia. He may make it through tonight or he may not. There is not much I can do about the heart until we get the pneumonia under control. If he does pull through this crisis, he is going to be weak. Sarah, the work will fall on you. I hope you can keep him here. I know it's a lot to ask but he really can't be moved."

Sarah thought of Geronimo Barse dying alone in the barn without even the horses to keep him company. Tears dripped from her eyes onto the oilskin cloth covering the table, her tears matching the dripping of the water outside. She nodded. "Doc, that isn't even a question. Of course he'll stay here."

"I figured you'd say that so I left medication on the bedside table along with directions. Dusty, I have another horse you might want. Come over this weekend and let's do some horse trading. Jake and Janice, go surprise him. I didn't tell him you were here. I need to get home to my family so, goodnight all. Sarah, I'll check in on him on my way to Spearfish tomorrow."

Doc finished his coffee, picked up his bag, and walked to the door. He pulled it open and started to step out into the coming night. He paused a moment and turned back to where Sarah and Dusty stood.

"Sarah, Dusty, find out who his people are and what they want to do. If he makes it through tonight he certainly won't be here by summer. Call me if you need anything. Goodnight."

Later that evening, Sarah, Dusty, Jake and Janice sat around the fire, none of them wanting to discuss the topic that was on all of their minds. Jake's stocky body lay relaxed in a recliner, his black snakeskin boots kicked off, a hole visible in the bottom of his left sock. Janice sat next to Jake's chair, her arms crossed over her knees as she stared into the fire. Sarah and Dusty sat together on the overstuffed couch. The small black-and-white cat had laid claim to Billy's rocking chair, her tail twitching as she dreamed of mice and little birds. The old brown dog lay on the rug in Billy's room, his snores clearly audible.

The great room was the heart and soul of the ranch. Lamps made of wrought iron in the shapes of cowboys on bucking horses topped with dun-colored shades were scattered on the tables constructed of small and large pieces of polished wood. The couches and chairs were of leather and dun-colored cloth while the pine rocker Billy used during the day was covered in green plaid. A picnic table sat just inside the sliding glass door, a discordant note in the room but it would be moved outside when Spring truly arrived. Long evening hours were passed in the great room, its comfort inviting conversation but also offering the solace of silence.

Finally, after watching the cat twitch and dream as she lay in the chair, Sarah cleared her throat. "Jake, you know the old man better than all of us. Who do we call?"

"Sarah," Jake said in a low voice, his face averted from the other three, "Billy is my great- grandfather. He raised me from the time I was one. There is no one in the family left but the three of us."

Sarah uttered an exclamation of surprise and started to speak but Jake held up his hand, asking her to wait. He continued on in a somber voice, heavy with loss. "I have no brothers and sisters and my parents died long ago. They were hit head-on by a drunk driver coming home from Pine Ridge. My grandmother was Billy's daughter. She died of breast cancer a long time before I was born. Billy and Janice are the only family I have."

A bitterness and sadness crept into Jake's voice. "That's the way it is on reservations. No one wants to hear it but we are a Third World nation in our own land. Don't get me started on it."

Janice shifted her weight and leaned over to rub Jake's feet. Dusty and Sarah kept quiet, not wanting to interrupt the story.

"Janice and Billy took me in. She is my aunt, the only one I have left. These two people mean everything to me and we are so grateful you have cared for Billy. Janice, you finish the story. I can't."

Janice pushed her turquoise bracelets up and down her arm. She leaned back against Jake's chair and ran her fingers through his hair. "Billy is my great-uncle. He raised me when my mother and grandfather left the reservation and never came back. I never knew my father. My mother and grandmother died in a fire set by one of my mother's boyfriends. It's Billy's ranch out there at Parmalee where Jake and I live. Jake's right, there is no one left. Billy left the ranch two years ago. He told us he was going to die and wanted to say goodbye to his people and to the land. He made it to every rodeo that Jake rode in but we were never sure where he was staying most of the time as he would only send us a postcard or call about once a month. We were so glad that day in Cheyenne when you took him home."

The fire had burned down until there were only a few embers left. Jake got out of his chair and put two more logs into the stone fireplace. He did not return to the chair but chose to sit, instead, on the hearth, his feet resting on Janice's legs. Sarah, watching the scene, suddenly saw in that motion the unmistakable mannerisms that Jake shared with Billy. She shook her head; astonished she had not noticed it before. In the low light from the fire, she could also see the fine lines in Janice's face and the shape of her long, elegant hands. Jake's arms were braced on either side of his body, his fingers splayed and showing a grace identical to Janice.

How did I miss it all? Sarah asked herself. *How could I be so blind? They were so loving and comfortable with each other that first day. How could I not see it? No wonder Billy laughs at me. How did I miss this? What else did I miss?*

She looked down at her own hands and slid her palms back and forth against each other. She thought of the graceful old man in the other room and prayed for his peace and asked God to spare him from pain and suffering. Startled, Sarah realized she had missed much of what had been said in the past moments. She looked up to hear Jake say, "Go on, Janice. Tell them the rest." Jake's voice was barely audible in the quietness of the room.

"Well, there isn't much left to say. I never married or had any children. Jake and Billy are it for me. You know, it's an old story, alcohol, grief and suicide. It runs in our family and its path broke Billy's heart years ago. What Jake hasn't said is that Billy taught him both our language and our traditions. The other thing Billy probably hasn't told you is how he knew Geronimo Barse. They were in the same boarding school in Nebraska. They had their hair cut and were beaten for speaking Kiowa and Lakota. It is so amazing that neither of those men was bitter for one day and they both raised their children in their traditions. Too bad their families never understood the gifts they had been given.

"Geronimo and Billy stayed in touch until Geronimo died. That's how we knew about you and Henry. Geronimo loved you all. We were glad to hear you had the herd. We were also glad to hear his great-grandson has the ranch. But, you know, Billy is about the last of the old ones left. Thank you again, Sarah and Dusty, for your kindness to both of those old men. Excuse me, now. I need to go to bed. Jake, we need to get going early in the morning."

Janice pushed herself to her feet. She bent down to where Jake sat and ran her hand across his face, gently patting it. "You're a good boy, Jake. A lousy bull rider but a good boy!"

She straightened up, her slender body lean and hard in the light, her silver and turquoise jewelry gleaming in the ambient glow of the fire.

"Sarah, don't worry. He won't die tonight. He told Jake and me he wouldn't go until the white buffalo calf is born. Good thing we don't have any buffalo on the ranch."

Jake and Janice were gone by the time Sarah got up the next morning. She had been up and down through the night, checking on Billy and pacing the kitchen, a plan formulating in her mind. Dusty had found her there at three a.m. and had led her back to bed, refusing to hear her plan or discuss anything until at least six o'clock. Sarah, fatigued from her lack of sleep, had not awakened until nearly nine o'clock with both the cat and dog standing by the bed, pleading for breakfast and to go outside.

Sarah checked on Billy when she passed his room. He was sleeping, his breathing shallow but regular. She tiptoed out of the room, not wanting to wake him, and went to the kitchen. She sat at the plank table with a pad of paper and a pen in front of her. She began to write and then stopped. She pushed away from the table and ran up the stairs to grab the laptop from its usual spot by the rocking chair. She sat down in Billy's chair, turning the machine on and listening for the rattling of the old dog's collar, signaling his readiness to come back in.

Through the sliding door, she could see Dusty coming up from the barn and across the lawn. Despite most of the sky being overcast, there were slight patches of blue. Overnight, a few purple and yellow crocuses had pushed through the earth. The grass seemed greener and it appeared Spring was actually going to make its way back to the valley. Sarah laughed and clapped her hands and waved to Dusty, blowing him a kiss. She ran back down the stairs and out the back door, grabbing Dusty and hugging him as tightly as she could.

"Dusty, quick, come in. I have something I need to tell you. I have a wonderful idea. Please, come in for a minute!"

"Sarah, what is it? Is Billy okay? What are you doing?"

"Dusty, I want to invite our special people back to the ranch for Easter. Lola, Forrest, his wife, Marie, and especially, Jones. Lola can bring Istie and the baby. Billy would love this. Jake and Janice can come, I am sure. We can find the room for them all. Dusty, we really need to do this!" Sarah was nearly dancing in her excitement. "I will take care of everything. Just say Yes!"

"Sarah, I think that would be fine but if you are going to have that many people here, I better get busy!"

"Dusty, do you believe this ranch came to us by accident? Do you think it was a coincidence that we met Geronimo the way we did and then Billy? Do you think all of this was just by serendipity? Look, I know this sounds crazy but think how healing this place is for everyone who comes. Everyone that has ever been our guest comes back, over and over, and brings someone new with them.

"Think about it, Dusty. We had only the bunkhouse and no horses to start with. Now we have so much and it has all come so easily. Think about it. Whenever we thought we could not make it through the month, people came and helped us. Dusty, don't you see? That's the whole purpose of the ranch."

"Sarah, slow down. Shh! Just a minute, let me breathe. Okay, go on. Let's hear the rest." Dusty laid a finger across Sarah's lips, kissed her cheek and then put his hand on the table in front of him.

"Dusty, you know that spot up on the trail behind the pond? The one where there is that big gouge in the ground, the one where the horses always roll? Billy told me that was an old buffalo wallow. Think about that! Our ranch is 'Buffalo Springs Ranch!' Oh, Dusty, I finally understand it! Think of all those people who have come into our life. Dusty, that's what we are supposed to do, make this a place of healing!"

Dusty slowly nodded his head and leaned over to kiss his wife. "Sarah, if that is what you believe, we will make it work. I have to go to town today and pick up some grain. I love you. Keep an eye on Billy. I'll be back by dinner."

Four weeks later, Sarah hung up the phone after giving Jones directions. The invitations had gone out and had been received with enthusiasm and confirmation of attendance. Forrest had called, telling Dusty and Sarah that he and Marie would be coming and asked if they could bring Jamie, their daughter-in-law. Lola had reserved three spots for herself, Istie, and Liliana, Janice and Jake had agreed they needed to be present and had promised to bring a home-cured ham with them.

Sarah, almost at a run, had spent the past week making beds, hanging towels, vacuuming rugs, baking and freezing pies, scrubbing bathrooms, and washing and ironing curtains. In the afternoons, if the day was warm enough, she would help Billy out to the deck to sit and enjoy the view. He had made it through the crisis in March but was thin and pale. He now spent most of his days dozing with the old brown dog, the two of them snoring in unison, a racket that never failed to make Sarah laugh.

Sarah turned away from the window she had rubbed clean and picked up the basket of laundry. She started to walk down the hallway to the room she shared with Dusty. The cat and dog had long ago deserted them to sleep with Billy. As she turned, the phone rang again.

"Buffalo Springs Ranch. This is Sarah."

"Sarah, this is Janice. Jake and I are almost there. We're at the Barrs' ranch, you know, the C-Bar-C, down by the Tower. Sarah, a white buffalo calf was born there this morning. Sarah, Sarah, are you there?"

Sarah slowly bent over and dropped the basket of clean clothes on the floor. She leaned back against the cabinets and folded her arm across her chest, feeling her heart stutter and skip.

"Janice, are you sure? Oh, Janice, I can't tell Billy. I just can't. You know that's what he was waiting for. Janice, I just can't tell him." Sarah began to cry and the wind seemed to increase its howling, sounding for all the world like a grief-stricken child.

"Sarah, don't cry. This is Creator's gift for him. Billy needs to go home. You have to let him go. We all have to let him go. We will be there as soon as possible. The weather is getting bad and we want to get to the ranch before the road gets too icy. Don't cry, Sweetie. This is a good thing. We can tell him together."

The phone clicked in Sarah's ear. She slid to the floor and wrapped her arms around the basket, pressing it against her chest. The room suddenly seemed very chilly and an icy gloom permeated the air.

"I can't believe it. He fought so hard this last time. God, I can't let him go now. Not now. Please, don't take him now."

A sharp rap on the sliding door upstairs startled Sarah. She wiped her eyes on her denim shirt sleeve and pulled her hair back from her neck. A second, more impatient rap sounded on the door. Sarah pulled herself to her feet and made her way around the table and up the stone-lined stairway. As her head reached the top of the stairs, she could see the feet of at least five people standing on the deck. Reaching the top of the stairs, she could see that Billy had awakened and was trying to stand.

Sarah's heart began to beat rapidly and she nearly ran across the great room to the sliding door.

"Billy, sit down! I will let everyone in! Billy, sit down!"

Sarah helped Billy back into the rocking chair and then pulled the door open and tried to hug everyone at once.

"Forrest, I am so glad you are here. This must be Marie, and, oh Forrest, this has to be Jamie. She is so beautiful. Lola, you made it! Istie, welcome to the ranch and this tiny thing must be Liliana. Oh, my gosh, you all made it. Come on in, get out of the cold. Come and meet Billy. Lola, you will never guess, Jones is coming. We haven't heard from him in years but he is on his way! I am sure you remember him from four years ago."

Billy coughed and grabbed the arm of the rocking chair.

Alarmed, Sarah turned around but saw he was only clearing his throat. Sarah laughed and waved her guests in ahead of her. A gust of wind blew a smattering of snow into the great room, tugging at coats and pants as everyone moved into the heat of the room.

"Hand me your coats and just drop your bags. Let's just get everyone a seat and make introductions. Oops, hold on. Let me get the other door and I'll be right back!" Sarah's face was flushed with excitement as she ran downstairs to answer the knock on the wooden door. Three people, wrapped in heavy coats and scarves, stood outside, stomping their feet and grinning at Sarah. Her heart came into her throat and she could barely choke back the tears, for standing between Jake and Janice was the long-lost Jones.

"Come in, come in. I just can't believe it. Jones, where have you been? We were so worried when we didn't hear from you all these years. We could never get you out of our minds. How are you? Janice and Jake, this is Jones. Oh, for goodness sake, Jones, can't we call you Terry?" They took the steps to the great room where the other guests waited.

Jones smiled at Sarah and shyly put his hand out to shake those around him as Sarah made introductions.

"Forrest, Lola, Istie, Jamie. And Marie and Janice and Jake and, our most special of guests, Billy Hawk. I am so glad that you are all here." Sarah shook her head to clear her eyes.

"Dusty will be up in a minute. I can't believe it. You all came! We have missed you so much. Please, everyone, have a chair. We'll show you your rooms in a few minutes!"

Forrest pulled Sarah to him in a silent hug and then turned to the small gray-haired woman who stood next to him. Her smile was sweet and she gently touched her husband's arm.

"Sarah, this is Reed's mother, my wife, Marie." Forrest said.

"Sarah, Forrest has spoken so much of you, Dusty and the ranch." Marie said. "I feel like I have been here for years. I am so glad to finally meet you. This is Jamie, Reed's wife. Jamie is our daughter. We had to convince her to leave the peach blossoms of Georgia but she came. She wanted to see where Henrietta, our former canine pet, lives now. The last time Forrest saw him, he was running down the side of Devils Tower with a new mate."

Sarah turned to the petite black-haired young woman who stood behind Forrest and Marie. She took Jamie's hand between hers and gently squeezed them. Outside the window, the storm increased in velocity. She could see a bent figure struggling against the wind, a flap of coat loosened by a gust. She dropped Jamie's hand and went to peer out the window. As she watched, Dusty came up to the house and disappeared under the deck. She heard the door downstairs open and close and

Dusty stomping the snow off his boots. He was whistling as he came up the stairs to where everyone else waited.

"Well, as I live and die! Sarah, where did all these people come from?" Dusty gave Lola a huge bear hug, shook Forrest's hand and then turned to where Billy sat in his chair.

"Old man, you're sitting there and laughing. What's the joke?" Dusty leaned down and placed his hand on Billy's knee. His touch was kind and his look tender. "Has Sarah introduced you to all these good folks?"

"Lola, is this Istie? And, lordy, I bet this is Liliana. Hello, baby! Aren't you the pretty one? Oh Lola, they are as beautiful as you said."

Dusty held his hands out to Liliana who smiled and slipped from her mother's arms into the ones Dusty held open. Her bright black eyes slid from Dusty's face to where Billy sat. She laughed, clapped her hands and leaned down to the old man. She cooed and giggled as Dusty placed her on the old man's lap. The room suddenly grew quiet as everyone stopped and watched Billy hug the little girl and rock her in his arms.

Several minutes passed with only the sound of the ticking clock, the squeak of the rocker, and the popping fire. Sarah watched the scene and then cleared her throat.

"Janice and Jake are Billy's niece and great-grandson. Billy has been with us all winter. We are so blessed to have him here. I don't know what I would have done without him to keep me company this winter. We just love him so much."

Sarah's voice dipped low and she dropped her eyes. "Istie, " she said, "we are so sorry for your loss. We couldn't believe it when Lola told us. There is so much evil in this world. That's why we feel so grateful to have this place of peace.

"We are so happy, though, that you have chosen to spend this time with us. Liliana is so beautiful. Do you want to come with me and I will show you where you and the baby are sleeping?"

Istie seemed unable to take her eyes from Billy and Liliana. She crossed her arms over her chest and hugged herself. Lola went to stand by her niece and, with the warmest of smiles, placed her hands on Istie's shoulders.

"Come on, Istie. Leave the baby with Billy. She's fine with him!"

Sarah stopped in her footsteps and bent down to look Billy in the eye. "The buckskin outfit is for her, isn't it, Billy? You knew she was coming. We never said a word. You just knew!"

Billy just grinned and bounced the baby on his knee, kissing her cheek. The group of seven looked at each other, wondering what Sarah was talking about. Billy's enigmatic smile gave nothing away. Sarah, laughing, broke the quiet.

"Come on, everyone. I'll show you your rooms. Lola, you and Istie are in your regular room. We put up a crib for the baby. Jones, you are in the same room you had before, across from Lola and Istie. Hold on a minute, Forrest and Marie and Jamie, Dusty will walk you out to the bunkhouse. That's where you all are staying. Jake and Janice, you two have the hand's quarters at the back of the barn. Really, they are lovely. You'll see. Jake, don't look at me like that! Like you are deprived." Sarah laughed.

Dusty put his arms around Janice and Jake's shoulders. "Get your coats on and I'll take your bags, Janice! Jake's younger than all of us! Jake, you can be a pack mule and help me out! I'll toss you a beer for this later!"

"Jamie, we had heard you were beautiful but Forrest understated how lovely you are. We are so glad you and Marie came. We wish we had been able to meet Reed. We have something special for you waiting in your room. Grab your coats, too. We don't want you to freeze in our Wyoming Spring."

Marie went to stand between her husband and her daughter-in-law. She laid a tender hand on Jamie's arm. "Forrest and I have not seen Jamie since just after Reed's death. We were so afraid we had lost her, too. We are so blessed she came and so grateful for you and Sarah inviting us."

Billy, holding Liliana close to his heart, smiled in quiet contentment. The fire in the stone fireplace burned lower, the embers throwing shadows around the room and casting a golden glow on Liliana's tiny face. In the soft light, Billy and Liliana had the appearance of angels, smiling at each other as if they had known each other for a thousand years.

Forrest watched the old man and baby snuggle with each other. A gentle smile touched his lips. He finally broke the silence, clearing his throat and asking, "Dusty, where's the wood box? I don't want the baby and Billy to get cold. I didn't see the horses out in the pasture. Where are they? I wonder, do you ever go to the Tower? Do you ever see Henrietta? I always wonder where he is and if he is safe. Sometimes, I cannot believe he's gone."

A look passed between Jamie, Marie, and Lola. All three of the women silently nodded their heads, knowing Forrest was talking more of his lost son, Reed.

"Come on, everyone." Sarah spoke up. "Let's get you settled in. I want to hear about all of you. We're having elk stew for dinner tonight. It isn't salmon or Georgia peaches but we think you will like it."

Tears began to run down Jamie's face. She sniffled, hugged Marie, and went to stand by the sliding door. "Sarah, your place is so wonderful. I feel so much peace. I can see why Forrest wanted us to come. Billy, it is an honor to meet you and, Lola, I finally get to spend time with you. This is such a Godsend in my life. I miss Reed every day and some days it is more than I can bear. But I am so glad to be here.

"Forrest, there are the horses. Look, they are coming up to the fence! Dusty, how many do you have now? Probably too cold to ride but I bet the ranch is beautiful in the snow!"

Dusty smiled at Jamie. "Well, we hope the weather will clear up. We have ten horses, now. You can meet them all later. If it clears, we can ride to where you can see the Tower. It's a favorite place for Forrest. Let's go face the elements and get you folks settled in!"

Dusty, Jamie, Forrest, Marie, Janice and Jake clattered down the stairs and, as they went, Jamie could feel the heat coming off of Jake. She stole a look at him and he was stealing an equally furtive one at her. Jamie was shocked as a tiny thread of heat ran between the two of them. She had been so engulfed in her grief over Reed, she had never considered even recognizing another man was alive. Janice, watching the two of them as they went down the stairs ahead of her, smiled to herself. She snickered and shook her head, pleased to see Jake take an interest in something other than Angus cattle and rodeo buckles.

Keep an eye on those two. she thought to herself. *Looks like Jake's getting ready to pick her out, just like he does with a horse. Whoo hoo! Will that young man be in for a surprise? That is one strong little girl!*

Back in the main house, Lola, Istie and Jones followed Sarah down the hall. Stepping into their rooms, Lola beamed at the sight of the bunk beds, the horse lamp with the plaid shade and the star quilt. Istie looked around in satisfaction. "Well, Sarah, this will do! Thanks so much. I better go get Liliana from Billy."

"Istie," Sarah said, "Liliana will be fine with Billy. He's spent the whole winter waiting for her. Istie, I know there is so little I can say to make things right for you but we wanted you to know we are so sorry about Sean. We know you must miss him terribly.

"It seems so odd, both you and Jones losing your loves to terrorists and Forrest, Jamie, and Marie losing Reed. So many people gone and so much sadness. Istie, take a look in the crib. There is something there for you and Liliana. I think Billy snuck in here this morning and put it there!"

Istie, who had been taking in the room, bent to look in the baby's crib. There was a pink crocheted baby blanket, an embroidered pink pillow with delicate lilies on it, and plastic spinning toys attached to the sides of the crib. Then she noticed the tiny buckskin dress with moccasins, leggings, and a red shawl covered in lilies, a tiny matching belt and purse, and the tiniest of a red beaded crown, also with lilies on it.

Istie reached into the crib to stroke the softness of the items. She looked up in wonder at Sarah. "Where did all of this come from? Sarah, did you make all of this? It is so beautiful. Is this all for Liliana?"

"Istie," Lola whispered. "That old man, Billy, did all of this, didn't he, Sarah? He knew she was coming. I cannot believe those old hands and eyes did such exquisite work. Sarah, did you talk to him about the baby?"

"Istie, can you believe all of this? It is so amazing. The only thing ever said about these items was when I would ask Billy who they were for. He would never tell me. He knows everything. He knew you were coming but we never told him Liliana's name. We wanted to surprise him. He knew her. Look at how he took her on his lap. I guess we should go out and get the baby. He tires easily and I need to make sure he is covered by his blanket."

The three women tiptoed down the hall to where Billy now slept with a sleeping Liliana curled up in his arms. The fire was still warm and Billy had pulled the plaid wool blanket up over the two of them. All three women smiled as Sarah leaned over to kiss both Billy and Liliana on their foreheads.

A quiet footfall sounded behind the women. Jones reached out and placed his hand on Istie's shoulder as he came to watch the quiet, tender scene.

"Lola, did you tell her?" Jones asked. "I know she was there when you found the wallet. Did you tell her?"

"Tell me what?" Istie asked, finally looking closely at Jones. He had an odd look on his face, one of immense sadness and one of great appreciation.

"The brown wallet you two found at Ground Zero belonged to my wife. Annie Jones was my wife."

Jones peered intensely into Lola's face. "You never told her, did you? I can't believe that. Why didn't you tell her?"

Lola stared down at her hands, a typical gesture of hers when in doubt or embarrassed. Once more, she studied the lines and creases on them. Finally, after several seconds, she looked straight into Jones's eyes. "I couldn't tell anyone. It was your grief. After Istie and Sean left for England, she was so busy. She used to ask about the wallet. I just couldn't tell her. I have always wondered what happened to you and Annie's parents. They seemed like such kind people and it was clear they loved Annie to pieces. I just couldn't talk about it."

Istie leaned down to kiss Liliana and to gently brush Billy's hand. She could feel the heat from Jones's hand as he laid it on her shoulder. It felt strangely comforting, the first comfort she had felt since she had last held and kissed Sean as he lay dying on the floor of London's Hilton.

"I understand, Auntie Lola. I really do understand. Jones, I lost my husband in the London subway bombings. I understand the sense of helplessness and anger over losing a loved one to fanaticism and ter-rorism. I understand that feeling of standing on quicksand and of being so overwhelmed. I am so glad I have Liliana and I am so sorry you and Annie did not have a child. I am so sorry. I knew my Auntie Lola and Sarah and Dusty had ulterior motives in bringing us here. I feel so at home. I am so sorry for your loss but Jones, I do understand. I feel I have so little of Sean left. He never even got to see Liliana. I wake up at night and hold her hand. I think, sometimes, I can feel Sean in the room but he's never there."

Istie sighed and moved away from Jones's touch.

"Look at her. I think she has found her niche in the world on Billy's lap. Poor baby. No father, another LeFleur female with no man in her life."

Sarah coughed into the room, startling the others. "Come on down for lunch everyone. Istie, I will check later on Liliana but she and Billy look pretty content. I am so very glad you are here."

As the tender tableau played out in the great room, Dusty walked Marie, Jamie and Forrest to the bunkhouse across the yard. The snow blew up around them and they could see the horses stomping in the paddock, steam rising from their coats. The little buckskin whinnied when he saw Jake and Janice and ran along the fence, nickering to them.

Dusty laughed. "Look, he must remember you two from last summer. He is fat and sassy, Jake, if it clears, we will go for a ride. Oh, and by the way, Janice, that little boy rides like a dream, never a buck out of him."

Dusty opened the door to the bunkhouse. "Jamie, this room is yours and Forrest and Marie, this one is yours. The bathroom is at the back and there are towels out for you. Lunch is in about ten minutes. Come on back to the house but make sure you keep warm."

"Come on, you two trouble makers. Your rooms are out here." He pushed Jake and Janice ahead of him down the stone path towards the barn, the yellow buckskin running back down the line of the fence that led to the red barn. He shook his head, calling to the three of them. He reached the paddock by the barn and looked back at them, his ears moving forward to hear their voices.

"Dusty, I know you think we are a couple of reprobates, but do we really have to sleep with the horses?" Janice laughed and kicked some blowing snow at Dusty. He laughed back and then led the way through the fences and across the paddock. The little yellow buckskin walked forward and nudged Janice's arm. She laughed and gently pulled his forelock, shooing him back to the pasture with the rest of the herd.

"Well, Janice," Dusty replied, "I think you will be pleasantly surprised. Look at that snow coming down. Real blizzard. I'm glad everyone beat the storm. I heard you have something special to tell Billy, about the white buffalo calf. I am curious, how did you find out about the calf?"

Reaching the side of the barn, Dusty pulled open a door that was underneath the white B/S surrounded by running horses. Inside were two rooms and a bathroom. The rooms were clean and neat, the beds made up and covered in buffalo robes. On the rough-hewn walls were pictures of Jake, Janice and Billy, taken over the course of the trips Dusty had made to Parmalee. One of the pictures was Jake being thrown from a huge brown bull, his hand in the air, and his feet just clearing the back of the bull. Janice laughed at the picture. "I always knew you were a lousy rider, Jake! Those championship buckles must have been guilt gifts from the judges!"

Janice suddenly grew serious. "Dusty, the birth of the white buffalo calf has been news via the moccasin grapevine. But, you do understand what this means? Why we haven't told Billy? He said he would die when the white buffalo calf came again. I can't bear to think it is true. We know he has been so sick this winter. I don't know what we would have done without you two taking such good care of him. I know he went down to Geronimo Barse's ranch. Said Geronimo's great- grandson has turned the ranch into a showplace.

"He got married, you know. A girl from Louisiana, Cajun and Seminole I think. I think her name was Alley Dupree. They have a little boy, named after Geronimo. He's three years old. I hope to get down there in a few weeks. Jerome said he has three new horses from a farm in Kentucky and we want to take a look at them. Junior here wants a pony to practice on!"

Dusty laughed and Jake scowled at his aunt. "Well, old lady, I think you were the last one to get bucked on that sorrel. Time for me to give you some lessons. Come on! Let's get some lunch."

Jake's voice became somber. "Janice, we have to tell Billy. He has the right to know. Besides, you know he always knows what's going on. When have we ever been able to keep a secret from him? Dusty, do you think we could take him down after lunch to see the calf?"

Dusty nodded and opened the door to the outside. The storm had abated and the horses were milling around the paddock. He stepped out into the cold and pulled open a gate, shooing the horses out into the lower pasture. Jake and Janice followed behind, linking their arms and pulling each other close, the tall, lanky woman and the stocky young man, clearly fond of each other and in sync with each other built on love and nurturing.

Inside the snug warmth of the main house, the others had gathered at the plank table. Billy had made his way down the stairs, a rare treat. He stood at the head of the table, Liliana still tucked in his arms.

Istie reached for the baby to put her on her lap as she moved to the table. It had been set with plates painted with running horses and tall glasses with the Buffalo Springs ranch logo etched in each glass. The placemats were scenes of the ranch and the silverware had tiny buffalos on the handles. Billy sat down and reached to take the baby back from Istie. She hesitated but at the look on Billy's face, she handed Liliana back to him. He held her up and kissed her tiny face. Liliana patted his face with her tiny hands and grabbed one of his braids to put in her mouth. Billy laughed and disengaged his braid.

Istie sat down, taking care to avoid the smug look on Sarah and Dusty's faces. Jones sat down on the bench next to her. His shoulder bumped Istie's but she did not move away. Lola watched the little interlude and smiled at Sarah. The great scheme Sarah and Dusty had hatched appeared to be working.

Marie, Forrest and Jamie had taken their places across from Istie, Jones and Lola. The dining room suddenly seemed to be filled with lightness, joy, camaraderie, and love. The heat from the stove steamed up the windows and sank around the group at the table, carrying with it delicious aromas. Sarah and Dusty carried dishes heaped with food to the plank table. When all the food was placed in front of their guests, Sarah grabbed Dusty's hand.

"Grandfather, Creator, our Lord Jesus. Thank you for this gathering of friends. Thank you for the blessing of these people and thank you for the food for our bodies. Amen!"

Jamie spoke up, her voice light and sweet. "Sarah, I want to propose a toast, if I may. This is to my beloved in-laws. You never lost me and I feel, right here and now, that I have never lost Reed. Lola, I am so glad to meet you. You have been such a comfort to Forrest. Marie, I have to tell you what was beside my bed, an incredible gift."

Jamie reached into her purse lying beside her on the bench. She pulled out a James Lee Burke book, *Black Cherry Blues*.

"Sarah and Dusty, how did you know he was our favorite author? I have a feeling a gentle angel named Marie told you. Reed was reading a James Lee Burke book when we met. And, look, everyone. It is even signed. Sarah and Dusty, I can't thank you enough."

Billy grinned and held up his free hand, the other holding Liliana close to his heart.

"We have a blessing song to sing, Jake and Janice help me out!"

In a strong voice, belying his frail frame, Billy started to sing. Janice and Jake joined in, the Lakota words soaring over the table and through the room. When it ended, a silence filled the space. Billy coughed, caught his breath, and began speaking. He stroked Liliana's black hair and tiny back as he spoke.

"The white buffalo calf has been born. I can feel it in my bones. He is close. He has come to take me home. Liliana is the answer to my prayer. I know of the grief you carry, all of you; Sarah, your grief over losing me; Dusty, your grief over Sarah's sadness; Jones and Jamie and Istie, for the losses of your mates, and Janice and Jake, for all of our relations who have left us. Lola, you have lived your whole life in grief.

"But look at this child. She is the blessing to bring us all together. This is a time for joy. Janice, you and Jake have to take me to see the calf today. Istie, the dress is for Liliana. I would be honored if you would dress her in it and come with us to see the blessing of the calf."

He coughed deeply and tears came to his faded eyes. "Don't mind an old man," he said. "This is a time for celebration."

The meal passed with laughter and jokes. Liliana was passed from person to person, smothered in kisses and bounced on knees. Jones, holding the baby up, eye to eye, saw the child he and Annie would never have. Jamie saw her own black eyes reflected back to her. Marie and Forrest saw the grandchild they would never have. Sarah and Dusty saw the love and hope that came in the shape of a baby, watching Liliana coo and giggle at the faces that smiled down at her.

Finally, Sarah got up to clear the table. She hated to break the spell that seemed to have taken hold of the room and the people in it. It was snowing again, big flakes filling the air. Through the misted windows, she could see the herd moving slowly back to the lean-to by the barn. She could barely make out the B/S on the barn. She thought of the old Kiowa man and his grandson. She thought of the horses that had come north with them on that long ago trip. She thought of the old man who sat at the end of the table.

Suddenly, with a gasp in her throat, Sarah saw a vision. The white buffalo calf and his mother were slowly moving through the fields of the ranch. They walked through the fences as if they did not exist, disappearing up the hill, their shaggy heads plowing the way through the deepening snow. In the reflection of the window, Sarah could see Billy's beloved face, his head nodding at her.

"Dusty," Sarah said in the quietest and gentlest of voices, "it's time to take Billy down to the C-Bar-C. Forrest, can you and Jones both drive and take the rest of us? It won't take long. Istie, I'll dress Liliana. Lola, can you help me get some blankets to keep Billy warm? You can drive with us."

Startled at the suddenness of Sarah's request, they all looked toward Sarah and then Billy. Without a word, the table benches were pushed back and people began to reach for their coats. Istie took Liliana from Marie's lap and started up the stone stairs, Sarah close behind her. Lola pulled the truck keys from the hook by the door and grabbed her old parka and scarf.

Jake and Janice disappeared up the stairs behind Sarah and came back down with Billy's coat, his lodge drum, eagle feather fan, and his fur moccasins. When they reached the kitchen, Billy was standing by the wooden door that looked out to the pastures. His eyes gleamed and seemed to see something neither of them could discern.

Janice put Billy's sacred items on the table and walked up behind the graceful old man. She put her hands on his shoulder and laid her face against his still, straight back. Jake stopped short and closed his mouth as he started to make one of his smart remarks. He sensed the old man was watching something out in the pasture, something from the other world from the one in which mere mortals lived. He, too, went to stand next to Billy, wrapping his arms around the old man.

Sarah and Istie found them this way when they carried Liliana down the stairs and back into the kitchen. Liliana giggled and held her arms out to Billy. He turned from the hugs of Jake and Janice and took the baby from Istie. Liliana was dressed head to toe, in white buckskin, leggings, shawl and moccasins. Billy nodded his head and kissed Liliana on the top of her head. She grabbed for his red-wrapped braid and attempted to suck on it. Billy gave a chuckle and took it from her tiny hand.

"Istie, hand me her wraps. I don't want her getting cold. Are we all ready to go? Where are Forrest, Jones, Jamie and Marie? Are they coming, too? It's getting late. We need to go. They are waiting for us. We have to go." Billy's voice was firm as he herded everyone ahead of him, Liliana was now wrapped snugly in blankets and her baby parka, and her little face barely visible through the scarf Billy had pulled up to her nose.

Outside, a patch of blue sky appeared and, for the moment, beams of God's Light glistened on the snow of the fields, the house and barn. The herd was running from one end of the pasture to the other, snorting and shaking their heads. Liliana laughed into Billy's face and he turned her so she could see the galloping horses. All of a sudden, both Liliana and Billy grew quiet, both of them intently watching something in the midst of the horses. With a sigh, Billy stepped forward and, with a purposeful stride, headed to where Dusty, Forrest, and Lola had the truck and cars warming for the others.

Within a minute, everyone had settled themselves in the vehicles and the caravan began its slow journey down the dirt road. No one spoke. The only sound was the crunch of snow and the tick of the heater. After a half hour, the vehicles pulled onto the blacktop and crossed the highway to the long drive of the C-Bar-C ranch. The gate had been left open, a rare sight in the world of cattle ranches.

As Lola drove up the road, she could see dozens of cars lining the sides of the lane. Crowds of people dressed against the Spring storm made their way on foot towards the barn.

"Drive on up, Lola. There are spots up there by the barn. The calf is waiting for the baby. Go on up." Billy spoke with the assurance of his ninety-nine years and there, up against the huge yellow metal barn, were three parking slots. "Don't look so surprised, Lola. Janice told them that we were coming. Just park here and we can walk around to the back of the barn. They are waiting for us. Come on!"

Lola and Sarah could hear the excitement in the old man's voice. Beside them, the doors of the other cars closed. Jake went to take Jamie by the hand, a gesture that surprised Janice for he rarely showed tenderness to anyone other than her and the old man. Behind Jake and Jamie, Forrest and Marie came to stand, holding hands. The couple stood in comfort with each other, their long years together and their mutual loss drawing them as close as two people could be.

Marie smiled as she watched Jake holding Jamie's hand. Her fear for Jamie had been that she would never overcome her grief over Reed. It was one thing for two older people to mourn the loss of a beloved son but neither she nor Forrest had wanted Jamie to stay in an emotional limbo, waiting in vain for Reed's footsteps on the tile floor of the adobe house. Marie understood why Jamie had sold the house and moved back to Georgia to be with her mother and father. Late at night, she could hear Reed whispering her name and feel him shaking her by the shoulder to wake her up and tell her he was home. On those nights, she would turn and wrap her arms around Forrest, feeling his heart beat and his breath, slow and even. She would clutch him tightly to her body and try to pace her heart to his.

Forrest would not speak of his grief but spent long hours at the cemetery, bringing yellow roses and carefully clipping the grass around Reed's headstone. He never asked her to come and she grew to understand that this was the only way he could mourn his son. In the den, next to the pictures of his old Army friends, Henrietta and Roxie, now stood several silver framed pictures. There was one of Jamie and Reed, running in the surf off of Hilton Head, smiling into the camera and waving to Marie as she took the picture. Marie's shadow on the sand could be seen in the photo.

Next to this picture was another one Marie had taken, this one of Reed's last trip home. It was one of Lola and Forrest holding the bridles of the red pony and Roxie. The horses were saddled with their heads up and eyes soft and brown. Reed stood between the horses, an arm over a saddle on either side. At his feet lay Henrietta, his tongue lolling out with one black eye and one blue eye staring straight into the camera.

Marie thought of these pictures as Istie and Jones, also holding hands, came up beside them.

"Istie, I think you have lost that baby to Billy. Have you ever seen such love at first sight?" Marie shook her head and squeezed Forrest's hand.

With a sudden stop, Istie and Jones turned back to look at Marie. "Yes!" came the answer to Marie's question. Marie looked closely at Istie, her hand in Jones's, and smiled.

Inside the pen was a red buffalo cow surprisingly dainty-looking for an animal her size. Her head was down and she was licking the coat of a small calf, its coat as white as the snow that had fallen for most of the day. The eyes of the calf were closed with a blissful look on his face as his mother nuzzled him. To the side of the pen, Clair and Christian Barr, the owners of the C-Bar-C, stood welcoming their guests.

A large gathering of Native people from all the neighboring tribes and beyond the tri-state area crowded together. Several of the ranchers and townspeople were present and two of the elderly ladies from the next ranch grasped the metal fence that marked the edges of the pen. A low murmur flowed through the crowd but came to an abrupt halt as Billy stepped forward, holding Liliana in his arms.

Billy's joy in Liliana was evident as he took off the baby's wraps and scarf and handed them to Lola. He held the baby in one arm and pulled her dress down to cover her knees. He fussed over the leggings and moccasins. He straightened her shawl around her tiny torso, and re-tied the leather thongs that held the beaded belt around Liliana's waist. Lola and Istie watched silently, Billy's old hands trembling as he fussed with the baby's outfit.

Janice had carried Billy's treasures from the car and one by one, at his beckoning, handed them to him, a practiced movement that had passed between uncle and niece for nearly five decades.

As Billy moved forward towards the pen, the mother buffalo swung her head and stared deeply into Billy's eyes. Her calf, sensing her movement, moved to stand by his mother. Billy held Liliana in one arm and

reached through the metal bars of the pen to bless the buffalo with his eagle feather fan. Liliana held her hands out to the buffalo calf touching his forehead. Billy motioned to Istie to come to his side and take Liliana. Janice handed him his drum and, in the deep quiet of the barn, he began to sing an honoring song. The buffalo stood in complete stillness, listening to the old man's words. The crowd gathered in the cold of the metal barn grew completely still and silent.

"*Pilamayaye. Mita kuye ayasin. Thank you, Grandfather.*" The words slipped from Billy's lips as he finished his songs. From around his neck, he pulled a cord of sinew. Dangling from the end of the cord was an exquisitely carved white buffalo. With all the love accumulated in his extraordinarily long life, Billy kissed the totem and placed it around Liliana's neck.

"Sarah," Billy sighed, "take me home. I am tired and I want to sleep. I am tired. Istie, could you please wrap up the baby and hand her to me? We need to go to sleep, the sleep of the old and of the young. I am glad you all came with me but now I need to go home. It is time for me to sleep."

The crowd parted, allowing Billy and the baby to walk out into the snow. He held his drum and eagle feather fan in one hand and Liliana, once again tightly wrapped in blankets, in the other. His back was straight and stiff, bending only as he stepped into the truck, Liliana held tightly to his chest.

Once back at the ranch, Billy climbed the stone steps with labored breathing. He had refused to relinquish Liliana with the exception of Sarah helping him off with his coat. Janice had gone to the paddock to help Dusty feed the horses. Jake, Jamie, Istie and Jones started a game of dominoes at the plank table in the kitchen, the clink of the tiles a pleasant sound that drifted up the stairs to where Lola and Sarah helped Billy into the rocker. He still held Liliana in her white buckskin dress, leggings and moccasins, and tiny shawl tucked around her little body.

Lola had picked up the fan and the drum, and took them into Billy's room. Sarah pulled the plaid blanket up across Billy's chest. Liliana was asleep, her head with its fine black hair tucked up under Billy's chin. She was sucking on the thumb of her right hand, her left hand entwined in Billy's braid.

Lola moved to squat down by the fire and stir the ashes that barely burned. She added some paper and more wood, thinking of the night she and Krissie and Rona had stood along the river, the ospreys flying with their precious cargo of the silver salmon. As the embers glowed and flew up the chimney, they seemed to turn to turquoise, blue and green, echoing the bright lights that had sat in lodge with them. A breeze stirred in the room, and Sarah gave a loud gasp.

"Billy, oh no Billy, don't go. Not yet. Billy, don't go. Oh Lola, he's gone. He's gone. Quick, go get Dusty, Jake and Janice. Oh, Billy, don't leave. Lola, oh Lola, dear God. Oh, Billy, don't go!"

Lola jerked her head towards Sarah. Around Billy's head and covering the tiny baby sleeping on Billy's chest, was a golden glow. She slowly stood and went to place her hand on Billy's neck. Carefully loosening the baby's hand from Billy's braid, she picked up Liliana who cried as she was taken from Billy's chest. Lola held the baby over her shoulder, patting her back.

"Shush, baby. He's gone home. Shush. Sarah, you need to stay with him. I'll go get the others." Lola touched Billy's face and then moved to descend the stairs. At her approach, the four young people looked up into Lola's solemn face. Istie, in fear, pushed back the bench and came to her feet.

"Auntie Lola, what is it? What is it? Is Liliana all right? Auntie, say something. Sarah, where are you? Auntie, say something. You're scaring me!"

Lola took a deep breath and buried her face in the sweet softness of Liliana's neck. She felt the softness of the buckskin dress Billy had crafted and touched the baby's feet in the miniature moccasins. She raised her teary eyes to meet Istie's. Her voice came out flat and lifeless. "He's gone, Istie. Billy is gone. Can you take the baby? I have to get Janice and Dusty."

Jamie, Jake and Jones quickly stood up, Jake racing up the stairs, calling Billy's name. The others followed him and watched as Jake dropped to his knees beside his great-grandfather, grabbing for Billy's hand.

"Old man, I know you had to go but couldn't you wait?" Tears fell from Jake's eyes, and he rubbed his face on Billy's hand. "Sarah, look at his face. He's smiling. Oh, Sarah. He died happy. This is going to be so hard. I knew he would go once the white buffalo calf came. I could see it in his face. Oh, Lord, Janice. I have to get her."

At that moment, running footsteps could be heard coming up the stairs. Janice ran across the room, Dusty close behind her. Lola had run to get Marie and Forrest from their room where they had gone after coming home from the C-Bar-C. They were exhausted from the travels and emotions of the day. Forrest, not waiting to put on their coats, had dashed with Lola into the house. They, too, climbed the stairs, reaching the great room in time to hear Janice break into ragged sobs.

Jake stroked her hair as Janice sank to her knees in front of the old man. The others stood with their hands clasped and heads down in acknowledgement of Billy's passing. Sarah pulled Dusty to her.

"Dusty," she sobbed, "he knew he was leaving us today. He waited for everyone to come and to see the white buffalo calf. That is what he and Liliana were looking at today out the window. I thought I was crazy but I saw them walk across the pasture and up to the buffalo wallow. He knew he was going and so did Liliana. Jake and Janice, what can we do to help? I will call Doc Leighton. Oh, Dusty, I can't believe he left us. I just can't believe it."

In the background, the fire crackled and came to life. A burst of wind shook the sliding door and rattled against the windows. The small group of people standing around Billy all glanced at the door as the wind increased in volume.

"They've come to take him home." Janice said. "Jake, help me move him to his bed. Sarah, can you come with us? We have to wash him as soon as Doc Leighton gets here. Dusty, can you call Jerome and Henry? They will want to know."

Janice's knees popped and creaked as she came to her feet. She hugged Jake and ran her hands over his face. "He's gone, Jake. We have to prepare him for his last journey. We can cry later."

"Let me take the baby, Istie. Forrest and Marie, can you wait down-stairs for Doc Leighton and have him come up. It is such a blessing he went so quietly and Liliana was with him."

Lola started to take Liliana from Istie but Jones stepped ahead of her. "Lola, please let me have her. I can take care of her if you want to help out. Jamie and I can watch her."

Istie cast a sideways look at Lola who nodded and handed him the baby. Liliana squirmed around, still trying to see Billy and holding out her chubby hands toward him.

With some difficulty, Sarah and Dusty, helped by Jake, Janice and Forrest, carried Billy into his bedroom. Sarah moved the eagle fan and drum off the bed and pulled the plaid blanket from Billy's body. She folded his hands on his chest and touched the braids she had combed and plaited every morning. Janice and Jake sat on the edge of the bed, grief noticeably aging Janice. Jake grabbed his aunt's shoulder, lines of tears marking his young face.

"He knew, Janice. He knew it when he left the ranch two years ago. He knew we loved him, Janice. We've been lucky to have him for so long. I'm going to go talk to the others."

Jake squeezed his aunt's shoulders and stood up, pausing at the door to look back at Billy's peaceful face, and stepped out into the hallway, clearing his throat. Istie, Forrest, Marie, Jamie and Jones, carrying Lili-ana, slowly moved back into the great room. No one spoke as they made their way to the couches and chairs that filled the room. They watched as Jake sat down on the floor at the base of the recliner where Billy had passed. The fire had continued to burn and the wind continued to blow.

Forrest cleared his throat and shook his head. "Jake, we understand your grief. We have all been through it. Maybe that is why we are all gathered here. Sarah, somehow, she must have known. I think this is to be a time of healing for all of us. Time to mourn, and then time to celebrate our lives and move on."

Jamie and Marie stared in shock at Forrest. Neither of them could recall a time when he had shown such open emotion. Istie and Jones, not wanting to break the mood, held their breaths. The room was warm and a feeling of peace crept into the comforting space. Behind them, down the hall, they could hear the low murmurings of Janice, Dusty, Lola and Sarah. A soft thud sounded, Dusty dropping Billy's boots to the floor.

A knock on the sliding glass door announced Doc Leighton. He slid the door open and nodded to the small group. He held his black bag in his hand and wiped his wet feet on the mat in front of the door. He pulled the door closed against the cold. The others watched as he stepped into Billy's room and closed the door behind him. They could hear Sarah's voice and then Janice joining in. A half hour passed as the others waited in the great room. Jamie added more wood and stirred the fire. In Jones's arms, Liliana fell back asleep. Istie stared at the two of them, a small hope stirring in her chest. Jamie sat down on the hearth, raising her head as Jake came out of Billy's bedroom.

"He just died," Jake said. "He died happy. I think he wanted to go. He had been saying goodbye for two years. Janice and I have agreed to bury him on the ranch if Sarah and Dusty will let us. Doc is signing the death certificate and then we can prepare him. I cannot believe he is gone. He is the only father I have known. He watched me in nearly every rodeo I ever rode in. I don't know what Janice will do. He was her whole life."

Jake's voice cracked and he looked down at his feet. At that moment, Doc Leighton came out of the room. "It's done. I am sorry for your loss. I wish I had time to sit and get to know you. Sarah and Dusty have shared so much about all of you. I have to go now though. Got a page from the clinic. Looks like Mildred Anderson slid off the road in her jeep and broke her wrist. Jake, call me if you think I can be of further help. My condolences to you and your aunt."

He quietly let himself out of the room, his footsteps echoing as he made his way down the path to the parking area. Within a minute, the sound of his car engine was heard and then faded off into the distance.

Loud whinnying came from the pasture, the yellow buckskin calling across the paddock. Jake went to stand by the door and leaned his head against the cold glass. "I think they are saying farewell. That little buckskin Dusty got last summer is leading the herd. Look at them run. Aren't they beautiful? That old man loved his horses, just like Geronimo Barse. Now they are both gone. All of our elders are gone. Who will teach us now?"

In the bedroom, Sarah, Janice and Dusty carefully removed Billy's clothes. They washed his body with the greatest care, Sarah untying the red cloth from Billy's braids. She ran her hands through his gray hair and smoothed his forehead. Dusty, his back to the women, pulled out a drawer in the dresser where Billy had kept his jeans and shirts, meticulously folded. He pulled out a green shirt and a black pair of jeans along with underwear, socks and a snowy white undershirt.

"Are these the ones you want, Janice?"

"Dusty, it doesn't matter to me. But I have to ask you both a hard question." Janice stared down at Billy's still face. She searched for the soul of the old man who had raised her and Jake, singing songs, teaching them traditions, and wiping the tears of life away.

"I would like him to be buried here on your ranch. Up the hill from the buffalo wallow. I don't want to take him back to the ranch in Parmalee. He left that ranch to die and I know he loved you both so much."

Sarah nodded and in silence the three of them finished their task of dressing the gracious old man. Once more, Sarah thought of Geronimo Barse dying alone, not even his horses near him. She said a quick prayer to God and reached her hands out to Dusty and Janice, squeezing them as she said a soft "Amen."

The evening passed, marked by the slow tick of the clock. At eight o'clock, Sarah went to the kitchen and returned to the great room with fruit, sandwiches, drinks and hot coffee. At ten o'clock, Forrest and Marie gave their goodbyes and made their way through the dark to the waiting bunkhouse. The sky had finally cleared and the Milky Way shone its billions of stars down onto the snow. Forrest saw a large shadow and a smaller shadow moving across the pasture. It appeared to be that of two buffaloes, one a large female and the other a calf, the calf as white as the surrounding snow.

"Marie, look over there. Do you see that?"

Marie peered into the darkness and shook her head. "No, I don't see anything. Let's go to bed, Forrest. I am really tired. I think Jamie and Jake like each other. Same with Istie and Jones. I have a strong feeling, very strong, that Sarah is playing matchmaker. Forrest, I can see why you love it here. I know you miss Reed, but can't you feel his spirit?

Tomorrow, after the funeral, let's go to the Tower. Maybe Henrietta and his new mate will come to see us. Wouldn't that be wonderful?"

Marie and Forrest stood with their arms around each other, gazing at the stars and thinking their own thoughts about their beloved and much-missed son. Forrest shivered and opened the door to the bunkhouse, stepping inside after his wife.

In the main house, Jamie, Istie, Lola and Jones sat sipping the last of the coffee. Janice and Jake sat in vigil beside Billy's bed, the light spilling into the hallway. The fire in the great room died back to embers, the room chilling. With a reluctance born of new friendships and bonds of love, one by one, they said goodnight and went to bed, leaving Sarah and Dusty alone.

Jones carried Liliana down the hall and handed her to Istie. He stood in the doorway of the bedroom, watching Istie change the baby into night clothes, pulling the pink crocheted blanket up around her. He watched as Istie placed the white buckskin dress, shawl, belt and moccasins on the bedside table. Istie carefully slipped the carved white buffalo from Liliana's neck and held it in her right hand, stroking it with the fingers of her left.

Jones turned to leave and then, as an afterthought, went to stand next to the bunk bed where Lola sat, once again studying her hands. Jones squatted down beside Lola and placed his hands on her cheeks, raising her face to his. "Istie," he said, looking at Lola but his words clearly intended for both women. "Think about it, this very odd string of events. It was my wife's wallet your Auntie found that day. It was Annie's parents on the train with your Auntie Lola and Auntie Louella.

"I saw Annie fall that day. I saw her fall and watched her die. I know you lost Sean the same way I lost Annie, to crazy people. But, Istie, I have spent nearly five years in grief. When I saw you and your Auntie today, my heart was glad.

"I don't know if Lola ever told you, but it was here on the ranch, a year after Annie died, that your Auntie gave me back Annie's wallet. I carry it with me everywhere, Istie. We all have to have something to remember our dead. It's all I have left of her from that day. I worry that I might forget her face sometimes but thanks to your Auntie, I have it with me and I can look at her when I feel her starting to slip away. Istie, please bring Liliana and come to New York with me. I want to show you the city. Lola will give her blessing. Please, come with me. It's time for both of us to start living."

Jones rose to his feet and left the room. Istie and Lola stared at each other, a silent message passing between them. Slowly, Lola nodded, and with the movements of all of her nearly sixty years, stood and closed the door. She undressed and dropped her nightgown over her head. She climbed in bed and from under the covers, spoke the words that had sat silent in her heart for years.

"Istie, I was wrong to fuss when I found out you and Sean were married and were moving to London. I simply could not bear losing you after losing Auntie Louella. I was wrong. I know you loved Sean, Istie. He would have loved Liliana beyond all sanity. But, Istie, I was wrong. Go to New York with Jones. I won't make the same mistake again. You have my blessing. I won't try to keep you with guilt this time. You deserve a second chance at love, Istie. Don't make the same mistake the LeFleur women have made all of these generations. Go on with you life, Istie. You have my blessing. He will be good to you."

The next morning, a thaw came to the ranch, water dripping from the branches of the trees and the fence lining the pasture. A crow called in the distance and was answered by the loud shriek of a jay. A small red squirrel scolded them both from his perch in the oak tree that, in the summer, shaded the lawn. The horses, feeling the sun on their backs, stomped their feet in impatience, waiting for Dusty to open the gate to the paddock.

Sarah had risen early, starting to climb the stairs for her morning ritual with Billy. She remembered he was gone and heaved a deep sigh. She gathered up the dominoes that had been left on the table and, one by one, dropped them back into the box, closing the lid with a pop.

A noise behind her made her look up as Jake and Janice came into the kitchen. Their eyes were red-rimmed with fatigue. Jake, without saying anything but giving Sarah a kiss, walked out the door towards the barn. Janice poured herself a cup of coffee and stood by the sink, staring out of the window.

"Janice, Dusty will be back in a few minutes. He took Jones and Forrest up on the hill to dig Billy's grave. I would like, with your permission, to bury him in the red plaid blanket. He slept under it every day. Do you mind?" Sarah's voice was low and shot through with grief.

"Sarah, I would be honored. I would like to bury him at noon. He was ready to go. I am so glad he was here with you when he went. I am sure going to miss that old man. Where is everyone? Lola and Istie, Jamie and Marie. Are they out, too?"

"I think so," Sarah replied. "There were dishes in the sink when I got up this morning. I think I have been a negligent hostess. I was so exhausted last night. I kept hearing Billy call me and then I would remember he was gone.

"Janice, go take a nap. You look exhausted. I will wake you in a few hours. Look, here they all come but Dusty and Jake. I think they are going to feed the horses. I called Jerome and Henry today. They send their love and condolences. Go on, get some sleep."

At noon, as the sun shone on the remaining snow, Dusty, Forrest, Jake and Janice carried Billy up the hill. Jamie, Marie, Lola and Istie followed behind, Jones once more holding Liliana. As the party made their way up the hill, Sarah began to pray, an Easter prayer that spoke of renewal and of the Spring, a prayer for healing and a grateful thank you for all of her guests and for her husband. She prayed for Billy's soul and for a hope that Istie and Jones would find love with each other and that Jake could bring a spark of life back to Jamie's eyes. She prayed for Janice's peace of mind and for Forrest and Marie to have each other for many more years. She prayed for Dusty and his love. She prayed for Lola's peace of mind and for peace in the world.

As Billy was laid to rest on the hill, a long howl of wind came from behind the low rise that shielded the ranch. The horses had followed the party up the hill. They nickered and nudged each other. Jake and Janice stood over the grave and laid Billy's eagle feather fan and drum on top of the red plaid blanket that covered the beloved old man. Dusty placed the first shovel of dirt into the grave. He began to sing a Kiowa song long ago taught to him by Geronimo Barse. His voice carried across the fields and into the valley rolling away from the ranch.

As the song faded, a hawk flew overhead, its scream a final farewell to Billy. All eyes lifted to watch the hawk fly up into the blue. Everyone but Jake, Forrest and Dusty turned to walk back down the path to the house. Behind them the muffled sounds of falling dirt could be heard. Liliana, her head over Jones's shoulders, reached out her tiny hands toward Billy's grave. She laughed and waved as Jones carried her away from the old man. She looked up into the blue sky and waved again, cooing in delight.

As they moved slowly down the hill, Sarah suddenly stopped and pointed to the ground, a soft cry escaping her lips. "Janice, look, look. There, in the snow. Look! That's what he saw."

In the snow, clearly marking a trail across the pasture and up to where Billy now lay in his grave, were the tracks of two buffalo, one large and one small. High on the hill, Billy's soul rose from the earth and circled with the hawk. Upon the back of his namesake, Billy went home. He gazed down on the people gathered in his honor. He threw a kiss to Liliana, dressed once more in her buckskin.

As he went to join the old ones, he took a final last look below him. There, standing by the buffalo wallow, were the white buffalo calf and his mother. Billy smiled and reached out to shake Geronimo Barse's hand, held out to him in love and welcoming him home. Together, the old friends moved into the beyond, peace coming at last to them as Janice murmured a final goodbye:

> "In the arms of an Angel;
> Fly away from here;
> You're in the arms of an angel;
> May you find some comfort here…"

⇥ Epilogue ⇤

Devils Tower

Gillette, Wyoming   **September 11, 2006**

Light sparked off the whirling propellers of the small cigar-shaped tube of the plane. Lola stared out the window, seeing each individual blade as they pulled through the bluish rain-spitting clouds. A shattering boom of thunder rocked the plane, shaking the cedar box cradled on her lap. A trembling whispering sound of water on sand rose in her ears as the sweet summer smell of cedar reached her nose. She turned to look out the rain-streaked window as the plane began to descend, her ears popping as the cabin pressure changed.

A weathered face, green-eyed with high cheekbones and the softening jowls of middle age, reflected back at Lola. Dark circles enhanced the tiredness in the woman's face. The lines at the corners of the eyes were reminders of laughter, now permanently engrained. A small scar, just under the right eye, deepened as the face grimaced and turned away from Lola's stare. The plane touched the ground at the Gillette airport with a shriek of smoking wheels and came to a shuddering stop, just shy of the neat, tidy brick terminal. The storm had passed and in its place was the sun and heat of the waning days of summer.

Lola, along with her co-passengers, descended the stairs to the hot tarmac, carrying a red Nordstrom shopping bag with frayed handle and edges. The four passengers waited in the hot sun as a dusty wind whipped around their legs. At long last, the flight crew delivered luggage to the waiting passengers. Lola gathered her possessions and slowly walked into the building. Temporarily blinded by the darkness of the terminal, she welcomed the air-conditioned coolness that swept over her.

She stepped up to the Hertz counter and presented the clerk her driver's license. After much ado regarding the car rental process, the clerk handed her a set of keys and chirped out a cheery "Drive Safely." Lola failed to hear the clerk's parting remark as she pushed her way out the sliding door, dragging her luggage behind. The weight of the contents, along with the thinness of the straps of the Nordstrom bag, cut a red welt into her arm.

Lola unlocked the doors of the white rental car and tossed her luggage along with the Nordstrom bag onto its back seat. Sliding into the driver's seat, she started the engine. Slowly, she backed the car out of the slot and cautiously drove away, pulling onto the frontage road that led to the highway.

As she headed northeast, the countryside changed from red and brown dust to a greener, softer landscape. To her right, a huge open pit coal mine disgorged its treasure onto an enormous conveyor belt, sending energy and pollution to the millions of people living to the south. Lola's imagination saw the power plants as the fires of hell, burning into eternity. She chided herself for her dark thoughts and slid an Eagles CD into the car's player.

"It wasn't really sad the way they said good-bye...

Or maybe it just hurt so badly, she couldn't cry..."

She patted the cedar box beside her on the passenger's seat. The red and yellow wood gleamed in the sun and she thought of the task ahead. An hour into the drive, the landscape changed yet again. The pine trees began to mingle with the yellow grass.. Above, the hawks and crows rode the currents of the late summer air. The wind slid over the white car just as it slid under the wings of the birds. Lola sang along to the songs on the CD, sighing to herself as she listened to the words about wasted time and unrequited love.

They had come to this place in time, a journey of two generations. As she drove over the ridge, the familiar monolith came into view. Once again, the ground squirrels saluted her with their shrill whistles and sharp barks. The smell of dust and pinesap floated aloft on the dry end-of-summer air.

Lola's eyes moistened as she eased the car up the road and into a parking spot at the base of the Tower. She stepped out of the car and opened the back door, pulling out the red shopping bag. Reaching into its depths, she drew out a large round, flat bag with a black shoulder strap running across its top. She swung the bag over her shoulder and turned to pick up the cedar box. Again the sound of waves on sand rose from the box and caressed her ears. She turned once more to pull two large plastic containers from the Nordstrom bag. She held them in her left hand as her right hand gripped the cedar box as tightly as the talons of a Red-tailed Hawk holding its prey.

Above, the sun glistened off the helmets of the climbers descending from the flat platform atop the Tower. Lola took a moment to take in the magnificent view. The last rays of the sun cast a pink and orange glow over the few clouds gathering over the plains below. The flat river crossing the plain seemed motionless from the distance. Lola took a deep breath, closed her eyes, and took a last look at her car, parked in the same spot as it had been five years before.

"Aay, ya, aay ya, Saghalee Tyee, Mahsie Mahsie, aay ya, aay ya…"

The words to the ancient song quietly escaped Lola's lips, each sound bursting into the cooling air as she began her slow and methodical walk up the asphalt path. Her sneaker-clad feet knew the way, leaving her free to look skyward as she sang her song.

Her words still hung in the air as she reached the altar with its medicine bundles and offerings. She stopped and placed the cedar box on the ground under the altar. She unzipped the red bag and pulled out the drum, the face painted with a green and red thunderbird clutching arrows in its talons.

"Aay ya, aay ya, Saghalee Tyee, Aay ya, aay ya.. " As Lola sang again, she hit the drum with the leather-wrapped baton. The sound echoed off the rocks and carried into the approaching night. Finishing her honoring song, she dipped her hand into the clear plastic bags and pulled out a handful of chocolate-scented tobacco and sprigs of white sage. As she tossed them into the air, a stray breeze danced around the base of the Tower and carried the shreds of tobacco and sage up into the air. Up, up they went to where the sisters hid from their brother the bear; up, past the top of the Tower, where the Little Bear and Big Bear lumbered into the sky.

Lola sighed, and slowly replaced the drum into the red bag. She shrugged the strap back over her shoulder and, looking around her into the woods, she began her walk up the familiar trail. Approaching the bench, she again gazed at the view spread out beneath her, far away to where the Old Ones lived, far away to the land of Crazy Horse and his pony, far away to where the last of Sitting Bull's buffalo turned their enormous heads into the wind.

Lola sat down on the bench at the bend in the path, carefully placing the cedar box on the wooden slats next to her. She patted the top of the box and turned to again pull the red drum out of its bag. Carefully, she laid the drum on the ground, and placed the plastic bags of remaining sage and tobacco on it.

"Auntie," Lola whispered, "let's go home."

Lola softly placed the cedar box on her lap. Lovingly, she stroked its glossy lid. With a final murmur of "I love you," she opened the box and slowly stood. A small brown rabbit sniffed at her sneaker and the Red-tailed Hawk screamed as ruffled wings carried it off into the deepening blue of the coming night sky.

"Auntie," Lola whispered, "let's go home…."

"Yo, no, no, no nay ya… yo no no no, nay ho, ya yay, ya ho, ya ho… "

Lola crooned the words of the wind song and the wind answered as Lola's song grew louder. It matched her tone and tempo and, as she and the wind sang in harmony, Lola turned the cedar box into the breeze. The ashes of her beloved auntie flew into the sky and spread out in an ever-increasing arc.

Auntie Louella was going home. The Red-tailed Hawk screamed a farewell to the graceful old lady now joined with the Old Ones. The sound faded with the last light of day. Lola gently closed the lid of the cedar box and turned to make her way back to the car. She walked in solitude. No visitors were on the path and the climbers had long since gathered their ropes and left the God's Headstone. Lola and the Tower were alone in the night.

A fine thread of light struck the top of the Tower and reflected down to where Lola made her way, more by feel than sight, to the parking lot. She slid her shoe along the edge of the path, the soft soil giving way at the rim of the blacktop. Just off the path to her right, a small object gleamed, capturing her attention. Bending down to pick it up, she gasped as she realized what it was. Entwined into one were the black cords of several small fetishes, a wolf, snake, horse, elk, crow, falcon and wolverine. The stone figures swayed from the ends of their cords, grinning at her. The mountain air grew cool and the stars began to shine as she gazed at the carvings. Lola smiled into the forest surrounding the Tower and continued her way down the trail.

Reaching the altar once again, she hung the intertwined cords of the animal fetishes in the branches of the tree behind the altar. She rubbed each surface, feeling their coolness under her fingertips. Kneeling in front of the altar, Lola shut her eyes. The cool mountain air washed over her and cleansed her soul. She listened to the night sounds of the forest and smelled the earth. A richness filled her nostrils. No cries came from the woods, no sounds of tumbling rocks or smells of fear.

Lola longed to stay in the safety of the altar but she knew it was time to leave. Slowly she rose to her feet and continued her retreat to the parking lot below. Farther down the trail, she could see the gleam of the white rental car. It was as alone as she felt. At last she reached the car and opened the door, returning the sage and tobacco, along with the drum and the cedar box to their hiding place in the Nordstrom bag. She slid her knees under the steering wheel, and closed the door behind her.

The faint stars and full moon beamed through the windshield onto her face as she started the car's engine and shifted into reverse. Rays of moonlight reflected off the spectacular monument, the rock that had stood for forty million years and would stand another forty million. The silence of the woods beckoned to her once more as she eased the car out of the parking lot and drove down the mountain.

A deep sadness ran through her as she remembered the ones she had lost and the ones never to be found: James and Andrew, Geronimo and Billy, Reed and Auntie Louella, Annie and Curt and Todd. She tuned the radio to a station and there it was—one of the songs she had murmured into the night, the same one on the Eagles CD she had listened to on the trip to the Tower only a few hours earlier.

> "You never thought you'd be alone this far
> Down the line
> And I know what's been on your mind
> You're afraid it's all been wasted time..."

"No," Lola mused, "it wasn't all wasted time..."

She drove past the field of sleeping prairie dogs and past a pair of spotted fawns that startled into flight as she approached. As Lola drove away from the trees and into the open space of the prairie, two small animal figures began to run towards the pines, their coats black and their feet silver. The animals stopped and glanced back towards the car. Lola pulled to a halt and sat in stunned silence. In the early night's light from the moon, caught by the car's headlights, were two young wolves. Each had one blue eye and one black eye. The two wolf pups stared back for a moment, then darted into the woods disappearing from her sight.

The smell of sage and tobacco she had placed on the altar wafted through the car. Sliding her foot off the brake pedal, she sighed as the car rolled forward. Down she drove, down to where she and Auntie had stopped the day before the world changed. She gently coasted to a halt at the same stop sign, now pockmarked with buckshot and faded by the Wyoming sun. Glancing into the rearview mirror, she saw the reflection of the black owl hanging at the base of her throat. The owl's calm eyes shone at her and seemed to blink. A wistful smile came over Lola's lips, deepening the creases at the corners of her eyes. Winking back at the owl, she pulled her car seat an inch forward.

Lola took a deep breath and ran her hands over the smoothness of the steering wheel. In the field across the road a light mist rose in swirls above the ground, hovering and then disappearing. A strange light glowed within the mist; thousands of eyes staring at her and then slowly closing. She sat transfixed as the words of an ancient song surrounded her in the warmth of the car:

> *"Amazing grace, how sweet the sound that saved a wretch like me. I once was lost, but now I'm found, was blind but now I see."*

Lola thought about the grace that, despite the horror of September 11, 2001 and two endless wars, had come into her own life in the past five years: the restoration of Annie's wallet to Jones; the passing of the red pony from the loving hands of Geronimo Barse into her own; the kind and tender hearts of Sarah, Dusty, and Billy Hawk; the flicker of hope in Istie's eyes as she left for New York with Jones; the blessing of the white buffalo calf; the birth of Liliana; the healing touch of Madeline on the frozen faces of the twins, and the infinite peace of Devils Tower soaring above the ground behind her.

Turning to the south, she accelerated into the night, away from the Tower, and into a future full of hope and redemption. The Tower still stood as it had from all eternity, standing when other Towers had fallen; standing through time, standing through the ages, standing as a beacon of peace and hope for anyone in its presence. As Lola sped away, a single small stone fell from the top of the Tower, bouncing over the striated sides of the monolith, the sound echoing with only the owls and coyotes to hear it.

⋙ Afterword ⋘

The Story of Diamond L Ranch

I believe there are few places in the world that merit the label "paradise on earth." To me, the Diamond L Ranch in Hulett, Wyoming, deserves this title with no caveats, hesitation, or question.

I first came to the ranch in 2001, two days before the horror and pain of 9/11. It was befitting that this was my first visit, for out of that evening—with my aunt Lucile LaDue sitting beside me in the warmth of that place—grew friendship, love, renewal, and redemption.

The Diamond L Ranch sits at the end of a ten-mile dirt and gravel road on the edge of the Black Hills. To get there, one must cut through hay fields and cliffs of red rock. It is a place where time stands still and at night the stars dart across the sky, reminding us of the infinity of the Creator and the hope of the future.

I have returned to the ranch nearly every year for the past twelve years, basking in the gracious company of Carolyn and Gary Luther, the owners. In their presence, I returned to faith in the Creator and in the basic goodness of people.

The Diamond L Ranch is officially a guest ranch and bed and breakfast, but many of us are no longer treated as guests but as cherished members of the Diamond L family. This book would not have become a reality if it was not for the sanctuary of the ranch, which sits a very short distance from the majesty of Devils Tower. In the space of these two places, I could not help but be touched by the hand of the Creator, and surrounded by peace, joy, love and redemption.

Robin A. LaDue, August 2013

TOTEMS OF SEPTEMBER
FAMILY TREES

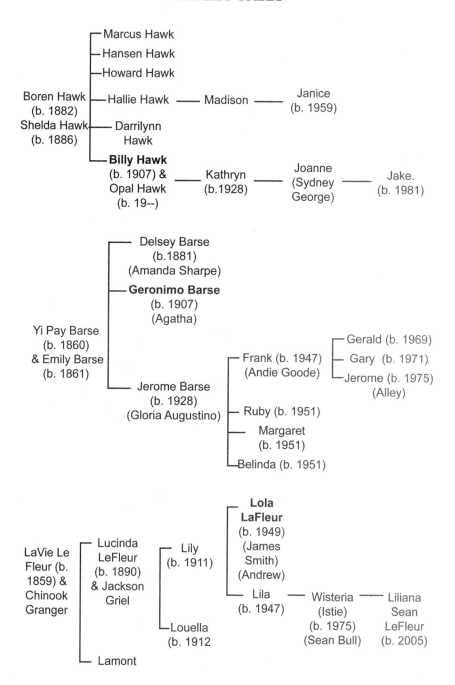

Marcus Hawk

Hansen Hawk

Howard Hawk

Boren Hawk (b. 1882)
Shelda Hawk (b. 1886)

Hallie Hawk — Madison — Janice (b. 1959)

Darrilynn Hawk

Billy Hawk (b. 1907) & Opal Hawk (b. 19--) — Kathryn (b.1928) — Joanne (Sydney George) — Jake. (b. 1981)

Delsey Barse (b.1881) (Amanda Sharpe)

Geronimo Barse (b. 1907) (Agatha)

Yi Pay Barse (b. 1860) & Emily Barse (b. 1861)

Jerome Barse (b. 1928) (Gloria Augustino)

Frank (b. 1947) (Andie Goode)

Gerald (b. 1969)
Gary (b. 1971)
Jerome (b. 1975) (Alley)

Ruby (b. 1951)

Margaret (b. 1951)

Belinda (b. 1951)

LaVie Le Fleur (b. 1859) & Chinook Granger

Lucinda LeFleur (b. 1890) & Jackson Griel

Lily (b. 1911)

Lola LaFleur (b. 1949) (James Smith) (Andrew)

Lila (b. 1947) — Wisteria (Istie) (b. 1975) (Sean Bull) — Liliana Sean LeFleur (b. 2005)

Louella (b. 1912

Lamont

About the Authors

Robin A. LaDue, PhD

Dr. Robin LaDue is a retired clinical psychologist formerly in private practice in Washington State. She was born in Seattle but raised in the Sacramento, California area.

Robin's grandfather and great-uncles were survivors of the Cushman Boarding School, having been removed from their parents and experienced the horrors of having their hair cut, not being able to speak their language, and losing their culture. This heritage, along with Dr. LaDue's passion for helping Native women raise healthy babies and addressing the problems of oppression and loss in Native communities, were driving forces in her personal and professional life.

She received her Master's and Doctorate degrees from Washington State University; has been affiliated with the University of Missouri, Kansas City, and with the University of Washington's Department of Psychiatry and Behavioral Sciences, the Native American Center for Excellence, and Waikato University in Hamilton, New Zealand.

The award-winning author of the *Journey through the Healing Circle* books and video, Dr. LaDue has lectured worldwide on the effects of prenatal alcohol exposure and historical trauma in Native American communities, as well as the treatment for and consequences of psychological trauma, including traditional Native methods of treatment. She is an enrolled member of the Cowlitz Indian Tribe of Washington.

This is her first historical novel.

Mary Kay Voss

Mary Kay Voss was born in West Texas and grew up in Houston. She has lived in Texas, California, Tokyo, and Washington State and considers herself a misplaced Texan in a Washingtonian's body.

Mary Kay's professional career has revolved around the financial industry. She was a stockbroker, when that was unusual for women, and has had her own company for over twenty-five years. A former instructor in financial planning and insurance topics for continuing education, Mary Kay currently is an Associate with Agreement Dynamics, Inc, teaching communication styles and facilitating retreats.

An active member of a book club for fifteen years, Mary Kay credits the club with exposing her to a much wider selection of books than she might have ever chosen on her own. Her passion for reading also has led to an exciting journey into community theatre, where Mary Kay has been a regular performer on stage as well as on the managing board of the Driftwood Players in Edmonds, WA.

Of her collaboration with Dr. LaDue, she says, "Robin has an extremely creative mind, probably actually channeling the old Native Americans, and I had the pleasantly rewarding job of enriching the pages by smoothing the writing style and enhancing the readability. It is a great match of talents."

Mary Kay has been married to Didrik for over thirty years; is a mother and grandmother.